AS A YOUNG NATION PURSUES ITS DESTINY AGAINST ALL ODDS, OLD PASSIONS CATCH FIRE, IGNITING A DEADLY CONFLAGRATION

Renno—Through war and peace, the legendary Seneca warrior has earned an honored place in the white man's world. But now another terrible battle beckons, threatening to destroy his legacy . . . and his children's future.

Little Hawk—Renno's son and a decorated war hero, he faces his severest challenge ever, not only as a soldier but as a husband and father, pursuing the rebel Creek leader who has taken his family captive.

Naomi—Little Hawk's beloved wife, she and their two sons fall into the bloody hands of Calling Owl, her husband's ruthless enemy and a man whose brutality knows no bounds.

Gao—Nephew of Renno and son of a Seneca shaman, his loyalty to the white man's army turns to bitter hatred when he is falsely accused of rape and murder. Escaping death, he brings his fierce passion and fighting skill to a new cause: driving the white man from Indian land.

Tecumseh—Passionate and eloquent, he dreams of one great, united Indian nation. His vision flashes like a meteor across the sky—brilliant, inspiring, destined to become legend. And for one brief but unforgettable moment in history, his holy war scorches the American frontier.

The White Indian Series
Book XXVI

RED STICK

Donald Clayton Porter

 Producers of **Children of the Lion,**
The Holts, and **The First Americans.**

Book Creations Inc., Canaan, NY • *Lyle Kenyon Engel, Founder*

BANTAM BOOKS
NEW YORK • TORONTO • LONDON • SYDNEY • AUCKLAND

RED STICK

A Bantam Domain Book / published by arrangement with
Book Creations Inc.

Bantam edition / December 1994

Produced by Book Creations Inc.
Lyle Kenyon Engel, Founder

DOMAIN and the portrayal of a boxed "d" are
trademarks of Bantam Books,
a division of Bantam Doubleday Dell Publishing Group, Inc.

ISBN 0-553-56142-1

Published simultaneously in the United States and Canada

Bantam Books are published by Bantam Books, a division of Bantam
Doubleday Dell Publishing Group, Inc. Its trademark, consisting of the
words "Bantam Books" and the portrayal of a rooster, is Registered in
U.S. Patent and Trademark Office and in other countries. Marca
Registrada. Bantam Books, 1540 Broadway, New York, New York
10036.

PRINTED IN THE UNITED STATES OF AMERICA

OPM   0 9 8 7 6 5 4 3 2 1

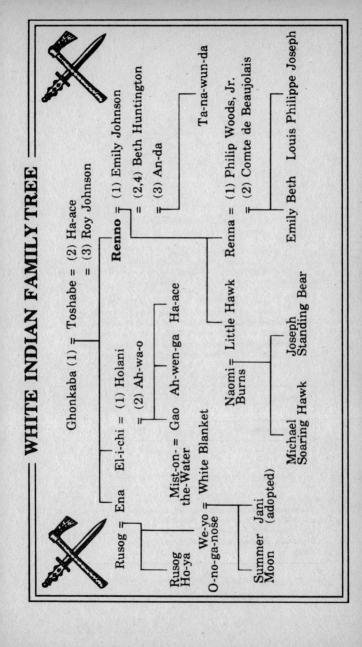

WHITE INDIAN FAMILY TREE

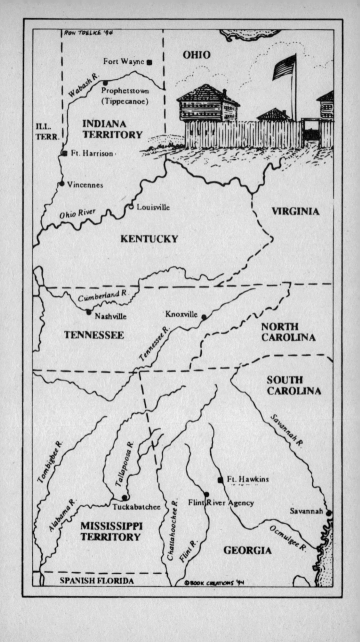

RON TOELKE '94

OHIO

Fort Wayne

Wabash R.

Prophetstown
(Tippecanoe)

ILL.
TERR.

INDIANA
TERRITORY

Ft. Harrison

Vincennes

Ohio River

Louisville

VIRGINIA

KENTUCKY

Cumberland R.

Nashville

Knoxville

NORTH
CAROLINA

TENNESSEE

Tennessee R.

SOUTH
CAROLINA

Savannah R.

Tombigbee R.

Tallapoosa R.

Ft. Hawkins

Alabama R.

Tuckabatchee

Chattahoochee R.

Flint River Agency

Savannah

MISSISSIPPI
TERRITORY

Flint R.

GEORGIA

Ocmulgee R.

SPANISH FLORIDA

©BOOK CREATIONS '94

Chapter One

Running Mink, sister of the war chief Main Poche, had seen fourteen winters when she discovered the comfortable and effortless world she could reach through the magic of the white man's potent medicine. Her brother laughingly offered her a brown crockery jug and said in an aside to his fellow warriors, "Let us see how my little sister likes fire in her throat."

Main Poche, although young, was a fully mature Potawatomi warrior, and he was fresh from a raid. Liquid booty and two bloody scalps of the white enemy had lifted his spirits. Although he was an admirer of the mighty Tecumseh, also called the Panther Passing Across and Chief of the Beautiful River, he did not share the Shawnee's dislike of whiskey.

Running Mink rested the heavy jug on her shoulder as she'd seen the men do and turned her head to suckle at the opening. A conflagration of taste, aroma, and sensation brought tears to her eyes. She took big, gulping swallows before lowering the jug. Within a few minutes she saw the lights in the sky more sharply than she'd ever seen them before, and she could hear the music of their singing. While the men danced and chanted long-winded accounts of their latest foray, she lifted the jug again and fell into a state blessed by the spirits. She was fourteen. From that day forward no price was too high to pay for the fiery medicine.

In the days following the aching defeat at Fallen Timbers of the united tribes of the Ohio by Mad Anthony Wayne, the Chief Who Does Not Sleep, it was unusual to see a solitary white man in the wilderness to which the tribes had fled. It had not always been so. In the time of Running Mink's grandfather, white men came from the north by canoe to trade for beaver skins. Those ragged men of the woods spoke French, and many of them took Indian wives for warmth and comfort.

Charles Lefont was a man out of his time when he came alone into Main Poche's camp, calling out friendship in a mixture of French and northern Indian dialects. Not all his words were understood, but the whiskey jug he waved aloft spoke a universal language. By the time Running Mink was able to claim her share of the Frenchman's bounty, Main Poche and several senior warriors were under the spell of the white man's fiery potion, and Lefont was eager to offer whiskey to a pliant Potawatomi maiden.

It was only because Main Poche had been mellowed by a successful raid on settlers to the south and by Lefont's whiskey that the Frenchman continued to live after being discovered using the chief's sister's sleek young body expertly and passionately. Although some of the old ones objected, there was a quick wedding at which both bride and groom were unsteady on their feet. After being promised all the whiskey she wanted, Running Mink went away into the deep woods with Lefont. There she helped her husband run trap lines. She carried wood, built fires, cooked for him, warmed his bed, and berated him often when there was no whiskey. Only occasionally did Lefont take her into a settlement where he could trade hides for provisions and ammunition, as well as for the commodity Running Mink desired most.

A daughter was born to Charles Lefont and Running Mink in the winter of 1796 on a day when warm air poured up from the south and formed a fog over the lake beside which Lefont had made his temporary camp. It was Lefont who gave the infant her name, Mist-on-the-Water.

It seemed to the trapper that the child marked the beginning of his bad luck. The winters were colder, game was scarce, and it became more and more difficult to find an area where his trap lines produced results. Running Mink, who lived only for escape into the world of the white man's medicine, became tiresome. She nagged when there was no whiskey, and that was more and more often as her little girl passed the toddler stage.

Mist-on-the-Water was eight years old when she first came to understand what was happening when her father took them into a town. Lefont earned more money by trading Running Mink's body to white men than by selling his pelts. At first Mist-on-the-Water simply accepted Lefont's drunken statement that when she was old enough, she, too, would be set to work earning money for the family. She had just begun to realize what that meant when the Frenchman sold her and her mother to an American army sergeant for two dollars, a horse, and a stolen army rifle.

At first it seemed that Mist's world had changed for the better. Running Mink had whiskey—not all she wanted, but enough to keep her happy. Mist-on-the-Water's new father ignored the eleven-year-old girl as long as she kept the cabin neat and had food ready when he came home at midday and in the evening. She also brought fresh water for drinking and washing and replenished the woodpile regularly. It didn't take long, however, for the cruel nature of Sergeant Jeb Martin to make itself evident.

Martin, too, liked his whiskey. When he drank, he took it upon himself to punish Running Mink for her past sins. As old bruises faded, he added new contusions to her face, arms, and legs. She seemed not to feel the blows, for she had drunk herself into semipermanent torpor. Mist-on-the-Water had to coax her into eating a few bites now and then, or she would have starved.

So it was for four years, while the little post on the Wabash River called Fort Sackville became better known as Vincennes, and the slim, boyish body of Mist-on-the-Water began to blossom. She had counted thirteen winters when Martin first punished her by turning her over his knee, lifting her doeskin skirt, and applying his big, hard hand to her swelling, soft, girlish rump. There was nothing she could do. She had come to feel responsible for her helpless mother, and it frightened her to think of being alone in the vast wilderness that surrounded the town. She could only hope that Jeb Martin would not claim her for himself or sell her body to white men as her French father had once threatened. Mist-on-the-Water knew that she was the niece of an important war chief, but that and his name, Main Poche, were the extent of her knowledge.

Because the heavy-caliber rifle ball had cut its way through the flesh and muscle of Gao's upper thigh, it had taken time for his body to repair the damage. Long after the visible entry and exit wounds were covered by smooth, new scar tissue, weakness lingered within the injured limb.

Gao, son of the Seneca sachem El-i-chi, was able to put most of his weight on his wounded leg as he walked with the aid of a crutch fashioned from a stout elm branch. His favorite promenade extended from the western end of the Vincennes parade ground to the bank of the Wabash River. He was young, and the restless blood of the white Indian flowed in his veins. Eager to be about his work, he stayed on his feet even when healing muscles protested with spasms, and he hissed through his teeth as he reached awkwardly to massage the painful knot. One low moan came from deep in his throat as the agony abated. He looked around guiltily and felt a flush of heat creep up his throat. The girl was coming down the slight slope from the parade ground, and he wondered if she had heard his unmanly expression of pain.

It was not the first time he had seen her. He knew that her name was Mist-on-the-Water and that she was the daughter of a white soldier's squaw. He guessed her to be fifteen years of age, for she had the bearing of a girl just beginning the wondrous bloom into womanhood. Her waist was small, her breasts were youthfully pert under well-worn doeskin, and her hips flowered outward in a sensuous curve. With one upraised hand she balanced a large ceramic water jug on her head.

Gao ignored the residual aches left by the muscle spasm and limped to intercept her. She smiled, and the bright day became radiant.

"I will help," he said.

Mist-on-the-Water worriedly looked over her shoulder toward the log cabin where she lived with her mother and the white man who called himself her stepfather.

"That is good of you," she said, "but you're in no condition to—"

As he took the water jug from her head, his hand brushed hers, and the tingling thrill of the touch awed him. She walked at his side as he limped along with the jug cradled under his free arm.

"You push yourself too hard," she said. "I have watched you. If it is painful, you should not walk on the injured leg."

His heart pounded. She had watched him. She had noticed him.

"I am Gao of the southern Seneca."

"I know."

"And you are Mist-on-the Water."

She tilted her head at him in teasing inquiry. "How do you know my name?"

"I asked the army surgeon who treated my wound."

"And what else do you know about me?"

"That you are more beautiful than that for which you are named." He swallowed hard, amazed at his own daring. Encouraged by her smiling silence, he continued. "That you are like silver moonbeams on a quiet lake and yet like the lightning that shimmers in bright sheets before a storm."

"I think that the young Seneca warrior's tongue has taken on the sly skill of the fox," she said.

"The words come from my heart."

"They are good words, but spoken too quickly," she countered.

Gao positioned himself at the edge of the river, squatted, and put his crutch aside. He leaned out to fill the water jug and lost his balance. His effort to catch himself pulled his healing thigh muscle painfully, and he grunted and splashed heavily into the river. He came up holding the water jug in front of him as he stood in waist-deep water.

Mist was laughing, one delicate hand in front of her mouth.

"Your jug is filled," Gao said solemnly as water dripped down his nose.

He thought her trilling laugh was the combined song of all the birds of the forest. The delight of it filled him and overflowed so that he laughed with her as he stood dripping water back into the stream.

"It is an interesting way to fill a water jug," she said. "Give it to me."

Still smiling, she took the jug, set it down, then reached out a hand to help Gao up the bank. He sat down heavily.

"Are you hurt?" she asked with sudden concern.

"Only my dignity and pride," he said.

"Pfffft," she said, springing lithely to her feet.

"Don't go."

"Jeb Martin is waiting for the water."

Gao glanced in the direction of the cabin, which was hidden from his view by the slope. He knew Sergeant Jeb Martin. He was regular army, a member of the Vincennes garrison under Governor William Henry Harrison. While recuperating from his wound, Gao had made it a point to get to know all the soldiers at the army post that had become the town of Vincennes, capital of the Indiana Territory. He and Ta-na, his cousin whom he called brother, served Harrison as scouts. It was in their interest to know the men who would follow them into the northern wilderness, where warriors from many tribes were gathering under the leadership of Tecumseh.

"You will come this way again tomorrow?" Gao asked.

"I usually do."

"I will be here."

"As you wish," she said, with a swish of her braided hair, but her smile told him that she was not indifferent to his promise.

Dr. Armand Henri was sitting in a bentwood rocker on the wooden stoop of the cabin assigned to Gao and his absent cousin, Ta-na. Henri was a small man, wrinkled and withered by the frontier elements. As Gao came swinging up, putting most of his weight on the healing leg, the doctor gave himself a dose of the whiskey with which he treated his patients.

"C'est bon," he said, "that you do the exercise of the leg, but does not one usually undress before swimming?"

Gao sat on the edge of the porch.

"How is it, the leg?"

"It grows stronger."

"Do not overstrain it," Henri said. "The new muscle is tender."

Gao pondered ways to phrase his question obliquely but failed. It was his inclination to attack a problem head-on. "The girl Mist-on-the-Water," he asked, "what has she to do with Sergeant Jeb Martin?"

Henri raised one bushy eyebrow. "Were I you, I would avoid Martin as much as possible. He is harsh with members of your race."

"In this is he different from other white men?" Gao asked with a hint of belligerency. The hatred that many whites bore for all Indians was not unknown to him.

"Only in degree, *mon ami,*" the doctor said.

"And yet he has a squaw," Gao said.

"True. She is Potawatomi. Her name is Running Mink."

"And Mist is her daughter?"

"*Oui.*" Henri leaned down toward Gao. His breath was a testimony to the potency of the whiskey in the silver flask he always carried with him. "You find the young one to be *trés belle,* eh?"

"So," Gao said noncommittally.

"Understandable, it is, for she is half French." He preened his mustache with one finger and smirked. "And we French are a uniformly handsome people, *non?*"

Gao laughed. He had suspected that Mist's blood was not pure Indian. As was true of Ta-na-wun-da and him, white blood had come down to Mist from her father's side.

"Take my advice," Henri said. "Find yourself another girl and leave Jeb Martin's stepdaughter alone."

Gao heeded the doctor's warning only to the extent of waiting the next day below the slope of the riverbank so that he could not be seen from the Martin cabin. His patience was rewarded. When the sun was no more than two hours high, Mist-on-the-Water walked by, carrying her water jug. This time Gao managed to fill her jug without falling in the river, and after he put it carefully on the ground, she sat down on the bank beside him.

"I have not heard how you received your wound," she said.

She spoke English with a charming French accent.

Gao knew some French from his late grandmother Toshabe, who, like Mist, had had a French father.

"My brother and I wanted to leave a certain place, but there were those who disputed our desire."

"Now I know everything," she said with sweet sarcasm.

"It is a long story."

"The sergeant is at his duty. My mother is sleeping."

Like many Indians, Gao, being three-quarters Seneca, loved to tell or hear a rousing tale. He found himself speaking easily to Mist, telling her how he was shot in the leg while leaving Prophetstown, where Tecumseh, the Panther Passing Across, had pursued Ta-na and him down the river and engaged in a swift and deadly encounter in the dark of night.

"I look forward to meeting your brother," Mist said.

Gao felt a quick stab of concern. Once before he had been attracted to a girl, the Cherokee Head-in-the-Cloud, only to have Ta-na win the fickle maiden's affections. Gao pushed away such unworthy thoughts. Had it not been for Ta-na he would have died at the hands of Tecumseh's men that night on the bank of the river.

"Tell me about you," he said.

She, too, talked easily, although he could tell she left out certain aspects of her life with the Frenchman. Gao was properly impressed that she was the niece of the war chief Main Poche, but he was also troubled, for it was known that Main Poche was an ally of Tecumseh.

"And now Jeb Martin is your father," Gao prompted as Mist fell silent.

She delayed her answer long enough for Gao to guess that her relationship with the sergeant was not ideal.

"He provides us with a place to live," she said. "We do not go hungry."

A few days after he had plunged face-first into the Wabash while filling Mist's water jug, Gao discarded his crutch, and as long as he moved slowly he could walk with only a slight limp. On that same day he saw Mist's mother, Running Mink, for the first time. It was early morning, not yet time for Mist-on-the-Water to make her daily trip to the river, but Gao was drawn to the parade ground near Jeb Martin's cabin. When the door opened, the young man's heart stood at attention until his eyes told him that the squat, barrel-shaped woman who came out of the cabin was not Mist. Curious, he went up to the woman as she walked unsteadily to the trading post.

He was shocked by Running Mink's appearance. One of her eyes was swollen shut. A cut on her lower lip had a fresh scab, and on her bare arms and legs was the evidence of many blows.

"I greet you," Gao said.

Running Mink's eyes seemed to be incapable of focus as she turned her bloated and bruised face toward him, then wobbled past without acknowledging his greeting. Saddened, he turned to watch. She was almost at the trading post when Jeb Martin came striding toward her. He seized her arm and turned her roughly. Gao, made uneasy by the display, walked toward the river. When he looked back, Martin was dragging Running Mink along at a trot. Then he opened the door to his cabin, thrust her inside, and disappeared after her with a loud slam of the door. Gao thought he heard a single, pained outcry.

It was not unheard of in his world for a husband to "correct" a wife, but beating such as Running Mink's was rare. A Seneca husband would not sleep easily if he violated decency to half that extent, lest he awaken to find his wife wielding a sharp blade in retribution. A Cherokee woman would simply pile her husband's belongings outside the door of the lodge, as Head-in-the-Cloud had done with Ta-na's possessions, and be rid of an abusive husband. Gao didn't know Potawatomi custom, but he was certain that Martin's abuse of his wife would not meet with approval in any tribe.

He was downcast, but soon that emotion was replaced with concern for Mist-on-the-Water. His fears were confirmed when she had no smile for him that day. Walking directly to the river, she refused his offer of help and dipped the jug herself, then turned to go. He put his hand on her arm to stop her, and she winced at his touch. The soft flesh of her arm was hot under his palm, and it was red and purple. Anger flared in him.

"If he struck you—"

"No," she said, trying to pull away.

"Listen to me."

"I must go. He is waiting for the water."

"He did strike you."

"No, please."

He had no choice but to release her. The next day she changed the time of her walk to the river in an obvious effort to avoid him, but he had been waiting within view of the cabin all day. He intercepted her before she reached the riverbank.

"You must tell me what is troubling you," he said.

"It is nothing," she said, trying to walk around him.

He blocked her way. "I will not let you go until you tell me."

Her sob surprised him, and she dropped the water jug heedlessly to the ground and wept against his shoulder. He held her close and tried to control the mixture of fury and love that filled him.

As he crooned his love for her, her sobs subsided. He wiped her face with the fringe of his sleeve, and her tears left wet smears on her smooth cheeks.

"When he touches me he makes me feel unclean," she whispered. Her eyes went wide, and she tried to pull away.

"He hit you, here," he said, touching the bruise on her arm.

"He has never done that before."

"What else did he do?" Gao demanded.

"Oh, how I wish that my mother and I could go back to our people," she said.

"He beats your mother."

She nodded, sniffing back a sob.

"Has she relatives other than Main Poche to come for her?"

Mist shook her head. "They are dead. Her parents. Her other brothers and sisters. All dead."

"When Ta-na comes back from his scouting duties—" He paused. He could not speak for Ta-na. "There is a way. We will find it, you and I."

"I must go now."

He was reluctant to release her from his arms, and though he knew he should not, he let his lips touch her forehead. Kissing was a white man's custom, but she made no objection when he turned her face upward with his fingers under her chin and touched his lips to the fullness of her mouth. An uncontrollable shivering overtook him. It was as if he had been exposed to a winter storm without proper clothing, and he had to concentrate to keep his teeth from chattering. He deepened his kiss, and Mist sighed into his mouth and pressed her body to his in a gesture of willing submission.

She looked at him with her eyes wide. They were the black of midnight under sooty lashes, and the remains of a tear glistened. She put her hands on his arms and felt the quivering of his muscles.

"I do that to you?" she asked in awe.

"Come to me tonight, after Martin is asleep," he whispered.

"I would be too frightened. He would be so angry."

"This afternoon, then, while he is still on duty."

"Not here."

"No." The riverbank was too open. Anyone who walked to the top of the slope from the parade ground could see them.

"Just downstream there is a grove of willows," she said.

"I know the place. I have walked there."

"As soon as I can, then."

"Yes."

As in the story of Joshua, as told to Gao by his aunt Beth, wife of the sachem Renno, the sun stood still. Time became eternity as he walked to the spreading, feathery thicket of willows, and the memory of how Mist had felt in his arms made the wait intolerable. With boughs and a blanket he made a secluded nest among the shimmering trees.

When Gao saw Mist coming down the riverbank at last, he was filled with joy and anticipation. He took her hand, led her into the sheltering thicket, and lowered her gently to the blanket, then lay beside her and traced the proud line of her delicate nose with the tip of his finger.

She shivered. "That tickles," she said with a giggle.

"And this?" He kissed her neck. She laughed. His mouth brushed her cheek, then her lips. His hand found a firm mound of breast. With a sigh she pushed him away, sat up, and tied her skirt into a loose knot between her legs, thus marking the boundary of his explorations.

He lost himself in her, submerged himself in her kiss.

Again she laughed. "It is our white blood, is it not?" she asked, as he pecked little kisses on and around her mouth.

"This?" he asked, kissing her soundly.

"My mother will not allow men—I mean Martin—to kiss her."

"They say this is the way the French do it." Gao thrust his tongue deeply into the sweetness of her mouth. He felt as if he were a hummingbird delving for nectar into the heart of a flower.

"Do you like this?" he asked.

"I like everything you do," she whispered.

He unlaced the leather thongs of her shirt, exposing the twin mounds of her breasts. He measured them with his hands and worshiped them with his lips, then pressed himself to her, his arousal hard against her thigh.

"You will be mine," he said.

"Yes, oh, yes."

For a few more heated moments his hands explored the curve of her waist and her outflowing hips. He was so enthralled he did not react immediately when he heard a sound behind him. He was just pushing himself up and turning when Jeb Martin's iron-hard fist smashed into the side of his face, knocking him off the blanket and rolling him in the dirt.

"You Injun son of a bitch!" Martin bellowed as he leaped over Mist and aimed a kick at Gao's head.

The fog that clogged Gao's brain cleared just in time for him to roll away, and Martin's boot grazed his shoulder. Gao stood up.

He had inherited his father's lithe body and was taller than average, but Martin was over six feet and outweighed him by fifty pounds. Gao had a feeling that if the contest came down to pure strength, the white man would be the stronger. But the Seneca had his youth; he had agility and quickness and the indignation of a proud man struck without warning. He anticipated Martin's next bull-like rush, stepped lightly aside, and buried his fist in Martin's soft belly as the big man hurled past.

Martin's breath exploded outward. He bent over and gasped but came back to the fight quickly. Gao laced two quick blows to his face, but the man's powerful fist smashed against his cheekbone and sent him reeling.

It quickly became evident to him that he could not stand up to Martin in a fistfight. He closed with the sergeant, putting into use the skill and speed he had developed during years of wrestling with Ta-na and other young warriors in Rusog's Town, the Cherokee-Seneca village where he had grown up. He used his legs to trip the larger man and twisted in midair to land atop the sergeant and pin one of his arms under his body. Gao gained a fingerhold on the exposed hand, and Martin jerked and cried out in pain as the hold took effect. He struggled to get his right arm out from under him, to no avail.

"Listen to me," Gao said.

"I have nothing to say to you, Injun."

"You will hear what I have to say. You will never again molest Mist-on-the-Water."

Martin struggled briefly, then went limp as Gao applied painful pressure to his fingers.

"You will never touch her again," Gao said.

"I have done the girl no harm," Martin grunted.

"Nor will you, ever."

"What is your interest in the girl?" the sergeant asked.

"I want to claim her as my wife."

Martin's face darkened; then he grinned. "Well, why in hell didn't you say so?"

"You gave me no opportunity."

"She's of marriageable age. She has a mind of her own." Martin turned his head to look at Mist, who had been watching the combat with a mixture of fear and pride in Gao's mastery of the situation.

"I will be his wife, Stepfather," Mist said.

"Let me up and we'll talk this over," Martin said.

Warily releasing the sergeant's fingers, Gao leaped to his feet. Martin pushed himself up slowly but then spun around and launched a kick at Gao's groin. Although the blow did no real damage, it sent sheets of pain into the healing thigh muscles, leaving Gao vulnerable. He was sent sprawling with another blow, and when he rolled back on his feet, crouched for action, he faced the seven-inch blade of a hunting knife in Martin's hand.

The sergeant moved forward, squinting murderously, then thrust the knife toward Gao's midsection. The boy leaped aside and looked around desperately for a weapon, a stick, a rock. There was nothing. Martin was moving in remorselessly when Mist-on-the-Water threw herself on his back.

"Stop it!" she cried. "I will not allow you to kill him."

Martin halted and straightened from his knife-fighter's crouch, shrugging Mist off his back as he did.

"No, I will not kill the son of a bitch this time." He put his
knife back into its sheath. "Stay away from me and mine,
Injun."

Gao burned to avenge the kick that had set his
wound to aching, but he knew that to continue the fight
would lead to either his death or the sergeant's. In his
youthful confidence he was unconcerned about the first
possibility, but to kill Martin would only make a bad situation worse. The sergeant was an important man in the
Vincennes garrison, and Gao would have to work with
him when he returned to his scouting duties. It would be
wise, he decided, to forget Martin's treachery; and, although the thought of it made him feel desperate, he
would have to avoid Mist-on-the-Water until he could
find a way out of the dilemma of duty versus love.

He watched Martin lead Mist away. Once she turned
her head to look back, but the sergeant jerked her arm
and spoke to her in a harsh voice. Gao couldn't hear the
words, but his blood boiled at the white man's tone.

Gao's leg hurt; he limped as he crossed the parade
ground to his cabin, desperately trying to resolve his
plight. He had pledged himself not only to Ta-na but also
to William Henry Harrison. He was of the blood of the
original Renno, of blue-eyed Ja-gonh, of dark Ghonkaba.
Gao's father, El-i-chi, his uncle Renno, and his grandfa-
ther-by-marriage, Roy Johnson, had served with Harrison
under the Chief Who Does Not Sleep, Mad Anthony
Wayne. He and Ta-na had answered Harrison's call, which
had been intended for Renno and Roy Johnson. A warrior
with the blood of the white Indian in his veins honored
his commitments. He could not leave Vincennes to take
Mist and her mother back to their people because of his
pledge and the fact that he and Ta-na were enemies of
Main Poche and all those who heeded the call-to-arms of
Tecumseh, the Panther Passing Across, and his brother,
Tenskwatawa, the Prophet.

He could take Mist south, back to the Cherokee Nation, but breaking his word to Harrison was as unthink-

able as leaving Mist-on-the-Water to the whims of Jeb Martin.

When he reached his cabin he lay down on his bed to ease his aching leg and was dozing when the door burst open. Three uniformed soldiers aimed their rifles at him.

"On your feet and follow me!" bellowed the corporal who stood in the doorway.

Gao was careful not to make any sudden moves as he rose from the bed. He knew the corporal by sight, but at the moment the man's name escaped him.

"You'd better bring a blanket," the corporal said. "Where you're going, the accommodations ain't too grand."

Gao folded an army blanket and put it under his arm. The two privates marched behind him as they crossed the parade ground. He didn't have to ask where they were taking him, and he berated himself for not having anticipated it. Although he had resolved to forget Martin's attack, clearly Martin had no such intention.

The post guardhouse was a converted cellar with one tiny window and a door cut so low that Gao had to stoop to enter. Both door and window had iron bars embedded in mortared stone. Inside there was a bunk made of rough-sawn planks on top of which a few handfuls of hay served as a mattress. On a table made of the same rough lumber sat a washbowl and pitcher; under it was a night jar that, judging by its smell, had not been properly cleaned.

"Am I to be informed of the charge against me?" Gao asked.

"Don't he talk purty?" one of the privates asked.

"Right civilized fer an Indian," the corporal said.

"By whose order am I here?" Gao asked as the corporal started to close the door.

"You picked the wrong 'un to mess around with," the corporal said. "Sergeant Martin, he's right upset 'bout what you done to his stepdaughter."

The door slammed shut. Gao heard the key turn in

the lock. He spread his blanket on the wooden bed, sat down, and looked around. The cellar, no more than eight by ten feet, was dark and dank. The rock wall at the front was well built, with small mortar joints. But the inner walls, also made of native stone, were not as skillfully joined. With some sort of tool it would be possible to dislodge a rock and dig outward and upward. For that matter, he could tunnel through the dirt floor, under the wall, and then upward. But it would take the guards no more than a casual glance through the window to see what was happening. Given time and privacy Gao could escape by digging his way out, but he suspected that he would not be allowed the opportunity. At the very least they would check on him twice a day, when he was given food.

The door opened within an hour, and in the dimness of the prison Gao recognized Lieutenant Stockton O'Toole, the youngest officer in the Vincennes garrison. Gao stood up.

"Sit down," O'Toole said. He had a thin, reedy voice that went well with his frail appearance.

"Am I to be informed of the charges against me, then?" Gao asked.

"You are." O'Toole sat on one end of the hard bed. "You're charged with striking a noncommissioned officer."

"I did not hit him first," Gao said.

"That doesn't matter. You are a quasi-official member of the United States Army by virtue of your employment as a scout. You are governed by the same rules as the men in uniform. Disobeying a direct order from a noncommissioned officer is a grave enough breach of discipline. To strike a sergeant while in contempt of his orders is serious indeed."

"The first I knew of Sergeant Martin's presence was when he knocked me over with a blow to the face," Gao protested. "Does that constitute an order? If so, it was an odd and rather painful one."

"Do you deny, then, that you were told by Sergeant Martin to leave his daughter alone?"

"I deny that I was given an order. I deny that I disobeyed."

"Do you also state that you were not molesting Sergeant Martin's daughter?"

"I do," Gao said.

"And yet the sergeant says that you and his daughter were, and I quote, rolling around on a blanket like dogs in heat."

"The girl who has agreed to be my wife was lying with me on a blanket," Gao said. "Neither of us was rolling around in any fashion."

"But you were in, ah, intimate contact with the sergeant's daughter?"

"Sir, I was kissing her. She was kissing me back. We had just promised ourselves to each other in marriage."

"And Sergeant Martin did not ask you—order you—to unhand her, to leave the scene?"

"He came up behind me. I heard him at the last minute. I turned my head, and he hit me in the face, knocking me off the blanket. He then tried to kick me in the head, and I hit him—"

"Ah."

"—more than once, because he was doing his best to hit me. I put him to the ground—"

The lieutenant raised his eyebrows. "You put Jeb Martin to the ground?"

"I did. I held him there and talked to him, asking him to understand that I love his daughter and she loves me. He seemed to be willing to listen to reason. I let him up, and he tried to kick me in the groin. He then drew his knife, and only the intervention of Mist-on-the-Water prevented him from attacking me with it."

"You held Jeb Martin on the ground?"

"So," Gao said.

"The sergeant says that it was you who drew a knife. He says that he disarmed you and, out of respect for the sensibilities of his daughter, did not continue the fight at that time."

"That is not true."

"He has brought charges against you. You will face a court-martial. I have been named to defend you. Are you sure you don't want to change your story and admit to the charges? I think that the court would be reasonable in its sentence. No more than a year at hard labor, I'd guess."

"You're going to defend me?"

"So it has been decreed by my superior officers."

"Then wouldn't it help if you believed me?"

O'Toole shrugged eloquently. "It really doesn't matter one way or the other whether or not I believe you. Jeb Martin is a veteran noncommissioned officer. He fought with Anthony Wayne at Fallen Timbers. He has served with every officer on this post under trying circumstances. If it comes down to your word against his, whom do you think they'll believe?"

"I see."

"Of course, there's the girl. Will she support your version of the story?"

Hope surged in Gao but faded rapidly. "You will not involve her," he said.

O'Toole shrugged again. "Your choice."

Even with Mist supporting him, there was still a very good chance that officers of the United States Army would take the word of one of their own against that of an Indian. If that happened, Mist would be left in the excruciating situation of having testified against the man who supported her mother and her, a man who would be in a position to make her life miserable.

"When will the trial be held?" Gao asked.

"We'll have to wait until the militia comes back from a reconnaissance into Tecumseh's territory," O'Toole said. "There aren't enough officers on post at the moment to staff a court."

"And when will that be?"

"A week, perhaps. Ten days." O'Toole rose. "A guilty

plea would go a long way toward making it easier for you. Think about it."

"I will," Gao said.

At last he slept. He was awakened when the guards opened the door to give him his evening meal of venison stew and corn bread. After the meal he was allowed to take his slop jar to the river. In the nights and days that followed he had time to nurture a bitterness that slowly began to change him.

Chapter Two

With great care Ta-na-wun-da, second son of Renno, approached Vincennes from the north. William Henry Harrison's militiamen, not yet hardened in the crucible of battle, tended to see a hostile Indian behind every tree and had been known to shoot at the slightest sound. After having survived constant danger for three weeks in the territory where Tecumseh's name was honored by many tribes, Ta-na had no intention of being shot by a nervous young picket standing guard duty at the fort.

He easily located the army outpost by the smell of tobacco and unwashed white bodies. With skills learned from his uncle El-i-chi and the Seneca-Cherokee senior warriors of Rusog's Town, he made his way to within hailing distance. He could hear the voices of at least two men, and he shook his head in wonderment. A Shawnee raiding party could be on the guard post before the inexperienced soldiers who manned it knew that a hostile Indian was within ten miles.

It was a dangerous time of day. The sun was nothing more than a red glow in the western sky; lengthening shadows merged to bring dim twilight to the forest. Ta-na took cover behind a large tree and called out, "Hello, the outpost."

Instantly the mutter of voices stopped, and he heard the click of metal on metal as someone cocked a rifle.

"Hello, the outpost," he repeated.

"Who goes there?"

"I am Ta-na, scout for General Harrison."

There was a long pause.

"Show yourself, whoever you are," a voice shouted.

There was just enough tension in the man's tone to alert Ta-na. He stepped from behind the tree but leaped back instantly as a shot rang out. The heavy-caliber slug made a *snick* of sound as it cut leaves above his head. Another shot followed.

Ta-na shook his head in exasperation. He was tired. He wanted to make his report to General Harrison, get some food into his belly, and check on Gao to see how his leg was healing.

"Did you get him?" one of the sentinels asked excitedly.

Ta-na rolled his eyes toward the darkening heavens and let out a great groan.

"You got him."

The Seneca grinned. He moaned again and added a hacking cough at the end.

"You got him!" the guard yelled again.

Ta-na kicked rhythmically at a pile of leaves in imitation of the spasmodic jerkings of a dying man.

"Go out and see who the bastard was," a voice ordered.

"You go see," the other man said.

"Damn it, that's an order," said the first man.

"You get another stripe to go with that one you got and you'll be dangerous."

Ta-na waited behind the tree as a man came crashing through the growing twilight toward him. Silently he leaned his rifle against the tree and took his knife out of its sheath. The approaching soldier had apparently reloaded his rifle, and he carried it at the ready. Ta-na moved to the other side of the tree and let him pass.

"I don't see anything," the soldier yelled over his shoulder.

"Here I am," Ta-na said, stepping forward quickly to put his hand under the soldier's chin and press the razor-sharp knife to the bare skin of his throat. The soldier froze in panic.

"One move and I'll give you a new mouth," Ta-na said.

The soldier swallowed hard. His rifle fell from his numbed hands, and he shivered violently. "Don't—" he said in a strained voice.

Slowly Ta-na took the knife away from the man's throat. "Turn around," he ordered.

The soldier's eyes were wide with fright.

"Look at me," Ta-na said. "I told you that I am Ta-na, scout for General Harrison."

The soldier seemed to wilt in relief. "God. Yes. I've seen you around the post."

"Call out to your corporal," Ta-na ordered.

"He's not a corporal. He's just—"

"Tell him that two of us are coming in."

The soldier obeyed, but Ta-na kept his rifle at the ready until the one-stripe soldier in the trenched guard post lowered his own weapon.

"It is good to be alert," Ta-na said, for they were both young and frightened by the vastness of the forest around them.

Ta-na himself had just turned eighteen. He had the Seneca eyes and hair of his mother, An-da, who had died when he was a babe in arms. His grandmother Toshabe, who was now with her ancestors in the west, had told him that he had the nose, cheekbones, chin, and body of his great-grandfather Ja-gonh. His three-quarters-Indian blood gave his skin a coppery richness. He moved with the litheness of youth and the agility of an athlete; his long, lean muscles were those of a runner.

It was dark when Ta-na finally walked through the walnut grove that surrounded the general's house. Called Grouseland, the brick mansion was two-and-a-half stories in height. Four tall chimneys were outlined against the starry sky, and the windows of the lower floor were illuminated by candlelight.

Ta-na was escorted by one of Harrison's brood to the general's study. The room had wainscoting of polished black walnut, and over the large fireplace was an ornate, hand-carved mantel. The outer walls of the house, eighteen inches of solid brick, had narrow portholes to accommodate rifles. The glass in the six-foot-high windows in the study had come all the way from England and were fitted with heavy shutters inside and out.

"Well, my boy," Harrison said, rising from his desk to extend his hand, "you've come back to us."

Harrison's long, sharp-nosed face seemed small above his peaked collar and sloping shoulders. His hair was beginning to recede; by accident or design a lock fell over his broad forehead as if trying to make up for nature's lack. He wore an ornate lounging coat over white linen, and a large black bow was tied at his throat.

"I am eager to hear your adventures," the governor said. "You are overdue, you know. You shouldn't worry us that way."

Ta-na leaned his rifle against the walnut wainscoting and lifted his bow and small quiver of arrows from his shoulder.

"Sit, sit," Harrison said, indicating a leather chair in front of the tall windows. He sat in an identical chair, leaned back, and put his feet up on a matching leather ottoman.

"The Panther Passing Across states that the chiefs who signed the treaty at Fort Wayne sold land that was not theirs to sell," Ta-na began.

Harrison sighed. "It seems that I have heard that story before. There were at least fourteen hundred Indians at Fort Wayne, Thomas. More than agreed to the treaty of Greenville in 1795."

It was not the first time the governor had applied that Christian name to Ta-na. The Seneca made no objection. He was aware that Indian names made some men uneasy.

"Tecumseh spits on such chiefs as Lapoussier and Little Eyes," Ta-na said. "He has traveled far, from the northern lakes to the Great Smoky Mountains of my homeland, from the Saint Lawrence to the Ohio, and from the banks of the Susquehanna to the plains of the Father of Waters to take his message to a score of tribes. It is his contention that the United States has no right to the land running southeast from a point north of Vincennes on both sides of the Wabash to the east fork of the White River. He tells everyone that your agreement with the lesser chiefs at Fort Wayne was fraudulent."

"Did you see Tecumseh this time?" Harrison asked.

"No. He was away. I heard his brother the Prophet speak."

"From a safe distance, I trust."

"From a very safe distance," Ta-na said with a smile that lit his face. "Moreover, I was dressed as a Miami squaw."

Harrison broke into laughter.

"I tell you this in confidence," Ta-na said uneasily.

"Of course, of course." Harrison allowed himself one more chuckle. "But I wonder what your father and your step-grandfather would say if they knew you had hidden behind the skirts of a squaw." Harrison knew both Roy Johnson and Ta-na's father, Renno, from having served with them in Anthony Wayne's American Legion.

Ta-na laughed. "My father would say that I had

pulled a good trick, and if I know my grandfather, he would advise me to do whatever it takes to keep my hair."

"So he would."

"The theme of Tecumseh's oratory does not change," Ta-na said. "He preaches that all Indians are of one blood and that to insure the survival of the race they must unite to form a single armed front against the white invaders."

Harrison nodded.

"There is this." He paused, as if unsure of himself.

"Go on," Harrison said.

"Mind you, sir, this is conjecture on my part. In defense of that, let me say it is opinion based on observation. I believe that Tenskwatawa, the Prophet, is nothing more than a voice for Tecumseh. I think it is the Panther Passing Across who put the startling predictions of things to come into the mouth of his brother."

"Yes, I have always wondered how Tenskwatawa could have known his astronomy well enough to predict an eclipse of the sun back in 1806."

"Tenskwatawa cannot read."

"I would have guessed as much. So it was Tecumseh who knew about the eclipse." Harrison reached for a cigar and prepared it for lighting. "Why do you mention this?"

"It is said by some of those who have visited Prophetstown that now and again it is necessary for Tecumseh to deflate his brother's pride lest Tenskwatawa forget who gives wisdom to his lips."

"Ah," Harrison said. "Trouble in paradise?"

Ta-na shrugged. "Not yet. In the future?" He shrugged again.

"That is something to consider." Harrison lit the cigar and with a few puffs filled the room with a cloud of blue smoke. "I've always wondered what Tecumseh would do for an encore to the eclipse." He looked at Ta-na expectantly.

"I don't understand everything that I have heard," Ta-na said. "Last year, in early summer, Tecumseh had craftsmen carve elaborate wooden slabs. Each of the slabs was covered with symbols. They were delivered to the chiefs of thirty major tribes. With each of the message slabs were thirty carved sticks that had been painted red. One red stick was to be discarded each month beginning with the Wind Moon. When one stick remains, a nightly vigil will begin until the sign of Tecumseh is seen in the sky."

"A meteor?" Harrison asked.

"That is my guess, for he is named for a flaming ball of green fire, the Panther Passing Across, that lit the sky the night he was born."

"Nonsense," Harrison said, puffing smoke. "The man can get his hands on an almanac and know that there's going to be a solar eclipse. He cannot—I repeat—he cannot predict that on a certain night so many months after the Wind Moon a meteor will flash green across the sky."

"So," Ta-na said.

"There's more?"

"When the sign of the Panther Passing Across is seen, the final red stick is to be cut into thirty pieces, one of which will be cast into the fire each night. When the last piece is burned, Tecumseh will send the world a powerful sign."

"Damn, I'll check the almanac for another eclipse."

"The whole world will dance to Tecumseh's prophecy," Ta-na said.

"Dance?"

"The very earth will be riven, and the rivers will flow backward."

"Earthquake," Harrison said.

Ta-na nodded.

Harrison chuckled. "Well, the old boy has bitten off more than he can chew this time. Have you any idea when the last of the red sticks will be discarded?"

"I'm not sure," Ta-na said. "It will be after the large bear in the sky empties his color pot to make the leaves flame."

"In the autumn, then?"

Again Ta-na nodded.

"I think we can discount an earthquake," Harrison said. "Could it be that when the last piece of the message stick is burned, it is the time intended for Tecumseh's uprising?"

"I think he would be reluctant to start his war with the cold of winter so near. Perhaps he expects the sign to bring more tribes to his confederation in time for war in the spring."

"Hmmm. Yes, you have a point." Harrison waved his cigar. "Well, let's table that for a while. Were you in Tippecanoe again, or should I call it Prophetstown as the Indians do?"

"Yes, I was."

"Are warriors still joining the cause?"

"Main Poche, the Potawatomi, arrived with a body of warriors while I was there, and several groups of Kickapoo came from the valleys of the Sangamon and Vermilion rivers. Small delegations of Delaware and Miami arrived at different times."

"So, the population of Tenskwatawa's town is growing."

"Tecumseh has not yet achieved his goal of uniting all Indians," Ta-na said, "but I fear that he has already built the greatest confederation of tribes ever assembled."

Harrison rubbed his clean-shaven chin. "Can you get messages to the tribes who have not yet joined Tecumseh?"

Ta-na nodded.

"I'll prepare papers for you. I want to tell each and every one of the uncommitted chiefs that if war comes, even friendly Indians will die, because in the heat of battle our soldiers won't be able to tell friend from foe."

Ta-na hesitated before speaking. "Sir, I fear that some of them will take that as an open threat."

"Threat? No. It is simply a well-intended warning."

"To a white man all Indians look alike?" Ta-na asked with a little smile.

"Now, don't you start hinting that I'm a bigot, young sprout," Harrison said. "I have many Indian friends, and I'd trust my life to your father, for example."

"Who is half white," Ta-na said.

Harrison leaned forward. "Believe me, I'm thinking of the best interests of those Indians who are friends of the United States. I simply don't want to see them caught between two warring forces." He puffed on his cigar. "Is there anything else?"

"No, sir." Ta-na rose and gathered his weapons.

"How many warriors would you say are encamped at Tippecanoe, uh, Prophetstown?"

"Three thousand, give or take a couple of hundred."

Harrison whistled. "There's one more message I'd like to have you deliver—or see that it is. I want to meet with Tecumseh's brother Tenskwatawa to see if I can talk some sense into his head. Can you do that for me?"

"I would not want to deliver any message to the Prophet in person," Ta-na said.

"But can you find someone who can?"

"I will try."

"Good, good. If you'll go out to the kitchen, my boy, Cook will give you a meal."

"That's generous of you," Ta-na said. "I'll get something when I have joined my cousin in his cabin."

"As you wish," Harrison said. Long after Ta-na had been shown out, the general sat in his study puffing on the diminishing cigar. "Three thousand," he whispered. "Three thousand."

There had been only one thousand Indians at the Fallen Timbers, along with about a hundred British regulars and Canadian militiamen. Arrayed against that force had been the most stalwart American army since the days of George Washington. They were General Anthony Wayne's American Legion, men so well trained that they marched in ranks into the muzzles of the Indians and British hidden among the storm-tangled trees. At Vincennes Harrison had only two short companies of militia and a handful of regulars. It was time, he decided, to start beating the drums.

His first action was a request to Secretary of War Eustis that the Fourth Regiment of Volunteers, a regular army unit recruited in New England, be sent down the Ohio with all possible haste. Although his plan had not been approved by the secretary of war, Harrison, as governor, had the authority to call out all the militia units in the Indiana Territory.

Ta-na found Gao's cabin dark and empty, but some of Gao's clothing was still there. He lit candles and rummaged in the kitchen for food, but aside from a container of flour there was nothing. He was tired from a long day of running at a warrior's pace, and he lay down on the bed, pulled a deerskin over him, and closed his eyes. His cousin was a warrior and capable of taking care of himself.

But Gao had been badly wounded. What if the wound had festered?

He leaped from the bed, gathered his weapons, and ran out of the cabin. A larger cabin at the east end of the parade ground served the garrison's surgeon as both infirmary and quarters. The windows were dark, and Ta-na pounded on the door with the butt of his rifle until he heard sounds from within. There was a crash and a torrent of curses before a light blossomed and the door opened. The surgeon reeked of his own remedy, and he was unsteady on his feet as he tried to rub a barked shin and look at Ta-na at the same time.

"What in hell do you want?" Dr. Henri demanded.

"My brother," Ta-na said, fearing what he would hear.

"I don't know your damned brother." The surgeon started to close the door, but Ta-na put his hand on the wood and pushed.

"You treated my brother for a wound in his thigh," he said.

"Oh, that one."

"Yes. Where is he? Is he all right?"

"He is all right as far as I know," Henri said.

"His wound healed properly?"

"Oh, *oui*. I do not know what Jeb Martin has done to him, though."

Ta-na took hold of the surgeon's arm and squeezed hard. "Where is my brother?"

"The last I heard, he was in the guardhouse," the surgeon said. "Will you break my arm for that? It was not I who put him there."

"Thank you," Ta-na said.

A lone sentry stood guard outside the converted cellar in which Gao was imprisoned, and he came to attention when Ta-na approached.

"Stand and identify yourself," the guard ordered.

"I am Ta-na, chief scout to General Harrison."

"What do you want here?"

"I want to see my brother."

"Come back tomorrow."

"I will speak with my brother now." Ta-na lifted his rifle and pointed it directly at the soldier's belly.

"He'll be asleep," the guard said. "That man can do some sleeping."

"Stand aside." Ta-na backed down the steps, still holding his rifle on the guard, and called out Gao's name.

"Ta-na?"

"So."

"Open the door."

"I can't," Ta-na said.

"I'm going to call the sergeant of the guard," the sentry said.

"You are going to keep your mouth shut," Ta-na said, cocking his rifle.

"I will keep my mouth shut," the guard said. "But if you try to break the prisoner out I'll have to shoot you."

"Fair enough, if you have time to load your weapon before *I* shoot *you*."

"Get me out of here," Gao pleaded.

"First tell me how you got in."

Gao told the story as quickly as possible. The guard, hearing how Gao had bested Sergeant Jeb Martin in a fight, leaned his rifle against the wall and listened with Ta-na as Gao wound up the tale.

"It's true that the sergeant beats the living daylights out of that squaw," the young soldier told Ta-na. "I'd have to see it to believe it, though, your brother whupping ol' Jeb Martin."

"If my brother says it is so, it is so," Ta-na said. "What will happen to him?"

"Soon as they get enough officers here they'll try him before a court-martial, and then they'll probably give him a public flogging before putting him to work at hard labor for a couple of years."

"Ta-na, get me out of here," Gao said with passion.

"Yes," Ta-na said.

No lights were visible in the lower story of Grouseland when Ta-na ran through the walnut grove, but candles were still gleaming from two windows on the bedroom floor. Ta-na pounded the elaborate brass knocker again and again until an upper window opened and Harrison called down, "Who the devil is there?"

Ta-na moved out into the yard, in Harrison's view. The moon was so bright it cast shadows. "They have thrown my brother into the guardhouse," he said.

"Ta-na? Is that you?"

"Yes, sir. My brother has done nothing wrong, General Harrison."

"Can't we take this up in the morning?"

"My brother is locked in a cave."

"Blast and damn," Harrison said. "All right. Wait there."

It was a full ten minutes before the front door opened to reveal the governor in his dressing gown, carrying a candle. "Come in."

He led the way to the study and put the candle on

the mantel, but he did not sit down. "All right. Let's have it."

Ta-na repeated Gao's story. Harrison's anger gradually faded. "It's hard for me to believe that Gao took Jeb Martin down."

"Gao did nothing wrong, sir," Ta-na repeated.

"Well, hitting a noncommissioned officer isn't exactly in accordance with army regulations, boy."

"Sir, we came here in good faith, my brother and I, to serve the United States as our fathers and our grandfather did before us. Is this to be Gao's reward?"

"Take it easy," Harrison said. "I'll see that justice is done."

"Thank you, sir."

"If you'll just get the hell out of here and let me get some sleep." Harrison lifted one hand. "I know, I know. Your brother is locked in a cave, but he's been there for a week or more now, and he's survived. I think he'll live through the next few hours, don't you?"

"Yes, sir," Ta-na said grudgingly.

"You find Lieutenant O'Toole and tell him I said I want to see everyone involved in this affair at headquarters first thing in the morning. That means Sergeant Martin, your brother, and the two women."

"Thank you, sir," Ta-na said.

The following morning Gao was the last to arrive at post headquarters. His buckskins were soiled, his hair matted and tangled, and he smelled rather high. Already gathered in Harrison's office were Ta-na, Lieutenant Stockton O'Toole, Sergeant Jeb Martin, and the two Indian women.

Running Mink stank of stale whiskey. Her eyes were bloodshot, and there was a fresh, vivid bruise around one swollen eye. Mist-on-the-Water stood against a wall, her head down. When Gao was escorted into the room by an armed guard, she looked up briefly.

"All right," Harrison said. "I've read your report, Sergeant Martin, and I've heard this boy's account of the affair secondhand. What I want to know is how it all started. It seems that there's some difference of opinion."

"Sir," Martin barked. "You have my word as a noncommissioned officer that this Injun was molesting my stepdaughter."

"Yes, yes, I know what you've said." Harrison thumped Martin's written report with his finger. "I want to hear what the young woman has to say. She was, after all, directly involved."

Mist-on-the-Water glanced around with wide, frightened eyes, as if she were looking for a means of escape.

"It's all right, girl," Harrison said. "Gao, here, says that you two were talking marriage. Is that true?"

"Yes, sir," Mist said softly.

"Was he molesting you?"

"No, sir."

"What was he doing?"

Mist-on-the-Water looked at Gao as if for help.

"Well?" Harrison demanded.

"He was—we were . . . kissing."

"I told you the son of a bitch was after her, sir," Martin said.

"Control yourself, Sergeant," Lieutenant O'Toole said sharply.

"Was this kissing against your will?" Harrison asked Mist.

"No, sir," she said so softly that she could scarcely be heard.

"Now," Harrison said, "tell me how the fight between Gao and Sergeant Martin started."

Mist looked at Martin fearfully. A look of defiant determination crossed her round, pretty face. "Neither of us knew my stepfather was there until he put his hand on Gao's shoulder, turned him, and hit him in the face."

"Without prior warning? Without an order to cease and desist his amorous activity?" Harrison asked.

"Yes, sir," Mist said.

"And did Gao draw a knife on the sergeant?"

"No, sir. Gao wrestled my stepfather to the ground and held him and tried to talk to him. When my stepfather agreed that there was nothing to fight about, Gao let him up. But then my stepfather kicked him on his injured leg and attacked him with a knife. That's when I jumped on my stepfather's back and begged him to stop."

"You lying Injun slut," Martin said.

"Lieutenant O'Toole," Harrison said, "you will clear this room of everyone except Gao and Sergeant Martin."

"Sir," O'Toole snapped, clicking his heels. He ushered the two women and Ta-na out of the room.

"Sergeant Martin," Harrison said in a mild voice, "I am quite familiar with your record. It is an admirable one. In view of the service you have given this country I would not presume to call you a liar, and I will do all that is within my power to see that not even so much as a hint of such an accusation goes into your file."

Martin's face darkened, but he stood rigidly at attention.

"Sergeant, I served with this boy's father, his uncle, and his grandfather. You, too, since you were at the Timbers, may have heard of those men: the sachem Renno, the shaman El-i-chi, and Anthony Wayne's chief of scouts, Colonel Roy Johnson."

"Yes, sir, I have," Martin said, his anger giving way to uncertainty.

"It is difficult for me to believe that this boy attempted to rape your stepdaughter and that she would lie about it."

"Well, sir, maybe it wasn't as bad as it looked," Martin said.

"Do you want to change your story?"

"Well, sir, he was lying beside her on a blanket."

"Fully clothed?"

Martin was silent.

"Since he was in a position to get to his feet and engage you in a fight, I have to assume that he was dressed," Harrison said.

"Yes, sir," Martin said sullenly.

"It is a serious matter when a noncommissioned officer engages in fisticuffs with a subordinate," Harrison said, "especially if the superior strikes the first blow. I would think, Sergeant, that you would be as interested as this boy in wiping any mention of this affair from the record."

Martin glowered at Gao.

Gao felt a chill of warning, for there was pure hate in Martin's eyes.

"When you put it that way, sir," Martin said.

"Shall we consider this matter closed?" The governor shifted his gaze from one combatant to the other.

"So," Gao said stiffly.

"Sir," Martin snapped.

"I warn both of you," Harrison said, and there was iron in his voice. "I will not abide a resumption of this affair. Regardless of whose fault it is, I will hold both of you responsible. Am I understood?"

"Sir," Gao and Martin said together.

In the afternoon Ta-na and Gao walked beside the river. The summer sun warmed them, and the water of the river looked cool and inviting. At a spot below the willow thicket where Gao had lost himself in the sweet kisses of Mist-on-the-Water, they stripped and plunged into the stream to surface and blow and splash at each other like two young otters. When they came out and sat on a mossy bank, Ta-na stared at the large scar left by the rifle slug that had torn its way through the big muscle of Gao's thigh. He had, of course, noticed that Gao walked with a limp, but the entire leg looked shrunken. Concerned, Ta-na pointed.

"It is much better," Gao said.

"A good run will complete the healing," Ta-na stated.

They dressed, and Ta-na set off at the warrior's pace. For a few minutes Gao stayed at his side, then fell slightly behind, breathing in sharp, shallow bursts. When Ta-na sneaked a look at him, his lips were pulled back so tightly that the blood was forced from them. He was clearly in pain.

"Enough," Ta-na said, stopping.

"It is much better." Gao stood straight, looking his cousin in the eye. Suddenly his face contorted, and he bent to massage a severe cramp in his weakened leg.

"So," Ta-na said, pushing Gao to the ground and rubbing the knotted muscle with both hands. Gao moaned a little as the spasm relaxed.

"It does this often?" Ta-na asked.

"Only when my inconsiderate brother forces me to run with him," Gao said.

"What does the surgeon say?"

"That it will grow stronger with time."

Ta-na shook his head. "When I leave you behind, you get into trouble. If I take you with me, I will have to carry you."

"May dogs bark at your spirit," Gao said, not too playfully.

"Come," Ta-na said, giving Gao his hand and hauling him to his feet.

They walked slowly toward the parade ground.

"You go out again, then?" Gao asked.

"I am to deliver messages to those chiefs who have not yet decided to fight with Tecumseh."

"A peaceful mission. We can deliver messages at a walking pace."

"And if the friends of Red Horse or the others who died by our hands in the fight on the Wabash strike our trail?"

"All right. I will stay behind and get married, and when I am lying in my bed in comfort with Mist-on-the-Water beside me, I will say a prayer to the manitous that you are having to sleep in a swamp."

"It is good to know that the brother of my heart truly cares for me," Ta-na said in the Seneca tongue of his father.

*   *   *

Each day brought new strength to Gao's leg. He ran short distances and swam against the river current with his legs doing most of the work.

Ta-na had been gone from Vincennes eight days when Gao was awakened by a pounding on the door of his cabin. He leaped to his feet, his hand closed over the handle of his tomahawk. He recognized the keening of a woman in mourning and heard sobs as he jerked on his clothing. When he opened the door, Running Mink rushed into the room and fell heavily on the floor. Gao lifted her to her feet. Her nose was bleeding, and her doeskin tunic was torn.

"Help her," Running Mink wailed. "Help her."

Concern for Mist-on-the-Water welled up and became a ball of panic in Gao's throat. "Where?" he asked.

Running Mink pointed.

"Your cabin?"

She wailed acknowledgment.

Love and fear banished caution and common sense. Leaving his weapons behind, Gao ran from the room, sprinted across the parade ground, and burst into Jeb Martin's cabin. He saw Mist's long, graceful legs kicking as she struggled under the weight of her stepfather. As she fought and squirmed Gao caught a glimpse of her bare breasts. Her shirt had been ripped down the front, and Martin was trying to pull her skirt aside.

"Martin!" Gao yelled.

Swaying drunkenly, the sergeant came to his feet. Mist crawled off the bed and tried to pull her torn shirt together.

"You," Martin said with such malevolence that Gao reached for his tomahawk, only to remember that he'd put it aside when he helped Running Mink to her feet.

For a few breathless seconds the two men faced each other. Mist-on-the-Water edged around the bed, putting distance between her and Martin.

"Get out of my house," Martin said.

"I will," Gao said. "And I will take Mist-on-the-Water with me."

"Like hell you will," Martin said.

"Mist—" Gao began.

He was interrupted by Running Mink, who came through the open door at full speed and threw herself at Martin with her hands extended like claws. Martin tossed her aside as easily as if she had been a limp rag, and her head struck the corner of the rock hearth with a sound that told Gao she was seriously injured. Mist-on-the-Water cried out and ran toward her mother.

Martin backhanded Mist across the cheek. "Leave the Injun whore alone."

The force of Martin's blow sent Mist tumbling back onto the bed. A red mist of rage before his eyes, Gao leaped toward the larger man. Martin whirled and picked up a tomahawk; Gao aborted his rush and went into a defensive crouch. Sneering in satisfaction, Martin advanced toward the young Indian. Gao dodged under a swinging blow that would have split his head but, in so doing, allowed Martin to get between him and the door.

With no room to maneuver, Gao looked around frantically for a weapon as the sergeant positioned himself to corner his opponent. Gao went low and knocked Martin's feet from under him. The big man tumbled but quickly regained his stance. Gao picked up a small table and used it as a shield, but Martin's blade split it into two pieces, and the table legs were too fragile to be of much use.

"Gao," Mist-on-the-Water called frantically.

He glanced toward her, and she tossed a tomahawk to him, handle first. He plucked it out of the air and tested its heft. It wasn't as well balanced as a Seneca tomahawk, but its iron blade was sharp. He lifted the weapon in time to parry a killing blow toward his throat.

"I don't want to kill you, Sergeant," Gao said as Martin backed away to assess the altered situation.

Martin laughed. "That's the least of your worries." As he advanced, he feinted first to the left and then directly toward Gao. Gao knew Martin's strength and backed away, alert for any sign of weakness in Martin's defense. When the sergeant rushed, he danced aside and fell over the table, sending it crashing to the floor. Martin's blade smashed wood near his head, and then he was on his feet.

Iron rang against iron. Martin's hand closed over Gao's wrist. Gao seized the sergeant's weapon hand, and they stood face to face, muscles straining, Martin's cold eyes staring into Gao's.

"Sergeant, I will take Mist and go," Gao said, his voice strained by his effort.

"Injun son of a bitch," Martin said.

Gao twisted his wrist out of Martin's hold and released the sergeant's hand at the same time. Martin's blade whistled past his ear as he dodged aside to backhand a glancing blow to Martin's head. The sergeant went down heavily. Panting with exertion, Gao stood for a moment, then took a step toward the fallen man to check on his condition.

"What in blazes?" asked a uniformed soldier as he burst in the door, rifle at the ready.

"The Indian has killed the sergeant," said a second man.

As the first soldier brought his rifle to bear, Gao could see death in the man's eyes and in the way his finger tensed on the trigger. The second rifle was moving as well.

"No!" Mist-on-the-Water screamed. "No."

Gao took three running steps. A rifle blasted, and he felt the hot brush of the ball on the back of his neck. He jumped as high as he could and smashed through the glass of a window just as the discharge of the second rifle filled the cabin with smoke and sound. He landed on his shoulder, rolled to his feet, and ran toward the shelter of the trees along the river. Behind him he heard shouts of alarm and feared that a hundred soldiers would soon be after him.

Moving swiftly along the river toward the grove of

willows, he thought of Mist, and the pain of loss was added to the pain in his leg. He could never go back. The governor had said that both he and Martin would be held responsible if there was more trouble. If Martin was dead, the white man's justice would demand Gao's death in return.

He didn't know what he was going to do, other than avoid being punished for killing a man who deserved to be dead, a man who beat his wife and attempted to rape his stepdaughter.

He guessed that the garrison would assume he had fled to the south, toward his home below the Ohio, beyond Kentucky and Tennessee. Instead he waded into the river, swam to the western bank, and began a northward circle around Vincennes.

Chapter Three

B eth Huntington Harper's house in the Cherokee Nation was as grand—if not as solidly constructed—as Governor William Henry Harrison's Grouseland. It was the finest house west of the North Carolina Piedmont cities and north of New Orleans. No one remembered who had first called it Huntington Castle, but even those who lived there had come to accept the name. Since there were no brick kilns in the autonomous Indian nation, Beth's sprawling home north of the big bend in the Tennessee River was constructed of native timber; the clapboard exterior had been painted gleaming white. The beams, rafters, floor supports, and wall joists were rough-sawn pine, and the interior finish was the work of craftsmen who had been brought to Rusog's Town from Knoxville and Nashville. Some of the furnishings had made the long voyage across the Atlantic from England.

Pecan trees planted during construction lined a broad, straight lane that led to the pillared front porch. Split-rail fences enclosed green pastureland, where spring colts gamboled and splendid mares regarded visitors with friendly curiosity. Meadows and a line of trees separated the house and its surrounding pastures and fields from Rusog's Town, where Cherokee and Seneca lived side by side in mutual regard.

When the flame-haired mistress of Huntington Castle was in residence, the permanent staff of freed slaves moved a step faster. The outbuildings took on a fresh coat of whitewash; weeds along the fencerows fell to swinging scythes; dust flew as each of the twenty rooms received what amounted to a spring, summer, fall, and winter cleaning all at once. At night the windows were lit, and the great rooms rang with singing, laughter, the bawling of babies, and the deep voices of warriors speaking a mixture of English, Seneca, and Cherokee.

Renno, the master of Huntington Castle, was content to let his wife run the place as she saw fit. Whether the dwelling was a traditional Seneca longhouse, a Cherokee lodge, or a mansion, it was the woman's realm. A man, even one like Renno who could shift successfully between two worlds, had the duties of providing meat for the table and protecting the home. A worthy man, like the husband of the virtuous woman described in the last chapter of Proverbs, was "known in the gates, when he sitteth among the elders of the land."

Using the excuse that he wanted to tell Renno and El-i-chi about having given hospitality to their sons Ta-na and Gao on their way north, Andrew Jackson arrived at Huntington Castle. Actually, Jackson was afflicted by the very condition that beset most frontiersmen: He was curious to see the other side of the nearest ridge, and one excuse for a trip was as good as another.

Jackson was a popular man with the senior warriors of Rusog's Town, in spite of his reputation as an Indian fighter. The days of blood were past, the days when Jackson and John Sevier, first governor of the state of Tennessee, vied with each other to see how many Indian scalps they could accumulate. For over a year Jackson had been living quietly with his family at the Hermitage, near Nashville, where he owned six hundred and forty acres, a square mile of land. For the moment, at least, he'd had his fill of politics. However, he maintained his commission in the Tennessee militia, just in case some interesting little war came along.

In Jackson's honor, Renno had invited friends and neighbors to gather on a balmy night in the back garden of Huntington Castle, where a pig was roasting on a spit. While watching Aunt Sarah, the black cook, supervise the kitchen crew, Jackson quoted to his audience of household members, family, and senior warriors—both Seneca and Cherokee—the biblical description of a godly woman and a worthy man.

"Miss Beth," Jackson said, "if I hadn't found my Rachel when I was younger, I would have challenged this aging warrior for your hand."

"You would have made my choice difficult," Beth said.

Renno put a fierce scowl on his face and used his forefinger as a blade to indicate what he would have done to Jackson's hair in such an event.

Jackson chuckled, mellowed by sharing a jug with his old friend Roy Johnson—twice Renno's father-by-marriage, due to Renno's marriage to his daughter, Emily, and Johnson's marriage to Renno's mother, Toshabe.

"Yep," Jackson said, "the Good Book points at you, Miss Beth, when it describes a virtuous woman."

Beth was no stranger to the Bible. She had taught it to her stepchildren, her nieces and nephews by marriage, and other youngsters from Rusog's Town who had chosen to attend her informal school.

" 'Her price is far above rubies,' " she said with a smile.

Renno nodded as the next verse of the Thirty-first

Proverb came to him. " 'The heart of her husband doth safely trust in her.' " He winked at Roy. "But I don't see my virtuous woman rising while it is yet night to giveth meat to her husband."

"Shall I go plant a vineyard?" Beth asked, smiling sweetly.

"Wheat and corn do better in this soil," Renno said, smiling back.

At forty-seven, Renno was the eldest son of Ghonkàba and Toshabe, and great-grandson of the white infant who had been taken and raised as his own by the wise Seneca sachem, Ghonka. Known as the white Indian —as were his ancestors before him—he held informal audience while seated in a bentwood rocker. His younger brother, El-i-chi, sachem and shaman of the Seneca, who lived in Rusog's Town, was with him, as was his brother-by-marriage, the stocky, solidly built, and ever redoubtable Cherokee Rusog.

Renno's older sister, Ena, named for the wife of old Ghonka, was also present, still a striking woman at forty-nine. Her dark brown hair was touched with hints of silver, and her green eyes expressed compassion and wisdom. When she and Rusog were at the Castle she alternated her time between participating in the men's conversations on the front porch and watching in awe while her flame-haired sister-by-marriage cracked a velvet whip over the staff as the house acquired a final polish.

To Renno, there seemed to be a sadness about Ena. Except for her husband, she was a woman alone. Her son and her daughter had migrated to the west, taking her grandchild with them. Grief over the death of their mother, Toshabe, was still with all three of the siblings, but since Ena was her only daughter, the loss had affected her in ways unknown to Renno and El-i-chi.

Renno could empathize with his sister, for two of his children were far away as well. Pale-haired and beautiful Renna, living image of Renno's first wife, Emily, was in

France with her husband and their son and daughter. Their letters were pored over eagerly. Ta-na, Renno's son by the lovely Seneca, An-da, was with El-i-chi's son, Gao, in the Ohio country acting as a scout for Governor William Henry Harrison.

Renno's elder son, Os-sweh-ga-da-ah Ne-wa-ah—Little Hawk—sat nearby listening to the talk and watching his five-year-old cousin, Ah-wen-ga, daughter of El-i-chi and Ah-wa-o, play with his twin boys on the lawn. Little Hawk's four-year-old twins, Michael Soaring Hawk and Joseph Standing Bear, were chasing lightning bugs with great enthusiasm.

It was stolid Rusog, the Cherokee chief, who took the conversation to a more serious topic, speaking in a low, somber voice of the persistent encroachment into Cherokee lands by the white tide of humanity that continued to pour over the mountains from the east. "General Jackson," he said in his deep, accented English, "we have heard from the south, especially from the Creek Indians, that war is likely in the Floridas."

Jackson took a puff on his pipe. "I've just had some correspondence about that area, as a matter of fact. All we read about in the papers is the situation at sea, but it seems to me that if war with either England or Spain comes, it will begin right down there in Florida."

"Ummm," Rusog said, reluctant to voice an overt question but interested in hearing what else Jackson had to say.

"There are twenty thousand people in West Florida," Jackson said. "Four fifths of them are Americans, but we're still expected to leave the best port along the coast in Spanish hands. It's my contention that the fort and harbor at Mobile were a part of the Louisiana Purchase. Mr. Madison, up in Washington, is going to have to come to a decision about that, and right damned quick, or the Americans in West Florida will take matters into their own hands."

"But wouldn't that bring the British into it?" Roy Johnson asked. "After all, Britain and Spain are allies."

Jackson puffed clouds of smoke. "Yep, the Brits have made noises about moving into Florida. They say they'd be doing it to protect the interests of Spain, but any man with a grain of sense knows that the British lion is land hungry. Let him loose in the Floridas and he'd have to be driven out at the point of a bayonet."

"Reckon the Creek will side with England?" Roy asked.

Jackson shrugged. "The Creek will side with whoever offers them the most money, the best arms, and the rawest whiskey."

Rusog grunted. His early experiences with the white man's ideas of fairness and justice had left him more doubtful than some about Renno's contention that the future of the Indian lay with the United States.

"No offense meant, Rusog," Jackson said. "It's just that I don't consider the Creek to be as civilized as you Cherokee. I think you'd have to agree with me that there is a difference in the tribes, wouldn't you?"

"According to Tecumseh," said El-i-chi, speaking for the first time, "we are all brothers, we Indians."

"Well, so are we *all*," Jackson said. "All sons of Eve, after all, but some of us have taken divergent paths. Admit it, El-i-chi, how far can you trust a Creek?"

"About as far as I can trust a white horse trader," El-i-chi answered.

"There you are, then," Jackson declared with a laugh. He poked the stem of his pipe at Rusog. "How close are we to war with England in the south? Let me tell you this. Mr. Madison ordered Governor William Claiborne of the Orleans Territory to keep his militia out of West Florida, but some of the boys didn't listen. They took the Spanish fort at Baton Rouge, hoisted the Stars and Stripes, and said that West Florida was an integral and inalienable portion of the United States. What did England do? Not a dad-gummed thing. And they won't, because in spite of all their big talk, Napoleon is giving them all they can handle. The European war is bleeding them dry. They don't have the men to fight a land war on the North American continent. They'll continue to harass our ships at sea as long as we let 'em, and what we ought to do right now is call out the militia and march into West *and* East Florida and then into Canada as well. We can make this continent American from the North Pole to the Mexican border in six months, and after that, if the spirit moves us, all the way to South America."

"I think I'll let you young sprouts fight the next war," Roy said.

Jackson laughed. "You're an old warhorse, Roy. Let a bugle blow and you'll be up looking for your tomahawk and rifle, rarin' to go." He relit his pipe. "Fact is, boys, I can't think of anyone I'd rather have with me if war comes either with the tribes who are listening to Tecumseh or with England."

"Thank you, General," Beth said, "but I'm going to keep my husband at home for at least a month or two before he takes on another cause."

Although it was no easy jaunt from Rusog's Town to Knoxville, there was considerable travel back and forth, enough so that a letter addressed to Captain Hawk Harper, United States Marine Corps, had lain in the Knoxville post office for only a week before it was brought to Rusog's Town by a warrior from the Cherokee village who had gone to Knoxville to trade. As it happened, Little Hawk was in the pasture in front of the house when the Cherokee arrived. Hawk took the letter, and his eyes widened at the title before his name. Casting a guilty look toward the house before breaking the battered wax seal, he glanced first at the scrawled name on the bottom of a sheet of White House stationery. President James Madison's signature was inked heavily, but the letters were cramped and run together.

The message was brief and to the point. Hawk's commission in the Marine Corps had been reactivated, with an immediate promotion to captain. He was ordered to travel south to serve as military liaison to Benjamin Hawkins, agent to the Creek Nation. The last paragraph of the letter stated Madison's intent.

> *"Your primary duty is to report to me with regularity on the state of mind of the various Creek chieftains regarding the possibility of their remaining neutral in the event of war between the United States and England; and the reactions of said chieftains to the preachings of the Shawnee Tecumseh."*

Naomi, Little Hawk's wife, was a daughter of the western frontier. She had been brought into the troubled Tennessee Territory as a child by her parents, Frank and Sadie Burns, who were killed not by the hostile Cherokee Indians whose lands had been invaded by white families from east of the mountains, but by renegade white men. As a cotton-headed girl she had given Little Hawk his first kiss, and from that time their romance had been a now-and-again thing interrupted by Little Hawk's duties and, most recently, by his term as an impressed seaman aboard a British ship of the line.

At twenty-eight, Naomi's hair was corn-silk yellow, and her sable-brown eyes were large and expressive. Only a few of her youthful freckles remained, two of them on the tip of her nose. Her mouth was wide, her lips sensuously full. Following the birth of the twins, she had recovered her tiny waist, and her breasts had shrunk back to the size of large apples.

As soon as Little Hawk walked into the kitchen where she was supervising the pulling of a batch of taffy by little Ah-wen-ga and the twins, Naomi knew something was troubling him. She lifted her face for a quick peck. Since she'd been sampling the taffy it was a sweet kiss.

"Ummm," Little Hawk said, coming back for more.

"Behave," Naomi said teasingly, rolling her eyes at the children.

"You're going to save some for your father, I hope," Little Hawk said to Joseph, the more serious-minded twin.

"Naomi says there'll be enough for everyone," Ahwen-ga said. She slapped at Little Hawk's hand as he stuck his finger into the taffy bowl.

"Have you seen my father?" Little Hawk asked.

"He and Beth were going riding," Naomi answered.

"When you and your helpers finish with this rather sticky project, I'll be outside," Little Hawk announced.

"Husband?" Naomi said quietly as he turned.

He looked over his shoulder.

"What is it?"

"I'll be on the porch," he said.

She could not hurry the process, and then a considerable period of time was required to remove taffy from the hair, ears, and fingernails of her three small helpers. She left the children in the kitchen with Aunt Sarah and found Little Hawk sitting in his favorite bentwood rocker, staring moodily into the distance.

"All right," she said as she sat down in a chair beside him.

He handed her the letter. She read it, and her heart sank for a moment before a look of determination firmed her mouth. "The twins and I will go with you, of course."

"I gave that my consideration," he said.

"This is a decision that will be made by both of us," she said, "so don't use the past tense. We *will* give it a *lot* of consideration."

He took her hand and smiled at her.

"And don't try to soften me up by showing me your pearly whites," she said sternly. "We have been apart more than we've been together during our marriage, and I will have no more of that."

A fond smile brightened Little Hawk's face. He

leaned toward her and kissed her on the cheek. "We'll see."

To know that he was considering her protest was enough for the moment. He would be fair, but in the end the decision would be his. She sincerely believed that another separation would be as painful to him as to her; she had come to feel secure in his love. Sometimes at night when she lay awake beside him after they had been together as man and wife, the past would invade her, and she would be back in a frontier cabin made filthy and crowded by the men who killed her mother and father, the men who used her as if she were an animal. She would never be able to forget that shame, but thanks to the love of the man who had saved her, she usually managed to keep it deeply submerged. Little Hawk's unquestioning and uncritical love had begun the cleansing of her soul. In giving birth to Joseph and Michael the purification of her body was completed, for God would not have gifted her with such perfection had not the taint of that terrible time been wiped away.

During the evening meal Little Hawk told Renno and Beth about President Madison's letter. Renno voiced no immediate opinion, but Beth said, "Surely, since you are going to be living in a well-established and protected agency, it will be safe to take your family."

"I have been trying to convince him of that," Naomi said.

"Where are we going?" Joseph asked in a piping voice.

"Where do we go?" Michael seconded.

"Where is the Hawkins agency located?" Renno asked.

"Among the Lower Creek on the Flint River," Little Hawk said.

"That is not an inconsiderable journey," Renno said.

Little Hawk nodded. He had consulted the maps in Beth's library. To reach the Flint River he would have to cross the northeastern tip of the Mississippi Territory to the Coosa River, then travel through the towns of the Upper Creek. His best estimate of the straight-line distance was between one hundred fifty and two hundred miles, but the actual trip would by necessity be longer.

"Although there is still some youthful coup-counting now and then between Cherokee and Creek, the relationship between the tribes is peaceful," Renno said. "I would think that a man traveling with his family could do so without fear."

That would hold true almost anywhere in areas controlled by eastern tribes. Two or more warriors traveling alone would have to be alert to possible attack, for those in possession of the land were jealous of their ground and might mistake a desire for peaceful passage as intent to raid. When a man marched openly with women and children, his intentions were taken to be peaceful.

"We would not be traveling through areas where Creek warriors raid white settlements on the Georgia frontier," Little Hawk said.

"I have read about your Benjamin Hawkins," Beth said. "He has his family with him, a considerable brood, if I remember correctly."

"It's settled, then," Naomi said, reaching out to take Little Hawk's hand.

He laughed fondly. "I guess it *is* settled."

Only days later father and son faced each other on the front porch of Huntington Castle. The sun was an hour high, and the day was going to be a hot one, with clear skies until the usual afternoon buildup of thunderheads that would bring scattered showers.

"Do you have everything you need?" Renno asked.

"If we were taking more I'd have to hire a train of wagons," Little Hawk said.

Three pack mules were laden. Packing had been a family activity, and there'd been much discussion. In the end Naomi decided to leave her finer clothing at Huntington Castle, since there would be little call for dressing formally in the Lower Creek Nation. One pack held cooking utensils and flatware, a linen tablecloth, a sewing kit, a Bible, packets of herbal concoctions provided by Ena to ward off evil fevers and other ailments that plagued the muggy lands to the south, and toys carved for the twins by Se-quo-i, the talented and wise Cherokee and valued friend of the family.

Clothing burdened the second mule: sturdy, sensible togs for Naomi, spare buckskins for Little Hawk, and more things—so said Renno—than the twins could wear out before they grew out of them.

"If that happens," Beth had said as she helped Naomi pack, "you can give them to Creek youngsters so they get at least some use."

The third mule's pack contained camping equipment, sleeping gear, water containers, and food for the trail.

Little Hawk carried his most important possessions. At his waist were the ornately carved pistols that had once belonged to Meriwether Lewis, and he carried Lewis's fine rifle in addition to a tomahawk and a hunting knife.

Since returning to Huntington Castle he had let his hair grow, so it reached his shoulders when it was hanging loose. Now he wore it gathered at his neck and tied with a leather thong. It gleamed yellow-gold in the sun. He was dressed in buckskins and moccasins, and while Naomi and the boys wore hats, his head was bare.

Renno handed up the boys: Joseph rode behind Naomi on one of Beth's fine horses, and Michael held on tight to Little Hawk.

"The manitous will be with you," Renno said solemnly.

"God bless you," Beth told them as Little Hawk signaled to Naomi to move ahead. They made a rather lengthy procession as they rode down the lane and away, first the two horses, then the three pack mules in single file.

"Damn," Beth said heatedly, "how I do hate farewells."

Her eyes were wet, and Renno put his arm around her waist, but he didn't trust himself to speak.

"Now we're just old folks at home," Beth said.

Renno cleared his throat. "If you get lonely I'll have Ah-wa-o bring Ah-wen-ga and some of her playmates to run through the house and make much noise."

"It might just come to that." She smiled up at him. "Well?"

Renno's heart was heavy. One son was far away to the north and quite possibly facing danger with each sunrise and sunset. Renna and her two children were separated from him by almost half the continent as well as the Atlantic Ocean. Now his other son was just turning out of the lane, heading south. Renno lifted his hand in response to Little Hawk's last wave, and the voice of one of the boys came to him faintly. To answer the last, barely heard good-bye, he lifted his head and sent the mournful call of a wolf after the departing members of his family. Little Hawk answered, his voice rising and falling in a keening howl that wavered with distance.

Beth held tightly to her husband's hand. A shiver shook her, and she firmly told herself not to worry. They would be all right, those whom she loved. They would come back to her. But behind her the house seemed so empty, and the bright morning sun no longer seemed as warm. She turned her face quickly to the northwest and saw, rising over the forest that lay beyond Rusog's Town, a bank of low, purple clouds.

"Oh, dear," she said, "I hope they don't have to ride through a storm on their first day."

"First day or last, the rain is wet," Renno said.

"Old Indian adage?"

He shrugged.

"I have work to do," she said. "We're making pickles today."

"So," Renno said.

She knew him well. He couldn't bring himself to look at her. His eyes penetrated distances and saw things that were not visible from his stand on the porch.

"Oh, go on," she said.

He bent and kissed her. "You always understand, my Beth. Thank you."

He started to run after passing the gardens at the rear of the house, leaped over the small creek on the other side of the cultivated area, and was soon in the forest. His feet landed lightly, avoiding making noise as if they had eyes of their own. He began breathing with difficulty, and he felt the pull in the big muscles of his thighs and the long sinews of his lower legs. But he pushed past the pain, and his chest seemed to expand as he increased the pace and bounded up to the top of the ridge, then cast himself down, down, running full tilt across a grassy meadow that extended to the trees on the opposite slope.

He halted at the top of a bluff overlooking a stream and stared into the western distance. Out there was the northward bend of the Tennessee, and beyond that the oily, languid flow of the Father of Waters, the Mississippi River. His son Little Hawk had seen lands beyond the big river, having traveled from the Pacific with Meriwether Lewis and William Clark. He himself knew the lands of the Arkansas, the grassy plains of Spanish Texas, and the dry and awesomely beautiful vastness of the Apache far to the west.

But, ah, manitous, there were so many streams he had not crossed; so many mountains hid that which lay beyond them. He was forty-seven years old, and he was saddened by having been left alone by the blood of his blood. Always it had been he who had climbed the far ridge and forded the unknown stream. Now he was alone.

He ran. Running had always been cathartic for him; it was in his blood to cover great distances in a tireless flow of movement. He felt that he could run forever, and as he turned eastward to make a circle, he remembered other times when it had been necessary to cover vast distances quickly. He could smell the fresh, clean air of the north woods as if he'd been there yesterday, running southward from Canada to bring warning of the British threat against the embattled Americans.

With glowing pleasure he relived the time he'd spent with Beth in the northern forests as once again he traveled southward from Canada. He was not alone. He would never be alone as long as he had his flame-haired bride. Moreover, he was among his people. Although he had abdicated his position as sachem of the Seneca who had followed his father to the Cherokee lands following the Great White Man's War, he was respected by all. His brother, El-i-chi, was now sachem.

Renno camped beside a clear trickle of water that oozed from a natural spring at the foot of a ridge. The night was warm, and he felt cleansed after the day of exertion. Every sense was alert.

The fire he made popped cheerily as he fed it small, dry branches and stared into the flames and the bed of embers beneath. The wall of dark purple clouds that had been visible to the northwest remained low on the horizon. Overhead, the lights in the sky were brilliant and sharp-pointed. There was no moon.

It was not sleep that came to him. He could still hear the night sounds, the rustle of leaves as a breeze teased the treetops, the scurrying of some small animal on the far bank of the creek, the distant, mournful song of a whippoorwill. He saw the stars clearly, and the fire glowed with a pleasant warmth as the night cooled.

When he heard the disturbing sound of a weeping woman, he knew that it was useless to look around, for it was only a presence, a feeling in the night air. Renno lifted his face and felt pain, for the weeping held the pain of mourning. A heavy feeling of dread weighted his heart.

"Manitous," he whispered. "Manitous."

Emily's pale hair was visible to him first. Fine as spiderwebs, as blond as corn silk, a shiny wave of it moved as if a slight breeze caressed it. It materialized across the fire out of the blackness of the night. Her face, after all the years since her passing to the west, was achingly dear to him, but he was alarmed that her eyes were swollen and red.

"Why?" he whispered. "Why?"

She put her hands to her face, and her shoulders heaved with her sobs.

"Who?" Renno begged. "Tell me. Who?"

She looked at him with tears streaming down her face. Her voice was so familiar to his ears.

"It is red," she said. "Everything is red."

Never before had a message from the manitous been so enigmatic.

"Is it time for us to be together?" he asked.

Her tear-filled eyes smiled with her lips. Her voice caressed him. "Soon. Soon."

Twice now that promise had been made to him. He felt no dread. He had lived longer than many, and his life had not been futile. Questions came to him, of course, but underneath all was acceptance, for each man had, in his own time, to make the journey to the west.

"And yet you weep not for me," he whispered.

"It is red," the manitou said softly. "All is red."

When the vision began to fade, he leaped to his feet and stepped over the embers of the fire, but there was only empty air.

"Who?" he shouted to the darkness, to the sharp-edged stars and the crooning whippoorwill who had moved closer. "Tell me. Who?" If the time was near for him to join his ancestors across the river, that he could accept, but to think that crimson danger threatened someone he loved aroused fury in him.

The Coosa River was one of the most beautiful that Little Hawk had ever seen. The journey since the crossing of the Tennessee had been pleasant. The twins took to life in the open with unabated enthusiasm and an energy that taxed the ability of their parents to keep the boys seated behind them on the horses or force them to remain within sight when they made camp for the night.

That afternoon everyone wanted to go for a swim. Naomi was especially pleased, for a dip in the clear waters of the Coosa would clean away the dust and sweat of the trail. Little Hawk and the boys went right in with their clothes on to give them a wash, and Naomi did some scrubbing on the garments after they had been removed to make swimming easier. She swam naked as well, but only after Little Hawk held up a blanket to preserve her modesty.

Little Hawk had killed a turkey, and their evening meal was roasted meat washed down with water from the river. The next morning the family crossed into Upper Creek lands, and when they approached a village, Little Hawk announced his presence with signs of peace. Using a mixture of languages, he learned that the Creek town was called Tallushatche, and that Menawa, the speaker of the Upper Creek Indians, was there.

Menawa greeted the travelers in his lodge. Little Hawk was surprised to see that the speaker was, like Little Hawk himself, of mixed blood, that there was a white man in his ancestry. Menawa, also called the Big Warrior, wore traditional Creek dress, including a ribbed skullcap with a spray of feathers on top and a doeskin tunic decorated with beads. A sash crossed his full chest, and long earrings dangled from his lobes.

"You have come far," Menawa said in English.

"From the land of the Cherokee chief, Rusog," Little Hawk said. "I thank you, Great Chief, for your hospitality."

"Your woman and the children will be with the squaws," the speaker said.

Naomi opened her mouth to protest, but Little Hawk gave her a warning glance, and she allowed herself to be led away by two of Menawa's wives.

"You are not Cherokee," Menawa said.

"My blood is Seneca. I am called Os-sweh-ga-da-ah

Ne-wa-ah, Little Hawk. With my wife and sons I travel to the agency of Benjamin Hawkins on the Flint."

"Ah, yes." Menawa's face was broad, his nose impressive, his brows heavy over penetrating eyes. "He is a man who talks sense, this Hawkins."

"You know him, then?"

"I know him well. It was he who encouraged me to open my store to trade our furs with the white men in Pensacola. It was he who said to me that it would be good to raise cattle, which I have done." He waved his hand. "Once, when my blood was young, I raided with the other warriors on the Cumberland frontier. For fifteen years I joined other young ones in war against the whites of Georgia. Now I am different."

"My father, the sachem Renno, sought peace with the whites long ago," Little Hawk said.

"He was wise. It is peace that I desire. I no longer lift the hatchet against my white neighbors, and it is my advice to my people to stand aside when once again there is war among the whites."

"You are wise, Big Warrior. I pray that your wisdom is recognized by all of the Creek Indians."

Menawa shook his big head sadly. "I fear not. Some listen, but others agree with the oratory of the Shawnee Tecumseh, who preaches widely against the land-devouring white man."

"Among the Seneca and the Cherokee there are such men, but they are few. My father and my uncle, both of whom are sachems in their own right, will remain neutral if there is war with England. My Seneca clans have long been at peace with the United States, for my grandfather, my father, my uncle, and my aunt fought with George Washington against the redcoats in the Great White Man's War."

Menawa extended his arm to clasp that of Little Hawk. "May other sensible men be with us."

"I join you in that wish."

"The hospitality of my people is yours," Menawa

said. "And when you go to the Flint River Agency, you will give my regards to Hawkins. Tell him that Menawa and the Upper Creek have heard his urgings for peace."

"I will, Great Chief, with goodwill." Little Hawk returned Menawa's gesture with a Seneca warrior's clasp. "Thus do my people signify respect and friendship."

"It is good," Menawa said.

That night there was plentiful food and much oratory, and Menawa spoke of the greatness of the Creek Nation and cautioned his people to live at peace with the white men.

"It is true," he said, "that the ink is scarcely dry on one treaty before the Great White Father in Washington sends word of a new council to consider still another agreement, the result of which seems always to be a loss of Indian lands." He laughed. "I myself have attended more than one such council. I remember when the white general, James Wilkinson, demanded in insulting tones that we sell land in the east, those lands known to the white man as the Altamaha–St. Marys and the Oconee-Ocmulgee tracts. The great white general was surprised at the speed with which we agreed."

The speaker paused, smiled broadly, and let his eyes pass over his audience. "And why did we agree so quickly to sell the Altamaha land and the land between the Oconee and the Ocmulgee? Because we wanted to get home and tend to our crops. Because we knew from past experience that the Great White Father in Washington would continue to push and push and push until he got what he wanted. Meanwhile, our corn was ready for harvest, so we did the business and went home, lest our crops be taken by the deer and the raccoon.

"Look around you," Menawa continued. "You will see many of us living as the white man lives. We plow the earth with his iron-shod tool. We have learned the skills of the blacksmith in working metals. White women are among us, teaching our women how to weave cloth. The forts are there not to protect the white man from us but to

keep white settlers and frontiersmen from encroaching on
our lands. It is true that we are hemmed in on three sides
and that the white population along the Father of Waters
is growing at a rate that can be sustained only by those
who breed like rabbits. We have white men to the east, to
the west, to the south. We have agreed to let the United
States cut a road from the Ocmulgee to the Alabama
River, with the right to build inns and provide ferry service, but in exchange the United States has promised us
that our lands are now ours forever. We gave up any claim
to lands within the state of Georgia, but we have peace in
return."

When it was Little Hawk's turn to speak, he told of
the understanding that existed between the Seneca and
the United States. He spoke of his brother and his cousin
who fought with the white men in the north, and of the
desire of his people to live in peace with their Indian
neighbors.

Naomi sat with the women, her eyes gleaming with
pride as her husband held council with chiefs and warriors. "Listen," she told the twins. "Listen carefully and
remember, for this is your father, and he is a man among
men."

Chapter Four

Little Hawk and his family struck the Pensacola-New Orleans trace as they approached the Flint River from the west. A ferry was in operation, and the short ride across pleased the twins. Upriver from the ferry a fish trap had been constructed below a small waterfall. The orchards of the Flint River Agency and Benjamin Hawkins's private gardens were directly across the river. To the left of that were more than a score of log buildings arranged in two straight lines.

The family's horses and mules were left in the care of an obliging stable keeper who assured Little Hawk that they would be "done right" and that his belongings would be sent to the proper place once quarters had been assigned.

The Indian agent's office was in the first log building on the western end of the row of cabins nearest the orchards. From the size of the structure it was evident that it contained a living area for the Hawkins family.

The agency seemed to be thriving. A sawmill was in operation; the shrill sound of its huge blade tearing through wood was background for the metronomic fall of a blacksmith's hammer, the lowing of cattle from the surrounding pastures, and the laughter and cries of a herd of children at play. Small black faces were mixed with white. The disparity in dress bespoke the status of the black children, and the line of smaller log cabins with their barren yards confirmed for Little Hawk the presence of black slaves at the Flint River Agency.

Most of those who studied the newly arrived whites were Creek. The men wore loincloths, long shirts, leggings, and moccasins; some also sported close-fitting, turbanlike hats decorated with feathers. The women were dressed in petticoats that came to just below the knee; some wore a shift over them; others, young mothers, wore a chemise that opened in front to give their nursing infants access. Earbobs were popular with both men and women, and a few silver necklaces were in evidence, made with beautifully wrought silver beads.

A white lad of about twelve years ran to meet the newcomers. He halted, smiled self-consciously, and said, "Hello, sir, madam. May I help you?"

"You may," Little Hawk said, "if you can take me to Colonel Hawkins."

"Yes, sir, that's my papa." The boy led them to the porch of the agency office and pointed to the open door. "Just in there, sir."

Benjamin Hawkins looked up from his desk as they entered.

"Colonel Hawkins?" Little Hawk asked.

"I am he, sir," Hawkins said, coming to his feet.

Little Hawk snapped to attention and saluted. Hawkins returned the salute casually, and Little Hawk stepped forward and extended the letter from President Madison.

Hawkins was fifty-seven years old. His hair fell in a smooth, convex flow to his collar at the back and was rolled into a curl above each ear. He wore it as he had when he was one of the men included in John Trumbull's epic painting, *General George Washington Resigning His Commission to Congress as Commander in Chief of the Army at Annapolis, Maryland, December 23rd, 1783*. Age had broadened his prominent forehead, lightened his heavy brows, and seamed his strong nose and downturned mouth. He peered at Little Hawk from sunken eyes of unfathomable depths.

"Captain Harper, welcome to the Flint River Agency." Hawkins extended his hand. "And welcome to you, Mrs. Harper, and young gentlemen."

"I'm Joseph Standing Bear."

"And I'm Michael Soaring Hawk."

Although it was not obvious at first glance that the twins had Indian blood, Hawkins showed no surprise at the Seneca names. "My pleasure," he said, bending to extend his hand to each of the boys. "I have children of my own who will be glad to have new friends." He straightened. "I'm sure you'll want to get your family settled in, Captain Harper. We'll see to that, and then you and I must have a long talk. I'll be greatly interested in your analysis of the situation in Washington."

"I'm afraid my information about Washington City is out of date," Little Hawk said. "We came here after spending some months at my home in the Cherokee Nation."

"You interest me." Hawkins was about to continue but turned to Naomi instead. "First let us find a place for you and the young gentlemen, Mrs. Harper."

Hawkins escorted the group outside and pointed the way. "We are self-contained here, Captain," he said. "We have blacksmith shops, woodworking shops, a sawmill to provide lumber, a tannery where deerskins are prepared by methods a bit more modern than having the squaws scrape them by hand and chew them into softness. We grow our own vegetables, corn, fruit, and beef. We have a hatter, by the way, and I suggest you visit him. He's one of the slaves, but an accomplished fellow. You'll need to cover your head down here, Captain, for the sun is much more intense this far south, you know."

"Yes, sir," Little Hawk said.

"Here is the home of my assistant, Christian Limbaugh." Hawkins pointed to a well-built log cabin behind his own. "And there, just beyond, is, I think, the best place for you."

The house was almost identical to the Limbaugh cabin. As they walked toward it, Little Hawk noticed that the cedar-shake roof was sound, the logs appeared to be well chinked, and luxury had come to the land of the Lower Creek in the form of glass windows. Inside, the house was clean and adequately furnished.

"It's not a mansion, Mrs. Harper," Hawkins said, "but it's the best we can do here in our little enclave."

Naomi forced a smile. Although the rooms were larger than she had expected, the house reminded her of the frontier cabin she had shared with her mother and father, where she'd been savaged by Bearclaw Morgan and his two sons.

"It's fine, sir," Little Hawk said.

"If you need anything, Mrs. Harper, just call on my Lavinia and she'll be glad to help."

"Our things are at the stable," Little Hawk said.

"I'll have them brought over," Hawkins responded. "And at your convenience, Captain, you'll join me in the office?"

"Yes, sir."

"Mrs. Harper, I'll have Lavinia send a girl around to give you a hand."

"That isn't necessary," Naomi said.

"It's no imposition, Mrs. Harper." Hawkins inclined his head slightly and left.

The twins clambered up steep stairs to the loft. "Mother," one of them called out, "come look."

Little Hawk turned Naomi to face him. "Is it that bad?" he asked, seeing that she was upset.

She shook her head. "I'm being silly."

"Spoiled, aren't we?" he whispered, smiling fondly.

"Well," she said ruefully, "it's not exactly the White House, is it?"

Little Hawk felt a surge of guilt. Naomi sensed it and was immediately contrite. She tiptoed up to kiss him. "It will be just fine."

He looked around and grinned wryly. "You've known variety, at least. You've been a guest of the President in the White House. Guest of Dolley Madison. You've lived in Mother Beth's place in Wilmington, then Huntington Castle, and now this palace in the Creek Nation."

"I'm with you, and that makes everything right," she said. "Forgive me. I was being very silly."

Little Hawk's face was serious. "You and the boys should have stayed with Beth and my father at Huntington Castle."

"No, no," she said vehemently. "Of course I'd prefer the Castle, but I'm married to a soldier. I go where he goes." She stood on tiptoe again and kissed him quickly. "Let me say this again. I am with you. That's all that matters." She smiled. "I'll put up curtains, do some brightening up. I can make the house more livable."

"That's my girl."

"Mother, come look," one of the twins called again from a sleeping loft. "We'll have our own cave up here."

"Go talk to the colonel," Naomi said to Little Hawk. "I'll just go up and have a look at the cave."

Benjamin Hawkins motioned Little Hawk to a cane chair.

"You come highly recommended, young man," he said, picking up a letter from his desk and waving it around. "To know that the President has confidence in you would be ample, but to have a reference from Thomas Jefferson as well—"

"That's very kind of Mr. Jefferson," Little Hawk said.

"You were one of the first to attend Jefferson's little military school on the Hudson?"

"Yes, sir."

"If you're wondering, Thomas and I have been friends for a long time," Hawkins said. "We share many interests, among them the oddities of the various Indian languages. I once provided him with a basic vocabulary of Cherokee and Choctaw."

Hawkins paused, a thoughtful look on his face as he considered how best to satisfy his curiosity. The young man in front of him had a bronzed, golden look that was just dark enough to make the agent wonder about the Indian names of the twins. He decided upon an innocuous way to phrase his question. "I assume that you speak an Indian tongue?"

"Yes, sir. I speak my native Seneca, of course."

"Ah," Hawkins said. "I sense a story there."

"I am fairly fluent in Cherokee, since my people have lived with them from the time I was born. Since I know Cherokee I can get by in Choctaw. I have only a little Creek, enough to be a better listener than a talker."

"Good, good, because that's all I want you to do for the time being, just listen. I want you to get your family settled in so that you can accompany me day after tomorrow."

"Yes, sir."

"A Seneca in the Cherokee Nation—why does that sound familiar to me?"

"My people fought with George Washington," Little Hawk said. "Most members of the League of the Iroquois did not. After the War of Independence it was uncomfortable for my people among those who had sided with the British, so my grandfather led those Seneca who had been loyal to the United States to the south."

"And your father?"

"The sachem Renno."

"Yes, of course."

"You know my father?"

"I know of him. Thomas Jefferson has mentioned him in his letters to me." He snapped his fingers. "Good Lord, you're not the man who made connections with Lewis and Clark on the Pacific coast?"

"I plead guilty."

"I anticipate some very pleasant evenings, Captain, if indeed we can convince you to tell us about your experiences."

Little Hawk laughed. "Sir, you should know that there is only one thing an Indian likes better than hearing a good tale, and that is telling one."

"Excellent," Hawkins said. "I look forward to it. Do you have any questions about our operation here on the Flint River?"

"I'm sure I will have, sir, and I assume you'll tell me what I need to know."

"I will," Hawkins said. "In the meantime, let's get one thing straightened out between us. Your orders from President Madison require that you report to him regarding the Creek state of mind. I only hope that does not mean that you were sent here to spy on me."

"No, sir," Little Hawk said quickly. "Of course not. I believe Mr. Madison thinks highly of you."

"Perhaps both Mr. Madison and you feel that your Indian blood will give you a better insight into all things Indian, and that may very well be true. However, I would like you to do me the courtesy of consulting me before you report anything that might have a detrimental effect on the Creek Nation. I know that there are still violent and hostile feelings between some Creek Indians and the white settlers on the borders, but you will see after you've been here a while that the tribe is becoming quite civilized. Most of them want peace, and many of them are adapting admirably to our ways."

"Yes, sir," Little Hawk said. "I was told much the same thing by Menawa, the Big Warrior, when we stopped in his village on our journey. He assured me that he wants peace with the United States. And I will, of course, consult you regarding the accuracy of my reports."

"Thank you."

"I do have one question," Little Hawk said. "Where are we going day after tomorrow?"

"To Tuckabatchee, on the Tallapoosa. I have called all the Creek into council. It will be a good time for you to meet the chiefs." He tented his fingers. "And if we're lucky we may get to meet a rare visitor."

"Sir?"

"It is rumored that Tecumseh will be there," Hawkins said quietly.

Lavinia Downs was a motherly woman with a pleasant face and a reassuring smile. At Naomi's invitation she came into the Harper cabin trailing a pair of young slave girls who peeked around her generously proportioned body in wide-eyed curiosity. The house slaves carried linens, curtains, and cleaning materials.

After mutual introductions, which included the twins but not the two servant girls, Lavinia said, "Now, you just stand back, my dear, and let these two work their magic."

Naomi made no protest, and the girls went to work with a will, starting by scrubbing everything in sight.

"Don't get in their way, boys," Lavinia warned, "or they'll scour you, too."

"Can we go outside?" Joseph asked.

Naomi looked doubtful.

"Let them go," Lavinia said. "It's perfectly safe." She followed the twins to the door and pointed. "Over there you'll find a little creek. Go down to my house and find my Ben. Then tell him to fix you up with lines and hooks for crawdad fishing."

"Yea," the boys yelled together. "Will you cook 'em, Mother?"

"You catch, we'll cook," Lavinia answered before Naomi could speak.

The boys dashed off.

"Don't worry," Lavinia said. "My Ben is twelve. I told him to keep an eye on your tots. The creek is no more than a foot deep anywhere."

In spite of having ordered Naomi to stand back, Lavinia took a hand in the cleaning, and Naomi joined her. They hung new white curtains. Men arrived from the stables carrying the family's few possessions, and soon the cooking utensils were in place in the kitchen, fresh linens were on the beds, and there was a clean smell of strong lye soap throughout the house.

"Now," Lavinia said when it was all finished, "this one"—she put her hand on the shoulder of one of the girls—"is Magnolia. She'll be yours. Magnolia, I want you to come here to Mrs. Harper's cabin each morning. Early, mind you. In time to build the cook fire for Captain Harper's morning coffee and his breakfast."

"Yes, ma'am," Magnolia said.

"Tonight I want you all to have dinner at our house," Lavinia offered, turning back to Naomi. "Bring the boys, of course. The colonel likes to eat at five."

"You've been so kind I don't know how to thank you," Naomi said.

"It's lovely to have someone to talk to," Lavinia responded. "I pray that we'll become good friends."

"I'd like that very much," Naomi said.

"So shall it be, then." Lavinia swept out the door and turned to look over her shoulder. "Well, shortly before five, then, my dear."

"Mrs. Harper," Magnolia said, "is there anything else y'all want?"

"I think you've done a wonderful job, Magnolia."

"Yes, ma'am."

"I think both of us have earned a sit-down and a cup of tea."

"Yes, ma'am. I'll fix it."

Naomi followed the girl into the kitchen and was pleased to see that she knew the proper way to make tea.

Magnolia was reluctant to sit down at the table with Naomi but did so when Naomi made it an order.

"I want you to tell me all about life here," Naomi said.

"Well, you know."

"No, I don't. Are there always so many Indians in the enclosure?"

"Yes, ma'am. They're here most of the time."

"Is there ever any trouble with them?"

"No, ma'am. Master Hawkins, he keeps the peace."

"Why did Mrs. Hawkins introduce herself as Lavinia Downs?" Naomi asked.

"Well, Master Hawkins and Mrs. Downs, they ain't married."

"What?" Naomi asked, startled.

"No, ma'am. They ain't."

"But they have children."

"Yes, ma'am. Six of them, but they ain't married."

"Lord a'mercy," Naomi said.

The assembled Creek national council was composed of the wisest and most skilled warriors and chiefs from both the Upper and Lower Creek Nations. Dressed in their finest ceremonial clothing, they sat row upon row in the *chunkey* yard, a sunken rectangle in the common at the heart of Tuckabatchee, the traditional Creek war capital. The three-hundred-yard-long area was surrounded by banks for seating spectators.

The coppery skin of the Creek leaders gleamed at hip and thigh under their loincloths. In honor of the occasion the frontal flaps were decorated with beads and metallic lace. Cloth leggings covered their lower legs above fine deerskin moccasins, and scarlet and blue cloaks were draped from their shoulders. Tattoos of blue stars, animals, birds, flowers, and images of the sun and moon decorated bare breasts and arms. Necks, ears, and wrists were adorned with silver medals and gorgets, gold and silver chains, bracelets, and earbobs of fanciful design.

Heads were shaved except for a central comb of hair worn long at the back and accented by beads, feathers, ribbons, and colored stones. Every article of clothing was ornately bedecked with bells, lace, fringe, beads, ribbons. Some of the Indians wore turbans of fine cloth with a brooch at the front from which extended a plume of feathers. Others wore broad headbands.

Big Warrior, Menawa, speaker of the Upper Creek, was the first orator. It took him only an hour and a half to welcome that great friend of the Creek Nation, Benjamin Hawkins, to council. He could have spoken much longer but for the anticipation among his listeners of news of Tecumseh's approach.

Following the speaker's opening oration, the smoking cook fires gave forth their bounty. Creek women outdid themselves in preparation of the feast. There was roasted pork, chicken, duck, turkey, and venison; rice, potatoes, bean bread and dumplings, pumpkin fritters, ground peas, chestnuts, as well as hickory-nut oil for seasoning; rum, water, and tin cups of boiled, chewy coffee to wash it all down.

Big Warrior sat with Little Hawk. Hawkins was conversing animatedly with a group of chiefs enjoying the abundance of food.

"Never have I eaten better," Little Hawk said.

"Not even in the halls of the great white chiefs?" Big Warrior asked.

"Not even there."

"You have counciled with the chief of all the whites in Washington, I am told," Big Warrior said.

"I have listened to his council," Little Hawk responded with a grin. "I myself didn't do much talking."

"Why does he not put an end to the wars between our people and the whites?" Menawa asked.

Little Hawk was silent for some time. "Perhaps Mr. Madison is wise enough to do just that," he said finally. "However, it would require goodwill from all. He would hear your words, Big Warrior. He would understand your desire for peace. Perhaps he would say to you: ' Keep your young men under control, Menawa. Stop them from raiding along the border.' "

"And would he then ask that I sign another paper giving up more land to the whites?"

"I can answer that only from my own experience," Little Hawk said. "I fear that eventually he would ask you to sign another paper."

"That is my fear as well."

"The Seneca blood in me cries out that it is an injustice for the whites to push always toward that which is the Indians'; but I am the son of Renno, who believes that in order for the Indian to continue to survive he must become like his white neighbors."

"And do you feel so?"

"I can't answer that simply."

"Answer as best you can," the older man said. "There is yet time left in the day."

"Let me say that I don't think labor is slavery," Little Hawk said.

"A very un-Indian belief."

"Yes, but what is labor?" Little Hawk asked. "That definition lies at the heart of the dilemma. It is true that if a man becomes like the whites and owns a little piece of land, he must work to make that land produce food. Most Indians feel that if they give up that which they have always considered theirs—the freedom to hunt and share the resources of vast tracts of tribal lands—they lose dignity and liberty. However, such liberty also has its price. To provide food and clothing for his family a warrior must leave his home, his woman, his children. There are times when he must travel far. When his hunt is successful, it is necessary for him to dress his kill, butcher the meat, preserve it by drying, and then carry it home on his own shoulders if he does not have a horse or a mule. While engaged in this activity—which must be repeated time after time—he faces cold, thirst, hunger, and the danger of accident, of being killed by a wild animal or by an enemy. Often he fails. And yet he does not consider this to be labor. He is a slave to the tyranny of the need to hunt as much as he would be a slave to farming a plot of ground or of raising domestic animals for his meat."

"I think I understand," Big Warrior said. "I raise cattle, and I am not a slave. I grow food on my land, and I am not a slave." He nodded. "But neither am I a white man. I want my own people around me."

"President Madison might say that if you are to be a full citizen of the United States you cannot dictate who will own the land beside you. You cannot say that you are like the white man in all ways but you don't want him to live next to you."

"It is something that will require much thought and wisdom," Big Warrior said. "I fear that a resolution of the problem will call for much more blood."

"If your people listen to bad council, yes."

"Such as the council of Tecumseh?"

Little Hawk nodded. "Will they follow the Shawnee?"

"Some will."

"So I feared."

"Some consider him one of their own," Big Warrior said. "It is told that his parents were born not far from here, at the Shawnee town of Sauvanogee, which was once a part of the Creek Confederacy." He looked intently at Little Hawk. "Yes, some will listen to Tecumseh, and still others will hear the words of such men as Colbert of the Chickasaw and Pushmataha of the Choctaw."

"And what say they?"

"You know that Tecumseh is coming?"

"So I have heard," Little Hawk said.

"He has already crossed the Tennessee on Colbert's ferry to bring his call to war to the Chickasaw and the Choctaw. Pushmataha said in answer to Tecumseh that his tribe enjoyed good trade with the Americans, that without such trade there would be no cotton gins and therefore no looms on which his women could make cloth. There

would be no farm tools, and once again the ground would
have to be tilled with sharpened sticks. There would be
no white man's medicine to heal the sick."

"How do you know this?" Little Hawk asked.

"We watch the Shawnee's advance toward us by runner."

"Colbert feels the same as Pushmataha?"

"Yes. Colbert agreed when the Choctaw said that to
go to war with the United States would bring only death,
hunger, grief, and devastation."

"And so say you?"

"So say I," Big Warrior stated emphatically.

Just as Hawkins was about to speak, there was a stir
in the audience, and all eyes turned to see Tecumseh arrive at the council. He was escorted by two dozen
splendid warriors who had been picked for their physical
perfection. Tall and powerfully built, they wore new buckskin shirts and leggings heavy with rich, silver decora-
tions. Their faces were painted red and black, and they
carried gleaming new rifles, war clubs, and tomahawks.
The visitors were welcomed with much ceremony and
quickly shown to their quarters.

The Creek reassembled and listened carefully to
Hawkins. Little Hawk was impressed by the way the
Creek chiefs accepted and honored Benjamin Hawkins.
In addition to those who sat in all their finery in the
sunken yard, five thousand people heard Hawkins deliver
his report on tribal affairs. He made recommendations for
expansion of trade and for better relations with white
neighbors, and he praised the wisdom of the leaders and
the greatness of the Creek Nation. They approved the
speech with grunts and nods.

The chairman of the national council, Hawkins's
good friend Tustunnuggee Thlucco, was getting to his feet
to state his agreement with the things that Hawkins had
said when Tecumseh's bodyguard of twenty-four warriors,
shrilling out war cries, burst into the common next to the
yard. They were naked except for breechclouts and orna-

ments, and their faces and bodies were painted with black patterns. Eagle feathers swayed from their heads, and buffalo tails streamed out behind them as they broke into a wild ceremonial dance.

The Creek chief lifted his hands in protest, but Hawkins caught his eye and silenced him. The American agent stood with his arms crossed and watched with evident interest as the costumed warriors performed.

Tecumseh, also stripped for war, stood beside Tustunnuggee Thlucco, thus upstaging Hawkins.

"Brothers," Tecumseh thundered, "there you see the dance of the lakes." He lifted high a carved wooden slab, the same type he had sent to thirty tribes. "It is a dance of triumph, my brothers."

Hawkins kept his face neutral, prepared for more warlike talk from the Shawnee, but to his surprise Tecumseh spoke no more.

In the days that followed, Hawkins became more and more irritated. With Little Hawk at his side, he sought out Big Warrior and Tustunnuggee Thlucco.

"You are my friends," Hawkins said, "and I yours. Tell me, then, why have the chiefs of the Creek forgotten the purpose of this gathering?"

Both the Creek chiefs were glumly silent. It was evident that Hawkins was right. For two days there had been no council, only rituals, singing, and dancing. It seemed that every young Creek warrior wanted to learn the dance of the lakes, and Tecumseh's two-dozen-strong guard of honor held the attention of all.

"When will the man speak?" Hawkins asked. "When will he make known to all the reason for his presence in the peaceful land of the Upper Creek?"

"In truth, my old friend," Tustunnuggee Thlucco said, "he will not speak as long as you are here."

"Then by the God that made me, he will never speak," Hawkins thundered. "Am I not among friends? Is the Shawnee more welcome than I?"

"You know that you are always welcome here," Big Warrior said sincerely. "But if we are to have the chance to hear the Shawnee and to counter his mad-dog talk of war with the wisdom of the elders of the tribe, perhaps, my friend, you should go."

Hurt and frustrated, Hawkins stubbornly remained in the old war capital until, on the eighth day, he again sought out the Big Warrior, who was taking food with Little Hawk.

"Menawa, my friend, you spoke wisdom, and I had not the humility to hear it."

Menawa made a sign with his hand to negate the statement.

"I now recognize the truth that if the war council of the Shawnee is to be proven false, it will be men like you, my friend, who will do it. The young warriors would not listen to me, a white man, in spite of my true and proven friendship for all Creek."

"You are always wise," Big Warrior said.

"Captain," Hawkins ordered, "you will remain here."

"Yes, sir," Little Hawk responded.

Tecumseh was forty-three, a man at the height of his physical powers. The meteor that had announced his birth had given him the gift of leadership. His years of struggling to unite the tribes had taught him how to motivate his brothers.

He was dressed simply. He was not a chief, after all, although many called him the Chief of the Beautiful River. He was a warrior, a catalyst, a needle in the side of his Indian brothers, a reminder of past wrongs and an assurance of future tragedy unless they joined him in his quest to reclaim their land from the white invaders.

Little Hawk had found a place along the bank of the sunken chunkey yard, close enough to see the Shawnee's face clearly, to hear his soft words. The man's power was unmistakable.

Tecumseh spoke softly. "As soon as I was strong

enough to draw a bow I fought against the white-eyes
who crossed the Ohio into the lands of my Miami brothers. I saw my father die in the cause of stemming the
white flood. Two brothers of my blood gave their lives.
And still I fought on. When others signed papers drawn
up by the Chief Who Never Sleeps after the battle at
Fallen Timbers, I was not there to agree to give away the
lands of my brothers.

"Now I speak to you, my Creek brothers, among
whom my parents were born. I speak to you thoughts that
trouble all Indians. You have heard of our brothers the
Narraganset, our brothers the Mohawk, the Mohican, the
Pequot, the Tuscarora. Where are they now? Where are
all of the once powerful tribes who had the misfortune to
occupy land near the great salt sea which was a watery
highway for the invasion of the white European hordes?"

He paused and let his expressive eyes fall on—or so
it seemed to those who listened—each individual face in
the gathering.

"Where? Vanished. Eaten by the greed of the white
man. And soon their broad roads will pass over the graves
of *your* fathers." He fastened his magnetic eyes on the
Creek chief Opothie Micco. "Is it not true, my brother,
that the white man built a road through the lands of the
Creek, a road from the Ocmulgee to the Alabama?"

"It is true," Opothie Micco said.

"The soldiers of the white chief in Washington laid
out the road, and now it swarms with white invaders. But
even this is not enough. Now the white chief in Washington asks that white traders from Tennessee be allowed to
navigate the Coosa River on the way to the settlements at
Mobile."

There was a stir among the listeners, a growl of protest.

Opothie Micco stood. "I have said no to those who
want to give access to the heart of our land by way of the
Coosa. I have said what land we have left is but large

enough to live and walk on. My chiefs and warriors will never say yes to a white invasion along the Coosa."

Tecumseh's voice soared and showed its magic. "Our race—all men of Indian blood—will pass and be forgotten unless we unite in common cause against the white flood. They seize our land. They force our women into corruption. They have no respect for the bones of our fathers. They come leaving a trail of blood, and it is in a trail of blood that we must thrust them back. All the tribes of the north are dancing the dance of the lakes. The British have promised to send us arms. Accursed be the race that takes our land and makes women of our warriors."

His voice grew in intensity.

"Wipe away the mist that clouds your vision, my Creek brothers. Look about you. You have only to lift your eyes to see what the *Shemanese,* the whites, have done. Even now their iron ax is chopping at your trees, and their saws cut your forests into little pieces to provide shelter for their women, who breed like the mice of the field."

He cupped a hand behind his ear. "I hear our fathers. I hear them in the wailing winds. They mourn our lack of action. Our fathers are asking, Who are these white people that you fear them so much? We killed many of them. Are we the sons of our fathers, or are we women?"

A group of young warriors howled a war cry, and immediately the shriek was taken up by others.

Tecumseh let his eyes fall full on Menawa, the Big Warrior. His tone was scornful. "You hear the words I speak, but your blood is white."

Big Warrior seemed to swell with resentment.

"I know that you do not mean to fight," Tecumseh went on. "And I know the reasons. You do not believe that I was sent by the spirits, but you shall know. I will now return to the north, but when the time comes for all things to be brought together, I will stamp my foot and awaken our mother the earth. She will flex her muscles in protest against the cowardice of those who continue to endure the desecrations of the whites against her. She will rumble and roar out her anger. Your water jugs will fall to the ground and be smashed. Your houses will crash to the earth. Your bones will tremble with the fury of the earth. When that happens, then you will cease to be women. You will drop your mattocks and your fish scrapers, and you will pick up your war axes and rise up with one mind and one heart against the white invaders."

Considering the number of people gathered in the common, it was unnaturally quiet. Tecumseh stood with his head bowed, looking down upon the ornately dressed chiefs. The silence lasted for a long time before the Shawnee lifted his hand, in which he held a red stick.

"My brothers who have fought with me in the north have left among you the means of knowing when the time is near. Watch as one red stick is burned each day. When the last is consumed by the fire, be ready to hear the earth mother answer when Tecumseh stamps his foot. All you who join in this holy war will be invulnerable. You will be protected by the spirits. You will share in the power that will guide the white armies to perish in the quagmire of the swamps and will drive those who survive back to the coast, all the way to Savannah. Then once more the land that was Creek will be in the hands of its proper owners."

Little Hawk recognized in Tecumseh a potent threat to the status quo. He was eager to return to the agency to report to Hawkins and then to pen a letter to President Madison warning him that Tecumseh's fiery oratory had not fallen on deaf ears at the Indians' national council. He hurried to Big Warrior's lodge to express his gratitude for Menawa's hospitality and to make his farewells.

"My friend," Menawa said, "I am confused. The Shawnee reminds me that the land is the Indian's whole being, his flesh, his blood, his heart, and once the land is gone the Indian will be as nothing. I fear that the young warriors find him to be persuasive."

"Is this the same Big Warrior who convinced me that peace with the United States is the only wise choice?"

The Creek frowned and shook his head. "I have heard one of my young men ask this: Do the whites even now not kick us and strike us as they do their slaves? The young warrior asked how long it would be before the whites tie *us* to a post and flog us."

"It will not come to that as long as I can lift an arm to fight," Little Hawk promised.

"Still, I am confused," Big Warrior said. "There are too many differences between us and the whites. I have heard the teachers of the white man's black book say that I should love their God, and they do not understand when I tell them that I see God everywhere, in a newborn baby or a young colt frolicking in the pasture with his mother, in the trees, in the fields, in the very grass that covers the earth, in a bird flying. They shake their heads when I tell them that I have heard the same word of God that they speak from our old ones, that we know God without having to capture him in a book. How can such different ways of thinking be reconciled?"

"I only wish I were wise enough to answer you," Little Hawk said.

Chapter Five

Dolley Madison didn't like what the presidency was doing to her "dear little husband." It seemed to her that the whole world had been conspiring against James Madison during the first two years of his Republican administration. Malcontents within his own party in the Congress sided with the Federalists in the Senate to criticize his every action.

Madison, however, was made of stronger stuff than his small, fragile-looking frame suggested. He was standing up well under the continued threat of war with England and France, but—although he would not admit it to Dolley—the continued frustration of his goals on the domestic scene was taking a toll.

Late in 1810 Napoleon had issued the Decree of Rambouillet, which ordered the sale of all United States ships that had been seized by France. For a while this belligerent action drew attention away from England's continued undeclared war against U.S. shipping, but the War Hawks soon renewed their clamor against Great Britain and against the persistent threat of an Indian war on the western frontier. In the midyear elections of 1810 the western War Party, aroused by Tecumseh's efforts to organize all Indian tribes, made gains in both houses of Congress.

In Europe, Sir Arthur Wellesley, who had been awarded the title Viscount Wellington after his victory over superior French forces at Talavera in 1809, had been driven back into Portugal by the French generals Masséna and Soult. Although he was holding the line before Lisbon at Torres Vedras, once again Britain's old struggle against Napoleon was in doubt. Like a snake with a broken back, England was striking out in all directions in her desperation. The poorly armed merchant marine of the United States continued to be an easy target.

The beleaguered Madison needed help. Political expediency and the need for regional balance had saddled him with a weak cabinet at one of the most crucial times in the history of the young republic. He often turned to an old friend, Albert Gallatin, who had been Jefferson's secretary of the treasury and continued in that job in the Madison administration. Madison wanted Gallatin to be his secretary of state, but the coalition of anti-Madison Republicans and Federalists in the Senate had recently refused to confirm Gallatin to the post; hence the inept Robert Smith still held the position.

Dolley did her best to ease Madison's burdens by presiding over one social triumph after another at the White House. With her husband's indulgent approval she did not hesitate to break Thomas Jefferson's tradition of Republican informality.

"It is evident, my dear James," she maintained, "that a certain amount of elegance and style do credit to the dignity of a great nation. We are almost eight million peo-

ple now. We are no longer a hasty conglomeration of rebellious little English colonies. This country stretches
from the Atlantic to the Pacific. You could drop both
France *and* Great Britain down inside our borders and
have vast areas left over."

"You realize, my dear," Madison said fondly, "that
some members of my own party are accusing me of having become a Federalist and of trying to establish a regal
presidency."

"Some misguided souls called General Washington
King George," Dolley retorted.

"Actually, I do agree that a modicum of cultured
grace is not totally out of place in a republican setting,"
Madison said.

The President and his Dolley were conversing over
tea. Dolley had established a precedent of giving James a
midmorning reprieve from official visitors and the affairs
of state. Their few minutes together had become sacro-
sanct.

"I *am* upset," Dolley said.

Madison lifted his pale brows in concern.

"I do not want to put Robert Smith's name on my
invitation list for Saturday night."

A wry smile lifted the corners of Madison's solemn
lips. "Protocol, my dear. Protocol."

"After what the man has done to you? He actually
told foreign representatives that there are powerful forces
in the United States ranged against your policies," Dolley
said indignantly.

"Well, you see, Mr. Secretary Smith takes the concil-
iatory position of the Federalist Party in regard to our
relations with England."

"Albert says that the man actually thinks his attacks
on you will put him in line for the presidency in 1812.
When *will* you fire him?"

Madison's smile was genuine, for he himself had
been looking forward to just that for over two years.

"Because of that ambitious, bungling fool, both the

French and the British ignore your policy statements," Dolley went on.

"I should have appointed you secretary of state, my dear," Madison said, with the sweet, gentle fondness that always melted Dolley's heart.

She steeled herself against a desire to leap up and give him a kiss on his broad forehead. "Now, don't you try to jolly me out of talking sense to you, James."

"Would I do that?" he asked with wide-eyed innocence.

"Ha," she retorted. "Listen to me. I am getting tired of you having to do your work *and* the work of the State Department as well. Don't you think I know when you're forced to take on tasks that have been neglected or are beyond the capability of Robert Smith?"

Madison smiled again. "You have asked me a question, my dear, that begs a thoughtful answer."

"Does that mean you're going to give me one?"

"As a matter of fact, madam, I am." He picked up a sheet of paper. "This is a letter from Albert Gallatin withdrawing his name from consideration as secretary of state."

"Ah," Dolley sighed.

"That does not mean absolute defeat," Madison said. "At least not in addition to those already suffered. While it is true that I have lost Albert as my right-hand man, his gesture in writing this letter was neither vindictive nor empty. As you know, the Congress has just gone into adjournment, and the honorable senators will not be in session again for a period of eight or nine months."

"You have something up your sleeve," Dolley said.

At that moment there was a timid knock on the door. Dolley pursed her lips and turned her head. The President's tea interlude was never to be interrupted.

"My fault, my dear," Madison said. "I left orders." He raised his voice. "Come."

Madison's male secretary stuck his head in the door. "The governor is here, Mr. President."

"Good, good," Madison said.

"If this is important, James," Dolley said, rising and gathering the tea things, "I will leave you to your work."

"Stay for a moment, dear," Madison said. And to the secretary, "Show the governor in, please."

Madison rose and extended his hand to a distinguished-looking, smiling man dressed in formal black.

"Why, it's James Monroe," Dolley said.

"Good morning, Mrs. Madison," Monroe said, making a small bow.

"It's been ever so long," Dolley said, extending her hand. Only her husband knew her well enough to hear the false note in her voice. She had not forgotten that James Monroe had opposed her husband for the presidential nomination in 1808 and that Monroe's backers had called Madison a Federalist in disguise.

Monroe was all Virginia elegance, from his swept-back, graying hair to the silver buckles on his shoes. He had a broad forehead, a heart-shaped face with a strong, dimpled chin, and a prominent nose.

"We have not had the opportunity to congratulate you on your election as governor of Virginia," Dolley said as Monroe took her hand briefly.

"I'm afraid that your husband considers the august governorship of the Old Dominion to be of transitory importance," Monroe said.

Dolley looked to her husband in question.

"My dear, you may congratulate Mr. Monroe on being the new secretary of state," Madison said, his eyes holding hers warningly.

"Oh, wonderful," Dolley said. "So that's what you're up to, is it?"

"It may be," Monroe said, "that my stint in the office will be brief, no longer than it takes the Congress to reconvene in the new year."

"We'll have you so well established that they wouldn't dare refuse to confirm your appointment," Madison said. "It's going to be good to work with you, Governor Monroe."

"The honor is mine, Mr. President," Monroe said.

"You have kept this from me, James," Dolley said in teasing accusation.

"It required some rather delicate negotiations," Madison responded.

At that moment Dolley made up her mind. Whatever had divided the two men from Virginia in the past, she knew that James Monroe was an honorable man. He would not have accepted Madison's offer if he were not able to give the President his full loyalty. He was also a man who always made his position clear, sometimes painfully so, as when he had loudly voiced his disapproval of the Jefferson administration's rejection of the Treaty of 1806, which had been hammered out by Monroe. If James Monroe disagreed with something or someone, he let it be known. There would be no backbiting from him.

"I'm so pleased," Dolley said sweetly. "Another Virginian." She turned to Madison. "Did Thomas Jefferson have something to do with this?"

Neither man answered.

"And are you two already looking forward to 1816?"

Madison laughed. "First of all, my dear, we must think of 1812." He winked at Monroe, an uncharacteristic informality. "My opponents, as you must know, Governor, are actively looking for a new candidate for the Republican party in 1812."

"We will find a way, Mr. President, to block their ill-advised efforts," Monroe said.

Dolley couldn't help smiling. Another Virginian, a man of honor, a friend, a man of experience was coming into the battle on the side of her dear little husband. She sensed that from that day forward things were going to be different. The nadir had been reached when her husband's vice president, George Clinton of New York, deserted him in the effort to recharter the Bank of the United States. Clinton, as president of the Senate, cast the tie-breaking vote against Madison's policy and won Dolley's everlasting enmity.

James Monroe was, of course, a guest at Dolley's table that evening. She seated him to the President's right to give the city of Washington the message that her husband had a new ally. During the course of the meal she announced she had received a letter from the charming young comtesse de Beaujolais.

"I'm sure you gentlemen remember Renno's fair daughter, Renna," Dolley said. "I can barely imagine that the comtesse has two children of her own already. The Lord only knows how the letter finally made its way here from Paris, but it did, and in only four months."

"She is a lovely woman," a congressman said. "What ever happened to that English scoundrel, the one who tried to kill her husband in Lisbon?"

"He ran like the coward he was," James Madison said, "lest he have to face Beaujolais in a duel."

"Well, they are all safely back in Paris now," Dolley said. She sighed. "I do pray that this silly and inconvenient state of belligerency that plagues the world will be ended by the time my husband has finished his duty in Washington. It would be so wonderful to visit the comte and his lovely wife."

"And to shop in Paris?" Madison asked laughingly.

"That is only one of the things one does in Paris," Dolley said, giving him her most dazzling smile. "Will the wars be ended by 1816, when you've finished your second term?" Dolley asked.

Madison laughed loudly. He started to say that it wasn't likely the war would be over by the time he finished his first and probably last term in 1812, but he decided that such wry self-deprecation was not worth the negativity with which it would be received by some of those present.

Had the choice been Ta-na's, he would have pushed on to the fort at Vincennes in order to arrive no more than three hours after dark. It was Lieutenant Stockton O'Toole's decision to make camp north of the territorial capital. The officer was in command of a company of thirty men who had been led by Ta-na to a point a little over fifty miles north of Vincennes. They were on a twofold mission.

William Henry Harrison, fearing that war with the tribal confederation being assembled by Tecumseh and his brother Tenskwatawa was inevitable, had given O'Toole orders to stake out a suitable site for a log palisade fort to be built halfway between Vincennes and Prophetstown. Secondly, the patrol was to assess the presence of war parties in the area immediately north of the capital.

The jaunt had been almost leisurely, and no hostiles had been encountered. There was some grumbling among the regular soldiers who had wives and children at Vincennes about O'Toole's decision to spend one more night on bivouac, but for the most part the complaints were good-natured; it would be an easy march home the next morning after a sound night's sleep. Soon fires were burning, and the smell of roasting meat scented the air.

Ta-na had supplied two young bucks for the evening meal. He had come upon them almost by accident, having seen their sign as he scouted the trail ahead of the company. He had appropriated a choice piece of shoulder for himself and was turning it over his fire when he heard the soft call of a mourning dove. All senses alert, he waited until the call was repeated. It came from quite near the camp, so near that he suspected the sentinels were not giving full attention to their duties.

He moved the venison roast to one side of the fire, glanced around to make sure that no one was watching him, and slid into the shadows of the nearby trees. After he'd moved in complete silence about a hundred feet, the call of the dove came again. He halted and answered with three mournful notes. Like a shadow Gao moved soundlessly to his side, and Ta-na put a hand on his arm to indicate continued silence as he led him farther away from the camp.

"If you had your wits about you, you would have brought the roast with you," Gao said in Seneca.

"Has my brother lost his skill for the hunt?"

"Your brother did not want to draw the attention of your friends, the soldiers."

"Ah," Ta-na said in anticipation. "What has gone wrong now?"

Gao told his story quickly. When he voiced his belief that he had killed Sergeant Jeb Martin, Ta-na made a sound of sadness; when Gao finished his account, Ta-na mused silently.

"I have waited for you," Gao said, "to inform you that I will go to the home of my father, El-i-chi."

"That is one choice," Ta-na said.

"That is the only option I care to contemplate."

"General Harrison is a fair man," Ta-na said. "He has demonstrated that in the past."

"In the past I had not killed a United States Army sergeant in his own home."

"But you did it in self-defense. He had injured Running Mink and was attempting to rape Mist-on-the-Water. Your action was justified."

"Ha." Gao spat on the ground.

"Gao, you can go home," Ta-na said, "but to run from the situation will be an admission that you bear the guilt for it. The accusation will follow you forever. Should the army decide to label you a murderer, the long arm of the white man's law can touch you even in the Cherokee Nation."

"I don't like the sound of your voice; nor do I like your words," Gao said.

"The general will give you a fair and unbiased hearing," Ta-na said. "You will have Mist-on-the-Water as a witness." He put his hand on his brother's arm. "We came here together to follow in the footsteps of our fathers. We can still achieve that goal. Come with me. We will talk with General Harrison."

"Why do I feel," Gao asked with a wry smile, "that you are talking me back into the guardhouse?"

"We have been taught to speak the truth. We will do so, and then you will be with me again." Ta-na clasped Gao's arm. "How is the leg?"

"It has healed well."

"Good. Soon we will set a warrior's pace to the north and tweak the nose of the Prophet."

"In the meantime," Gao said, "is that roast nearly done?"

"Just as you like it."

Gao sighed. "Perhaps it is my stomach that is leading me into an action that is against my judgment."

Gao's appearance brought Lieutenant Stockton O'Toole to Ta-na's fire. The cousins nodded greetings without words, for their mouths were full.

"The leg has healed, eh?" O'Toole asked Gao.

"Yes," Gao said around a mouthful of hot, juicy meat.

"I guess you'll be going with us next time out," O'Toole said.

"My brother and I came here to work together," Ta-na said.

"I'll be looking forward to riding with you both," O'Toole said.

Ta-na cut off a small strip of pink meat and offered it to the lieutenant. O'Toole took the morsel and chewed with satisfaction. When he finished, he rose.

"May I suggest, Lieutenant, that you tell your guards to be more alert?" Ta-na asked.

It hadn't occurred to O'Toole that Gao had come into the camp unchallenged. He made a face. "Good point."

Ta-na looked at Gao and grinned, when, a minute or two later, they heard O'Toole applying army creole to the sergeant of the guard. For some time after that, as the cousins shared Ta-na's blanket, they heard the sergeant making the rounds of the posted sentinels. He was doing more than merely suggesting that the guards stay alert.

The column was under way shortly after sunrise, and Ta-na and Gao ran ahead of it along a well-used trace leading directly to Vincennes. Neither of them expected trouble that close to the capital. When chaos erupted behind them, they turned and sprinted back toward the advance element of the company. A half-dozen rifle shots buzzed around and past them. With a cry of surprise Ta-na threw himself in a rolling fall off the road and came to his feet behind a tree. Gao was safe nearby.

"It was my understanding that we were among friends," Gao said with a raised eyebrow.

"Hold your fire," Ta-na called out. "Lieutenant O'Toole?"

"Is that you, Ta-na?"

"Of course not," Gao yelled out. "It is Tecumseh and five thousand Shawnee warriors."

"Get back here, scouts," O'Toole ordered.

Ta-na emerged from the woods carefully. Gao followed but kept to the cover of the trees.

A soldier lay dead in the middle of the trace. Ta-na knelt and examined the feathers and construction of the arrow that had gone in one side of the young man's neck and out the other, severing the artery. His legs were still twitching.

O'Toole had dispersed the company into cover. Dozens of rifles protruded from behind the trees. The lieutenant, pistol in hand, asked, "Shawnee?"

"It is difficult to say." Ta-na noted that the iron tip of the arrow had been sharpened without notable skill.

Gao, who had disappeared into the woods, gave a signal to Ta-na to follow, and he did. Gao was kneeling near a large tree.

"Two of them," he said. "Here."

"So," Ta-na said, seeing the disturbed detritus.

"There." Gao pointed toward the north.

"You go after them and leave an easy trail," Ta-na

said. "I will send the column on its way and then catch up with you."

O'Toole had put his pistol away, but the men were still alert.

"Two warriors," Ta-na said. "We will follow them."

"Bring me their scalps" O'Toole pointed toward the town. "Can we expect others?"

"I think not," Ta-na responded.

"You will scout ahead."

Ta-na did not argue. He ran down the trace toward Vincennes and, once out of sight of the men, dashed into the forest and turned northward. He struck Gao's clearly marked trail just after he passed the column, which was moving in a body down the trace. The two warriors who ambushed them had run parallel to the road. After about a mile, the signs indicated that they had slowed to a walk. Within an hour Ta-na heard the soft call of a dove, and he crept forward to where Gao was lying behind a fallen tree. Down a slight incline the two men they were after rested on a mossy bank beside a creek.

Gao motioned, and Ta-na nodded. Gao left his cover to circle far to the left, and only minutes later Ta-na heard his signal from across the creek. He readied himself. When Gao emerged from the trees Ta-na leaped down the embankment, his rifle at the ready. Gao delivered a blood-curdling war cry.

Two frightened young boys scrambled for their weapons. One of them had his bow in hand but froze in the act of notching an arrow when Ta-na jammed the muzzle of his rifle into the boy's stomach.

"Children," Gao said in disgust. "Nothing but children."

"Their age makes no difference to the dead one," Ta-na said.

One of the boys spoke rapidly and nervously in a dialect that neither Ta-na nor Gao understood very well. Gao tried Seneca, then Cherokee, and Ta-na employed the combination of Indian dialects and French that had once been the lingua franca of the frontier.

After much gesturing they discovered that the boys were Ottawa Indians who had run away from home to join Tecumseh, and now they were lost. The single arrow they had fired at the column was an act of counting coup, and the boy who had drawn his bow with such deadly effect was proud of it.

The boys obviously assumed that all the Indians they encountered in the Ohio lands were loyal to Tecumseh, and they made it clear that they were pleased to meet two such seasoned warriors. One of the boys politely asked the way to Prophetstown, where he and his brother would join Tecumseh's confederation.

Ta-na looked at Gao. "The lieutenant ordered me to bring him the scalps of those who killed his man," he said in Seneca.

"I will not help you obey that order," Gao said.

Ta-na lowered his rifle, then drew a map in the dirt with a stick. "You have but to follow the river," he said to the two boys, then pointed. "The river is there. When you strike it, turn north. You will reach Prophetstown in three days' march."

The young Ottowas disappeared after a final friendly wave from the treeline across the creek.

"When war comes, perhaps one of them will put an arrow in *your* throat," Gao said.

Ta-na grunted and motioned to Gao to get under way.

By alternating the warrior's pace with walking, they arrived at the outskirts of Vincennes by late afternoon. A company of militia was drilling raggedly on the parade ground, and the smoke of cooking fires drifted upward from scores of chimneys. Ta-na's intended destination was the governor's house, Grouseland, and the shortest way to the walnut groves that surrounded it was through the town. Jeb Martin had anticipated their route, and six armed soldiers stepped out from behind a cabin and leveled their rifles at the cousins. Martin, his head heavily bandaged, followed.

"Put him in irons," Martin said, pointing to Gao. "If he resists, shoot him."

Ta-na lifted his rifle, and instantly three of the muzzles pointed at his heart.

"You stay out of this, Injun, or join this murderer on the scaffold," Martin snarled.

"We have come to speak with Governor Harrison," Ta-na said.

Gao, surprised to see Martin alive, looked at Ta-na and shook his head. "This one will not listen."

"Both of you drop your rifles," Martin ordered.

"I will see the governor," Ta-na said to Gao. "Go with these men, and I will come to you immediately."

"It's by the governor's orders that I'm arresting this murdering bastard," Martin said. "But do as you like."

"I go," Ta-na said, making no move to drop his rifle. He turned and walked away as, behind him, soldiers took Gao's rifle and clamped the heavy irons on his hands and legs.

Harrison was at his evening meal, and it took him a while to answer Ta-na's urgent summons. Ta-na was pacing in the parlor when he entered, still chewing.

"Ta-na, you have a genius for bringing trouble into this house when I'm either eating or trying to sleep."

"It's my brother, sir. I brought him back so that he could personally explain to you what has happened, but he has been arrested by Jeb Martin."

"What did your brother tell you?" Harrison asked.

"I'd rather you heard it from him, sir."

"Well, I reckon I'll have that chance, because he'll have to stand trial this time. Sergeant Martin says that he killed that Potawatomi squaw of his and was trying to rape Mist-on-the-Water."

"General, my brother gave me a full account of the affair. It was Martin who repeatedly struck Running Mink. If she is dead, it is the result of Martin's actions.

My brother prevented Martin from raping Mist-on-the-Water and defended himself when Martin attacked him with a tomahawk. He thought he had killed the man. When soldiers came in and shot at him, he had no choice but to escape."

Harrison shook his head. "Damn, why couldn't the boy have left Martin's daughter alone? None of this would have happened if he'd just stayed away from the Indian girl."

Ta-na decided it was not a proper time to explain to Harrison that it was nature's way for an Indian boy to notice an Indian girl.

"General, they have Gao in irons, and I'm not at all easy in my mind about his being in Martin's custody."

"There's bad blood there, sure enough." Harrison scratched his chin. "Look, Ta-na, you're both of good stock, you and your cousin. I've never served with more honorable men than your father and your grandfather." He walked to his desk, sat down, and wrote a note that he handed to Ta-na.

"Take this to Lieutenant O'Toole. I've ordered him to take the irons off Gao and bring him here." He shook his head and sighed. "I don't suppose either of you will object to his being a guest in my house until we can get to the bottom of this."

"No, sir."

"Then get out of here and let me finish my supper."

Lieutenant Stockton O'Toole had known that Jeb Martin intended to arrest Gao. The garrison was still humming about the fray in Martin's cabin that had resulted in the death of Martin's wife and the wounding of the sergeant. O'Toole intended to take the matter up with the governor, but it was late, and he didn't want to bother him after hours. He knew that there'd been trouble between Gao and the sergeant over the sergeant's daughter, but he found it difficult to believe that Gao had killed Running Mink and then tried to rape Mist-on-the-Water. It was a sticky situation, however, for it was the word of a U.S. Army sergeant against that of an Indian. O'Toole would leave the untangling of the situation to higher authorities. In the meantime, he didn't want Martin doing anything rash, so he decided to go to the guardhouse and check on Gao immediately after chow.

Gao did not resist as the heavy cuffs and chains were attached to his arms and legs. The metal edges chafed his skin as he walked between two files of soldiers to the guardhouse. Martin shoved him in so violently that he fell onto the hard bed; then, as Gao raised himself to a sitting position, Martin viciously backhanded him, his knuckles cutting into Gao's lips. Gao lashed out with his feet, but the chains prevented contact. Martin slapped Gao again and stepped back.

"Sleep well, murderer," he said.

Gao's eyes were points of black ice.

"But then again, maybe you won't make it through the night," Martin said insinuatingly.

It was difficult to get comfortable with the irons on his legs and arms, and his mouth was still bleeding when Lieutenant Stockton O'Toole arrived and peered into the cell.

"Is it necessary to keep the irons on him?" O'Toole asked the guards.

"Sergeant Martin's orders, sir," said a guard. "This Indian's a tricky one. He escaped once."

"I think that we'll remove the irons," O'Toole said.

"But sir—"

"The last time I read the regulations, an officer's order took precedence over a sergeant's," O'Toole said.

"Yes, sir."

"Lieutenant O'Toole," Gao said as the officer entered the cell with the two guards, "Martin is going to try to kill me during the night."

"Come now," O'Toole said. "I don't think Martin is a complete madman."

"He killed his wife," Gao said. "He was attacking Mist-on-the-Water when I came into the house. He knows his lies will be disproven when put to the test. He can't afford to have me appear at a court-martial."

"There'll be two guards here," O'Toole said. "You'll be all right."

"Lieutenant, if you'll just ask Mist-on-the-Water what happened, she'll tell you that I'm speaking the truth."

"That's rather difficult," O'Toole said. "You see, she ran away either during or after your fight with Martin. She's probably on her way back to her people in the north."

A cold chill crept up Gao's back as he extended his hands to let a guard remove the cuffs. Mist-on-the-Water had told him that she was frightened of the wilderness, and he feared she might not reach her relatives in the north.

The leg irons fell away with a clang. As the guard straightened, Gao moved with all the urgency and speed of overwhelming grief and youthful hate. His hand closed over the haft of a long hunting knife at the guard's waist, and in a flashing blaze of action he drove the blade into the man's stomach, thrusting upward into the vee between the ribs. In an instant Gao was on his feet. O'Toole reached for his pistol, and the other guard raised his rifle, but Gao lashed out with the heavy iron chains, and the force of his blow smashed O'Toole back against the bars. Gao grabbed O' Toole's pistol, and even as the guard's rifle filled the small cell with an ear-splitting roar, the pistol blasted, and as if by magic a hole appeared in the guard's forehead.

Gao leaped over O'Toole's crumpled body and raced out the door, stopping only to seize the fallen guard's rifle, bullet pouch, and powder horn. He heard voices call out in confusion and knew that men were running toward the guardhouse. After taking the shortest route across the parade ground to the trees, he was safely hidden among

them before the first shot was fired. The long shadows of
evening had become the full gloom of twilight under the
canopy of the forest, and he felt certain that no one would
catch him now.

He ran into the wilderness toward the north simply
because he had no plans other than to put a safe distance
between himself and those who had twice imprisoned
him falsely. After he had gone only a hundred yards he
stopped and listened carefully, but he could tell no one
was pursuing him yet. Only the memory of the advice
he'd heard many times from his father and his uncle prevented him from going back to kill Jeb Martin. To return
to the compound now would be to enter a fight that he
could not hope to win. At some later time, perhaps, he
could creep back, isolate Martin, and cut his throat, but
not when the entire settlement was aroused.

A vision of Mist-on-the-Water's face came to him,
and he knew once again the terrible pain of loss. He lifted
the soldier's rifle and pointed it toward the town.

"You will pay," he whispered, letting the words form
slowly on his lips. Although Jeb Martin had not been the
only one to put him in irons, Martin would be the first to
die for attempting to rape Mist-on-the-Water and killing
the woeful Running Mink; but others would pay for the
abrasions that the irons had left on his arms and legs.

He moved toward the river and struck the trace. It
seemed an age, not merely hours, since Ta-na and he had
run toward the town, Ta-na confident that the man who
bore the true guilt would be punished. It came to him
that Ta-na was his father's son, that Renno, too, trusted
the justice of the white man. But neither Renno nor Ta-na
had ever been unjustly accused of murder. Neither of
them had felt the bite of irons at ankle and wrist. His
uncle Rusog would understand, for once Rusog had been
falsely accused and had narrowly escaped execution.

Gao drank from the river and sat on a mossy bank,
his head tilted back so that he could see the lights in the
sky. There was the North Star. By traveling in the oppo-

site direction he would reach the Ohio, and Kentucky, and eventually Tennessee and the Cherokee Nation beyond; but as Ta-na had said, the arm of the white man's law was long. Now he was guilty, for he had killed two soldiers, and he could not go home and bring shame upon his family.

To the west was the Father of Waters, and somewhere beyond were his cousins, Rusog Ho-ya and We-yo O-no-ga-nose, twin son and daughter of his aunt Ena and her husband, Rusog. They had been right, after all, in leaving the world of the white man as far behind as possible. Perhaps he could find them.

He thought of the vastness of the country. He had heard the stories of the travels of his relatives—of his cousin Little Hawk, who had crossed the enormous distances from the Pacific; of his uncle Renno, who had traveled far to the north in Canada; and of his own father, El-i-chi, who had seen the arid deserts of the southwest. The land was an immense expanse. It would be like a blind man looking for one star among all the lights in the sky to find Ho-ya and We-yo in the lands beyond the Father of Waters.

He was suddenly very tired. The tensions of the day closed in on him all at once. He kept thinking of Mist-on-the-Water. It seemed logical that she was dead, for he could not believe that she could survive the wilderness alone.

Dead. Pain swept through him. Trying to force the thought from his mind, he found a thicket of brush, made a hidden bed of grass, and lay down. Sleep came to him as a pleasant surprise.

Chapter Six

Calling Owl, nephew of the Creek chief Opothie Micco, was fourteen when he killed his first white man. He was ten years older when he heard Tecumseh speak at the national council in the ancient Coosa town of Tuckabatchee. Calling Owl's hatred for the white man and all he stood for had grown each year. He had been a member of many war parties and had taken prized white scalps along the Georgia, Florida, and Tennessee borders. He had chosen his own name, and some felt that it was in defiance of fate, for to hear the hoot of an owl in the dark of night was a sinister sign, a death sign.

"That is true," Calling Owl agreed. "The sound of my name means death for the whitefaces."

He was a solidly built, well-proportioned man with wide, powerful shoulders, heavily muscled thighs and calves, a narrow waist, and bulging biceps. His eyes were wide-set, and his eyebrows arched down toward the thin bridge of his nose and gave him a look that could be taken

for either mild pain or intense concentration. There was
about his lips and nose a suggestion of white blood, although he would have killed any man who said so, and
there was no hint of it in his family's oral history

Because Calling Owl could boast of the blood of
chiefs, he dressed as befit his station. At Tuckabatchee he
wore a purple tunic tailored in the style of a military uniform, with shoulder epaulets and silver buttons, and his
coarse, heavy black hair was hidden under a turban. A
huge half-moon ornament of hammered silver hung
around his neck on a thick silver chain below twin strings
of Gulf Coast pearls, and for the formal occasion long
bobs of pearls and silver dangled from his ears.

To many, Calling Owl was a living representation of
the ideal Creek warrior. At twenty-four he was at the
height of his manhood. No challenger had ever defeated
him at wrestling, and in mock and real warfare his speed
was unmatched. Although he did not have sufficient rank
to speak at a national council, his voice was respected.

The words of Tecumseh, the Chief of the Beautiful
River, sang in Calling Owl's ears like an exaltation of soaring larks, and his logic was as seductive as the charms of
the Creek maiden Calling Owl had taken as his wife. He
could not get enough of Tecumseh's wisdom, could not
hear enough of the stirring words that stayed in his brain
and spun storms of emotion. He had listened in polite but
sullen silence to the blandishments of the Indian agent,
Benjamin Hawkins, but he knew from experience that the
words of the white man were but the hissing of serpents.
He had heard the white man call his people a tribe of
wandering hunters who did not really own the lands over
which they roamed, and he knew that the white man believed that his God intended that the interloper wrest all
the land from the hands of nature and tear it open with his
iron plows.

To Calling Owl's mind Benjamin Hawkins was a fool
to waste his time trying to convince true Creek warriors
such as he and his uncle Opothie Micco that all Creek

should breed the bland-tasting, mild-mannered cattle of the whites as Menawa the Big Warrior did. It was Tecumseh, the Shawnee, who spoke true. Tecumseh understood that the land was the Indian's flesh, the waters of the land his blood, the animals of the forests reflections of his spirit. Tecumseh knew that as long as the Indian kept his land he could never be subdued as the white man tamed animals and slaves to his own use.

The land was life to Calling Owl. In its own season the sweet earth provided wild peaches and plums, tangy muscadine grapes, nuts, persimmons, berries, tobacco, and medicinal herbs and barks. In times of hunger the bog potato was nourishment. The land gave of itself, everything from meat to acorns. Treated with respect, it would be fruitful forever; and it had no objection to the scratchings of the topsoil made by the women who planted corn, pumpkins, beans, squash, and potatoes. The Indian ate the produce of the earth and became a part of it and a part of the whole, a part of the Master of Breath, who was everywhere.

Wanting to hear more of Tecumseh's words, Calling Owl followed the Shawnee toward the northwest and the wide Mississippi, accompanied by his own coterie of young warriors who shared his feelings about the white man.

At a camp between villages Tecumseh sat beside a fire and spoke in a quiet voice. "I was not pleased by my reception among the tribes of the south," he said sadly.

Calling Owl felt immediate distress.

"Pushmataha and Colbert are deceived by the white man," Tecumseh went on.

Calling Owl could be silent no longer. "But there are many of us who see with our eyes open."

"Yes, yes," Tecumseh said morosely. "Some will rise up when I give them the great sign. Some will even come to the north to join us at Prophetstown. Others—" He shrugged eloquently.

"I will fight," Calling Owl said. His companions seconded the statement with assenting yips and grunts. "I will go with you now to the north, my brother. I and those who are my true friends are at your command."

Tecumseh clasped Calling Owl's shoulder. "I would have your company gladly, brother, if I were selfish. I would see your determined face and share your spirit with much pleasure, but there will come a time when you will serve the purpose best by voicing your wisdom among your own people."

"As you say," Calling Owl responded softly.

So it was that Calling Owl and his young warriors watched Tecumseh and his party cross the Father of Waters at the mouth of Nonconnah Creek in canoes furnished by the Creek Chief Chacalissa. The Shawnee's horses swam behind the canoes.

Calling Owl turned to his men. "You each know what we must do."

A young warrior who had not yet tasted white blood lifted his blade and shrilled a war cry.

"I have heard a tale," Calling Owl said. "I have heard a story of a Cherokee brother to the north."

The young men exchanged puzzled glances, for it was well known to them that the Cherokee were traditional enemies of the Creek.

"It was in the old days," Calling Owl recounted, "when the whites were just beginning to cross the river they call the Ohio. Chiefs from both the Cherokee and Creek nations attended a great council with the British redcoats. In those days Creek, Cherokee, and Shawnee fought as brothers against the white general Anthony Wayne, and Chief Glass of the Cherokee destroyed a blockhouse at Muscle Shoals and killed all the whites therein. When the whitefaces were all dead, Chief Glass ripped their scalps from them using nothing but his teeth and his bare hands."

A chorus of awe and approval sounded from the young warriors.

"So we must be," Calling Owl said, his voice soaring.

"Our hatred must be as strong as that of the Cherokee Glass as we fight the battle for all Indians in our land."

Not far from Muscle Shoals, where Chief Glass had demonstrated his enmity for the invaders of his territory, Calling Owl and his warriors came upon a log cabin in a clearing. A farmer was working a small field with one scraggy mule pulling a plow. A woman's voice floated an old English hymn through an open window of the log cabin.

> *"Now Satan comes with dreadful roar,*
> *and threatens to destroy*
> *He worries whom he can't devour*
> *with a malicious joy."*

The words were lost on Calling Owl and his followers. He motioned to the youngest among them, he who was not yet blooded. The youth was called Coweta, after the town of his birth, and would be given a warrior's name as soon as he proved his valor.

The unsuspecting man plowing his field did not hear the last line of the woman's song.

The boy drew his bow, and the iron-tipped arrow sang a song of mortality as it sped through the air. Dust flew from the farmer's shirt when the arrow pierced his back, exactly in the middle of the spine. With his spinal cord severed just below the neck, the white man fell. His weight broke a plow handle, tipping the blade up out of the earth. Its burden lessened, the farmer's mule surged forward a few feet, halted, turned its head, and snorted at the smell of blood.

"There is our evening meal," Calling Owl whispered.

Two arrows flew, and one pierced the mule's heart.

The woman's voice peaked at a crescendo and halted. The front door opened, and a warrior drew his bow but was prevented from releasing the arrow by Calling Owl's hand on his arm.

"That one is much female," Calling Owl said, awed by the sheer bulk of the woman.

She was indeed of ample girth. Her bosom bulged out and down almost to her waist. Under her long, soiled dress Calling Owl guessed that her thighs were as thick as Coweta's waist.

"Our little one has drawn his first blood," he said. "Let him now taste the fruits of victory."

The woman saw her husband lying in a plowed furrow and took one impulsive step toward him, but was warned by the arrow in his neck. She spun around into the cabin.

"Go," Calling Owl ordered.

The warriors rushed across the field. Calling Owl shouted a warning as the muzzle of a rifle appeared at a window. The weapon blasted smoke, but no one was hit. Two Creek rushed the front door and burst through. As he walked calmly across the clearing, Calling Owl heard the screams of a child. Thuds and grunts and the smashing of furniture told him that the woman was putting up a fight. He mounted the log steps to the porch and halted in the doorway.

Coweta, eager to claim his spoil, was clinging to the big woman's neck. So strong was she that his feet were lifted from the floor as she tried to dislodge him. The older men were calling out encouragement to the boy.

Cringing beside the fireplace was a girl child of no more than two years. The men roared in laughter as the woman finally dislodged Coweta and sent him sprawling onto the bed. The little girl screamed, and a chamber pot smashed down from the sleeping loft and broke atop a warrior's head. As he was inundated with an odorous liquid, he yelled in disgust and raised his rifle. The blast filled the small cabin with smoke and thundering sound. A boy of about eight years tumbled down from the sleeping loft and landed limply at his mother's feet. She moaned in anguish and lunged for the nearest man, the one who had just been drenched with the contents of the chamber pot, but he turned agilely and smashed the butt of his rifle into her face. She staggered backward and sat down heavily against the log wall.

Calling Owl motioned toward the loft. A warrior scampered up the ladder, gave a whoop, and reappeared holding a small boy. The screaming child was trying valiantly to strike his tormentor, but his blows fell on empty air as he was suspended by his hair. In a quick, almost casual motion, the warrior drew his knife blade across the boy's throat, and blood gushed out with arterial force. The warrior dropped the boy, who landed on top of his brother and tried to crawl to his mother. Dazed and bleeding, she reached out but failed to touch the dying boy.

"That one," Calling Owl said.

A warrior smashed the little girl's head with his tomahawk. Like the others, he was eager to get on with the fun.

"Now, Coweta," Calling Owl said with a grin.

The dazed woman fought until Calling Owl stepped forward and kicked her solidly in the temple with his heel. Coweta was struggling to free her heavy skirts when one of the men bent, slashed material, and denuded the woman from the waist down.

"He is a man, indeed," said one of the warriors as Coweta dropped his loincloth to reveal himself. There was laughter and good-natured advice as the boy who had drawn his first blood that day took the age-old prize of the victor.

There was further laughter when Coweta, buoyed by his new status as a man, sank his teeth into the woman's forehead in an effort to get a fingerhold to remove her scalp.

"Let us say, New Man, that willingness is equivalent to the deed," Calling Owl said. He was pleased. The boy would be an inspiration to others, for he had shown the same ferocious spirit that had been displayed by the legendary Chief Glass.

Calling Owl slashed open the woman's stomach with his tomahawk and left her as wolves often left a dog that had made the mistake of giving battle when it was outnumbered by the pack. He plunged his hand into the bloody cavity and stretched her intestines out on the cabin floor. She was still alive when one of the warriors scattered the burning wood from the fireplace around the room and tossed one flaming brand onto the bed.

Others died along the Tennessee border as Calling Owl and his band slowly made their way toward the southeast.

El-i-chi, sachem and shaman of the Seneca, was preparing to celebrate the birthday of his second son. The four-year-old boy, Ha-ace, was named for the Seneca senior warrior who had been twice his grandfather—by blood, as father of the boy's mother, Ah-wa-o, and by marriage, as the second husband of El-i-chi's mother, Toshabe. Both Ha-ace and Toshabe were in the west with their ancestors.

El-i-chi missed his older son, Gao, who had gone with Ta-na to join William Henry Harrison's army in the Indiana Territory; but the grace and beauty of his younger children were an acceptable balm. At six years old, little Ah-wen-ga was her mother's daughter in every way. Ha-ace was darker of skin than his father, having only one-quarter of the blood of the White Indian, but was a perfect copy of the sachem nevertheless.

"I do not understand," Ha-ace was saying with a maturity that belied his tender years, "why I must spend my mornings in a cave made by the white man learning things that are of use only to the white man."

"I would hardly call your aunt Beth's classroom a cave," El-i-chi said.

It was evident that Ha-ace was learning something in Beth's school. He spoke English with the upper-class accent of his aunt Beth, who was the daughter of an English peer.

"It is a prison," Ha-ace said. "I don't think the Father

of Life wants his people to be cooped up in a classroom when the summer grapes are ripe."

"Today you will not go to school," El-i-chi agreed, switching to Seneca. "Today, on the day when your mother gave you life, you will do what you like."

Ha-ace, too, grinned and shifted to his native tongue. "I have always known that my father is wise."

"I have learned quickly," said Ah-wa-o, "that my son has picked up the gift of blarney, probably from his grand-father-by-marriage, Roy Johnson."

"My beautiful mother is always right," Ha-ace said with a wide grin and a little bow.

Ah-wa-o rolled her eyes but could not hide her proud smile.

"And what is your pleasure today, my young warrior?" El-i-chi asked.

"We will hunt."

"Good," El-i-chi said.

Ha-ace quickly gathered his weapons. He had a bow fashioned of *bois d'arc* wood by the talented Cherokee, Se-quo-i, and El-i-chi had worked with his son to shape arrows of ash, carving the shafts himself but leaving the polishing and finish to the boy.

"I think I would like to go with you," Ah-wen-ga said, when the two hunters were ready to leave.

"Girls don't hunt," Ha-ace said.

"Ha. Tell that to Aunt Ena," Ah-wen-ga retorted.

"Let them go," Ah-wa-o said. "Let them be men together."

"Just don't ask me to clean your silly animals if you should be *lucky* enough to bag something," Ah-wen-ga said haughtily.

"I can clean my own deer," Ha-ace retorted proudly.

"Ha," said his sister.

El-i-chi and his son walked past the last cabin toward a line of trees. "I don't think we'll try for deer today, if you don't mind," El-i-chi said.

"That's all right," Ha-ace said. "I'm not big enough to carry a deer yet."

El-i-chi actually wanted to cut the hunt short because Beth had planned a party complete with a huge white cake and other surprises at Huntington Castle. Fortunately one foolish rabbit had managed to survive the young hunters of Rusog's Town, and the animal, pretending to be invisible, obligingly sat still long enough for Ha-ace to notch an arrow. The ash shaft flew true, and the boy leaped into the air in excitement when the little animal fell.

Ha-ace needed help cleaning the animal and made his father laugh aloud when he said that no wild game smelled worse than a rabbit in the process of being eviscerated.

"Can we cure the fur?" Ha-ace asked as they walked back toward the village.

"You can ask your mother if she'll help you," El-i-chi said.

When the hunters returned, Ah-wa-o said, "Since you were marksman enough to shoot the rabbit in the neck so that there is no hole in the fur of its body, I will be happy to help you. We will make a soft and lovely hat for you."

"Thank you," said Ha-ace. "What must I do to help you?"

Ah-wa-o smiled at El-i-chi. "Since this is your birthday, let *me* prepare the skin for drying."

El-i-chi stepped to the door and looked out at the sun. It was no more than two hours above the horizon. "We'll need to leave for the castle soon."

"It won't take long," Ah-wa-o said.

She had the rabbit skin scraped and salted in short order, and El-i-chi fastened it to a drying board and hung it outside their cabin. He and most of his people had long since given up living in Seneca longhouses with dozens of others and a few dogs; instead they had constructed log cabins.

* * *

When El-i-chi and his family arrived at Huntington Castle, its master and mistress were entertaining unexpected, but always welcome, company. Andy Jackson was seated on the front porch with Renno, Rusog, Roy Johnson, and Se-quo-i. After formal greetings that included the warrior's clasp, El-i-chi took his place in a bentwood rocker.

"Andy's come recruiting," Roy Johnson said, puffing on his pipe and sending a cloud of smoke billowing up to be wasted by a soft breeze.

El-i-chi lifted an eyebrow and waited.

"The Creek Indians," Jackson said.

"Ah," acknowledged El-i-chi.

"You haven't heard?" Jackson asked.

"I didn't get my newspaper today," El-i-chi said.

"Anything I hate, it's a smart-assed Indian," Jackson said with a grin.

El-i-chi laughed. "All right, Andy, what is it that I haven't heard?"

"War party hit three times on the border west of Muscle Shoals," Jackson said. "Eleven people dead. Men, women, and children. They strung one woman out like wolves string out a dog. Cut her open, pulled out her guts, and left her to die slow, but maybe not before the fire got to her."

"Uhnn," El-i-chi said, shaking his head.

"They've been at it along the Georgia and Florida borders, too," Jackson said. "What we're gonna do is call out the militia."

"I trust that you will prepare your militia well," Renno said. "The Creek are warriors. They have been forced to be, since they've long been caught in a nutcracker between the United States and Spanish Florida."

"Ten thousand of 'em," Jackson said.

"Creek?" El-i-chi asked.

"Militia," Jackson said. "Enough to exterminate the Creek Nation."

El-i-chi shifted uncomfortably. "General Jackson, it

makes me uneasy when someone starts talking about wiping out an entire people."

"I know how you feel, El-i-chi," Jackson said. "But we simply can't go on year after year letting them kill our women and children."

"I have heard," Renno said, "that the speakers of both the Upper and Lower Creek have said repeatedly that they want peace with the United States." He let his cold blue eyes seize Jackson's in a challenging stare. "You know that my son Little Hawk is in the Creek Nation."

"I'd heard. With Benjamin Hawkins at the Flint River Agency, isn't he?"

Renno nodded. "I've had a letter from him. He met with Menawa, who is called Big Warrior, even before he reached the Flint River and was told that the Upper Creek want to live in harmony with the whites. Big Warrior, it seems, raises cattle and tills the earth."

"Just as certain people, both white and Seneca, have been advising for some time," Roy Johnson said, with a wink at Renno.

"Wouldn't it be wise to meet with Big Warrior and the speaker of the Lower Creek before you go marching south with ten thousand soldiers?" El-i-chi asked.

"I've always wanted to believe that coexistence with the tribes was the right choice," Jackson said. "You know that, Renno. And you and Rusog have proven that coexistence is possible, at least temporarily."

Rusog looked at El-i-chi and nodded grimly. His English was heavy but articulate. "I think you are saying, General Jackson, that the pressure to dispossess all Indians of their land will not end, that it will eventually be directed once more against the Cherokee."

"Rusog, you know there are unanswered legal questions," Jackson said. "Under current law the Cherokee and others have nothing more than the right to occupy and use the land. The sovereign nation, meaning the United States, has the ultimate title to the land and, therefore, the right to dispose of it."

"Is it not true," Rusog asked, "that the United States merely *claims* ownership of the land? Is it not true that the land is ours by ancestral right?"

"In the best of all possible worlds, yes." Jackson waved his hand expansively. "I don't think you have anything to worry about. The Cherokee are becoming downright civilized. Aside from a drunken knife fight or the like, there hasn't been any hostility from the Cherokee Nation in quite some time."

"If things aren't exciting enough for you, Andy," Roy said, "I can stir up a few of the young ones to go out and count some coup."

"No, thanks," Jackson said.

Dressed in a formal gown for the occasion, Beth appeared at the door, and her radiant beauty brought the men to their feet.

"Gentlemen, we are about to cut the cake," Beth said.

"We don't want to miss that," Roy declared, leading the way.

"I appreciate you men giving me your views," Jackson said. "I count you all as my friends, and I hope it'll stay that way forever, in spite of that fellow Tecumseh and the blasted Creek." He put his hand on Renno's shoulder. "I won't push you for an answer right now, Renno, but when we march south against the Creek Indians I'll damned sure need a good chief of scouts."

"What in tarnation are you doin'?" Roy asked indignantly. "Promoting this young sprout over a man of experience? I was chief of scouts for Mad Anthony Wayne. Ain't that good enough for Andy Jackson?"

"Hell's bells, Roy, you're older'n I am," Jackson said.

"I can still put you in the shade," Roy said, holding the door for Jackson to enter the house.

"You want to go, you go," Jackson said. "I'll let you and Renno decide betwixt you who gets the title of chief of scouts."

"We'll think on it, Andy," Roy said.

Renno, El-i-chi, and the others sang happy birthday wishes to Ha-ace, and Jackson's voice was as loud as any. He seemed at home in Beth's big house, in the company of a Cherokee chief, two Seneca sachems, Se-quo-i, and several children with predominantly Indian blood. He laughed and teased the birthday boy and gave him a jack-knife as a gift, but even as he lifted Ha-ace high into the air El-i-chi was remembering what he'd said.

"I've always wanted *to believe that coexistence was the right choice."* Meaning, it seemed to El-i-chi, that the man could not actually bring himself to believe it, not even with people like Renno's Seneca and Rusog's Cherokee.

El-i-chi feared the day that pressure against the Cherokee lands would be brought to bear again. Right now the wrath of the United States was targeted against Tecumseh's northern confederation and the Creek. Tomorrow would it be the Cherokee and the Seneca?

Renno, El-i-chi knew, was looking at Jackson with different eyes as well. The man had been a guest in his home many times. They had hunted together. Roy Johnson considered Jackson one of his best friends. How could Jackson believe that the Cherokee had no right to the land of their fathers?

There was no more serious talk that night. The children played games, and after Ha-ace's playmates from Rusog's Town had been sent home, tales were told over coffee and the last of the cake. The family and their friends sat on the great front porch as twilight came and lightning bugs flashed over the pastures and the lawn, and the resident whippoorwill began his nightly serenade from the trees along the creek. Since it was Ha-ace's day, Renno told stories that would interest the boy. He spoke of the senior warrior for whom Ha-ace was named, how he had come from the Seneca homeland far to the north with Ha-ace's grandfather Ghonkaba and how the Seneca had been welcomed by old Loramas, then principal chief of the Cherokee.

"Will we go back to the homeland someday, Uncle Renno?" Ha-ace asked sleepily.

Where will we go? El-i-chi asked himself silently as Renno answered aloud.

"That, my young nephew, is in the hands of the Master of Life."

Far away in the Flint River Agency, Little Hawk found his wife and the twins in the garden. A cloth bonnet shaded Naomi's eyes as she worked diligently, back bent, to pick string beans. Putting his fingers to his lips to silence the twins, he sneaked up on his wife and seized her by the waist. She yelped in surprise and turned in his arms.

"You," she accused, laughing.

"Can't Magnolia do this work?" Little Hawk asked, turning one of Naomi's hands in his to look at the green stains on her fingers.

"It's so nice in the fresh air," Naomi said. "I just wanted to be outside for a while." She smiled. "Besides, I am a dutiful squaw who knows that it is a woman's place to prepare the food."

"Good, good," Little Hawk said. "If you're such a dutiful squaw who believes in doing things the Indian way, I think I shall take a second wife."

"How will you see her with your eyes scratched out?" Naomi asked.

"It is a custom of the Creek," Little Hawk responded. "Polygamy is perfectly all right. The wives live together in harmony."

"It is the custom for the man to get the first wife's permission before taking a second wife." Naomi smiled in satisfaction. "You see, I, too, have learned something about our neighbors."

"I suppose, then, that I should stop looking at the pretty young maidens with an eye to bringing one of them home with me."

"I would strongly advise you to do just that." Naomi

looked up at the sun, which was only midmorning high. "It isn't time for dinner."

"No," Little Hawk said. "I came to tell you that I'll be away for a while."

"Ohhh," Naomi said in true disappointment.

"A runner came just now from Big Warrior. He requests an immediate meeting with Colonel Hawkins."

"Why can't he come here?"

"This is to be a joint conference with the speakers of the Upper and Lower Creek. William McIntosh is meeting Big Warrior at Cusseta. Hawkins wants me along because he suspects the meeting has to do with the raids on white settlements that sprang up after Tecumseh was here."

"How long will you be gone?"

"Three, four days, I'd guess. It depends on how long the chiefs talk. You know how we Indians like to talk."

"Well, I know I'm going to miss my Indian," she said, turning her face up for a quick kiss.

"And I my squaw," he said.

Cusseta was the largest town in the Creek Nation. The Lower Creek called it their white town. Coweta, not far away, was the red town, where war tactics were planned in times of trouble. All other public matters were discussed at Cusseta, including the declaration of war.

"That concerns me," Hawkins said after explaining the customs to Little Hawk as they rode through one of the small villages that surrounded Cusseta. "I would feel better had they come to me, or had they called the conference at a spot other than Cusseta. After all, we know that Big Warrior was swayed by Tecumseh's call to arms. I have been told in confidence by Creek friends that he promised the Shawnee his people would rise up when the big sign comes."

"Perhaps he was temporarily influenced," Little Hawk said. "The Shawnee is a persuasive orator. But I think that after reflection, after the passions of the moment have had time to cool, Big Warrior will now feel differently."

"Let us pray so," Hawkins said.

The satellite villages that surrounded Cusseta looked alike. Dwellings were arranged around the public buildings and a common area. Depending on the size of the family, some of the houses consisted of up to four separate buildings. They were rectangular structures built on pole frames; the walls were plastered with straw-reinforced mud, and cyprus bark formed a waterproof roof. Each house had a garden plot, where the tobacco, almost ready for harvesting, was turning yellow. The corn crop was excellent this year; drying stalks were laden with heavy ears.

In Cusseta Hawkins and Little Hawk were greeted with much ceremony. They feasted on roasted duck, pork cooked with fresh greens, rice, potatoes, mushy beans, and a very sweet creation that Little Hawk guessed to be a mixture of cooked squash and honey.

Throughout the meal the conversation was limited to commonplace things. There were polite inquiries about their families and a discussion of the weather and the chances of a bounteous harvest.

Both Creek chiefs wore their formal finery and were equally solicitous of their guests, offering them more food until Little Hawk and Hawkins begged for mercy. Chief William McIntosh, half Scot, half Creek, spoke excellent English.

The council took place in the square, in the small house reserved for the meetings of local officials. The room was crowded with lesser chiefs and important warriors.

Menawa, the Big Warrior, stated the purpose of the council. "You were there, my friend," he said to Hawkins, "when the Shawnee Tecumseh came to Tuckabatchee with his red sticks, with his tall and powerful warriors dressed for conflict, with his sweet-tongued urgings toward war."

"I was," Hawkins said, choosing not to remind Big Warrior that Tecumseh had refused to speak until the Indian agent left.

"His words caused some of our young men to burn," Big Warrior said. "The flames of the Shawnee's oratory consumed their reason, and they killed white settlers."

"Of this I have heard, my friend," Hawkins said.

"For the whites of Georgia and the Spanish of Florida, this was nothing new," Big Warrior went on. "It was only a continuation of the old war between the Creek Nation and those who would push us to the banks of the Father of Waters and beyond."

"I have been informed that most of the killings took place along the Tennessee border," Hawkins said.

"That is true," William McIntosh answered, speaking for the first time, "and that is why, Colonel Hawkins, we seek your counsel and the opportunity to say that both Menawa and I, as speakers of the Upper and Lower Creek, deplore the actions of some of our young men."

"We have word that the whites of Tennessee are even now engaged in calling up a great army," Big Warrior stated. "They talk not just of war but of the extermination of the Creek Nation. They call us savages and blame the folly of a few young hotheads on the entire Nation."

"We have sent messages to the governor of Tennessee, Mr. William Blount, telling him of our wish for peace," McIntosh said. "We have told him that war would be a bad thing for both our people, that many men on both sides would die. We have told him that we, the Creek Nation, will punish our own people who have broken the peace between us."

"I would guess," Hawkins said, "that you have not received an answer."

"There has not been time," McIntosh said. "In the meantime we ask you, as a representative of the United States, to confirm our good intentions by sending a letter of your own to President Madison."

"I would be happy to do so," Hawkins said. "I am

convinced, my friends, that you are men of goodwill and that your wish for peace is as sincere as mine."

"That is good," Big Warrior declared.

"It would strengthen my hand considerably," Hawkins said, "if I could report to President Madison that the Creek have indeed punished the culprits."

"That will require only a short time," Big Warrior said.

"Do you know who made the raids?" Hawkins asked.

"We know who led the war party on the Tennessee border," McIntosh said.

"May I inquire?" Hawkins asked politely.

"Perhaps you know him," McIntosh said. "He was present at the national council. He is Calling Owl."

Hawkins's face showed his quick concern. "Yes, I know him. He is the nephew of Opothie Micco."

"That is true," Big Warrior affirmed.

"What will Opothie Micco say if you punish one of his brother's sons?" Hawkins asked.

"Opothie Micco counsels war in alliance with Tecumseh and the tribes of the north," McIntosh said, shrugging. "Perhaps we will have to deal with him as well."

"If so, so be it," Big Warrior proclaimed. "If we sit idly by and allow warriors like Calling Owl and Opothie Micco to raise the war club in the name of Tecumseh, the result will be the march of thousands of white soldiers into our lands. That we cannot allow. I will not permit a few who have been inflamed by the Shawnee's call to war to bring death and destruction down upon all our towns, upon all our people. Before I will do that I will run away and join the Sim-e-no-luh-gee, the wild people, in the swamps of Florida."

"You have made a wise and a very difficult decision," Hawkins said. "There is nothing sadder than when fate and necessity dictate that brother kill brother."

"Yet it must be," McIntosh said.

"How soon can I expect news?" Hawkins asked.

"Two days. Three days," Big Warrior answered.

"I will await word from you at the agency." Hawkins looked at Little Hawk thoughtfully, then back at the two chiefs. "Would I be presuming too much, my friends, to ask you to allow Captain Hawk Harper to go with your warriors? In that way I can be assured of receiving word of your success in the swiftest possible manner."

"My Seneca friend is welcome," Big Warrior said.

That same afternoon the punishment party was formed, and thirty warriors were chosen equally from the Lower and Upper Creek towns. Colonel Hawkins stood with Little Hawk as William McIntosh and Big Warrior instructed the men.

"Fierce-looking gunmen, aren't they?" Hawkins asked in a low voice. It was his habit not to call armed, renegade Creek Indians warriors. He felt that the application of the ancient and honorable word to those who perpetuated the tradition of strife among neighbors was undesirable.

"They look quite capable," Little Hawk said.

Big Warrior finished his speech to the gathered warriors, then stood beside Hawkins. "They are all good men," he said. "Many are veterans of clashes with the Spanish or the Georgians." He chuckled. "Some of the older men can remember counting coup on raids into your home territory, my friend Hawk." He made no attempt to conceal his pride. "Perhaps, Seneca, you will learn something by fighting side by side with Creek warriors."

"Captain Hawk is going along strictly as an observer," Hawkins said quickly. "It would not be wise for a Marine officer who is a representative of the agency and the United States to become involved in what is essentially an internal tribal matter."

William McIntosh, who had joined them in time to hear the exchange, laughed. "Perhaps the captain should hang a large sign around his neck to advise Calling Owl and his followers that he is present only to watch."

Chapter Seven

In the cool of evening Calling Owl came to his followers, who were lounging under a brush arbor that had been hastily built to provide shade from the sun. The group had grown since Calling Owl and his few had followed Tecumseh to the Father of Waters and, after leaving the Shawnee, had fired the flames of war along the Tennessee frontier. Some were drawn by Calling Owl's charismatic personality, others by the fetid scalps that decorated the red clubs of those who had killed the enemy.

"These are the words of Tecumseh as best as I recall them," Calling Owl said when the group fell silent at his approach. "The white race will perish. No longer will they seize our land and defile our women. Never again will they disturb the bones of our ancestors. We will drive them backward in a flood of white blood. The tribes of our brothers to the north dance war. The English king has promised to send us arms, and the Chief of the Beautiful

River and his prophets will stand between us and the
enemy. We shall be untouched by their bullets. Tecumseh
has said this. If there is one among you who does not
believe, then it is time for you to leave us."

"We fight with you, Calling Owl," cried New Man,
the young warrior once known as Coweta.

"New Man wants another nice, fat white woman," a
warrior said.

New Man happily shrieked a war cry.

Calling Owl lifted his hand for silence. "Even now
the white man's dogs howl on our heels," he said. "It is
not enough that we who believe must join in the extermination of the white man. We must fight against our brothers who in their lunacy would see us in the white man's
chains."

That it might be necessary to lift their weapons
against their fellow Creek caused a nervous exchange of
glances among the men.

"While you rest and tell grander and grander tales of
your bravery," Calling Owl said, "others have been on
guard, and with good reason. Now comes Big Warrior
with thirty men to rebuke us for our attacks on the white
men's farms."

"But Big Warrior promised his honor to Tecumseh,"
someone shouted.

"He has forgotten his words because he quakes under the threat of reprisal from the whites. He now vows to
punish those of us who have killed the enemy." Calling
Owl paused and looked at each man in turn before saying,
"Perhaps it would be best if I surrender with all those
who were with me in Tennessee."

"No, no," several warriors called out at once.

"I have just come into my adulthood," New Man
said. "I will not forgo my right to kill more whites."

"It is not whites who mark our trail," Calling Owl
said. "It is Big Warrior with thirty of the finest men from
both the Lower and Upper Creek. It may be that your
uncle or your brother's son will be among them."

"Surely Creek will not fight Creek," someone said.

"Big Warrior will fight," said Calling Owl. "Will you, or are you possessed of chicken entrails? Will you surrender and face what white men call justice?"

"Will you surrender?" New Man asked.

"No, never," Calling Owl said.

"Nor will I."

"Then two of us will face thirty-one," Calling Owl said.

"Three," said a grizzled warrior, stepping forward.

"Four."

"Five."

After that the count was lost.

"We are threescore," Calling Owl said.

"We will meet them face-to-face in the meadow," New Man said, "and if they want a fight we will teach them that it is dangerous to be the white man's dog."

"No," Calling Owl said. "We will not meet them in open battle."

There was a chorus of disappointment, protest, and curiosity.

"We have greater things to do," Calling Owl said. "We will not waste our lives fighting the white man's dogs. We will await the arrival of Big Warrior and his men at a place of *our* choosing. My brothers, believe me when I tell you that the blood that will soak the earth will not be ours."

Menawa was a devout man. He traveled with his own personal prophet, whose job it was to inform him of the designs and wishes of the Master of Breath. As stringy and tough as a wild turkey, the old Creek prophet called He Who Sees had no difficulty keeping up with the younger warriors. At night when they made camp he consulted the spirits by staring into the glowing embers of a dying fire and pronounced that justice was near for those who had defied the will of the Master of Breath by break-

ing the peace between the Creek Nation and the whitefaces of Tennessee.

"Will we catch them tomorrow?" Menawa asked in a
respectful voice.

"Tomorrow or tomorrow," chanted He Who Sees.
"Tomorrow or tomorrow or tomorrow."

Little Hawk hid a smile behind a half-consumed
roasted woodland dove. He was reminded of his uncle El-
i-chi, who had learned the same trick from old Casno, the
Seneca shaman who had come from the homeland in the
north with Little Hawk's great-great-grandfather. He had
never doubted that El-i-chi was a reverent man, nor did
he doubt the piousness of Big Warrior's prophet, but in
the words of a skilled shaman, prophecy could be made to
sound both definitive and ambiguous. From what Little
Hawk had learned in his brief sojourn in the Creek Nation, Creek and Seneca beliefs had much in common. The
Seneca spoke of the Master of Life and of *orenda,* that
nebulous oneness of all things. The Creek believed in the
Master of Breath and his prophets, who could foretell
drought or flood, and they believed the legends that said
the prophets could command thunder and lightning. Little Hawk suspected that the Creek were more susceptible
to mysticism than the Seneca or Cherokee and had fallen
more easily under the spell of Tecumseh, who promised
them immunity to the white armies' bullets.

It was interesting to watch He Who Sees, and Little
Hawk had to admire him for his sincerity even when he
doubted the carefully couched words that came in a near
whisper from the prophet's lips.

"Tomorrow or tomorrow," the old man said. "But justice will not be without its price. I see blood, Menawa,
much blood. I say to you, Menawa, have care. Pray to the
Master of Breath, and success will be yours and good will
triumph over evil."

As a Seneca, Little Hawk knew that he was never
alone when danger threatened, for the warriors of his nation faced all peril in the company of their ancestors. That

he knew from his own experience, for in a far land, with his back against the tomb of a pharaoh of ancient Egypt, he had seen his ancestors take solid form.

Here, only a few days' journey from the home of the southern Seneca, from the earth that had accepted the mortal remains of his great-grandfather Ja-gonh, the manitous would be with him in strength. But when the smoke of black powder filled the air and bright, sharp blades gleamed in combat, it would be his arm, his rifle, his pistols, his tomahawk that would determine whether he would live or take his place among his ancestors in the west. The words of a Creek prophet would have little effect when the fight began, and if the offenders were to be punished there would certainly be blood.

True, he was only an observer, but he remembered well the words of William McIntosh, chief of the Lower Creek. Little Hawk did not have a sign hanging around his neck to inform Calling Owl and his men that he was there only to watch. A bullet would not respect his neutrality.

Just as the sun rose above the horizon, Calling Owl led his followers to a spot where the Chattahoochee hugged a hogback ridge. Riverside bluffs made approach from the east impossible, and to the west open meadows would expose any attacker to rifle fire from the high ground. There was but one feasible approach to the position of Calling Owl's warriors atop the ridge: A game trail climbed the southern end of the slope and widened into a tall-grassed rabbit meadow with a forty-five-degree treed slope on the west. Calling Owl assigned each man a spot. Those who owned rifles were ordered to hold their fire until the main body of Big Warrior's men was fully exposed, and bowmen were hidden behind boulders on the river side and among the trees on the west.

The Creek Indian who was scouting for Big Warrior made his way cautiously up the game trail to the edge of the meadow and halted in the cover of a tree trunk. He listened but heard only the lazy drone of bees gathering nectar from yellow wildflowers scattered among the tall grass of the glade. Suspicious because the fugitives' trail had been too easy to follow, he circled the meadow to the west, moving from tree to tree as his eyes sought the slightest motion, his nose strained for scent. His ears seemed to enlarge the soft sounds of late summer: the hushed kiss of wind in the upper branches of the trees, the twitter of a wren berating him for intruding, the distant all's-well call of a crow. He was skirting the slope when he encountered a dense growth of underbrush and had to circle toward the meadow. He did not see Calling Owl, nor did he feel anything, for the blow of Calling Owl's red-painted war club was swift and deadly. The only sound that broke the summer quiet was a loud crack made by the warrior's breaking skull.

Little Hawk was riding with Menawa when the advance element of the force reached the lower slope of the hogback ridge and disappeared into the woodlands along the game trail that climbed upward. Only ten members of the punitive expedition had horses, and Menawa sent two of them and four of his fleetest warriors ahead to scout the trail. The sun was at midmorning, and a wind moved the grass on the open meadow to the west of the ridge. The gleam of water could be seen through the line of trees along the river. The ridge towered two hundred feet into the sky.

Big Warrior reined in, and Little Hawk followed suit. The Creek lifted his eyes to the top of the ridge. "If Calling Owl chooses to fight he will make his stand at just such a place."

Little Hawk nodded.

"I will ride ahead, my friend," Big Warrior said, "and caution my people to take care." He lifted his hand and gave orders to the force to stand where it was.

Little Hawk lifted one leg from the stirrup, crossed it

over the horse's neck, and sat in a comfortable position as he watched Big Warrior's horse disappear into the trees. The Seneca agreed with Menawa that the ridge, with bluffs on one side and a steep fall on the other, would make an excellent place of ambush. Menawa's men would be squeezed into a compact group by the narrowness of the approach. But if there was an ambush, the lead scout was to send back a warning in the form of spaced rifle shots.

It was not signal shots that broke the quiet of the morning. A volley of musketry blasted from atop the ridge, and smoke rose in a semicircle through the trees. All around Little Hawk the Creek warriors cried out in surprise, and several shouted war whoops and leaped forward. Another volley of rifle fire was heard from the top of the ridge. Quickly Little Hawk diagnosed the situation. Calling Owl's men had blocked the ridge in an arc of rifle muzzles. The blood that He Who Sees had foretold was flowing, and Little Hawk feared that it was the blood of Menawa's men.

A Creek horseman kicked his animal into motion and raced toward the foot of the ridge, but Little Hawk turned his horse sideways and blocked the trail for the other mounted warriors.

"Not that way," he told them. "Follow me and we will come upon them from the rear."

Without waiting to see if his orders were being obeyed, he spurred his horse to the grassy meadow west of the ridge. Yelps and war cries told him that some of the Creek were with him.

Rifles spoke from the ridge, and the deadly balls made thuds of sound in the air around Little Hawk's ears. He bent low and urged his horse onward. Behind him six Creek warriors followed his example, but a horse was struck, and it fell heavily. Its rider was tossed through the air, landed on his head, and lay still. Little Hawk and the surviving men raced on, and soon they could no longer hear the rifle fire.

*   *   *

Calling Owl cried out in disgust and disappointment
when one man opened fire with only six of Big Warrior's
men exposed in the rabbit grass. Other rifles blasted, and
four men went down, but one of them crawled back into
the cover of the trees, leaving a trail of blood.

"Fools!" Calling Owl raged at the top of his voice.
"Fools who cannot obey orders."

Four or five rifles fired from the tree line, and Calling
Owl shook his head. They were shooting at shadows, for
his men were well concealed. Near him New Man said,
"Let us go forward now, and take the others by surprise as
they climb the ridge."

"I am surrounded by fools," Calling Owl whispered
to himself. Aloud he said, "Hold where you are. Now we
must protect our retreat."

"Why must we retreat?" a warrior asked. "We are
twice their number."

A ball snipped leaves just above Calling Owl's head.
It angered him to think that members of his own tribe
were trying to kill him. Did they truly not understand the
righteousness of the cause? Were they so spoiled by the
toys and the promises of the white man that they were
blind to the true call of Tecumseh? Perhaps some were.
Others would listen to reason, but they would listen more
attentively if they were taught a lesson. The lesson was
that the true Creek who fought in the consecrated struggle against the white race were invincible.

Menawa arrived at the edge of the meadow in time to see
the wounded man dragging himself back into the shelter
of the trees. He leaped from his horse and ordered the
others to fall back, but two or three men fired before
obeying. The main body of his warriors was running up
the slope in full cry, eager to join the battle, but he stood
in the trail and blocked them. When he had quieted their
war cries, he informed them that those who had seen the

burst of rifle fire estimated at least forty men, perhaps more.

The old prophet had managed to keep pace, and now he looked at Menawa solemnly. "It must not be allowed," he pronounced. "Young and rebellious warriors must not be allowed to defy tribal authority, or we will cease to be a people."

"Perhaps the Master of Breath will make you invulnerable to bullets as you lead the charge through the rabbit grass," Menawa said.

"If that is my chief's wish I will do so," He Who Sees said quietly.

"Leave me, old man." Menawa turned to a group of experienced warriors. "They are deployed in a half circle around the rabbit meadow. To cross in the open would be to see most of our men fall. We will form two groups and advance under cover to the right and the left, for their line will be thin when it is approached from the flank instead of head-on."

He divided them into two groups. He himself led the eastern attack, for there was less cover on the brink of the riverside cliffs.

"Horsemen on the far edge of the meadow," a breathless warrior reported to Calling Owl.

"How many?"

"Six."

"They are of no matter," Calling Owl said. "Place four men with rifles to our rear to guard against them in the event they find a way up the northern end of the ridge."

He was not as calm about the report as he appeared to be. Even six men coming at his position from the rear would be a serious matter. He had not anticipated such quick thinking on the part of Menawa and had hoped that the speaker's outrage at being defied would lead him to charge head-on through the rabbit grass. Calling Owl spotted movement among the trees across the glade, but no charge materialized. Precious time was passing.

"New Man," he said, "pass the word to all. Upon my signal we will attack. We are twice their number. We will cross the clearing and be upon them before they are prepared."

It took several minutes for New Man to reach all the men in the arc around the meadow. When he returned, Calling Owl cast a glance at the blue sky and muttered a prayer to the Master of Breath. His signal was a three-part whoop. From all around the arc, men leaped to their feet and rushed toward the opposite line of trees, only to be met by a devastating hail of fire from the sides, for Menawa had split his men into two groups and caught Calling Owl's charge in enfilading fire. Everywhere men fell, and screams of mortal agony ripped the summer day.

"Back, back!" Calling Owl cried.

Some of his men were already running for cover. The others followed suit, but two more men fell before the force was back among the trees.

"Pass this order to all," Calling Owl hissed to New Man. "We will retreat in a column of twos. I will be in the rear."

New Man rushed off. Calling Owl saw movement, then leveled his rifle and fired in one smooth motion. He was rewarded by a howl of pain from an unseen man across the meadow. Scattered fire started to his right and then to his left. He knew well what Menawa was doing, but it was too late to make a countermove with concerted attacks coming from both sides.

"Fall back!" Calling Owl shouted. "Fall back in good order."

Calling Owl had no way of knowing that some weeks before, nature had taken a hand in the outcome of the battle at the rabbit meadow. In that unpopulated area along the river, no one had witnessed the violence of a whirling storm that had cut a straight swath through the thick trees on the northwestern slope of the ridge. The tornado had touched ground in the grassy meadow and traveled due east. Flowing hundreds of miles per hour, the twisting winds had uprooted and removed the trees, leaving a plowed pathway to the top of the ridge.

Little Hawk, riding hard in search of a quick way to the top, heard the firefight reach a crescendo, then fade. He prayed that Menawa had not mounted a head-on charge into the muzzles of Calling Owl's rifles. The disturbed earth was too soft, the grade too steep for the horses, so Little Hawk led the way on foot. He and the Creek warriors crawled and scratched until they gained the top of the ridge.

A brisk exchange of rifle fire told him that the battle was coming their way. He positioned his men in the trees on the north side of the tornado's path across the top of the ridge and waited. Four of Calling Owl's Creek warriors burst out into the soft ground.

"Fire," Little Hawk said softly.

But the fleeing men were also Creek, and faced with the choice of killing their own, the men with Little Hawk hesitated. One of them stood, revealed himself, and cried out, "Brothers, give yourselves up and face justice."

The last word had not completely cleared his lips when a rifle ball took him directly between the eyes and knocked him violently backward.

The rifles of the men with Little Hawk spoke almost as one, and the other Creek, running with difficulty in the soft, disturbed earth, fell.

"Load quickly," Little Hawk ordered.

Once again the rifles spoke from concealment, and once again men died.

Calling Owl heard the blast of Little Hawk's rifles and realized that he had delayed his withdrawal too long. Motioning for his men to follow him, he ran toward the sound of Little Hawk's second volley. It took him only a moment to see the difficulty facing him and his retreating warriors.

He counted five rifles firing from the cover of the trees.
There were more rifles than that behind him, and all evidence of discipline was gone from his force. He had little
choice.

"There are only a few of them!" he shouted. He led
the way and then cursed as his feet sank into the soft dirt.
A group of ten warriors burst into the open from his left
and closed with the riflemen on the other side before his
own group was well under way. Five of them went down
before they reached the trees. A white man leaped into
view, swinging his rifle like a club, and another warrior
went down. The white man drew two pistols and killed
two more before finishing his bloody work with a swing of
his tomahawk, which eliminated a fourth Creek.

The men with Calling Owl screamed out their hatred
and continued their charge. The Creek Indians who
fought alongside the white man were loading their rifles,
and it was evident to Calling Owl that they would win the
deadly race, that the rifles would fire point-blank into his
charging men.

Hatred shrieked from Calling Owl's throat. He
turned in midstride and was soon back among the sheltering trees. Men rushed past him, and some tumbled down
the steep slope on the west side of the ridge. He could
hear the battle cries of Menawa's men. He ran toward the
river, then poised for a moment atop the cliff. Far below,
the water swirled at the bottom of the sheer drop. He left
his rifle behind as he leaped out and away, falling feet first
forever until, with a shock that stung the bottom of his
feet, he hit the water.

He went deep, deep. He could see up through the
clear water and the storm of air bubbles left by his impact,
to the sun above, to the blessed air. Fighting his straining
lungs, he kicked upward. At last his head burst clear of
the water, and he gulped a breath. Something hit the
surface of the water so near his nose that his face was
splashed. A rifle ball. Another and another followed him

as he dived below the surface and swam strongly with the current.

When he breached the water again he was out of sight of the riflemen atop the cliff. He swam for the opposite shore, where he pulled himself up on the grassy bank and fell on his face, panting with exhaustion and hatred. Finally catching his breath, he sat up and lifted his clenched fists to the sky.

"By all that is sacred, by the Master of Breath and all of his prophets, I swear that I and mine will be avenged," he vowed in a voice that carried across the river and echoed back to him. "I know you, white man. I know you, and I know whence you came. I swear by the Master of Breath that you will pay. The others as well. Menawa. All those who betrayed their brothers and shed Creek blood. But above all, Hawk Harper, above all you will pay, and before I am finished you will pray for death to release you from your sufferings."

Calling Owl was Creek. He could not believe that Creek would kill Creek. It was as clear to him as the light of the afternoon sun that Creek blood dampened the earth atop the hogback ridge not because of Menawa, Big Warrior, and the Creek Indians who had fought with him, but because they had been led along the terrible path of fratricide by Captain Hawk Harper and the counsel of the white enemy.

In the depth of his hate and rage was the realization that the white man had fought well. So much the better. A man's worth was measured by the ability of his enemy; thus to kill such a warrior would bring power and honor. But Calling Owl vowed that before this white man died, he would know much sorrow.

All the horses were needed to carry the dead, so Little Hawk walked beside Menawa in silent respect for the Creek's mourning. All of the dead were Creek. Eleven of them had fought with Calling Owl, six with Big Warrior, but they were all of the same blood.

It was Menawa who broke the silence. "I would almost prefer to fight the thousands of soldiers from Tennessee. Killing a brother is a terrible thing."

"If law is to be respected, it must be enforced," Little Hawk said, knowing before he spoke that the words were lame, helpless.

"Now we must stop it," Menawa said. "Now we must go to Opothie Micco and all the others who were impressed by the Shawnee, and we must say to them, 'Brothers, let there be no war between us, for we are of the same blood.' "

"Surely not even those who carry red clubs and believe in Tecumseh's cry would countenance civil war," Little Hawk said.

"Let us so pray," said Menawa.

Although the Creek had not advanced as far toward adapting the ways of the white man as had the Cherokee, some among them knew white men well and had regular dealings with them. When Calling Owl, weaponless and alone, escaped the fight on the ridge, he sought the help of a man who could exercise influence in both worlds, a man with connections to one of the most powerful families in the Creek Confederation. He was a man of two names and two bloods: His white-blood name was William Weatherford, his Creek name Lumhe Chati, Red Eagle. He had inherited his hatred of the United States from his uncle, Alexander McGillivray, son of a renegade Scot and a Creek woman, a great chief who fought all of his life against the land greed of both the westward-pushing whites of the United States and the Spanish to the south.

Weatherford's father was a white trader who had deserted his half-Indian paramour, Alexander McGillivray's sister, while his son was quite young. So although Weatherford—Red Eagle—was three-quarter white, his sympathies lay with Tecumseh and anyone who was of a mind to take white scalps. He heard of Menawa's punishment of

Creek warriors and fumed against both the speaker of the Upper Creek and his own superior, William McIntosh.

When Calling Owl came to Red Eagle's house in the dead of night, he was greeted warmly and given food and a bed. In the morning they talked quietly. First Red Eagle listened to Calling Owl's account of the events leading up to the fight atop the hogback ridge. His face showed his anger when Calling Owl named those who had fallen in battle.

"So you have come to me for help," Red Eagle said when Calling Owl was finished.

"I ask only that you supply me with weapons so that I might kill those who shed the blood of my brothers."

"You alone will kill them all? The white Indian, the speakers of both the Upper and the Lower Creek, and all the men who followed their orders?"

"I will kill as many as I can before I myself go to my ancestors," Calling Owl maintained.

"Did you not promise to stand with Tecumseh? Did you not vow to answer his call when the signal comes?"

"By the Master of Breath, I did."

"Then honor that vow," Red Eagle said sternly. "Don't waste your life. Wait for the Shawnee's call, and then all of us, all tribes, all Indians will rise up as one and send the white face floating back to the salt sea on a river of his own blood."

"You are wise, Red Eagle," Calling Owl said. "But my blood burns for revenge. Only one of my eyes will find rest in sleep until he who gave the orders, the white man Harper, is punished."

"Is the life of one white man so important when the time will soon be upon us to kill many of them?"

"May the spirits forgive me, yes," Calling Owl said. "His face is burned into my eyes. His every breath is a pain in my gut."

"I will give you weapons," Red Eagle said. "I can only pray that you use them with common sense and with the knowledge that you will be of great value when we all rise up to fight the final battle."

"Again, you speak wisely. I will honor my promise to the great Shawnee Tecumseh. I will gather my scattered brothers, and we will wait for the sign."

"Good, good," said Red Eagle.

The rifle he gave Calling Owl was of the latest design, a .75-caliber English flintlock with beautiful engraving. With it came a large supply of balls and powder, blades, a keen-bladed tomahawk, and a heavy, strong knife.

Calling Owl traveled toward the Flint River dressed not as the nephew of a chief but as a common man. The time would come when he would defiantly proclaim his identity to one and all, but for the moment—with both the Upper and Lower Creek towns following the lead of the speakers in condemning the raids on white settlements, with both William McIntosh and Menawa kissing the white man's *fumbe* and begging forgiveness—it would be wise to be anonymous.

Calling Owl arrived at the Flint River in time to take the last ferry across into the agency. His clothing was ragged, he was soiled from his travels, and he had let dirt accumulate on the nonworking parts of his fine rifle in order to disguise its quality. He walked the grounds of the agency at dusk and saw the swarms of white children—or so it seemed—at play. He also saw the white captain who called himself a Seneca, Hawk Harper. Calling Owl's hatred was acid in his stomach—there he was, he who had killed Creek Indians, he who had used his influence as a representative of the United States to convince McIntosh and Menawa to shed the blood of their brothers. The Seneca was even in the uniform of a soldier of the United States.

Good. His blood would stand out against the white of his linen and darken the blue of his tunic.

Calling Owl almost killed him then and there. It would have taken only a second to lift his fine rifle and put a .75-caliber ball through the bridge of the white Indian's nose. But he had promised both Tecumseh and Red Eagle to save himself for the final struggle. He would wait, impatiently. Perhaps, in the meantime, he could find a way to make the White Indian's life intolerable.

He followed at a distance as Little Hawk went to his home, a log cabin not far from the agency offices. A white woman with milky skin and pale hair met him at the door with a kiss, and two white boys of tender years seized him, one on each leg, and demanded to be lifted high in their father's arms.

Little Hawk and his happy family were hidden behind a closed door, and Calling Owl was reminded that in many Creek homes there was mourning. Because of this white man, Creek children were fatherless and Creek women were widowed. In the gathering darkness Calling Owl edged into the shadows of the cabin, lifted himself carefully, and looked in on the family eating at the well-laid table. It was clear that the white Indian loved his wife and his sons very much.

It was then that the thought came to Calling Owl, and he thanked the Master of Breath for sending such an inspiration. A brave man would give up his life in battle with honor and a good heart, so merely to kill Harper would be too little and too swift. He must be made to know the sadness that filled the lodges of those who had lost a father, a brother, a son, a husband, to the guns of the white enemy and Menawa.

Calling Owl concentrated on the woman's face. Never one to fancy pale skin, to him there was something grublike about the woman who served food to her men inside the cozy cabin, but when he had finished with her and the two young boys, their pale hair would make a startling decoration for his lodgepole.

He studied the boys. They were identical, but it would not be his concern to tell them apart. Let them continue to look alike in death. He wondered if he could kill each of them in an identical way to preserve their sameness. But it didn't matter—it was the woman who was his main target. A man could mourn his sons with great pain, but the greatest loss was that of a beloved woman, and if that loss carried with it shame and dishonor, so much greater the anguish.

For almost a half hour Calling Owl crouched below the window, looking in on Little Hawk's family. When he left to find a place to sleep in the stables, he was thinking that it might be interesting to sample her fish-white flesh himself, instead of turning the woman over to the ever-eager New Man and the others.

Chapter Eight

G ao awoke to the uncomfortable feeling of impending doom. As he walked to the river the events of the previous days clouded his mind. He knelt, splashed water on his face, shook it off, then lifted his cupped palms for a quick drink. He felt the sun on his back and a soft breeze on his damp face. A mockingbird was practicing its amazing repertoire. Gao knew that the vitality of a healthy nineteen-year-old, when combined with such a masterpiece of a morning, lessened the weight of the most onerous burden.

Actually, he had made his decision during the first hours of his escape from the Vincennes guardhouse. His period of agonizing reappraisal was over. His cousin Ho-ya had been right; it was impossible for a man of pride and honor to live with the whitefaces. Given a choice, he would have headed west to join Ho-ya and We-yo on the far side of the Father of Waters, but he knew that to undertake such a hopeless search was no choice at all.

Gao reasoned that if Ho-ya had been right to leave his home and family to postpone indefinitely his own clash with the ravenous white culture, it followed that Tecumseh was also right. The whiteface was without honor. An Indian could sleep more securely walled up in a den of angry rattlesnakes than he could live side by side with the whitefaces.

So it was with a sense of purpose that Gao turned northward. There was sorrow in his heart, but in the blessed light of the new day it no longer seemed certain that Mist-on-the-Water was dead. The wilderness was, after all, the natural habitat of the Indian, and Mist was Indian. Perhaps she would be frightened by night, but she could travel by day and reach the sanctuary of lands held firmly by the tribes who had answered Tecumseh's call.

As for Ta-na, well, that was a different matter. Gao would never lift a weapon against him, even if Ta-na failed to realize that he was fighting the wrong enemy. Cousin would not strike cousin.

On such a morning it was impossible to think that he would never see the cousin whom he called brother again. The land was wide, true, but Gao knew in his heart that they would meet again under better circumstances. If Tecumseh's war succeeded in driving the white enemy back across the Ohio there would be time for brothers to find each other and be together.

With a firm nod of the head he reformulated his thoughts. *When* Tucumseh's confederation of Indian tribes cleansed the land of the white intruders, he would see Ta-na and the rest of his family again.

He increased his pace slowly, testing his spirit as well as his bad leg. He was moving as a warrior moves who can run fifty miles in a day and go into battle before the sun hides itself, and he was pleased with the improved condition of his leg. Not once did it even threaten to cramp.

By evening he was hungry, and with a well-aimed stone he killed a fat rabbit and cooked it over a small, nearly smokeless fire. He was, he estimated, at least thirty miles from Vincennes, well out of reach of any pursuit from the fort. However, he was easily within range of scouting or war parties from Prophetstown, and after having spied on Tecumseh earlier and killing some of his men, he would need to do a great deal of explaining before Tecumseh would allow him to join his force. Gao reasoned that his best bet was to find the Shawnee and throw himself on his mercy, pleading his youth and inexperience with the white man's treachery. Whatever Tecumseh's decision might be, Gao was determined to seek the right to join him in his fight for the heritage of all tribes.

Gao had heard that Tecumseh had carefully chosen high ground on the north bank of the Wabash River, two and a half miles downstream from its conjunction with the Tippecanoe River, to build his village. Several rows of well-constructed cabins lined the river, and temporary *wegiwas* spread out from the center of the town. At one end of the village was a large log-and-bark building called the house of strangers, where comfort was offered to important visitors, and at the opposite end stood the *msi-kah-mi-qui*, a great log council house that could accommodate five hundred warriors. Next to the council house stood Tenskwatawa's lodge, a sacred place, a temple for his meditations. All around the permanent settlement were the temporary camps of Tecumseh's allies.

Gao approached the village and was within sight of the council house when a heavily built warrior wearing the paint and trappings of a Shawnee nodded a greeting, looked away in politeness, then stared back into his face. He walked quickly into Gao's path.

Gao halted, making no attempt to ready a weapon. He would not lift his blade against a brother.

The Shawnee threw back his head and shrilled a wild cry. Immediately other warriors crowded around.

"The dead man walks," said the Shawnee.

"I have come to see Tecumseh, the Chief of the

Beautiful River," Gao said, holding the eyes of the Shawnee with his, determined not to show fear or uneasiness.

"The dead man talks," the Shawnee said. "The white
man's dog who killed my brother's son, Red Horse, talks
like a man."

"This is one of the spies?" an older warrior asked.

"I would know him anywhere," the Shawnee said.
"His reptile face was burned into my eyes even before I
saw the blood of Red Horse mix with the black mud of the
riverbank."

"You are sure, Crooked Tree?" the older warrior
asked.

"I stake my life and my honor." Crooked Tree lifted
his tomahawk.

Gao directed his words to the older warrior. "I have
been wrong. Now I have come to right that wrong by
fighting with you and with Tecumseh. If I am to die I will
die with pride, knowing that I have at last found my place
among my Indian brothers. But before I am killed let me
make my explanation to the Panther Passing Across."

Crooked Tree howled. The tomahawk trembled in
his hand.

"Tecumseh is not among us," the older warrior said.

"Kill the spy!" a man cried.

Crooked Tree's arm ached with his desire to sink his
tomahawk into Gao's head.

"He should not die quickly," another said. "He is
young and strong. He will give the women much sport. It
will take him a long time to die."

There was a chorus of approval, and Crooked Tree
lowered his weapon. "So be it," he said.

Several warriors sprang forward and disarmed Gao.
He put up no struggle and in short order found himself
bound to a tree by a rough rope that cut into his throat
and made it difficult to breathe.

"Will you at least allow me to present my case to
Tenskwatawa, the Prophet?" he asked, after catching the
eye of the older warrior.

The warrior shook his head silently.

"They are not human, my friend," a voice said in English.

Straining against the tight rope around his neck, Gao turned his head. He could just see out of the corner of his eye a white man, also bound to a tree. His face was bloody and bruised.

To be treated the same as a white man was galling to Gao, and sorrow flooded his eyes with quick tears.

"If we're lucky they won't turn us over to the women," the white man rasped.

"Tecumseh has forbidden the torture of captives," Gao said.

"Ha," the white man spat. "Tell that to these savages. Beside, you heard them say that Tecumseh is not here."

Women and children gathered to stare at the captives. They carried lashes made of interlaced brambles, flexible but strong switches, ugly rawhide whips, and heavy clubs.

"We're in for it now," the white man said.

There was a babble of voices, laughter, and loud calls to those who had not yet gathered. Two lines were formed, with men, women, and children of all ages spaced about eight feet apart on each side of a corridor left open and extending almost to the council house. The women were especially eager. They brandished their striking tools and called impatiently to Crooked Tree to let the entertainment begin. Crooked Tree nodded to two young warriors, who freed the white man of his bonds and escorted him to the head of the twin lines of yelling, gesturing Indians.

The captive's clothing was jerked roughly from his body. The bruises and contusions that covered him were clear signs that his treatment thus far had not been gentle. He turned and looked at Gao, who had to admit that he was a brave man, for he was about to undergo the gauntlet. Every person in the village was prepared to strike the captive as he ran past.

"You know the rules," Crooked Tree said.

The white man nodded grimly. If he reached the council house alive and still on his feet, he would have earned not his freedom but a respite from pain.

"All right, you bloody heathen," the white man said, "let's have a little sport."

Crooked Tree whacked the captive across his pale rump with a heavy stick, and the white man leaped away. With shrieks of delight the women and young ones raked his bare hide with their sticks and brambles and whips. Before he had passed ten of the two hundred or more people in the lines his back and shoulders were marked with bloody streaks. Other than his heavy breathing, he made no sound as he ran with slowly diminishing strength and speed toward the council house. In spite of the brutal blows that rained on him from the top of his head to his shins, he almost made it to the msi-kah-mi-qui. He staggered within reach of a frail-looking old hag wielding a club that seemed far too massive for her thin arms. She smashed the club into the white man's face. Bones shattered, and he fell in a limp heap, dying almost instantly as shards of bone penetrated his brain. A whooping gaggle of young boys swarmed over the body, belaboring it with blows and kicks.

A sigh of disappointment arose from the crowd. A silence. Gao smiled to himself. The old woman's unexpected strength had saved the white man from a slow death by fire.

Two Shawnee warriors untied Gao and led him to Crooked Tree by the rawhide noose around his neck. Squaws leaped to pull Gao's clothing off. One woman pointed to his genitals and giggled. Gao dropped his hand and with a sneer of defiance waved his penis at her, much to the approval of the other women.

"You know the rules, traitor," Crooked Tree said.

"I know that if I were face-to-face with one who had killed my blood I would not leave vengeance to women and children," Gao said. "Give me a blade and face me, Shawnee."

Crooked Tree surged forward, only too eager to comply, but was met by a great shout of protest.

"He is ours, Crooked Tree," cried a pretty young woman who held a rawhide lash at the ready.

With difficulty Crooked Tree controlled himself. He drew back to strike Gao across the bare buttocks, but the blow never landed. Gao danced to one side, the heavy stick swished past him, and he bored in and smashed his fist into Crooked Tree's face. Off balance from the force of his misdirected blow, the Shawnee fell on his back. All Gao's shame and fury were directed toward Crooked Tree. He leaped toward the fallen man, and his feet were in the air when his arms were seized by two strong warriors.

The crowd roared a mixture of protest and admiration. Crooked Tree, dazed by Gao's blow, struggled unsteadily to his feet, his hand searching for the haft of his tomahawk.

"Loose him," he ordered.

Gao, naked and unarmed, prepared to sell his life dearly. The Shawnee lunged forward, aiming a killing blow at his throat, but Gao ducked, lashed out with his foot, and kicked the Shawnee in the genitals. Crooked Tree roared in pain and came once more to the attack. Gao danced aside, but he was being pushed toward the gauntlet, where women at the starting end were waiting for him.

Crooked Tree, his eyes clear, prepared himself for another attack. His tomahawk was raised high when a stern, powerful voice carried over the laughter and cries of encouragement.

All eyes turned to the newcomer, and many recognized the impressive-looking man dressed in the regalia of a Potawatomi chief. It was Main Poche.

"The Panther Passing Across has told you time and

again that captives are not to be tortured," Main Poche said in his large, deep voice.

"The death of this one will be swift," Crooked Tree said.

"And why is an Indian to die naked and unarmed?" Main Poche asked.

"He is one of the spies who killed Red Horse and the others in the battle on the banks of the Wabash River," Crooked Tree said.

"Is that true, naked one?" Main Poche asked Gao.

"It is true, great chief," Gao said, "but that deed was done in youthful ignorance. I have come to join my brothers in your fight against the whitefaces."

"It is my will," Main Poche said, "that this young warrior face the Panther Passing Across. Let Tecumseh himself judge him and decide his fate."

"He is a spy and a traitor to his brothers," Crooked Tree protested.

"He has stated that his beliefs have changed," Main Poche said. "In the town of our enemy he saved my niece from disgrace."

Gao's heart leaped. For the first time he noticed a girl standing behind Main Poche. She was draped in deerskin and a blanket, but the shape of her head and her shadowed face were dearly familiar.

Mist-on-the-Water stepped up and stood beside her uncle. "Hear me," she said. "This Seneca, this Gao, did indeed save me from harm and shame among the white men and later killed two of their soldiers."

A mutter of approval arose from the crowd.

"Tecumseh will judge," Main Poche said.

"Hear me, Main Poche," Crooked Tree shouted. "Look at my face." His nose, broken by Gao's blow, was swollen and bleeding. "This he did to me. I have the right to demand revenge not only for the blow but for the death of one of my blood. Is that not true, even in the laws of the Potawatomi?"

"It is true," Main Poche said.

"So be it," Crooked Tree said, dropping into a fighting stance, his blade at the ready.

Gao retrieved his deerskin trousers with forced casualness, pulled them on, and cinched them at the waist. "I will need a blade," he said.

Main Poche handed a gleaming, iron-bladed tomahawk to Mist-on-the-Water. She came forward with the weapon in one hand and a paint pot in the other. Her movements were graceful, womanly. Gao's eyes and heart were pleased.

"You are my warrior," she whispered to him as she put her forefinger into the paint pot and made twin black marks on each of Gao's cheeks.

The lines of the gauntlet had dissolved, the body of the white man kicked aside to give the two adversaries fighting room. The Shawnee circled in a crouch, making a feint now and then, but Gao stood calmly, his tomahawk hanging loosely at his side. He did not underestimate his opponent, for Crooked Tree was a mature Shawnee warrior, thick-chested and strong of arm. Gao remembered the instructions he had received from his father El-i-chi and his uncle Renno: *When facing a stronger opponent, let his power work against him, evade it, dance with it, let the enemy tire his arm with his own ardor.*

More than once Gao feared for a split second that he had waited too long to mount a counterattack. Crooked Tree's blade left a deep red cut on his shoulder. Again the Shawnee lashed out, and only swift action on Gao's part avoided a death blow to the head. But the Seneca boy had been well trained. Even as his heart leaped in quick panic and his stomach burned with a surge of war fever, he launched a counterblow that broke Crooked Tree's left kneecap and left him hobbled.

Still the Shawnee pressed forward, for he was desperate to end it now, knowing that his shattered knee could give way at any time, leaving him at the mercy of the Seneca. Iron rang on iron as Gao countered a blow.

Crooked Tree's leg gave way and he almost fell, but he righted himself and hopped forward on one leg.

Gao moved out of his path. "I care not to slay a cripple."

Crooked Tree roared his rage.

"There will be another day," Gao stated. "Let your wound heal, and then once more we will dance the dance of death."

The Shawnee limped forward and smashed a series of blows that taxed all Gao's skill and strength. The red haze of combat was taking control of Gao's emotions, and he no longer concerned himself with the Shawnee's physical handicap. Crooked Tree was his enemy, a man who was doing his best to kill him. There was only one cure for it. Gao lashed out forehand and then backhand, the backhand following the retreating swing of Crooked Tree's effort to block the first feint. Sharp iron buried its message of death in the Shawnee's temple, and he took two faltering steps backward as Gao wrenched his blade free. Gao leaped to the kill, but no further blow was necessary. The Shawnee sank slowly to his knees and then rolled onto the ground, his eyes already showing the glaze of death.

Main Poche lifted his hands for silence. "By Moneto, the Supreme Being of all things," he said, "I declare that this dispute has been judged. By Inumsi Ilafewanu, the grandmother who weaves the great net, the *skemotah* that traps men, Crooked Tree has been taken. By Moneto who rules all, the Seneca warrior is blessed. Until Tecumseh returns, let that be an end to it."

Mist-on-the-Water put her hand in Gao's, and it was a warm reassurance that he had, indeed, been blessed.

Happy to be reunited, Gao longed for the privacy of a place where he could devote his full attention to Mist-on-the-Water. As the young lovers followed Main Poche into Prophetstown there was little chance to talk.

"Jeb Martin still lives," Gao said heavily.

"He lives," Mist said. "Your blow glanced without cutting."

"You were afraid of the wilderness," he said gently.

"When I saw that Jeb Martin was alive, I was more afraid of him," she said. "As you see, the wilderness did me no harm."

"It was fortunate that you found your uncle so quickly."

"Moneto was with me," she said, smiling.

They stood among Main Poche's men as the chief greeted the Prophet, Tenskwatawa of the damaged face. In his empty eye socket the brother of Tecumseh wore a round pebble on which was painted a fearsome red eye.

Although Gao could not hear their words, the Prophet's stern, one-eyed stare told him that he was being discussed. Main Poche spoke quietly. The Prophet nodded. The Potawatomi chief approached the couple.

"Tenskwatawa agrees that Tecumseh will be your judge," he said.

"For all this, great chief, I am grateful," Gao said.

"If you prove false once again, I myself will forget that Tecumseh has forbidden torture," Main Poche promised.

"To my shame," Gao said, "one quarter of my blood is the blood of whites, but I will never again be false to the three quarters that is Indian."

"Then you will find a place among my people," Main Poche offered.

"Come," Mist-on-the-Water said, taking Gao's hand once again. "I will show you."

Mist led him to an empty lodge on the village outskirts. There was much activity around them as women prepared the evening meal, but once inside the structure the sounds of the outside world were muted and, as she came into his arms, forgotten. She gave him her mouth as a white woman would, and in that respect, at least, he was false to his Seneca blood as he tasted her sweetness and touched her tongue with his.

"How I did pray for you," she whispered.

"I feared that you were dead," he answered.

"The Great Spirit would not be so cruel as to take me from you before I know you as a woman would," she said, her voice soft, low, and heated. She pulled him with her as she walked backward to a pile of sleep skins, sat down, and drew him down beside her. He put his weight on her, torso to torso, and drank of her mouth like a hummingbird at a rose. She helped him bare her firm breasts, and this time her skirt was not drawn up and knotted between her legs.

He had never been naked with a girl before, and he could not absorb all of her wonder at one time. With his eyes and hands he explored her, and she clung to him, her breath hot on his cheek. He let his fingers trail down into small indentations spaced equally above the swell of her buttocks and looked in shivering wonder on the smoothness of her inner thighs and the dark vee of her womanhood. Although his need was great—once again he was shaking as if with cold—he felt no sense of urgency. He was content to get to know her body inch by inch, to see the passion on her face and in her eyes, to feel her hands on him as she let her palm trail over his biceps, his chest, his thighs and—with a mutual gasp—his manhood.

"It is Main Poche who must give you in marriage?" he whispered.

"Yes. I will speak with him."

"Will he not refuse his permission until the return of Tecumseh and my judging?"

"No matter," she said, pulling him atop her.

"We must wait," he said, although she was guiding him to a moist, heated softness.

"I almost lost you once," she said. "I will not risk that again, not without—"

She gasped.

He froze, in spite of being urged with every fiber of his being to thrust forward.

She put her hands on his taut buttocks and pulled him gently to her, and slowly, slowly, they were one.

It was evening, and fires sparkled throughout Prophetstown and its satellite encampments. Main Poche had been sampling the white man's medicine and had reached a state of pleasant mellowness. He could see—perhaps it was only his fancy that he could smell—the love of the two young ones.

"It would be unwise to permit this marriage until Tecumseh has said whether or not the Seneca will live," Main Poche stated simply.

"Uncle," Mist-on-the-Water said, "already we are married in fact."

Main Poche chuckled. "So my nose has not grown as old as my head." He sobered. "That is a serious matter, daughter of my sister. It is not good to defy custom."

"Let us be married by the laws of our tribe, then," Mist pleaded. "Please give the order to the shaman."

"And what of the bride-price?" Main Poche asked.

It was Mist-on-the-Water who answered. "With all due respect, Uncle, since I have no father and my mother is dead, no bride-price is required."

"Nevertheless," Gao said, "I will willingly pay whatever your traditions call for."

Main Poche laughed. "Is the young Seneca suddenly rich in horses?"

"Give me the number and a few days, and you will have them," Gao urged.

"We live in strange times," Main Poche said, his face becoming serious. "We have not the numbers of warriors that would allow us to waste them in counting coup or stealing horses to meet a bride-price." He lifted his hand. "Daughter of my dead sister, you remind me of her when she was a girl standing on the brink of life. Take this man as your husband. If you desire to participate in an official ceremony, so it will be done. If not—"

"I intend to marry only once, Uncle," Mist said. "I would have all that goes with it."

So it was that the drums beat out a happy rhythm and the warriors danced something other than the belligerent leaps and whirls of war. Unmarried maids chanted wishes for happiness and blessings as the Shawnee shaman waved his magic tassels and touched first Gao and then Mist-on-the-Water on the forehead. A great whoop of joy and celebration sounded.

The newly wedded couple retired to the lodge that they had claimed and with the haste that burns in youth were naked together, only to have the roof shake and the walls tremble. To gales of laughter and ribald teasing, half a dozen tongue-lolling dogs were tossed through the doorway. Gao struggled into his trousers and ejected the friendly animals one by one, but still whistles and whoops sounded as the hecklers danced around and around the lodge.

When silence fell, Gao dared not hope that the jolly harassment was over. Nor was it.

"We will hear a speech from the newly married man," a voice cried out, and others took up the chant.

Mist-on-the-Water giggled. "They will give us no peace until we show ourselves."

Now fully dressed, Gao stepped out the door. Most of those gathered were young, most of them unmarried. Heckling the lovers was a way of anticipating the time when they, too, would enter a private place with a loved one and close the door behind them.

"It pleases me to know that my brothers and sisters wish us well," Gao said.

There was a chorus of good-natured hoots.

"We want to see the new woman," a young girl cried out.

Mist-on-the-Water pushed open the door and stood beside Gao.

"She looks no different."

"How can I become a woman when scalawags

threaten to shake down the very house on my head?" Mist asked.

"My friends," Gao said, "it grows late. For you who are so young it is past bedtime."

There were hisses, jeers, and more loud laughter.

"Mist-on-the-Water longs to ride the bony pony," a young man yelled from the back of the crowd.

"Go to," another said. "We will count cadence for you."

"Uh, uh, uh," several young men grunted in rhythm. The sound was taken up by others. Gao took Mist's hand and led her back into the lodge.

"It's no use," she said.

"Uh, uh, uh," the crowd chanted.

Gao kicked out a portion of the lower wall of the lodge, pushed Mist through it, gathered up two blankets, and followed her. They ran silently into the darkness toward the river. As they strolled northward along the banks of the Wabash, the sounds of the laughter and heckling faded in the distance.

"I kissed you first in a willow thicket beside this river," Gao said.

"How well I remember."

At a good distance from the town Gao made a bower of grass and branches, spread one of the blankets over it, and gently lowered Mist to lie on it. He removed his clothing and lay down beside her to discover that she, too, had stripped. The midnight air was cool, and he pulled the other blanket atop them, but the warmth of their love soon overcame the chill. There were no young rascals to interrupt, only the night sounds—the murmur of the river, the glad voices of little frogs, and once the squeak of a bat searching for insects just above the tall grass of their hideaway.

With the morning Gao led his bride farther to the north. When hunger came upon them in the middle of the afternoon, Gao, pleased by the opportunity to show his skills to the wondrous object of his love, eased naked into the river, swam underwater, and seized a surprised duck by the legs. They made another bower beside the river and talked of childhood memories while the fowl roasted over a fire. Another day and another they roamed the virgin wilderness, stopping to love when the banked coals of passion glowed, swimming in the river to wash away the sweat and juices of their ardor.

"I have only just remembered," Gao said one evening as they lay, arms and legs entwined, the heat of their desire cooled for the moment. "My mother told the story only once, how she and my father, the shaman, El-i-chi, lived together in the wilderness north of the Ohio. They dwelt beside a beautiful lake."

"And now it is I who live in the wilderness with you," Mist-on-the-Water said.

"We have no beautiful lake, only the river," he offered. "But when my mother talked of that time her eyes glowed. I would think that she and my father knew the same happiness that is ours."

"Moneto is kind," Mist said.

"The Master of Life is indeed kind," Gao agreed.

For a time all was right with the world. Thoughts of separation from his family and from Ta-na were banished. Concern about Tecumseh's coming judgment of his past deed was forgotten. All worrisome thoughts were crowded out of his mind by his delight in discovering that man and woman together is one of the greatest gifts given by the Master of Life.

Prophetstown was astir when Gao and Mist-on-the-Water approached it from the north ten days after their brief but impressive wedding ceremony. A crowd was gathered around the council house, and the reason was soon clear, for everyone was eager to tell them that Tecumseh had returned.

"Let us postpone the moment of judgment," Mist begged.

"It hangs over my head," Gao said. "We will face it now."

He led Mist to the back of the crowd, where he could hear the penetrating, powerful voice of the Panther Passing Across. Tecumseh was talking about his reception among the Creek Indians.

Gao saw the head plumes of Main Poche near the front of the crowd. Muttering apologies, he pushed his way forward, pulling Mist behind him. When he reached the side of the Potawatomi chief, a finger to the lips told him to be quiet. Gao listened impatiently at first, but soon he, too was being carried on the smooth flood of Tecumseh's oratory, sharing in the Shawnee's travels, his blood heating as Tecumseh spoke of the determination of the Creek and others, even among the tribes that claimed allegiance to the United States. At last Tecumseh was finished. The silence following his final, ringing proclamation of death to the Shemanese lasted so long that men began to be uncomfortable.

Finally Main Poche stepped forward. "My brother," he said, "there is a matter to be judged."

"Speak, brother," Tecumseh said, "although I would agree in advance to your own judgment."

Main Poche nodded acknowledgment of the compliment. "This has to do with you and the ghosts of Red Horse and other Shawnee warriors."

Tecumseh's face darkened, for the memory of a black night on the banks of the Wabash when his life was spared by a mere boy had become a festering sore.

"Two spies came to us," Main Poche said. "When they left to carry their traitorous messages to the enemy, they were followed by Red Horse."

"And by me," Tecumseh said.

Main Poche pushed Gao forward. "This one was wounded."

"And yet he killed from ambush," Tecumseh said.

"This one, the Seneca called Gao, comes to us of his

own free will to beg pardon for past actions against his Indian brothers," Main Poche stated.

"Let the Seneca speak for himself," Tecumseh said.

"It is true that my brother and I fought against you, great chief," Gao said. "In my youth I heeded the teachings of my father and my uncle. I had been told from the time I could recognize words that in order to survive, all Indians must adopt the ways of the whitefaces."

"You are Seneca?" Tecumseh asked.

"My grandfather led his people to the south following the great white man's war."

"Your father, then, is the sachem Renno?"

"He is my uncle," Gao said. "My father is El-i-chi, shaman and now sachem of the Seneca."

"Your clan bedevils me," Tecumseh said. "I saw your uncle at the fallen timbers. He sat his horse next to the most deadly of our enemies, the Chief Who Never Sleeps."

"I can only say that when I became old enough to think for myself it became apparent to me that my father and my uncle had been fighting the wrong enemy. If you will allow me, Tecumseh, I will be yours to command. I will lift the war ax with you and follow you wherever you lead in pursuit of the whitefaces who claim our hunting grounds."

"What of Crooked Tree?" Tecumseh asked, looking at Main Poche.

"Crooked Tree claimed his right to trial by combat," Main Poche said.

Tecumseh's grief showed momentarily. "That Crooked Tree is not with us indicates the decision of Moneto and the Great Spirit," he said.

"So it was," Main Poche confirmed.

"So be it, then," Tecumseh said. "If one so young can best a warrior of Crooked Tree's skill, then he is one to be valued. Would you then be by my side, Seneca?"

"With all my heart," Gao said.

Tecumseh lifted his tomahawk. "Hear me," he said,

his voice growing to fill the air over the entire town. "This one, this Seneca, is now one of us, a brother of brothers, a warrior among warriors, a friend among friends. If there is one who would deny this, let him speak now."

There was only silence.

"One thing," Tecumseh said. "Your cousin, the son of Renno. Where is he?"

"He scouts for William Henry Harrison," Gao said.

"Perhaps you will see his face in the sights of your rifle one day."

"I will be honest with you," Gao said. "If so, I will turn my aim to another."

"I respect that," Tecumseh said. "For it would be a crime against Moneto to kill a blood brother."

That night there were no hecklers outside the lodge. Mist-on-the-Water had spent an hour of the afternoon patching the hole that Gao had knocked in the wall so that they could escape. The night was cool, but the blankets and their bodies were warm. The next day Mist visited the gardens and came home with corn, late-summer squash, and melons. Main Poche sent a haunch of venison, and the smell of the evening meal made Gao's mouth water.

A general council was held that night. Gao and Mist listened from the back of the crowd as Tecumseh spoke of the wrongs done by the European invaders. The grim prophet Tenskwatawa repeated Tecumseh's promise to shake the very earth with one downward thrust of his foot when the time came to send the signal for the final uprising to tribes scattered from the lakes of the north to the swamps of the south.

"Do you believe he can shake the earth?" Mist asked when they were cozily in bed.

"When I am within range of his voice I can believe that he could shatter the earth," Gao admitted.

"And when his voice is not in your ears?"

"I can only pray that he is not a false prophet. I can

only pray that his genius is so great that tribes all over the great land will hear and answer his call."

"To think of war frightens me," Mist said. "Jeb Martin said the number of soldiers the whitefaces can put in the field is unlimited. Truly, I have seen them. Their women pop out children like the mice of the cornfields, and there must be many of them, for they have devoured so much of the land already."

"They are many," Gao said. "But if all Indians join forces we can push them back to the sea."

"And if all tribes do not heed Tecumseh's call?"

"We will die with honor."

Mist shivered and drew close to him.

Chapter Nine

President James Madison and his new secretary of state, James Monroe, sat side by side in a carriage bouncing over a road only slightly less bumpy than the worst of Virginia's growing network of thoroughfares. For the President, it was good to be away from Washington. A pestilent fever had broken out in the heat of summer; some said it was caused by the stagnant water in an unfinished canal. Dolley Madison, however, said that it was God's way of telling people with good sense to seek the healthy air of the Virginia countryside at every opportunity.

Madison leaned over and looked out the window. Through the trees he caught a glimpse of the stately home that Thomas Jefferson called Monticello.

When the carriage came to a stop, Jefferson was standing on the front porch of the house he had designed and greeted the visitors.

"There, sir," James Monroe said with a wry smile, "is a splendid portrait of a retired private citizen."

The President chuckled. He knew well that Jefferson

liked to pretend he was nothing more than a devoted farmer who was done with politics and had banished all the passions of power from his life.

The men greeted one another warmly. Madison, the shortest of the three, was escorted into the house ahead of Monroe by the former president. It seemed to the secretary of state that Jefferson was having some difficulty getting around.

"I trust, Mr. President, that you are well," Monroe inquired as they entered a large, pleasant study.

"A touch of rheumatism," Jefferson said, "for which Dr. Benjamin Rush has sent me a list of remedies."

"Oh, well, doctors," Madison said with a shrug.

Jefferson smiled as he motioned the President to a seat of honor in the most comfortable chair. "I am not too proud to listen to medical advice, although I must confess that I have not tried Dr. Rush's simplest suggestion, which was to wear a piece of calico on the painful areas."

"Dolley used to dose her mother with spirit of turpentine and sassafras tea," Madison said.

"Yes, I, too, have tried that," Jefferson admitted as he sat down slowly. "I'm not sure which brings the most relief, the internal consumption of those noxious beverages or my daily bath with camphor, opium, and salt, and a final application of castile soap."

"When I have an occasional twinge of the rumatiz," the President said, "I dose it heartily with a good French wine."

Jefferson laughed. "That, Mr. President, sounds very wise to me. In fact, I was just about to offer you something a tad stronger than wine. I have just received a supply of French brandy that has a pleasingly full body."

"Thank you, sir. Yes," Madison said.

"Certainly, sir," Monroe agreed.

As if she had been listening, Jefferson's daughter entered the room and served an aged brandy in delicate crystal snifters. She returned greetings from Madison and

Monroe politely, left the decanter within her father's reach, and retired quickly, closing the door behind her.

"It's too bad that the French can't be as agreeable as their alcoholic beverages," Monroe said, after an appreciative sniff.

"If the statesmen of the world would join together at a table and share a glass of fine French brandy," Jefferson said with a smile, "perhaps things would be different."

"First you'd have to educate some of the so-called statesmen to the basic principles of appreciation of the finer things of life," Madison said. "I had dinner recently with Sir Augustus John Foster, the new minister from Great Britain, just before leaving the capital."

"An old friend of yours, as I recall," Jefferson said.

"Yes," Madison acknowledged. "We were often in contact when I was in London. As it happened, most of Sir Augustus's other guests were New England members of the Congress. The minister served Potomac River sturgeon caviar. The New Englanders thought that it was black raspberry jam, and they slathered slices of bread with it and tore into it only to spit it out in disgust."

Jefferson laughed heartily. James Monroe, seeing that Madison's legs were too short for the chair in which he sat, pushed a hassock across the floor with his foot, and Madison nodded in gratitude.

"I haven't had the opportunity to congratulate you for ordering Governor Claiborne of the Orleans Territory to move his troops into West Florida," Jefferson said when he finished savoring his brandy.

"It became a necessity," Madison stated.

"I am only a retired private citizen, mind you—"

Madison cast a wry look at Monroe.

"—but as a citizen I would like to see us take possession of both Floridas immediately. The signal should have been our occupation of Baton Rouge. At that time we should have seized Pensacola and St. Augustine."

"In for a penny, in for a pound?" Monroe asked.

"Exactly," Jefferson said. "We would not have offended the Old World any more than we did by taking all than by taking only part."

"It seems to me, Thomas," Madison said gently, "that you have become much more bellicose since leaving the White House."

Jefferson smiled and waved his hand in acknowledgment. "Gather all your Republican members of Congress, lock them in a room, and don't let them out until they agree that the time has come to make the Floridas a part of the United States. The Georgia militia can accomplish the task in a fortnight." The former president leaned forward and spoke quietly. "On a more pleasant subject, gentlemen, I can't tell you how much satisfaction it gave me when I heard that you had healed the unfortunate breach between you. This old man can now rest easy in his bed at night, knowing that the destiny of our nation is in the hands of fellow Virginians."

"Kind of you, sir," Monroe said. Madison smiled.

"Aside from the pleasure of seeing you again, Mr. President," Monroe said, "I wanted to hear your current views on the actions of our mother country, England."

Jefferson leaned back. "The fellow who now calls himself the Duke of Wellington has the French on the run in Spain. His defeat of the French general Masséna at Fuentes de Onoro in May has opened the road to Madrid. It's only a matter of time before Napoleon is forced to withdraw from Spain entirely. The British lion will be roaring in triumph soon, and I don't have to tell you that a cocky England is a dangerous England. Mr. President, I applaud your orders to Commodore John Rogers, by the way."

Madison smiled at his companions. The British had responded to an easing of tensions between the United States and France by once again impressing American seamen from ships near the northeastern coast of the United States. The President had ordered Commodore Rogers to use the powerful U.S.S. *President* to put a stop to the British attacks. Overtaking a British warship off the

Virginia shore in the dimness of twilight, thinking it to be the *Guerrièfre*, a powerful English ship of the line, Rogers and his crew rendered the British ship helpless in a quarter hour. Only after the spirited cannonade did they discover that it was not the huge *Guerrièfre* but a corvette, the *Little Belt*, and she carried only half the *President*'s guns. Nevertheless, Madison had stated that his naval commanders would continue to support the dignity of the flag of the United States.

"The *Little Belt* incident will end either in better understanding or an open rupture of relations with England," Madison said, "but I feel that this nation has grown tired of that country's hostility. In fact, I plan to say in my annual message to the Congress that it is time to put the nation into the armor and the attitude that is demanded by this continuing belligerence from England. I will recommend enlarging the army, strengthening and preparing the state militias, manufacturing a stockpile of munitions, and building new ships for the navy."

"I am told," Jefferson said, "that Mr. Henry Clay, the Speaker of the House, is going to appoint men under forty years of age, all of them War Hawks, to the major committees in the House of Representatives."

"So I am informed," Madison said.

"Some Federalists will say that Mr. Madison is using overcharged colors to describe Great Britain, while whitewashing the injuries administered to us by Napoleon," Monroe said, "but it is my feeling that the mood of the country matches exactly that of the Congress."

"We can no longer suffer quietly the British outrages," Jefferson said with a vigorous nod. "Henry Clay has expressed to me in his correspondence that if England persists in her attitude toward the United States he considers war to be inevitable."

James Madison finished his brandy and put the crystal glass carefully on a side table. He had already told Dolley that it would be necessary for them to return to Washington a month before Congress convened so that he could consult the cabinet regarding his annual message. In his mind, as he turned his attention from the conversation that continued between Jefferson and Monroe, he was composing phrases. He was saddened by the depth of his own determination to declare war on Great Britain, but before the coming session of Congress ended he was ready to authorize armed reprisals against the belligerent British.

Perhaps, the President thought, he had come to Monticello to hear exactly what Thomas Jefferson had just said about England, if only to serve as reassurance that he was right in asking the nation to gird itself for another war.

One afternoon soon after Gao and Mist-on-the-Water had returned to Prophetstown, Gao came back from a hunt and found Main Poche preparing for a journey.

"Governor Harrison has sent messengers to the tribes," the Potowatomi chief said to his nephew-by-marriage. "Tenskwatawa the Prophet has asked me to determine the content of these messages and to assess their effect on our people."

"I will go with you," Gao offered, and the chief assented.

It was not a long trip. The tribes that had been pushed west by Mad Anthony Wayne's Treaty of Greenville following the fight at the place of the fallen timbers were in close proximity. It was a matter of only two days before Main Poche's party arrived at the Wyandot village of Tarhe the Crane. Main Poche had deliberately chosen to visit Tarhe first because Tarhe's support of Tecumseh was, at best, fitful, wavering back and forth like a reed in the winds.

As the travelers approached Tarhe's village they encountered many Wyandot who were seeking the same destination. The Potowatomies were welcomed by Tarhe himself and directed to a suitable campsite. He informed them that he had called a council of all Wyandot chiefs to convene as soon as the evening star appeared in the sky. Although Main Poche knew his was not to be a voice in the council, his rank entitled him to sit among the chiefs, and he directed his nephew to sit by his side.

Tarhe the Crane spoke first, and Gao was surprised when the Wyandot dived into the subject of the council without the usual colorful oratory.

"You have all been visited by a white man's dog," Tarhe pronounced.

The assembled Wyandot chiefs voiced their confirmation.

"And did the white man's dog deliver to you the same insult that was directed to these ears?" He pointed to his head.

There was a chorus of assenting grunts.

"This white man who continues to steal our land is not content with that," Tarhe went on. "Now he delivers a deadly insult to us all."

"My friend," Main Poche said, "what was the nature of this insult?"

"The white chief Harrison in Vincennes has told us that all Indians are his enemy. He instructed his dogs to tell me, Tarhe the Crane, that in the event of war against those who follow the Panther Passing Across, the white soldiers will shoot any Indian they encounter because they will not be able to distinguish friend from foe."

"Ahhhh," said the assembled chiefs in unison.

"Is this not a declaration of war against all of us?" Tarhe asked in a loud voice.

"Yes, yes," the chiefs answered.

"Now there is no choice," Tarhe said. "It remains only for us to join Tecumseh's cause."

There were whoops of agreement.

"Some of you know that I was with Little Turtle at the fallen timbers," Tarhe said. "I have faced the guns and the bayonets of the white soldiers. I have seen Indians turn and run at the mere sight of the sun glinting on the long knives. War with the whiteface is not a game for young warriors counting coup. I am fully aware of the seriousness of my words when I call upon all my brothers, upon all Wyandot, to join me in swearing that my loyalty to the Panther Passing Across is unqualified, that I will fight at his side forever."

Tarhe paused and let his eyes fall on the face of each of the chiefs. "Are we all agreed, then?"

The short, stocky man who stood was in his middle years. His mouth was unusually large and dominated his face. "You know me, my brothers," he said.

"My brother Leatherlips," Tarhe the Crane acknowledged.

"I have heard the words of my brother Tarhe the Crane, and I note especially his remembrance of the defeat the Ohio tribes suffered at the place of the fallen timbers." He paused and looked around, then lifted his head high for emphasis. "Are we so blind to the past that we would let such a thing happen to us again? Are we blind to the numbers of the white soldiers of the United States?"

There were muttered words of protest.

"I say to you that to follow the Shawnee Tecumseh into still another war with the whitefaces will result in the destruction of our villages. Our crops will be trampled into the earth and our storehouses emptied of the provisions we have stored for the winter. Our women and children will weep as they face the cold snows without clothing and without food."

"Not so, Leatherlips," someone called out.

"It is so. They are too many. They have the newest rifles. We have—what? Old guns that they no longer want, so they are willing to trade them to us. We are few. Their numbers are like the leaves on the trees."

"The leaves fall," Tarhe said, "and there are fewer on the trees every day."

"I know you have heard," Leatherlips continued, "that I and mine will have no part of the madness preached by the Shawnee and his brother, who calls himself the Prophet. Prophet he may be, but what he predicts is death for the Indian."

"Traitor," a strong voice called out.

Leatherlips drew back his shoulders and put his hand on his tomahawk. "Let he who speaks face me."

"I face you," Tarhe said, his eyes cold.

"So be it," said Leatherlips.

"You will reconsider your words," Tarhe ordered.

"I speak my heart," Leatherlips said.

"He is a traitor!" another chief shouted.

"Hold," Tarhe cautioned, lifting his hand. "I hear two voices. Let the council speak."

One by one the stern-faced chiefs rose and confronted Leatherlips.

"My brother," Tarhe said to him. "You see how they feel, all of your brothers. Surely you will reconsider."

"That I cannot do."

"You know the law," Tarhe said.

"I know the law," Leatherlips said. "I question the right of this council to apply it."

"That vote has not been taken," Tarhe said.

"Take it, then," Leatherlips said defiantly, lifting his tomahawk from its place on his belt.

At a nod from Tarhe, two young warriors pinned his arms and took his weapons from him.

"This is a solemn moment," Tarhe the Crane said to the chiefs. "Not in many seasons has a Wyandot been accused of treason to his tribe. You all know the penalty. How say you? Is the law to be applied to our brother Leatherlips?"

One by one the chiefs took a step forward; each drew his tomahawk.

"So be it," Tarhe said sadly, randomly pointing to four of the chiefs. The chosen men stepped toward Leatherlips.

"Loose me," the condemned man said to the two young warriors who held him.

Tarhe nodded, and the two moved away from

Leatherlips, who refused to look at the four chiefs advancing toward him.

"It will be remembered that in solemn ceremony the law of the Wyandot was kept," Tarhe the Crane said. "Let the shaman say the words."

A Wyandot medicine man shook a feathered flail around Leatherlips and chanted the song of death. In silence the four chiefs lifted their weapons and, as one, smashed the blades down onto his head. All life instantly left the traitor's body, and he slumped to the earth like an empty sack.

"The frost comes early in the north," Gao said, looking out the door of his lodge. Mist-on-the-Water was still in bed.

"Close the door," she said.

"Come, see how pretty it is."

Wrapped in a blanket, she reluctantly tiptoed across the cold earthen floor.

Crystals of frost covered the earth and jeweled the dry grass. The smoke of newly rekindled fires rose straight up into an azure sky of brilliant clarity. In the stillness only Tenskwatawa moved within Gao's view, and the young man closed his door until only a crack remained. He watched as the Prophet halted before Main Poche's lodge and called out in an arrogant, commanding voice. The Potowatomi chief opened his door.

"My brother Tecumseh has called council," the Prophet said.

"He has only to name the time," Main Poche responded.

"Now," stated the Prophet, turning his scarred face away.

"I'll be back," Gao said to Mist-on-the-Water.

"Eat something before you go," she said.

"There's no time."

Gladly Mist ran to the bed and snuggled down into the blankets and furs, and Gao dressed and hurried to join

Main Poche. His uncle-by-marriage nodded a silent greeting.

Already many chiefs and warriors had gathered in the common at the center of Prophetstown, and Gao felt a surge of excitement when he saw the commanding figure of Tecumseh standing in front of the council house. Gao and Main Poche found a good spot but did not sit down, as the ground was still covered by frost. The Shawnee waited in silence, his head down, his eyes staring at the ground.

"All are present," said Tenskwatawa.

Tecumseh lifted his head. "I have called you here, my brothers, to tell you that I am going away once more and to report to you on my latest and last council with General Harrison. As I told you previously, I asked General Harrison to submit my protest against the terms of the Treaty of Fort Wayne to the chief of all the whites in Washington. I said at that time that if the Great White Chief's decision was not in favor of the tribes from whom General Harrison seized lands illegally, there would be war. It was with reluctance that I agreed to another meeting with General Harrison. Although I have yet to receive a reply from the chief of all the whites, an answer was demonstrated to me at Vincennes when General Harrison greeted me with eight hundred federal troops."

Tecumseh's listeners exchanged uneasy looks.

"I answered this threat with a promise of my own. I told him that blood would flow. I was told that more white soldiers are on the way from the east and that the Kentucky Militia stands ready to join in any fight."

The Shawnee looked toward the pristine blue heavens and paused dramatically. "There will be war, my brothers. We will face the white soldiers. We will face their artillery, and we will fight against their big guns and their long knives."

Some of the warriors mumbled nervously.

"So it stands. General Harrison's last words to me were these. He said that he would put petticoats on his soldiers sooner than he would give up the land that he bought from us."

There was a shout of protest.

"Yes," Tecumseh said. "You and I know that the weak, greedy chiefs who met with Harrison at Fort Wayne did not have the authority to sign away land that did not belong to them."

He raised both hands as if in blessing. "My brothers, we will fight. And when we fight we will fight alongside the Choctaw, Chickasaw, Cherokee, Biloxi, Creek, Alabama, Seminole, Calusa, Santee, Yazoo, Natchez, Tawakonia, and Caddo. Even now I leave you to reaffirm our alliance with other tribes, such as the Osage. I will be gone when the first of my predicted signs appears, when the panther passes across the sky at midnight. In my absence I caution you, under no circumstamces allow yourselves to be lured into premature action by any provocation of the whites."

Tecumseh turned and put his hand on the shoulder of his brother. "You, Tenskwatawa, my brother and my right hand—you who talk with Moneto the Supreme Being of All Things—it will be your responsibility to hold back the natural inclination of our people to strike at the enemy. It is not yet time, my brothers. Our enemy is strong, his soldiers many. It will require our combined strength to defeat him, and the great massing of warriors of all tribes will not occur until the first sign is seen in the night sky, until our allied chiefs have cut the final red stick into thirty parts and burned one piece each night. Then and only then will I stamp my foot and give the call for the final congregation of forces, for the full assault on the white man from the coast of the southern salt sea to the cold, clear waters of the northern lakes."

Young warriors waved their weapons, and war cries resounded in the chill morning air. Someone fired a shot upward, and that one shot generated a volley.

"Hold," Tecumseh roared in anger. "Shot and powder are not easy to come by. Save them for the enemy."

* * *

William Henry Harrison believed in the old adage: Once burned, twice cautious. He had been caught unaware by the Prophet's prediction of the solar eclipse and had vowed to be prepared for whatever might happen next. For the life of him he didn't see how Tecumseh or his brother the Prophet could call the time, even the hour, of a shooting star, but he was not unaware that members of thirty or more tribes had begun a nightly vigil waiting for the sign. He knew that the red sticks had been discarded one by one until only one stick remained.

The puzzling timing of Tecumseh's latest prediction had begun with the Wind Moon, and now the cold was well advanced. Snow flurries had fallen in northern areas, and frost browned the vegetation. There was cider fresh from the presses, sweet potatoes were stored in hills, pumpkins showed their iridescent orange from the porches of settlers' cabins, and the luscious smell of pumpkin pie flowed from many windows. Harrison could not bring himself to believe that Tecumseh's war would begin in the cold. Food would be scarce, and soon deep snows would hamper movement. Never before had the Indians mounted a major winter campaign.

Nevertheless Harrison's request for more troops was being answered, and reinforcements were being sent down the Ohio by flatboat. In Kentucky militiamen were training, and in Vincennes the governor kept his garrison hopping. Sergeants bawled orders on the drill field, muskets roared in target practice, and patrols covered the wilderness to the north, toward the concentration of tribes at Prophetstown.

On one such patrol the governor rode at the head of the column with Ta-na, on whom he had come to depend heavily. They were leading the patrol along a well-traveled track toward the site chosen for a new fort to support the army's advance on Prophetstown. "Ah, my young friend Thomas Harper," Harrison said, preferring not to use Ta-na's Indian name. "Tecumseh's a charlatan. He cannot possibly say when a large shooting star will move across the sky, much less predict that it will be green."

Ta-na remained silent, for he had learned that Harrison often used trusted aides as sounding boards without requiring an answer or opinion.

"He's undone himself this time," Harrison continued. "He has Indians all over the country sitting up half the night watching the sky. They're out there every night, even when it's cold enough to freeze a brass monkey. They'll get tired of it pretty soon, and when nothing happens he will lose his credibility."

"Governor," Ta-na said, "I'd feel better if you'd fall back and join the column."

"Don't worry about me," Harrison said.

Ta-na laughed. "Well, sir, it's not only you that I worry about. You make an inviting target, and I don't have that much confidence in the marksmanship of our friends out there."

Harrison answered Ta-na's laugh. "I get your point, Thomas, but your father and your grandfather could smell an enemy a mile off. I have confidence in you."

"More than I have in myself, sir."

"You'll have to admit, though, that it's a brilliant strategy," Harrison mused. "Thirty bundles of sticks, delivered during the Hunger Moon either in person or by runners to the primary chiefs of thirty tribes. They went west, north, and south. And I can imagine Indians all over the country watching the bundles of sticks grow smaller month by month. By God, if he *could* bring it off . . . what would members of your tribe think if, on the predicted night, a great celestial body burned across the black of the midnight sky?"

"My father speaks with the manitous," Ta-na said.

"Hmmm," Harrison said. "Do Tenskwatawa or Tecumseh?"

"That remains to be seen, doesn't it, sir?"

"Yes, it does," Harrison said. "What happens after the panther passes across? They cut the final red stick into thirty pieces. Does the number thirty have some magical meaning to Indians?"

"My uncle El-i-chi could tell you," Ta-na said. "I can't."

"Well, they are to cut the stick into thirty pieces and burn one piece each night. When none remains, Tecumseh has foretold that he will stomp his foot and the earth will tremble."

"There's the fort site up ahead, General," Ta-na said.

"Good, good. I'm getting rump sprung. I don't know why in holy hell some genius doesn't invent a comfortable saddle."

"Most Indians find it best to ride without a saddle."

"I've tried that," Harrison said, "but I always seem to be given a damned bony horse."

In response to a signal from the general, Lieutenant O'Toole spurred up alongside him.

"Put 'em in camp," Harrison said. "Double sentry postings. And tell Cook that I'm damned hungry."

Harrison's tent was soon pitched by enlisted men, and the cook wagon was in operation. The general sat in a folding chair and watched the sun fall toward the top of the trees to the west.

"Thomas, what day did we figure was the best for Tecumseh's prediction?"

"Sometime this month, sir," Ta-na said.

"It was today, wasn't it?" Harrison said sheepishly.

"Yes, sir."

The sun touched the tops of the trees, and the shadows began to lengthen. By the time orderlies brought the general's meal, with a generous portion for his chief scout, Thomas Harper, the autumn twilight was deepening. The men finished eating by firelight.

"Well, sir," Ta-na said, "thank you for a fine meal."

"Don't go just yet," Harrison said.

"It's been a long day."

"Damn it, you're not a chicken. You don't have to go to bed with them."

"No, sir."

"Not that I plan to stay awake until any bedamned midnight, mind you."

"No, sir."

"Foolish idea."

"Yes, sir."

"Find my orderly, Thomas, if you please. Tell him I'd like some of that fresh cider."

When Ta-na returned with a canteen of cider, Harrison was dozing, slumped over in his chair. Ta-na sat by the fire and watched the embers glow until Harrison moved, moaned, and stretched his cramped limbs.

"Time is it?" he asked sleepily.

"Not midnight."

"Hell."

Ta-na poured the amber liquid into a tin cup and handed it to the general. He drank gratefully, then let out a long sigh. "Since we're up this late—"

A brilliant moon lit the scene in silver as Ta-na put more wood on the fire. Somewhere close by, four men were harmonizing an old Irish song, and a horse snorted from the meadow where the animals had been hobbled to graze. With the latening hours came the chill, so he got a blanket and pulled it around his shoulders. Ta-na stayed close to the fire.

To pass the time Harrison told Ta-na the story of the Battle of Fallen Timbers and of the things he'd seen Renno, El-i-chi, and Roy Johnson do. He asked Ta-na questions about his life in the south, and Ta-na told Harrison about Mother Beth's house, with its gleaming white linens, massive silver pieces, and delicate china that had survived the long trip across the Atlantic and half a continent.

Harrison checked his pocket watch and glanced at the sky. "Quarter of midnight," he said.

The night was crisp and clear, and the lights in the sky sparkled in spite of the moonlight. The sound of a man snoring with the regularity of a metronome could be heard from the tents.

"I wish we had a clearer view," Harrison said.

The bowl of sky above them was circumscribed by the surrounding trees.

But when Tecumseh's sign came it was clearly visible. It streaked toward them from the west, a great chunk of rock that flashed brilliantly and burst into pieces. Particles of debris burned in dozens of small streaks of light. To their amazement three large pieces separated, diverging from each other. One moved northeast, the second directly to the east, the third to the southeast.

"By God," Harrison breathed.

As he watched, the three largest pieces of the huge meteor began to burn with an intense, eerie green fire.

"Oh, by God," Harrison whispered.

The northernmost segment of the panther in the sky filled the heavens from west of the Lake-of-the-Woods to the great falls of the Niagara River. The central bolt showed itself from the Missouri flatlands through the Illinois and Indiana territories and then onward to Pennsylvania and New York. In the south the Creek Indians who kept vigil —among them Calling Owl, New Man, and other survivors of the battle with Big Warrior and Little Hawk—saw the green fulfillment of Tecumseh's prophecy as it flashed silently over Tennessee, the Mississippi Territory, Georgia, and into Florida.

Opothie Micco, the Creek chief most inclined to answer Tecumseh's call, eagerly cut the last red stick into thirty pieces, one to be cast into the fire each night. He turned to the warriors who had kept watch with him.

"Go to your beds now, my friends, and pray," he said. "The sign of the Panther Passing Across has come. Next, when the earth trembles, it will be time for us to fight."

*   *   *

On the night the panther passed across the sky most of
the five thousand people congregated around Prophetstown were awake to see the meteor burst into three
pieces in the western sky and send the message on its
separate ways.

Gao and Mist-on-the-Water, well swathed in furs,
had joined the crowd outside the Prophet's temple. When
Tenskwatawa emerged just before midnight, he had
painted the stone that filled his empty eye socket a glowing red. It reflected the flames of a fire as he stood, arms
crossed, his head lifted toward the sky.

"Ohhhh," Mist-on-the-Water moaned as the aerial
display began, burst, and faded into the distance.

Till that moment Gao had believed only in the wisdom of Tecumseh's message, but now he gained a new,
awed respect for the Chief of the Beautiful River. He
could not bring himself to speak.

Tenskwatawa chanted prayers, and his voice rose to a
high falsetto before he lowered it and bellowed, "Do you
doubt now? How can anyone doubt now?"

Chapter Ten

Calling Owl, New Man—who had also survived Menawa's attack—and six recently recruited warriors looked down on the Flint River Agency from the pine-barren hills to the northeast of the fort. On their left the Ocmulgee Garrison road entered the enclosure. During the morning a few Creek Indians came and went through the open gate. Inside, beyond the line of shops and houses, was a garden browned by the season, stables, a large tent, and a smokehouse. Now and then an errant breeze brought the smell of curing hams to the stunted pines, where it tweaked the warriors' appetites.

"His house is there," Calling Owl said, pointing past the orderly row of shops and slaves' houses toward the large building that held the agency office and the Hawkins family living quarters. "Pay close attention. First there is the big house, then another, and then Little Hawk's."

Wild Wind, so named because he was born at the height of a violent spring thunderstorm, shook his head.

He was eighteen, impressionable, and had stood on the fringe of the crowd in Tuckabatchee when Tecumseh spoke. He had told Calling Owl how the Shawnee's words had stirred his blood, but true conviction had come only after he had seen with his own eyes evidence that Tecumseh was one with the spirits. Wild Wind had witnessed the green fire of the panther passing across, just as Tecumseh said he would, and with the passion of youth Wild Wind was ready to fight, but no one was ready to lead him into battle against the whitefaces.

It was by sheer accident that he encountered New Man and Calling Owl, who had already struck blows against the enemy. Now Calling Owl was about to fight again; the target was the enemy among them, the whitefaces of the Flint River Agency.

Wild Wind and his best friends, Red Runner and Gator Toe, couldn't wait to storm the establishment of Benjamin Hawkins, the white chief who spoke with the tongue of a snake, but they were surprised and a bit intimidated by the extent of the agency. The large enclosure teemed with people, most of whom were Creek Indians.

"We are but eight, and they are many," Wild Wind said to Calling Owl.

"Do not worry. The whitefaces in the agency are few," New Man responded.

"But there are many slaves," Wild Wind said. "And will not the deluded Indians who accept their charity side with the whites if we attack openly?"

"We are not here to attack openly," Calling Owl said.

"Are we not here to kill whitefaces?" asked Eneah, the youngest in the group.

"In time, in time," Calling Owl answered. "Tell them why we are here, New Man."

"There is one below who rode with Menawa, the Big Warrior, against those of us who had the courage to strike at the enemy," New Man said. "He killed our Creek brothers."

It saddened Wild Wind to hear of Creek fighting

Creek. Were there not enough enemy skulls among the whites to dull every Creek blade? He wondered.

"When the time comes," New Man said, "when Tecumseh's final sign is felt in the trembling earth, we will punish Big Warrior and those who rode with him, and their blood will soak the ground. But first I want to torment the white man who helped Big Warrior murder our brothers who had done nothing more than fight for land that the Master of Breath gave our fathers."

"We are after only one man, then? The man known as Little Hawk?"

New Man nodded.

"How do we kill him while he is among so many?" Wild Wind asked.

"Hear me." Calling Owl pointed to the small creek that crossed the southeastern corner of the enclosure. "He has twin sons who each day play along the rivulet that runs there, and since you show so much interest, Wild Wind, you will lead the party that will bring the white cubs to me."

Wild Wind was silent. He had not joined Calling Owl to make war on children, but on the other hand he knew that one did not kill the adult rattlesnake and leave its young to grow long fangs.

"And when we have the white cubs, what then?" Wild Wind asked.

Calling Owl gestured menacingly and looked directly into Wild Wind's eyes. "You will do what I tell you to. Or are you questioning my leadership or my bravery—or both?"

"He means nothing," New Man said under his breath to Wild Wind when Calling Owl walked away. "It is just that his tongue is loose at both ends."

It was midafternoon when the warriors saw three children leave the vicinity of the Hawkins quarters. The boys made their way past the slaves' houses and chased each other across the common to a point above the springhouse.

"Choose three warriors and go," Calling Owl told Wild Wind.

Pride swelled Wild Wind's breast. It was his first command, and he was the leader. He tried not to think about the fact that he was going out against children, two of them no more than five years old and one a boy not yet in his teens.

Wild Wind found a deer trail leading down the hill to the little creek, then followed the stream to the enclosure's palisade fence. The creek ran under the fence, leaving just enough room for a person to crawl through without getting too wet.

When the Indians gained the inside of the fence they stood up and brushed the mud off their clothes. They could see the three boys dangling their lines into the shallow water no more than fifty feet away. Pretending to engage his companions in conversation, Wild Wind waited while two slaves filled their water jugs at the springhouse and carried them back across the common to the row of houses. When he was sure they were not being watched, he signaled his men to follow and walked directly toward the three boys.

Young Ben Hawkins, who had been given the job of keeping an eye on Michael Soaring Hawk and Joseph Standing Bear, saw the warriors approaching. He lifted his hand in greeting and turned his attention back to the serious business of catching enough crayfish—he called them crawdads—to make more than a bite for each of them. He looked up once more just as one of the Indians smashed his fist into his temple. The world went black, and the boy's limp body rolled into the cold water; his head rested on a mossy rock.

Joseph, who was standing a few feet away, shouted a warning just as one of the Indians seized Michael and cut off his startled cry by clapping a strong hand over his mouth. Another warrior leaped toward Joseph, and the boy, using what Ben Hawkins had taught him about how to kill quail with rocks, picked one up from the ground and smashed the Creek's nose with a well-aimed throw. The warrior stopped, his hand flying to his injured face. Joseph then leaped toward the man who held his brother and launched a rabid attack on the Creek's lower body, but the Indian lifted the little boy by his hair and with strong arms smothered his struggles and prevented him from crying out for help.

Wild Wind cast a look toward the houses but saw no unusual activity. Gator Toe and Red Runner guarded the rear while Wild Wind and Eneah carried the struggling boys to the palisade and dragged them under it.

The water was cold and the twins were shivering when, at a safe distance from the enclosure, they were lowered to their feet and harnessed with a rawhide strap around their necks. Michael opened his mouth to scream, but one of the Indians jerked the tether to tighten the noose. The boy clawed frantically at the restricting strap until he could breathe again.

"Make noise, you die," a warrior said in Creek.

"It's all right, Soaring Hawk," Joseph whispered. "Our father will come for us."

"No talk," Wild Wind said.

The twins were led like two-legged cattle up the game trail to the spot where Calling Owl and the others waited.

Calling Owl was furious. He confronted Wild Wind and bellowed, "Fool! Witless fool!"

Wild Wind's hand went to his tomahawk.

"Yes," Calling Owl said venomously, "draw your blade. I wish you would."

"Think, Wild Wind," New Man cautioned.

"Look," Calling Owl said, pointing back toward the enclosure.

They could see the other boy trying to crawl up the bank of the creek. He made an effort to stand but fell heavily.

"You should have killed the white man's spawn," Calling Owl hissed.

"I did not leave my home and my family to make war on children," Wild Wind snarled.

The boy stirred again. It was clear to those who watched that he was groggy, but soon he would recover his wits and sound the alarm.

"Mark this well," Calling Owl told Wild Wind. "If through your foolishness I am frustrated here, I will give you a chance to draw that weapon. Now, since your tender heart created this situation, it will be up to you to undo the damage you have done. You will have to move quickly."

Naomi could not accustom herself to having a servant, even though Lavinia Downs kept telling her, "Be sensible, girl. Let Magnolia do the work. You have enough on your hands looking after those twins of yours."

But when there was work to be done, Naomi was uncomfortable and guilt-laden until she pushed up her sleeves and helped Magnolia. As a result, since there was only so much work in a small log cabin after the end of the gardening season, both Naomi and Magnolia had time on their hands.

At first the serving girl had seemed uneasy when Naomi would put the kettle to boiling, brew tea, and insist that she sit down with her. However, after working together to get in the small crop of corn they had planted and going with the twins into the woodlands outside the enclosure to gather wild walnuts, the slave girl had come to accept what was, for her, an unusual relationship. At Naomi's gentle insistence Magnolia found herself talking openly about her life. The only servants Naomi had known were the freed slaves who worked for Beth at Huntington Castle, and there was a world of difference between the old cook, Aunt Sarah, who ruled Beth's house with a benevolent but firm hand and the quiet, shy, young Magnolia.

She told Naomi that she had been brought to the Creek Nation as a child. Her mother was one of Benjamin

Hawkins's slaves who worked under the supervision of Lavinia Downs, the woman who had joined Hawkins's household as a housekeeper and then became his mistress and the mother of his children. Because of her association with the Indians, Magnolia spoke better Creek than she did English.

Naomi noted early on that the slaves who lived in the enclosure were on friendly terms with the Creek Indians. After Magnolia became more comfortable in her presence, she questioned the girl on that subject.

"Well, ma'am," Magnolia said, "it appears some Indians think black skin is beautifuller than white, begging your pardon."

In Magnolia's case, Naomi thought, that statement was true, especially in the eyes of a young Creek warrior who apparently seemed to find a multitude of reasons to pass by the gardens whenever the girl was working there. A handsome boy of Magnolia's age, he also appeared almost miraculously each night when she left the Harper house for the cabin she shared with her mother and two siblings.

"Well, ma'am, he wants me as his wife," Magnolia said one day in answer to Naomi's good-natured teasing.

"And how do you feel about that?"

"No matter," the girl said. "I belong to Master Hawkins, and he says who I marry and who I don't. And he's not about to let me marry an Indian."

"But would you like to?" Naomi insisted.

A smile spread slowly across Magnolia's round face. "Lordy, Miss Naomi, you oughta see that man dance," she said in a voice filled with awe.

"Dance?"

"I've seen him," Magnolia said. "Lots of times. They like dancing, those Creeks. They do the eagle-tail dance, and Nugee—that's *his* name—well, you just oughta see that boy shake his rear end. And when he jumps, Lordy, he's right pretty."

One evening, after telling Little Hawk about Magnolia's suitor, Naomi asked, "How much would it cost to buy Magnolia?"

Little Hawk smiled fondly. "More than I make in a year as a Marine captain."

"Oh," Naomi said. "Well, that's out of the question, then. Perhaps Colonel Hawkins will give her to Nugee." She mused in silence. "Maybe if I have a talk with Lavinia—"

"My gentle wife," Little Hawk said, taking her hand, "you know that I agree with you, and with my father, who would have no slaves at Huntington Castle."

"It wasn't just Renno," Naomi said. "Beth hates the institution of slavery as much as he."

"Yes. The point I'm trying to make is that I, too, deplore the laws that allow men to own other human beings, but that's the way things are. We can do our best to influence others to join us in opposition to slavery, but I don't think Colonel Hawkins would look kindly upon a suggestion that he give away a valuable piece of property to a Creek boy."

"They're in love," Naomi protested, and the emotion in her voice expressed her feeling that love was more important than *anyone*'s property rights.

Naomi did speak to Lavinia, but Hawkins's mistress told her that she was well aware of Magnolia's infatuation with the Creek boy, that it had been going on for a while, and that sooner or later Magnolia would present them with a half-Creek baby. While it was clear that Lavinia was unconcerned about that, she would not consider a marriage between her slave and Nugee.

On the day that Calling Owl's warriors kidnapped Michael and Joseph, Naomi and Magnolia were seated at the kitchen table shelling black walnuts. It was a tedious job, for the nuts were hard to crack. Naomi used a flat rock and a hammer because the shells were too thick for the nutcracker, but she occasionally applied her teeth as well. When a loud knock sounded at the door, it was

Magnolia who leaped to her feet to answer. To her embarrassment and Naomi's surprise, it was Nugee.

The Creek spoke to Magnolia in his own language, and Magnolia turned to Naomi. "Miss Naomi, he says there's a Creek out here who wants to say something to you."

Naomi brushed off the front of her dress and walked to the door. An armed Creek warrior stood about ten feet from the stoop on the swept, hard earth of the yard.

"He wants to know if you're the mama of the twin boys who fish for crawdads in the creek," Magnolia translated.

"What's wrong?" Naomi asked in quick alarm.

Magnolia listened as the warrior who had been sent by Calling Owl spoke for some time.

"He says Michael and Joseph, they're fine, but they left the agency and got lost in the piney hills."

"What?" Naomi demanded. "What about Ben Hawkins? He was supposed to be with them."

Magnolia asked the question. "There's only the two of them," she told Naomi. "And one of them's hurted."

"Oh, my God," Naomi gasped. "Ask him if he'll take me to the boys."

"Yes, ma'am," Magnolia said. "He says he'll take you right now."

Naomi grabbed a shawl, draped it around her neck, and ran to join the Creek warrior.

"I go with you?" Magnolia asked.

"No," Naomi said. "I want you to go find my husband. Tell him where I've gone and ask him to come quickly."

"Yes, ma'am." Magnolia ran toward the agency offices as Naomi followed the Creek toward the gate. When her mistress was out of sight she spoke to Nugee. "Find the Seneca captain," she ordered. "Tell him that I am going north with Miss Naomi to look for his children. Tell him that one of them is hurt. Do this immediately. Hurry."

"Soon I will follow," Nugee promised. "To protect you."

"Miss Naomi and I are fully capable of protecting ourselves," Magnolia said proudly. "Now go."

Nugee sprinted toward the office, and Magnolia ran in the opposite direction. She caught up with the Creek and Naomi just outside the gate.

"Did you do as you were told?" Naomi asked.

"Nugee. He did," Magnolia said.

"Oh, Magnolia—" Naomi sighed.

"Don't worry, Miss Naomi. He does what I tell him."

"Well, that will have to do, I suppose."

The Creek who called himself Wild Wind set a rapid pace and urged the women to walk faster. He looked over his shoulder nervously and relaxed only when they were in the shelter of the pines and no pursuit had materialized.

"Mother," Joseph wailed when Naomi followed Wild Wind into a clearing atop a hill. A steeply slanted drop of perhaps fifty feet allowed an overlook of the agency spread out on the flats below.

"What is the meaning of this?" Naomi asked angrily when she saw that her sons were tethered to a tree with rawhide leads around their necks.

"God almighty," Magnolia said under her breath when she saw the heavily armed Indians, their faces painted for war. She whirled around and had taken only a few steps when Calling Owl pointed toward her.

"That one," Calling Owl said sharply.

A warrior quickly notched an arrow. The missile buzzed through the air like an angry bee, and its iron tip pierced Magnolia's back just to the left of her spine. She took three more staggering steps and fell to her knees.

"Fetch her," Calling Owl ordered.

Naomi was momentarily stunned, but when she instinctively tried to run toward the fallen girl, New Man seized her arms and held her. She jerked one arm free and lashed out at him. Her nails left four parallel

scratches down his cheek and enraged him so that he
drew back his fist and hit her in the stomach. The blow
doubled her over and left her gagging for breath.

Gator Toe and Red Runner dragged Magnolia across
the ground and threw her down at Calling Owl's feet. She
was alive. She lifted her head, and her eyes found
Naomi's face.

"Run, Miss Naomi. Run," she whispered.

But before Naomi could say or do anything, Calling
Owl buried the blade of his tomahawk in Magnolia's forehead.

Naomi screamed the girl's name. When a warrior advanced toward Michael and Joseph, whose eyes were
wide with terror, she said in a high, quavering voice,
"Leave my sons alone."

The warrior loosed the thongs from the tree,
wrapped them around one hand, and jerked the boys
toward him. Naomi surged forward, trying to break New
Man's hold on her arms.

"Keep her quiet," Calling Owl ordered.

New Man smiled, then doubled his fist and hit
Naomi in the nape of the neck. Her knees buckled, and
she folded to the ground.

"You hit my mother!" Michael shouted. In a flash he
opened the noose around his neck and threw it aside.

"I did not tell you to kill her," Calling Owl said angrily.

"She lives," New Man said, kneeling beside Naomi
just in time to receive the full force of Michael's charge.
The little boy's head rammed into his face, and the young
Indian grunted with pain and lashed out in fury. Despite
the blow, which knocked him halfway across the clearing,
Michael was immediately on his feet.

"You hit my mother," he repeated quietly, adding a
prime insult in Creek.

As New Man's companions roared with laughter, Michael doubled his hands and smashed them upward into
the Indian's genitals. The warrior doubled over, howling

his rage, and Michael danced away and took up a fighting stance.

Naomi lifted her head and saw her son facing the furious Creek. "He's only a child," she whispered. "Please. He's only a child."

Enraged and moving with difficulty, New Man picked up his rifle and swung the weapon parallel to the ground. The long barrel hit Michael in the ribs and sent him tumbling over the brink of the fifty-foot drop. Sick with fear, Naomi crawled toward the bluff as New Man ran past her.

Arms and legs flopping, Michael tumbled limply down the almost vertical slope and landed on the rocks. When his body came to rest, his leg was bent at an odd angle. It was thus that Naomi saw him when she reached the edge of the bluff.

"Help him," she begged.

Calling Owl joined New Man.

"Son of a white whore," New Man said, rubbing his genitals.

"Finish him," Calling Owl ordered.

New Man lifted his rifle, and Naomi gasped in disbelief. "No, fool. In silence," Calling Owl warned as he struck the rifle down.

"Do you expect me to climb down there?" New Man asked.

Calling Owl sighed in exasperation, motioned to one of the others, and pointed at the fallen boy. "Do you think you can devise a way to kill the white man's spawn with an arrow? Or can you not hit such a small target at so long a range?" His voice was rich with sarcasm.

The warrior pulled his bow.

"Noooo!" Naomi screamed as an arrow buzzed downward. Michael's body twitched when the iron head penetrated, and Naomi burst into helpless tears.

"Calling Owl," Eneah said from the other side of the clearing, "observe."

Below them, two men ran out the agency gate to the road.

"These men are not the white man Hawk and his Indian dog," Calling Owl spat.

"Do we kill the other white cub now?" Eneah asked, unconcerned about the men and eager to taste blood.

Joseph, white of face and short of breath because of the fear that filled him, stood up straight. And while his voice was that of a child, his words were not. "Give me a weapon and let me face you fairly."

Calling Owl laughed heartily. "So, New Man, are you capable of beating this white cub?"

New Man growled in anger and leaped forward. Once again Calling Owl blocked his intent, stepping between him and Joseph. "Hold, my friend," he said. "This is for me to do." He brandished his tomahawk.

"Please don't, please don't," Naomi begged.

Calling Owl stood over her and answered in broken English. "Your man, called Hawk, killed my brothers."

"Then face *him*," Naomi said defiantly. "Where is your manhood that you kill women and children?"

Calling Owl laughed. "I will kill your man, too, white woman. But first I kill his heart so that he will be a dead man walking." Smiling, he whirled around and his metal blade flashed in the sunlight as it slammed into Joseph's head, smashing the skull just over the boy's left ear.

Joseph died instantly.

The sound of the fatal blow reverberated endlessly in Naomi's ears until the sun seemed to burst into white light and the stunted pine trees around her to diminish with distance. She thought she was looking down on the clearing from a great height, as if it existed only in a terrible dream. Pulling her legs under her, she arranged her skirts in a modest fashion and let her fingers toy with a twig. Very softly she began to sing a lullaby she had often sung when the boys were babes in arms.

"Do we wait for the Hawk here?" Wild Wind asked.

Once again Calling Owl carefully explained his purpose. "To kill him now would be too merciful," he said. "He will see his two dead sons. That will hurt his heart. He will also see the dead slave, but he will not see the body of his wife. That will hurt his heart most of all, for he will imagine what is happening to the mother of his dead children. That will turn his heart to lead, leaving only the small matter of sending his body to the spirits after it."

"What will you do with her?" Wild Wind asked.

Calling Owl laughed. "When we meet up later, my brothers, at the the cave by the waterfall, we will do to her what New Man did to the fat white woman in Tennessee."

"I will show you how it is done," New Man said with a smirk.

Calling Owl roared with laughter. "Yes, he does have some experience, but there is another who will taste this one first."

"You?" New Man asked.

"So that when I face Hawk, at last, I can tell him that it was I who first used the body of his wife for my pleasure. Now let us leave this place behind."

Nugee did not locate Little Hawk immediately. He ran with all his speed to the office, leaped onto the porch without bothering with the stairs, and burst in. Benjamin Hawkins, irritated, looked up.

"I seek Captain Harper," Nugee said.

"It is customary to knock, Nugee," the colonel snapped.

"No time, sir. Please. Where is Captain Harper?"

"I don't know," Hawkins said irritably. "Obviously he is not here."

Nugee was out the door and running toward the stables before Hawkins could continue his lesson in manners. If the captain had left the agency he would have done so on horseback, and the stable hands would know. He dashed through the large, open doors into the sweet smell of hay and horses. The old man who ran the stables was grooming a tall bay.

"Captain Harper," Nugee gasped.

"Easy, son," the old man said. "You excite yourself."

"Have you seen him?"

"Might have," the old man acknowledged reluctantly.

"Where?"

"Him and a couple of the Hawkins children went to check the fish trap."

Nugee ran out the enclosure's southern gate and angled toward the bank of the Flint River just below the falls. He saw Little Hawk and the Hawkins boys and yelled out before he reached them.

Little Hawk, just removing a wriggling fish from the trap, looked up and straightened as the Creek boy skidded to a halt.

"Captain Harper," Nugee said breathlessly, "your wife needs you."

In spite of Nugee's apparent haste, Little Hawk was calm. He knew that Naomi was among friends, safe in their cabin in the heart of the Flint River Agency.

"What is it she needs, Nugee?" he asked.

"She and Magnolia have gone up the Ocmulgee road after your sons."

Little Hawk's brow furrowed. "Why were the boys out of the enclosure?"

"I don't know, but I think we should hurry."

"Yes. All right." Little Hawk turned to the Hawkins children. "Look, boys, I've got to go. Can you finish by yourselves?"

"Sure thing, Cap'n," the oldest boy in the group said. "But don't worry. Ben's with your two."

Nugee's urgency was contagious. Little Hawk fell behind at first, but he quickly caught up with the young Creek, and they ran side by side toward the enclosure.

"We will get horses," Little Hawk said as they approached the stables.

"Quicker this way," Nugee said. "We cannot track them from horseback."

"What's the hurry, Captain?" the smith called out as they ran past the forge.

Little Hawk didn't bother to answer. They skirted the hatter's shop and the smokehouse and raced onto the bridge that crossed a drainage ditch and some low, wet ground.

Little Hawk saw three sets of tracks as they left the enclosure. "Magnolia?" he asked.

"It is she," Nugee said.

"And a Creek," Little Hawk observed.

"I did not know him," Nugee stated. "He came with the message that the twins had wandered from the enclosure and that one was hurt."

"There," Little Hawk said, noting that the tracks left the main road and followed a trail that wound its way up the slope through stunted pines. His breath was coming hard before they reached the top of the hill. The trees were thicker there, and the trail was not wide enough for them to run side by side. It was Little Hawk who was in the lead when they burst into the small clearing. An explosion of black, flapping things sent a burst of adrenaline into his stomach as he skidded to a stop.

A dozen turkey vultures struggled into the air directly in front of him, so close that he was assaulted by their stench. Behind them lay the body of a woman. A few yards away another group of vultures paid no heed to Little Hawk and only quarreled and squabbled as they worked at something smaller with their great, tearing beaks.

Nugee pushed past Little Hawk and fell to his knees beside Magnolia's body. His face was contorted with pain, and he was making an odd sound with each breath. He reached out to her but instantly drew back his hands, then shuddered when he finally touched her shoulder. The vultures had ripped her clothing, and he could see the broken shaft of an arrow protruding from her back. Gently he turned her body over and moaned when he saw what was left of her face: the birds had eaten her eyeballs, lips, and nose, and the brain tissue that oozed from the hole smashed in her skull.

Nugee began to chant a song of death and suffering. Little Hawk, knowing in his heart what he was looking at but unwilling to admit it to himself, walked slowly toward the second group of flapping, squawking birds. Under the black, stinking mass of carrion eaters he saw a small leg move. His heart leaped, but he quickly realized that the movement was caused by a large bird that had bared the skin of the small body's rump. He cried out, lifted one of the pistols he carried at his belt, and fired it into the mass of black. With great flutterings and hoarse protests the vultures flapped away.

"Ah, God," Little Hawk moaned, falling to his knees beside the body of his son—which son he could not tell, for as they had done to Magnolia, the birds had attacked the softest, most accessible features of the boy's face first.

Rage filled him, and he took aim at a vulture sitting patiently on a tree limb. The heavy pistol ball sent feathers flying and dropped the bird to the pine needle carpeting of the earth.

"Get away!" he screamed, rushing toward the birds still on the ground. They flapped away to a safe distance and glared at him with baleful black eyes. Nugee still sang of death and sorrow.

At first Little Hawk thought his mind was playing tricks on him.

"Father."

It was so faint, so distant, that small voice. He looked around, picked up a dead stick, and shied it toward the vultures.

"Father."

There was no mistaking it this time. Running toward the sound, he stopped at the edge of the drop, looked down, and saw his son crumpled on the rocks below.

"Father," Michael said, "they hurt my mother."

Little Hawk looked around frantically for the best way down the bluff. He ran to the side and scrambled down recklessly, banging against the trunk of a tree without noticing. At last he knelt over Michael.

"It hurts," Michael said, trying to smile bravely.

"I'll get you home, son," Little Hawk promised, his tears blurring his eyes. It was obvious that the boy's leg was broken, but the arrow that protruded from his midsection worried Little Hawk more.

"They hurt my mother," the boy whispered again. "And they hurt Joseph."

"Lie still, Michael. They didn't kill your mother?"

"No," Michael said, "but they hit her. I tried to stop them."

She was alive. Naomi was alive. That was all that mattered. He would not think about what the Creek might be doing to her. She was alive.

"Michael, this is going to hurt," Little Hawk said. "I have to do it. Do you understand?" He put his hand on the shaft of the arrow and held it while he cut away the buckskin tunic around it.

Tears formed in Michael's eyes, and he bit his lower lip, but he did not cry out.

Little Hawk was afraid to look. If the arrow had cut through organs and intestines the boy would die an agonizing death. He pulled Michael's shirt aside and breathed in relief. One inch to the right and the arrow would have missed entirely. It had penetrated the boy's side, going all the way through to bury its iron barb in the earth; but it looked to Little Hawk as if it had not broken into the stomach cavity at all, that it had merely pierced the layer of flesh and muscle that lined the outside of the stomach.

"It hurts, Father," Michael said piteously.

Little Hawk used his knife to cut the arrow in two, leaving the iron tip embedded in the earth.

"Take a deep breath, my son," he said. The little boy inhaled and held it, then screamed when Little Hawk pulled on the arrow. Blood gushed from the wound, and Little Hawk pressed pieces of Michael's shirt against the hole to stop the bleeding.

"I want to go home," Michael said, doing his best not to cry.

"We've got to do something about this leg." Little Hawk turned his attention to the twisted limb. "Lie still. I'll be right back."

He cut straight branches for a splint, and when he was ready he knelt beside Michael once more. The little boy's face was white with fear. He had seen his uncle El-i-chi fix broken legs, but El-i-chi had been trained by the old shaman Casno.

"I want you to be a brave boy."

"I'll try, Father."

Little Hawk put one hand on Michael's knee above the break, then seized the boy's foot with his other hand. There was nothing to be gained by waiting. He pulled, and Michael screamed and fainted. There was a grinding sound and a snap as the broken bone went back into place. While the boy was unconscious Little Hawk bound the leg with the splints, lifted the small body in his arms, and found a way up the slope to the clearing.

Nugee was still kneeling beside Magnolia's body, and the vultures had gathered again around Joseph. Little Hawk placed Michael carefully on the ground and chased the birds away once more. He controlled his revulsion but not his anguish as he lifted the mutilated little body and placed it beside Magnolia's. Nugee looked up questioningly, his eyes red from weeping.

Little Hawk was wrestling with the most difficult decision of his life. His love for Naomi urged him to follow the kidnappers' tracks. If he moved quickly they wouldn't have time to torture her or, if it was their intent, to rape her. The more time they had, the more likely Naomi would suffer.

On the other hand, Michael was seriously hurt. Aside from the arrow wound and the broken leg, he was badly bruised on his right side, and Little Hawk thought it was possible that one or more ribs was broken. His son had to have care, but he was alive, and with God's help and the proper treatment he would stay alive. Lavinia Downs was very good with wounds; she knew all the Indian remedies as well as the white man's medicine.

"Nugee, I'm going to take Michael to the agency," Little Hawk said.

"I will go to find the ones who did this," Nugee said, "and I will kill them."

"Yes," Little Hawk said, the fierce fire of vengeance burning in him. "But you must not go alone. You must stay here until I bring people from the agency to get Magnolia and Joseph."

"That will give them time to run far," Nugee argued.

Little Hawk pointed to the waiting vultures. "Is that what you want for her? Is she to be a meal for them?"

Nugee threw back his head and uttered a loud, wavering cry of grief and anger.

"Stay with them. Keep the birds away. I will bring others, and then the two of us will find the murderers."

"I will do as you say, Captain," Nugee reluctantly agreed.

Carrying his unconscious son in his arms, Little Hawk started down the trail. It was only then that the true extent of his loss hit him: One of his sons was injured, the other dead, his face dissected by carrion birds. And his wife was in the hands of the enemy. Beyond the next ridge, or the next, he might very well find her body.

He was afraid to run, lest the motion do harm to the boy, so he walked swiftly but carefully. It took forever to reach the bottom of the hill. He paused and looked back. A funnel of turkey vultures soared in circles above the clearing.

"Manitous!" he cried in a long, drawn-out moan as he looked beyond the birds at the clear blue sky. "Note this well and remember."

On the road he moved faster, and as he walked he

sang an ancient Seneca song, low and mournful. With a start he ceased his singing, for the chant had suddenly become a symbol of a brutal culture.

He could not cut open a vein and bleed away that part of him that was Seneca, but he could erase from his mind and his heart all traces of his Indian heritage. He was Captain Hawk Harper, graduate of West Point, a Marine officer in the service of the United States. From that day forward he would divorce himself from the culture that had produced the men who had split the skull of one son and pinned the other to the ground with an arrow.

He blamed himself for what had happened. Had he refused the assignment to serve in Hawkins's Flint River Agency among the hostile Creek Indians, Joseph would be alive, Michael would not be limp in his arms, and Naomi would be safe in their cabin. As soon as he had killed those responsible and returned Naomi to her place at his side, he would leave the fetid, steaming wilderness of the Creek Nation.

He found Lavinia Downs comforting her son, Ben. The boy had a huge, flowering bruise on the side of his face, but he seemed to be all right. Lavinia cooed with concern as she carefully examined Michael and complimented Little Hawk on how well he had set the broken leg. While she was cleaning the arrow wound and the other contusions on his body, Michael woke up and began to complain bitterly. He screamed only a little when Little Hawk held him and Lavinia cauterized the arrow wound with the blade of a white-hot knife.

Chapter Eleven

James Madison took a quick look at the clock in his office and put aside the papers he had been studying. He sighed deeply, rose, stretched, and walked stiffly to the door. His secretary looked up from his desk as the President went past.

"Show the gentlemen from the Senate into the office if they arrive before I return," Madison said.

It was but a short walk to the White House sitting rooms, and he was pleased to find his wife alone there. Dolley turned her head at the sound of the opening door, leaped to her feet, and hurried to meet her husband.

"James, dear," she said, taking advantage of the moment of privacy to kiss him on the cheek.

Madison's face, which was deemed by many to be pallid and hard, softened. "You are lovely this afternoon, my dear."

"Come, sit with me," Dolley said. "I must tell you what happened while my sister and I were shopping this morning."

Madison smiled in anticipation of the amusing trifle

that was to come. He could always depend on Dolley for a moment of diversion from his heavy responsibilities.

Giggling, Dolley told him that while they were shopping she and her sister had encountered one of the leading members of the Federalist opposition, a man who often accused the President and his wife of trying to establish a regal presidency. He had criticized Dolley's habit of doing her own shopping, saying that it was unseemly for the wife of the President to mingle with common tradesmen.

Dolley reported gleefully, "He stared at us with overt disapproval."

Madison was reminded of an Arab saying that had been voiced by Sidi Suliman Mellimelli, the rotund ambassador of the bey of Tunis, while he was visiting in Washington. In the sandy tracts of North Africa, he had told, when camel caravans passed through a sunbaked village, the native dogs rushed to nip at the heels of the beasts of burden, but the taciturn camels paid no attention.

"The dogs bark," Madison said with his wry, fond grin, "but the caravan moves on."

Dolley was pleased. She considered it a part of her duty to be available in the sitting rooms during the afternoon just to tell her dear little husband a bright story and give him a chuckle. To that end she had changed from the plain clothes she wore for her shopping expedition to something colorful and gay. James Madison had told her once that a few minutes with her in the midst of a trying day was as refreshing as a long walk.

He removed a letter from his coat pocket. "I have a note here from tonight's guest of honor."

Dolley raised her eyebrows hopefully. "He hasn't canceled his appearance, has he?"

Madison laughed. "I'm afraid not." He was aware that Henry Clay of Kentucky was not one of Dolley's favorite people.

"It seems, my dear, that he has requested permission to supply the wine for tonight's dinner."

"Oh, dear," Dolley said, rolling her eyes helplessly.

"Good Kentucky Madeira."

"Good?"

Madison chuckled. "I know you take great pride in your management of the White House social affairs, my dear. I can tell by the stricken look on your face that you are imagining your well-orchestrated evening turning into an embarrassing failure. I well remember once before when Mr. Clay brought Kentucky wine to the White House, to Mr. Jefferson's table. The wine had been injured during the process of fermentation and was, to put it mildly, of woeful quality. He says that he begs this chance to restore in some degree the credit of Kentucky wine."

"Do we have a choice?"

"I fear not," he said ruefully.

"Oh, well." Dolley smiled prettily as she poured a strong cup of tea for her husband.

Reluctantly President James Madison returned to his office for a meeting with several Republican senators, and the afternoon stretched on until, at last, he had some time alone in the presidential suite. That night when he escorted Dolley down to dinner he looked at least partially refreshed.

At Madison's request the guest list was small. Secretary of State James Monroe was there with his stiffly formal wife, the regal Elizabeth Kortright Monroe. He was dressed in off-white, old-fashioned knee breeches, matching vest, dark frock coat, and a gleaming white cravat. Elizabeth, seated at the President's right, wore a frilly formal gown of imperial purple silk.

Secretary of War William Eustis, an army surgeon during the war and ex-congressman from Massachusetts, had been given the chair on Dolley's left, directly across from Henry Clay. Both Eustis and Clay were without female companions that evening.

Henry Clay's Kentucky Madeira was served at the end of the meal and proved to be excellent. After his second glass Madison was visibly relaxed. Presidential rigidity abandoned, he related a ribald anecdote about a country coon hunter in Virginia that had the men chuckling.

Dolley looked at Elizabeth Monroe with a smile and said, "If you gentlemen will excuse us—"

"Certainly, my dear," Madison said.

Male laughter followed the two ladies from the room as the President told another of his indelicate tales about life in Virginia. When the chuckles subsided, Madison's face became serious.

"Henry," he said, "I asked you here with James and William to discuss something about which, I'm sure, you are very much concerned."

"If you mean the situation in the Northern Territories, Mr. President," Clay said, "I am *quite* concerned. It is estimated that there are more than five thousand hostile Indians massed north of Vincennes."

Clay was by far the youngest man in the room. At thirty-four he already had a distinguished career behind him and, some thought, enough fire and ambition to carry him to the highest office in the land. Although, like Madison and Monroe, he had been born a Virginian, he was a westerner by choice and by temperament. After studying jurisprudence in the office of the Virginia attorney general, he opened a practice in Lexington, Kentucky, where he specialized in criminal law. For a time, he had represented Aaron Burr but resigned that position when Thomas Jefferson persuaded him that Burr was guilty of treason. Clay was appointed to serve out an unexpired term in the Senate but left for the House of Representatives because he felt that members of the lower chamber more directly represented the people. His election as Speaker of the House in 1811 and his position as chief spokesman for the western War Hawks had brought him to the attention of the President and his principal advisers.

"Mr. Speaker," said Secretary of War Eustis, after Madison cast a glance his way, "the department is acutely aware of the threatening stance adopted by this fellow Tecumseh and his rather strange brother."

"Don't underestimate Tecumseh, Mr. Secretary," Clay said, exercising his vibrant, resonant voice to the full.

"I don't think we're doing that," Eustis said. "As a matter of fact, at the request of Governor Harrison, the Fourth Regiment of regulars is at this very moment on its way down the Ohio from Pittsburgh." He smiled. "They're New Englanders, you know."

Clay accepted the secretary's display of regional pride with a nod and a smile. "They'll be fighting alongside the Kentucky Militia, Mr. Secretary," he said. "Americans all."

"Hear, hear," Madison said.

"While we do not discount the threat of five thousand Indians allied under Tecumseh," Eustis continued, "I am still puzzled as to how the man can attract so many warriors from so many tribes to a cause which has proven time and time again to be of false promise. Did the tribes learn nothing from Little Turtle's war? It would seem to me that General Wayne taught them a lesson they'd never forget."

"Ah, but they also remember other generals," Clay said. "They were young men when St. Clair marched his men directly into the jaws of ambush. There are still warriors alive who remember the sweet sound of white skulls breaking under their tomahawk blades. But it's more than that. They believe that Tecumseh and his brother, the Prophet, converse with Moneto, the Shawnee god they call the Supreme Being of All Things."

"Superstitious nonsense," Eustis said.

"I wonder," Clay mused, his lips pursed. "How do you account for the prediction of the red sticks, Mr. Secretary?"

"I beg your pardon?" Eustis asked.

"William, that intelligence was in the report I passed along to you from my representative in the Creek Nation," Madison said. "Captain Hawk Harper."

"Ah, yes, that," Eustis said. "Some prattle about a panther passing across the sky after a certain period of time marked by burning or tossing away a specified number of sticks that had been painted red?"

"At exactly midnight, on the exact night predicted by Tecumseh's red sticks, the so-called panther did pass across," Clay said with a hint of impatience. "The panther in the sky was a shooting star. There was one on the night when Tecumseh was born; thus his name, the Panther Passing Across. And, by God, sir, there was not one but three, so the sign could be seen in all different parts of the country east of the Mississippi, at the very minute when Tecumseh said it would appear."

Eustis shrugged. "I'm sure there is some logical explanation, just as there was when Tecumseh had his brother, this Prophet fellow, predict an eclipse of the sun."

Clay laughed. "Give me the name of an astronomer who can prophecize the exact minute of a shooting star."

Eustis was silent.

"For my part," Monroe said, "I found Tecumseh's prediction of the meteor to be quite impressive." He laughed. "Now, if the earth actually trembles when he stamps his foot, I shall be even more astonished—and perhaps a bit frightened."

President James Madison agreed. At least *one* member of his cabinet had read the papers that had been passed along to him.

"I don't think the Indians will be as easily defeated as they were in General Wayne's campaign," Clay said. "For one thing, we've pushed them into a corner. For another, Tecumseh is a leader of much more ability than Little Turtle. He has support from Florida to Canada and from some of the tribes west of the Mississippi as well, and he has good men in charge of his rank-and-file fighters. I've met one of his war chiefs, an impressive man called Shabonee. He's killed at least twoscore white men himself, and he has a low opinion of us. He says our hands are soft, our faces sickly white, that half of us are calico peddlers and the other half capable of shooting nothing more deadly than a squirrel."

"It is my opinion," Eustis said, "that this man—Shabonee?—will be forced to change his opinion if Tecumseh insists on war."

Clay leaned back in his chair. "Gentlemen, as you are well aware, the days are not long past when the tribes raided across the Ohio, leaving scalped and mutilated women and children in the Kentucky settlements. Here in the East people have forgotten the cruelty of the Indians because almost all of them have either been exterminated or driven west. In Kentucky we're still reminded quite often, perhaps when we pass the gravestones of our loved ones, that we still face an implacable enemy who has nothing but hatred for us." He turned to face Eustis. "I am in correspondence with Governor Harrison. He has informed me of his intention to take an expedition up the Wabash, build a support outpost, and make a strong military demonstration within sight of Prophetstown."

"Yes," Eustis said. "Governor Harrison has informed the department of his intention."

"And what was the department's response?" Clay asked.

The President answered. "Governor Harrison has been advised by this office that we do not actively desire war with the Indians."

"Mr. President," Clay said, "war will come. That is inevitable. It is my contention that—since war cannot be avoided—we should strike a preemptive blow. Defang the snake, as it were, *before* it is coiled to strike."

Monroe laughed good-naturedly. "Mr. Speaker, do I get the idea that the War Hawks, and you in particular,

don't really care whether we fight the British or Tecumseh, just as long as we fight?"

"We'll fight both," Clay said, "and let us all pray that
we're ready." He caught Madison's eye. "In regard to
Great Britain, Mr. President, I am in agreement with your
old and good friend, Light-Horse Harry Lee. I believe I
can quote his words almost verbatim." He rubbed his thin
chin and squinted. "Let me see—General Lee advised
you to take the nation out of the odious condition of half-
war with England either by restoring amity between the
two nations or by drawing the naked sword."

"Mr. Lee was not so colorful in his wording," Madison said, "but you have captured the intent of his statement."

"Then by God, Mr. President, do it!" Clay thundered. "We stand ready to back you. The younger members of this Congress have little care for the old
Republican verities of peace, mildness, and frugality. This
Congress represents change, Mr. President." He grinned
mischievously. "Why, Mr. Randolph, who is the most republican of Republicans, has brought his dogs into the
House only once this session."

Madison, relaxed by the solid Kentucky Madeira,
roared with laughter. "Mr. Clay, I believe you will be
pleased with my position when I spell it out in my annual
message to the Congress."

"I pray so," Clay said.

Madison's speaking voice had not improved since his
election. The members of the Congress, in joint session,
strained to hear as the President called the attention of
the world to the "direct and undisguised hostility" of
Great Britain toward the United States. He promised to
"authorize reprisals" before Congress went home in the
spring, and he accused England of "hostile inflexibility."

Madison smiled when he noticed Henry Clay nodding in agreement as he recommended a larger army, a
well-trained and -supplied militia, the manufacture of

munitions, expansion of the navy, and an increase in tar-
iffs on imports to encourage the growth of manufacturers
whose products were vital to the national interest.

The President's message was clear. The British were
being given one last chance to cease their overt raids on
American ships at sea, and France was being invited to
cultivate the goodwill of the United States. In the meantime the nation would prepare for war.

An Eel River Miami, Tall Pine was one year younger than
his new friend, Gao, and half a head taller. The two young
men often hunted together and shared their kill with several families in the Potawatomi-Wyandot-Miami encamp-
ment at Tippecanoe. Tall Pine's father was a dignified
senior warrior whose opinion was respected in council,
and his younger sister, who admired Mist-on-the-Water,
looked to her for advice about becoming a wife.

Hearing the two women talk of marriage reminded
Gao that he had not yet fulfilled his pledge to Main Poche
to pay a bride-price for Mist, and while her uncle had not
asked for it, Gao so loved his wife that he wanted to show
her how much he valued her.

As the two friends were hunting west of the Wabash
one diamond-sharp autumn day, Gao looked toward the
south and said, "There is something I must do."

"My stomach says that we must make a kill soon,"
Tall Pine said, rubbing the ridged muscles of his abdomen
through his buckskin tunic.

"We will complete the hunt," Gao agreed, "and then
you will take the meat back to Tippecanoe."

"Ah," Tall Pine said, "if finding horses for the bride-
price is your intent, you will not cut me out of the fun so
easily."

"What I do will be dangerous," Gao told him. "Tecumseh has warned us not to waste our lives but to save
them for the last fight. I feel that I must fulfill my vow to
Main Poche, but I will not ask you to join me in the risk."

Tall Pine spat out a good-natured obscenity, and Gao

shrugged. If the situation were reversed he suspected that he would feel the same as Tall Pine.

"I have never owned a horse," Tall Pine said. "I think it would be a pleasant thing to ride rather than walk."

Gao had only one reservation about heading south—each mile put him farther away from Mist-on-the-Water. However, since it was for her that he was acting, he shielded his heart with thoughts of how it would feel to ride through the common of Prophetstown leading several fine horses. It would demonstrate to all his regard for the girl who had made his life so complete that he rarely thought of his own family—with the exception of Ta-na.

The two friends alternated the warrior's pace with walking as they traveled down the bank of the Wabash River. At a point a little more than halfway to Vincennes, Gao noticed signs of white intrusion.

"Eight or ten men," he told Tall Pine as they examined the tracks left by a patrol.

"They are far from the white man's fort at Vincennes," Tall Pine said.

After proceeding with caution for a few miles, they came upon the reason for the presence of a patrol so close to Prophetstown. Gao counted sixty men erecting a fort in a clearing near the river, and the ringing sound of axes from the adjoining woodlands told him there were many more.

"Tenskwatawa will be angry," Tall Pine said. "He will say that the white chief of Vincennes is invading Indian lands."

Gao's immediate concern was that the soldiers might move even farther north, and it would not be a good thing to be away stealing a bride-price if the enemy advanced on Prophetstown. But he could see that it was going to take the soldiers many days to complete the fort. If this push into Tecumseh's stronghold was intended by Governor Harrison to be the first move toward confrontation, it would be wise to have horses not only for the bride-price but also to take his wife away from danger. Much as he had come to believe in Tecumseh's cause, his first priority was to keep his wife safe.

There would be time, he decided, to accomplish his own purpose while gathering information. He led Tall Pine in a wide circle around the men who were felling trees; twice they had to lie low to avoid any small patrols.

Acre by acre, mile by mile, moving with the slow but irresistible force of a glacier, land-hungry immigrants from the east had been pushing into the settlements along the White River northwest of Vincennes, and it was there, late in the day, that Gao and Tall Pine made camp near the river. With only a small fire to warm them, they ate half-cooked meat, slept, and then awoke to a day of roiling, low clouds and a northwest wind with the bite of the Canadian snow fields behind it.

The first log cabin they came upon was buttoned up tight against the chill. Smoke rolled out of the stovepipe and flowed down the slanted shake roof like water, an indication that the weather was about to change.

In a lean-to near the house, two fat, broad-backed, bay-colored plow horses stood side by side, bridles and blankets near at hand. When the young Indians approached, the docile horses complied lazily, lifting their heads to accept the bits. One of them broke wind as Gao vaulted to her back.

Tall Pine immediately decided that riding was far preferable to walking. "I will never walk again," he said as they followed a trail downriver. "I will steal enough horses from the white man to keep me off my feet forever."

The next two cabins had nothing but mules, but luck was with them. At the third home a celebration was taking place. Although it was early in the afternoon, the sound of a banjo and a fiddle came through the chinks of the well-built, spacious cabin. Whoops of delight accompanied the music, and the stomping of feet on the floorboards was so loud Gao wondered why the walls didn't fall down. Three surreys were tied up near the house, each pulled by a span of horses. More horses were hobbled in a nearby grassy plot or tied to the fence of the corral that enclosed the barn and stables.

"We need go no farther," Gao said, smiling broadly.

"I am heavy of heart," Tall Pine muttered.

"With such riches in sight?"

"Because there are so many of them and only two of us. We can't hope to steal them all."

"We don't need them all," Gao said.

Gao went shopping. Keeping a careful eye on the cabin, where the celebration continued, he crawled to the stables and chose six of the best horses, quietly bridled them, and found a blanket for the finest of the lot. Meanwhile, Tall Pine, not as confident of his ability to handle the animals, settled for one to ride, three to lead.

Gao cut the hobbles of the remaining horses in the grassy plot, opened the corral gates, and sent them all trotting away into the woods.

When they were well away from the cabin, Tall Pine said, "I am almost disappointed."

"You have four fine horses," Gao said.

"But it would have been more exciting if we had been forced to kill a few whitefaces."

Gao laughed. The young men had ridden several miles from the cabin and were feeling very confident. "I did not want to stir up that hornet's nest," he said. "I have been among such men, my friend. With a Kentucky rifle each one of them could give you a third eye at a quarter of a mile's distance."

Once more they skirted Governor Harrison's new fort and once again had to dodge his patrols, but the ride home was pleasant, uneventful, and leisurely.

Gao purposely waited until late in the afternoon to make their entrance to Prophetstown. Most of the hunting parties had returned by then, and the women were outside feeding the fires over which they would cook the evening meal. The weather had turned clear and crisp, and men with blankets draped over their shoulders sat in the sun and discussed matters of greater or lesser import.

Gao and Tall Pine tried to look casual as they rode into the common on fine bay geldings followed by a parade of eight horses. A hush fell as all eyes turned toward them. A young warrior their own age, a friend of theirs, whooped his approval, and the call was taken up by others. The progress of the adventurers was marked by an ever-increasing wave of sound as they advanced toward Main Poche's wegiwa.

As they came near, Gao sent the call of a dove ahead of him, and his heart leaped when Mist-on-the-Water emerged from their lodge. Her hand flew to her mouth in surprise, and a proud, happy smile spread over her round, beautiful face.

The Potawatomi chief, Main Poche, stood with his arms crossed on his chest, his head held high. Gao brought his mount to a halt in front of him, threw one leg over the horse's mane and slid off the horse.

"Uncle-by-marriage," he said with great formality, "I pledged to you that I would bring you a price of honor for the hand of your niece. I am here."

Main Poche grunted acknowledgment.

Gao selected the four finest horses and put the reins in Main Poche's hands. "And yet this is but a token," he said. "For what your niece means to me, great chief, is beyond value."

"It is good," Main Poche said.

A quavering cry of approval spread through the gathering crowd, and the noise became louder when Gao led a well-built, glossy mare to where Mist-on-the-Water was waiting. His adoration for her showed on his face as he placed the reins in her hand.

"This, my wife, is my gift for you."

"My husband is a kind man," Mist said, bowing her head.

"And what of you, Tall Pine?" someone yelled. "Will you purchase a bride with your animals?"

Tall Pine threw back his head and gave the call of a turkey gobbler. Much laughter greeted him, and he repeated the call, put his heels to the flank of his mount, and trotted off to his father's lodge with his share of the captured animals.

Mist-on-the-Water helped Gao gather tall brown grass for the horses, who nibbled contentedly while Gao cut poles and boughs to build a shelter for them. Mist got corn from Main Poche's store and gave her mare a treat. The other bay, a gelding, nuzzled her hand until he, too, was allowed half an ear of corn.

And then came the best time of all. The food was still warm in the pot, and they were alone in the wegiwa. The wind was humming a mournful song around the edges of the roof, and the cold drafts tried but could not penetrate their snug blankets and softened hides.

"My Moonlight is a beautiful horse," Mist whispered into Gao's mouth as he kissed her teasingly.

"So you have named her already."

"Yes, do you like it?"

"I like whatever you like," he said.

"Do you like this?" she asked, doing naughty things with her hands. His answer was not made with words.

When they were quiet once more the wind sang softly to them, and they could hear the horses move now and then in the lean-to behind their wegiwa.

"But am I to be valued at only four horses?" Mist asked sleepily.

"Four hundred would not equal your worth to me."

"Just four hundred?" she teased.

"We must not make your uncle a poor man by forcing him to give all his stored food to the animals," Gao said.

"Well, there is that, I suppose."

"I am sorry if you think four not enough."

She clung to him. "Husband, I am so proud of you. Only you could set out to hunt and return with not one or two, but ten of the whiteface's finest horses. Only you would insist—even after my uncle told you that no bride-price was necessary—in honoring me so. If I tease you it is because I am so happy."

"I thank the Master of Life that he has given you to me." Gao sighed deeply. It had been a long day. He had triumphed. He had loved. He slept, and Mist slept in his arms, her breath warm on his neck.

Gao awoke abruptly with Mist's hand shaking his shoulder. "Wake up. Wake up," she begged urgently.

He opened his eyes and groaned.

"It is Tenskwatawa, the Prophet," she said. "He is here to see you."

Gao bounded out of the bed, dressed hurriedly, secured the rawhide string on his clubbed hair, slipped his feet into moccasins, and walked out into a bright, pleasantly warm morning.

Tenskwatawa stood a few feet away, his arms crossed, his empty eye socket glaring with the reflection of the sun on a white-painted pebble.

"You went to the settlements for horses," the Prophet said sternly.

"Yes," Gao said. "To pay the bride-price to my uncle-by-marriage." Suddenly he felt a wave of uneasiness. Belatedly he realized that he should have asked the Prophet's permission before staging a raid for horses. "It was not planned that way, great chief," he went on, hoping a bit of flattery would help the situation. "We left here to hunt and found ourselves near a settlement where something, perhaps a wedding, was being celebrated. There were at least two dozen horses."

Tenskwatawa glared at Gao with his one good eye; then his face creased in what was meant to be a smile. "It is good," he said. "You were with a young Miami, Tall Pine, is that not true?"

"It is true."

"Good. Good. That shows how young warriors from different tribes can work together."

Gao breathed a deep sigh of relief.

*   *   *

Two days later, however, two dozen heavily armed white men rode boldly into Prophetstown and drew rein in front of the Prophet's temple.

Gao, warned of the approach of the war party by a nervous Tall Pine, hurried to the temple in time to hear the leader of the whitefaces demand in a loud, rude voice the return of the stolen horses.

"Don't try to lie your way out of it," the man said angrily, "because we tracked 'em here. All ten of 'em."

A group of Shawnee warriors tensed, their hands moving to their weapons.

"I, the Prophet, do not lie," Tenskwatawa stated in a flat, deadly voice.

"Then you don't deny that the stolen horses are here," the white man said.

"It is possible that some of my young men, feeling in high spirits, played a joke on the whitefaces," Tenskwatawa said.

"The joke's over, Indian," the white man said. "Fetch the horses."

Tenskwatawa's face was wooden. His good eye glared at the unwelcome men with a darkness to match the black pebble lodged in his empty socket. Suddenly his face softened as he recalled Tecumseh's last words to him before he had left on his recent trip.

"Tenskwatawa, it is possible that Governor Harrison will do things while I am gone to tempt you to act recklessly. This must not happen. Take insult if you must. Swallow your pride. If Harrison should set his army against you, take all of the people and as much goods and foodstuffs as you can carry and scatter into the woods. If he attempts to attack Tippecanoe, let him. This town can be rebuilt. Our confederation, should it be riven by premature action, cannot. Do you hear me?"

When at last Tenskwatawa answered, his voice sounded rough enough to hurt his throat. "Get the horses," he ordered, looking directly at Gao.

Without question Gao ran to obey, and Tall Pine followed directly behind him. Main Poche, who had heard the exchange, made no comment as the two young men returned, leading only eight horses. It was clear to all the Indians assembled that Gao had chosen to keep the animal he had given to his wife as well as his own mount.

"There were ten of them," the white man said.

"You see," Tenskwatawa. "What you see, you see."

Some of the soldiers were getting uneasy, although the brazen leader refused to show any fear at being surrounded by thousands of armed Indians.

"Ten," the leader said through clenched teeth.

"To hell with that," one of the white men said. "Let's get out of here."

In icy silence the leader turned his horse and led the group out of Prophetstown.

A seething Tenskwatawa watched his enemies ride away, then turned abruptly and slammed into the medicine lodge. When he emerged an hour later, he had painted his face with the colors of war, and his good eye burned as red as the fiery pebble that filled his dead socket. His shrill voice rose to a shriek as he summoned the faithful to him, and he waited, standing tall and rigid, until the common was filled.

"Moneto, the Supreme Being of All Things, has sent me a vision," he announced in his oddly high, grating voice.

A moan of anticipation rose from the crowd.

"He has said to me that the eight horses that were taken from us were seized unjustly. He has said to me, 'Tenskwatawa, the horses belong to you and to your people.' He has said that the horses are the property of those who held them and that if there are those among you who will undertake to return the horses to their proper owners, no harm will befall you. No rifle ball will penetrate you. No blade will cut you."

War whoops sounded and reached a crescendo. Gao

caught Tall Pine's eye and smiled in agreement. Tall Pine
shouted and lifted his tomahawk high overhead.

It took the warriors less time to gather a raiding party
than it took to skin a hare. Gao rode Mist's mare, Tall Pine
rode Gao's gelding, and they galloped out of town in the
midst of fifty men and rode hard during the remaining
hours of the day.

As twilight deepened, Gao, scouting ahead along a
very fresh trail, saw the flicker of the soldiers' campfires
through the trees. He reported back to Shabonee, who
was leading the party.

Shabonee, who had killed twoscore white men and
was always willing to kill more, had also heard Tecumseh's
warning not to let the whites lure the tribes into war.

"We will claim our property in peace," he admon-
ished.

He positioned his men in a circle around the
soldiers' camp, and at the sound of an owl hoot everyone
moved forward, pushing two startled sentries ahead of
them until all fifty warriors surrounded the sputtering
fires. As a light, cold rain began to fall, fifty rifles were
leveled at the two dozen white men.

"We have come for our horses," Gao said in his re-
fined, upper-class English accent.

"Well, boys," the leader of the white men said, "I
guess this fancy-talking Indian has enough company to
just up and take 'em."

"And since you have invaded to the very heart of our
home village," Gao said, "we will take the horses you
were riding as payment for that insult."

Shabonee kept his rifle leveled at the nose of the
white leader as he gave orders to gather the horses.

"Tell them," Shabonee said to Gao when the animals
were in tow, one behind each of thirty-two warriors, "that
they should go back where they came from and should
not return to Prophetstown if they want to keep their
hair."

With a big smile on his face, Gao spoke slowly.

"I hear you, boy," the white man muttered. "I hear you well."

The warriors whooped with pride as the procession moved on. Only Gao had heard the venomous hate as well as the threat in the big man's calm words.

"I hear you, boy. I hear you well."

It was shortly before midnight when the victorious party reached Prophetstown, and soon almost everyone was in the common to greet the returning heroes.

There had been no violence. Not even one white man had been killed.

"Are you convinced?" Tenskwatawa asked as he stood in the torchlight in front of his temple. "Are you convinced that with Moneto on your side and the Prophet to guide you, you are now invulnerable?"

Shouts of joy and affirmation answered the Prophet's question.

Tenskwatawa lifted his arms to the cold, glittering stars and chanted a prayer of praise to Moneto. All the while he was thinking, *I am the Prophet.* He did not need Tecumseh to fill his head with wisdom. He could make his own prophecies. He was the Prophet.

"All will go well with you," he said to the people as horses milled and snorted and sleepy children clung to their mothers' legs.

"Moneto will be with each of you. When we stand together, nothing is impossible. The rifles of the white-faces will turn away from you, and their balls will not be able to find you."

Wrapped in a blanket, Mist-on-the-Water came to stand beside Gao's horse. For a while longer the Prophet spoke and then abruptly disappeared into his medicine house. Gao and Mist led their two horses to their lean-to, and soon they were abed, with Mist's warmth slowly penetrating the night chill that had crept into Gao's bones during the raid.

Chapter Twelve

Michael Soaring Hawk was sleeping. In the hours since Little Hawk had brought him back to the agency, the stick splint on his broken leg had been replaced with a sturdier one fashioned of slats. Lavinia Downs had confirmed Little Hawk's fear that the boy had at least two broken ribs, and she had bound his chest in clean white cloth and circled his midsection with another bandage to cover the cauterized arrow wound.

"He's a brave one, bless his little heart," she said in a whisper.

"I am greatly in your debt," Little Hawk said.

"Nonsense."

"May I impose on you further?"

"I know what you're thinking," Lavinia said, "and I assure you I will take care of this little fellow as though he were one of my own. Benjamin is waiting outside to talk with you. You run along. Find that dear girl and bring her back safely to us."

Little Hawk nodded grimly.

Benjamin Hawkins was waiting in his office. "Hawk, I know you're anxious to be on your way. I've sent a rider to the Ocmulgee Garrison. There'll be troops here by tomorrow morning and then—"

"With all due respect, sir," Little Hawk said, "I'll need a wagon and some men to bring back the bodies of my son and the slave girl."

"Yes, yes, of course," Hawkins said. "You shall have them, but you must not go off by yourself vowing revenge on the entire Creek Nation because of the actions of a few renegades."

"Thank you for your concern, sir." Little Hawk had no intention of wasting time arguing with the agent. One of his sons was dead, the other seriously injured. While outwardly he appeared calm, inside he was a caldron of emotions. For the first time in his life he knew consummate fear. The terror of loss was a debilitating force that threatened to overwhelm him.

A dead son.

Naomi.

The knowledge that the woman he loved was in the hands of the enemy who had so mercilessly killed Joseph and the slave girl bred an ogre of dread so formidable that to counter it he drew on a response as old as mankind: the drive for vengeance. He raced to his cabin, where he changed his clothing and packed a few trail provisions in a bedroll that he strapped to his back. He carefully checked his shot and powder and saw to the primings of the rifle and twin pistols that had once been the property of Meriwether Lewis. Finally he stuck a tomahawk—bright and sharp—into the waistband of his trousers.

When he emerged, armed and ready, a wagon drawn by two mules was moving slowly up the street from the stables. Putting his foot on the hub of the front wheel, Little Hawk leaped into the wagon, pushed the driver to one side, grabbed the reins, and lashed the mules into an awkward trot.

*   *   *

Nugee was still standing in the clearing with a long stick in his hand, keeping the turkey buzzards at a distance. The stench of the big birds and the presence of the dead caused the two soldiers in the wagon to look around uneasily. Little Hawk and Nugee wrapped the bodies in blankets and lifted them gingerly into the wagon.

"Go now," Little Hawk told the soldiers. "Do not make the mules run. Do you hear me?"

"Yes, sir," said the driver.

"Take them to Mistress Downs."

"Yes, sir."

"Go with them, Nugee," Little Hawk ordered.

The young Creek drew back his shoulders. His eyes were swollen and red from weeping, but his face was that of a man as he looked at Little Hawk and said, "That I will not do."

"Then do as you damned well please," Little Hawk said. He set off at the warrior's pace. The trail was easy to follow. He had not run a hundred feet before Nugee passed him. With a snarl he accelerated and caught the Creek by the shoulder, spun him around, and almost yanked him off his feet.

"Do not foul the trail, boy," he warned.

Nugee's face was expressionless. "You told me to do as I please. It will please me to find those who killed Magnolia, and that I intend to do."

"Run ahead of me once more and disturb the trail, and I will kill you," Little Hawk threatened.

So, for a long time they ran in file, the Creek behind, adapting his pace to the half-run of a Seneca warrior who had, in his mind, discarded his heritage. A hatred of all Indians and all things Indian flowered deep within Little Hawk's spirit.

So intent was he on catching the kidnappers and finding Naomi, he failed to follow the trail closely. Suddenly he realized that the number of tracks in the war party had diminished by three. He halted and cast around, trying to find a place where one or more of them had left the trail.

"They have been branching off one at a time," Nugee said. "It began several miles back."

Little Hawk's face darkened. He was chagrined by his lack of observation.

"One turned south to follow the small creek we crossed," Nugee said. "Another went north a half mile later, leaving the trail by walking along a large, fallen tree. The third left a hundred yards back."

Little Hawk was silent. He moved more slowly and spotted the place where a fourth man had left the main trail and checked it carefully. Naomi's smaller moccasin tracks continued westward. A feverish rage burned his face. The cowards were splitting up. But if he caught even one of them, he would make sure he learned the names of the others.

He voiced an oath under his breath as he ran. "By the God of my mother, I swear that each one will die. Each man who was there—whether he hefted the ax that killed Joseph, whether he pulled the bow that sent the arrow through Michael's side—each of them will die."

The Seneca no longer tortured enemy prisoners—at least not the Seneca he knew—but it would have been sweet to see each man who had been in the clearing die slowly and painfully. If Little Hawk could only hear the screams of each man as he was roasted by fire, he thought, it would help him forget how the vultures had torn away Joseph's nose and lips, how they had plucked out his eyeballs and torn into the softness of his small backside.

Just as a frog being pulled backward slowly and inevitably into a snake's fanged mouth feels nothing even though it lives and breathes, so Naomi felt nothing. Nature provided merciful shock for the doomed frog and for the woman who had witnessed horrors her mind was incapable of accepting. When Calling Owl moved his band toward the west, leaving the bodies of Joseph and Magnolia lying in the clearing, Naomi allowed herself to be led like a sheep by a rawhide thong around her neck. She did not feel the discomfort even when Calling Owl jerked on the lead to force her to increase her pace. She walked without conscious effort, for her mind was wrapped in a dark, all-enclosing cocoon of nothingness.

As the day passed, she became vaguely aware of tiredness in her legs and of discomfort at her neck. The rawhide leash had chafed her soft, tender skin, and she moaned in protest and lifted her hands to loosen the leather. Calling Owl jerked the lead, and she fell forward; gravel dug into her knees. For a moment she was aware of a strange, expressionless, Indian face looking down at her. She struggled to her feet, and once again her mind dived deeply into the soft, dark place to which it had retreated.

When Calling Owl started up the slope of the ridge, she followed the tug of the lead, going down on all fours from time to time, scrambling after the Creek in frantic haste to keep the noose from closing ever more tightly around her throat.

Calling Owl pulled her to her feet and with his hands on her arms guided her across rock surfaces so that no sign of their passage was left. He knew the ridge well and was able to move over the top of it and down the slope to its southern end without his moccasins, or the woman's, leaving a single mark for Little Hawk to follow. At the foot of the ridge a creek bubbled its way over a rocky bed. Calling Owl led the woman up the creek until the sun was brushing the tops of the trees to the west, and in the stillness of the evening he heard the sound of the falling waters and jerked the lead to force the woman to move faster.

Concerned about losing daylight, Little Hawk and Nugee arrived at the foot of the rocky ridge and noted that the remaining six members of the group they were following had split up. Four sets of tracks veered to the south. Two

continued onward, up the ridge, and from the size of the
footprints, Little Hawk knew that one of them was Naomi.

Naomi and one man. Little Hawk began to hope.

The abductors could have killed her at any time. In
fact, she might very well be injured, although not so se-
verely that she was unable to walk, for the imprint of her
small moccasins showed that she was moving under her
own power and that from time to time she fell to the
ground. It was not his most primal fear that she had been
molested, but he allowed himself to hope that the group
had been moving too swiftly for the Creek to vent their
lust.

Little Hawk bounded up the slope and overran the
signs, then turned and backtracked. Nugee was already
casting around among projecting rocks and smooth stone
surfaces.

"He has chosen his path well," Nugee said, unable to
find any tracks at the top of the ridge. "He could have
gone in any direction."

Little Hawk agreed. "We will separate. The signal is
the coo of a dove. Or if we are too far apart, the warning
call of a scouting crow, four quick caws followed by three
slower."

Nugee nodded and set off to the south, casting up
and down the slope.

Little Hawk walked slowly along the stream at the
top of the ridge and scouted it carefully in both directions,
but there was no evidence of recent human passage.

"Naomi, Naomi," he whispered. "Why didn't you
leave me a sign?"

According to plan, the Creek warriors who had served as
decoys to throw Little Hawk and Nugee off the trail circled around and rejoined Calling Owl at the waterfall.
Wild Wind had taken it on himself to be the rear guard,
and it was late afternoon when he caught up with the
main group. "They are but two," he said. "The whiteface

from the agency who calls himself Little Hawk and a Creek boy."

Calling Owl smiled with satisfaction.

"Give me three men and I will stop them," Wild Wind said, thrusting out his chest.

"I do not want to stop them," Calling Owl said. "It is late, and I want all of you but four to return to your families."

Wild Wind, New Man, Red Runner, and Gator Toe, all known for their lust for blood, remained with Calling Owl as the other warriors faded into the woods.

"Here is what you will do," he told New Man when the sun was no more than a hand's span high in the evening sky. "You will take these others and backtrack to a spot where you can surprise those who come after us. Do as you wish with the boy, but take the white man alive. There are four of you. Can you do it?"

"I will do as you say," New Man said.

"I will wait here with the woman at the place of falling water," Calling Owl continued. "Bring the white-face here. Bring him alive."

"It might be necessary to break him somewhat in order to bring him there."

Calling Owl laughed. "Break him only a little bit. We want him to enjoy himself as he watches his wife being mounted by Indian stallions such as you."

New Man felt a surge of interest and laughed at the thought of what was to come.

The cold water had washed away some of the dark, protective cushion in Naomi's mind. She looked around in puzzlement but did not recognize her surroundings. She could not understand why her feet were so cold until she realized that she had been wading in shallow water. The soles of her moccasins were slippery with moss from the rocks that lined the creek. She lifted both hands and seized the rawhide thong to ease the pull on her neck.

"What are you doing to me?" she asked, not recognizing the Indian who held her leash. "Where are you taking me?" He turned his head. "No talk," he answered in English.

Memory lanced through the haze. She relived the moment when Michael had rushed to her aide, glaring defiantly, and she thought how much he looked like his father. Then she heard the impact of the rifle muzzle as it slammed into his side and sent him tumbling over the cliff.

It was, she told herself, nothing but a nightmare. She would awaken in her bed with Little Hawk's arms around her, and he would soothe her and tell her she had just been having a bad dream.

But she heard the hollow sound of a tomahawk blade breaking Magnolia's skull, and she screamed aloud as Joseph died again in the mirror of her mind.

Calling Owl turned, took a quick step, and slapped her resoundingly. "No scream," he ordered.

The force of the blow swiveled her head, and the dull pain sent her back into the protective blackness. She followed docilely as Calling Owl led her into a cave near a small waterfall. She made no protest as he pushed her down; she only leaned back against the stone and closed her eyes.

The pleasant warmth of a fire near her face woke her, and without blinking she stared into the blaze. She grunted in feeble protest when Calling Owl put his hands on her arms and pushed her until she was lying on the hard-packed earth of the cave floor. As the Creek fumbled with her clothing and ripped away her underthings with a knife to expose her to his swift and penetrating attack, she was limp and unfeeling, closing her eyes against the pain.

Little Hawk and Nugee had failed in their effort to find a continuation of the trail. They had cast out in all directions from the ridge. Little Hawk crossed the creek and followed it in both directions for a half mile or more. Frantic with worry and frustration, he heard Nugee give the agreed-upon signal, the relaxed call of a crow that said to others of its ilk that all was well.

He found Nugee at the point where four warriors had turned south. "You found no sign of the small tracks?" he asked.

"It is my thought that we follow these four," Nugee said.

"No," Little Hawk said quickly, but reason changed that decision. Soon it would be dark. If he continued in his fruitless efforts to pick up Naomi's tracks he would waste the night hours. Following Nugee's suggestion offered the hope of accomplishing something: The four warriors would halt before full darkness, he would kill three of them quickly, and then he would question the survivor.

"We go," he said, motioning Nugee to take the lead since the Creek had followed the spoor left by the group of four for some distance.

Nugee was moving at a trot, covering ground steadily. Although the trail was easy to follow, it was difficult to run through the fallen leaves without making some sound. Visibility in the hardwood groves was good, so there was little danger of ambush. Nevertheless, something gnawed at Little Hawk. Something was amiss. The man with Naomi had skillfully thrown them off his trail, but the four who had turned south were making no effort to conceal the traces of their passage. Something was wrong indeed.

When the trail dropped down a slope into a densely brushed declivity through which a small stream ran, Little Hawk said, "Hold, Nugee."

The Creek stopped and turned. His chest was heaving with effort, for they had traveled far that day.

"Be ready," Little Hawk said.

Nugee, too, saw that the brush here closed in on both sides of the trail. He nodded and moved forward at a walk. It was Little Hawk who heard the almost inaudible *snick* as a rifle's hammer was cocked. He leaped forward and threw Nugee to the earth just as three muskets blasted, two from one side of the trail, one from the other.

                    *   *   *

New Man and Wild Wind stood side by side in the ambush. The other two warriors were in the woods across
the trail and had fired at the same time Wild Wind had.
The Indians had thought that three balls would take care
of the young Creek, leaving New Man with a round in the
event that it became necessary to stop the white one with
a shot to the leg or the shoulder.

New Man almost cried out in surprise when the
white one pulled the Creek to the earth as if he had
sensed the exact moment the rifles would fire.

The enemy must have guessed the Indians' position
by the smoke from their rifles, for he scuttled toward
them now on his hands and knees. Before they could
reload their weapons he burst through the brush and confronted them. He was on his knees when he drew his
pistols, but before he could fire, another shot rang out
from behind him, followed by a cry of pain.

New Man, recovering from his temporary shock, had
darted behind a tree, then lifted his rifle and fired in one
movement. The young Creek who accompanied the white
one fell over backward and lay still.

The white man's two elegantly decorated pistols
roared as one, throwing heavy-caliber lead with deadly
accuracy. Wild Wind took a direct hit to the head and
folded limply in the act of leaping toward the enemy.
Across the trail, Red Runner and Gator Toe, stunned by
their friend's swift, grisly death, turned and fled deep into
the woods.

Over the waning echoes of the shots, Little Hawk heard
the brush rustle behind him. There was no time to reload
the pistols, so he drew his tomahawk and whirled to face
New Man. New Man's raised tomahawk flashed downward, but Little Hawk swayed to one side and lifted his
blade to deflect the blow. Instead of retreating from the
Creek's headlong rush, he stepped into it, took the force
of New Man's movement against his own body, and

lashed out with his left fist to connect with his attacker's jaw.

For a moment Little Hawk feared that he had broken his hand. He yelped with pain even as the Creek went down in a heap, his blade falling from his fingers. Little Hawk gingerly shook his aching hand, looked at it carefully, and moved his fingers experimentally. To his relief no bones seemed to be broken, but his knuckles were already beginning to swell.

He turned his attention to the unconscious Indian and used the warrior's turban to lash his hands and feet. Only then did he go to Nugee's side. He rolled the dead Creek away and bent over the wounded boy.

Nugee was breathing. His eyes were open, and his lips parted in a smile when he saw Little Hawk. "Did we get all of them?"

"Two of the cowards ran," Little Hawk said, "and one yet lives."

Nugee was wounded in the shoulder. Little Hawk moved the boy's arm, but heard no sound of bones grating together. As he opened Nugee's tunic he saw that the ball had cut a groove in the flesh under his arm. He removed his own neckerchief and pressed it tightly against the wound until the bleeding stopped.

"It is not bad," Nugee said, half in question.

"It is only a little wound. It will heal swiftly, my brave friend."

Little Hawk removed the turban from the dead enemy and used it to tie the makeshift bandage in place. When he turned back to New Man there was just enough light to see that the warrior's eyes were open.

"Where has the woman been taken?" he asked.

New Man glared at him balefully.

"You will tell me where," Little Hawk said. "And you will tell me the names of every man in your party. We will start with the name of your leader."

New Man cursed Little Hawk, who stared at him through squinted eyes filled with hatred.

"Nugee, can you walk?" Little Hawk asked.

"Yes," Nugee answered.

Little Hawk retrieved his spent pistols and returned to his captive. He untied the warrior's feet and jerked him erect. He tied a noose around the Creek's neck but did not try to lead him, pushing him instead with the muzzle of his reloaded rifle.

Nugee chose to rest near a creek in a small, flat clearing surrounded by large trees. Little Hawk pushed their captive down to a sitting position and lashed him to a tree.

Although Little Hawk could tell that Nugee's wound was giving him pain, he was pleased that the boy gathered dead wood and soon had a fire going. When the blaze was high and the coals hot, Little Hawk placed the blade of New Man's knife in the fire. The Creek, fearing what was going to happen, struggled against his bonds but without success. The blade was white-hot when Little Hawk held it in front of New Man's face, then slowly lifted the Creek's tunic and placed the blade against the deerskin. The stench of burning leather filled the air.

"We will start with the name of the man who has taken the woman," Little Hawk hissed.

New Man spat directly at Little Hawk, but Hawk moved quickly to avoid the blob of spittle.

"So," Little Hawk said.

The blade was still white-hot, and as he lifted it he knew that New Man could feel the radiated heat against his cheek.

"Shall I blind you before I kill you, so that you will not be able to see the way to the place of your ancestors?"

New Man's eyes widened, but he controlled himself.

"Or shall I apply the blade to your manhood so that in the other world you will never know a woman's love?"

"I will be glad to see to that," Nugee said, smiling.

New Man's eyes jerked from side to side as if seeking help.

"I know that you are brave," Little Hawk taunted. "Death and pain are easy to face, are they not? But to think of not being able to find your way after death because your eyes have been burned is a terrifying thought. And I'm sure your manhood shrivels when you imagine the touch of the blade there. This is how it will feel." Little Hawk brushed the hot blade against New Man's cheek.

The Creek cried out in a high-pitched yelp as his skin smoked and charred.

"I think one eye first," Little Hawk said conversationally to Nugee. "And then we will remove his manhood and fill his mouth with it while he still has one eye left to watch."

"Uhhh, unnnnn, unnnn," New Man grunted in terror as Little Hawk lifted the knife toward his eye. "Wait," he cried.

Little Hawk pulled the knife back but kept it at eye level.

"It was all Calling Owl's idea," New Man said, the words spilling out of his mouth.

"Ah." Little Hawk felt a new surge of fearful despair as he began to understand. Calling Owl was the leader of the Creek Indians who had fought against Big Warrior's punitive expedition. "It is revenge he seeks, then."

"Because you fought with Big Warrior. Because you killed Creek warriors in a cause that was not your own."

"What is your name?"

"I am called New Man."

"Give me the names of all the others, slowly."

"He who lies dead is Wild Wind." New Man kept his eyes on the blade, which was no longer glowing but which Little Hawk knew was still hot enough that he could feel it on his cheek. One by one New Man named Naomi's attackers.

"Help him remember, Nugee," Little Hawk said, offering the smoldering blade to the young man.

"I will."

"Where has Calling Owl taken the woman?" Little Hawk asked.

"In truth, I do not know," New Man said.

Nugee touched the blade to New Man's cheek, and once more skin sizzled and New Man moaned in pain.

"Listen to me," Little Hawk said. "One of my sons is dead, the other hurt badly. It does not matter to me who struck the blows. Do you understand?"

New Man nodded, his eyes wide.

"Each time you spoke a name you called down death," Little Hawk declared. "Each of them will die. Do you see why it doesn't matter who killed my son and who shot the arrow into the side of the other one, since all of you will die?"

New Man shook his head. "If I am to be killed, why should I tell you anything?"

Little Hawk took the knife from Nugee and touched it to the underside of New Man's chin. "You will tell me where Calling Owl is so that your death will be quick and painless and you meet your ancestors whole and unmutilated." He turned and stuck the knife into the fire. "You have until the blade heats again to tell me."

Turning his face toward the darkening sky, New Man began to sing his song of death. Black blisters had risen on his cheek and under his chin. He was sobbing as Little Hawk lifted the blade, white-hot once more, and poised it a foot away from New Man's eyes.

"He has taken the woman to the place of the falling waters," New Man said desperately.

"There is a waterfall north of here," Nugee said.

"Is that the place?" Little Hawk asked.

"Yes. There is a cave beside the falling water. We were to meet him there."

"After you had killed us both?" Nugee asked.

"Only you, son of a Creek whore," New Man said, spitting in Nugee's direction.

"And what were you to do with me?" Little Hawk asked.

"We were to bring you to the cave," New Man said, "where you would watch as we used your wife, one by one in turn." He laughed. The sound was madness, a loon's cry, a realization of impending death, but his words rang out in the darkness. "Even now, white one, Calling Owl is enjoying the tender white flesh of your wife."

Nugee stood by Little Hawk, tomahawk in hand. "Have you finished with this dog's droppings?"

Little Hawk had to turn his head away quickly to keep exploding brain matter from striking him full in the face as Nugee smashed New Man's skull.

They left the bodies where they had fallen. It would be nothing more than justice to let the turkey buzzards feast as they had on Joseph Standing Bear and the slave girl.

Naomi felt as if she were being jostled by the pitching and rolling of a wagon traveling over a rutted road. The top of her head kept banging into something, but she refused to believe that it was a rock wall. Why would there be a rock wall in a carriage? she wondered. She hummed the lullaby that had been the favorite of the twins when they were babes in arms. She could not understand why Little Hawk slapped her and told her to be quiet. Soon the wagon was rolling smoothly, or it had stopped. No matter.

She lay as Calling Owl left her, with her clothing bundled around her waist, dreaming that she was back in the small log cabin her father had built on the Tennessee frontier. Her mother and father were dead, both victims of Bearclaw Morgan and his demented sons. She was a captive. She had fought the three Morgans until her heart threatened to leap from her chest; her face was bruised and her arms ached from their blows, but still they came at her to claim her body, one after the other.

She screamed, but no sound came from her throat as Calling Owl—or was it one of the Morgans?—vented his lust once more. When he was finished she tugged her skirts down, pulled her knees up under her chin, and lay on her side, staring unseeingly at the flickering shadows on the cave wall. Death seemed inviting, but something deep inside her repeated, *No, Naomi, death is not the answer.*

Little Hawk had forgiven her for that which she could not prevent. His love had purified her, and she had vowed she would never again be humiliated and used. In her love for Little Hawk she cursed herself for not having killed, if not one or more of the Morgans, herself.

But she had no weapon—only her revulsion, her shame, her anger, and her strong teeth and fingernails.

"We must wait for morning," Nugee said as Little Hawk prepared to move up the creek.

It was a dark night. The moon would rise later, but it would give little light.

"Stay here if that is what you want to do," Little Hawk said.

Nugee sighed. His wound was painful, but if he held his arm close to his side and walked with care he could match Little Hawk's pace. The brush along the creek made it hard going, and Nugee stumbled and grunted as the impact sent a wave of pain through his side.

"You don't have to follow me," Little Hawk said. "Take my bedroll. Rest. When I have Naomi I will come back for you."

"I want to see him die, this Calling Owl, the one who ordered the death of Magnolia."

"Then keep up with me and be quiet," Little Hawk said.

The little valley through which the creek ran made a sharp turn. Still more brush clogged the way. Little Hawk moved farther away from the stream. He thought he saw the ridge rising in the north, a mass darker than the sky.

"The place of falling waters," Nugee said, coming up to stand beside him "There."

"Stay here," Little Hawk said. "You'll be of no use in a fight."

"What fight?" Nugee asked. "There's only one. Calling Owl."

The song of the stream was becoming louder, its fall more pronounced. The clear water rushed around protruding rocks.

"How far?" Little Hawk whispered.

"A mile, no more."

"Once more, will you stay here?"

"No."

Little Hawk shrugged and saw to his weapons. When he moved forward he was sure he could hear the sound of the waterfall.

Chapter Thirteen

Naomi awoke to a nightmare. At first she thought she was only dreaming that she was awake and that she had been dragged back in time to the days when she was a beaten, cowed, enfeebled slave of the three odious Morgan men. It was dark, and she couldn't tell which one of them was rutting between her outflung legs, but she viewed each possibility with equal repugnance and fury. She arched her back in an effort to dislodge her tormentor and heard a hateful laugh. She remembered.

"I likes it when you fights."

Half-mad, her mind battered by the events of the day, she could not know that she was hearing Bearclaw Morgan's voice only in her imagination.

She lay still and squeezed her eyes shut. Soon it would be over, he would leave her alone, and she could cleanse herself and go back to sleep.

Words formed silently. Images flickered. "Help me,

Little Hawk," she prayed ardently. "Come quickly, my love."

The present and the past were mixed. She was puzzled. How could she expect Little Hawk to find her when she had seen him only once? For a blissful moment she relived the kiss that the beautiful boy had stolen from her. One kiss, and then for long and lonely months she prayed that he would come back, he of the sunlit hair and sky-filled eyes. She dreamed of his golden beauty, but he was nothing more than a dim and fading memory long before she saw the Morgans kill her mother and father.

How could she call on Little Hawk to save her when he was only a boy and had long since forgotten her?

A new terror caused her breath to catch in her throat. Bloodred pictures formed on the black inside of her closed lids, and she screamed as the war ax cleaved Joseph's skull.

"You are not Bearclaw Morgan," she said in a small voice.

When she opened her eyes she saw a round Indian face, and suddenly all the memories exploded into her conscious mind with a force that stunned her. She was certain that the man who was using her was the one who had ordered the death of Magnolia and her sons. His face was close to hers, his lips drawn back in the rictus of lust, and she could tell that he was near the end of his efforts. She stared at his strong, hawklike nose as he put his full weight on her and thrust harder. His face was so close she felt his fast, hot breath on her mouth. She timed her movement carefully, waiting until he went rigid and pressed deeply into her and squeezed her with his arms. His eyes were closed, and he did not see her head dart upward like that of a striking snake; into his moment of release entered swift and surprising pain.

Although she knew that it wasn't good for her, she had often cracked pecans with her teeth, and she had a very strong bite, which she now closed over the Creek's nose. She took as much of it into her mouth as she could manage and bit down with an animallike ferocity.

Calling Owl yelled and jerked his head away. Naomi's teeth slid, leaving behind deep grooves, and then locked on the soft tip of the Creek's nose and held. Calling Owl pummeled her sides with his fists. Although she could not breathe, she clung like a bulldog until her grinding teeth met and severed the tip of his nose. He aimed a blow at her, but she managed to turn her head, and the blow glanced off her shoulder. He touched his face and screamed in horror when his hand came away covered with blood.

"White witch!" he howled.

He hit her in the stomach. This time the blow landed, and she doubled up. He put his hand in her hair and lifted her head, drawing back his fist. At that moment she spat the top of his nose into his face, and the pulpy piece of flesh bounced off his cheek and fell onto the dirt. He howled again, let go of her hair, and crawled on his hands and knees to find it. Naomi scuttled away, crablike, and leaned her back against the stone wall of the cave.

Calling Owl could not find his nose. He was muttering to himself as he searched frantically in the flickering light of the fire. When he found it at last, it was covered with dirt. He cursed her as a white she-devil, all the while pushing the dirty fragment into the bleeding hole above his upper lip. It would not stay in place.

Then sanity seemed to return to him, and he stood over Naomi with his tomahawk raised.

For a few seconds she confronted death with clear eyes. Her mind accepted what was to come, for the man standing over her had killed both her sons and poor Magnolia. Gladly she would join the twins in God's place. That seemed so fitting, for they were little more than babies, and they needed a mother. She regretted leaving Little Hawk to mourn alone, but she would be with her sons. She was ready.

*   *   *

Calling Owl's muscles tensed. He shivered with his need
to smash the white bitch. The blade of his ax gleamed in
the firelight, and he cried out in frustration as he told
himself that quick death would be too merciful. He lowered the blade.

"No," he muttered. "No. That would be too easy."

With his fingertips he could feel the twin cavities of
his exposed nostrils. She had ruined his male beauty, and
as long as he lived he would be an object of scorn. No
woman would want him—and for that the colorless bitch
would suffer.

Outside the cave a late moon had risen. New Man
and the others were overdue. They should have finished
off the white man's dog and captured the white enemy
before dark, and it should not have taken them this long
to get to the place of falling waters. Something had gone
wrong. He jerked Naomi to her feet. He could see that
her eyes were once again empty and her spirit was somewhere else as he led her away from the cave by the noose
around her neck.

Little Hawk set a swift pace, for he was driven by devils.
The mutilated face of his dead son urged him on. Guilt
screamed at him, "Hurry, hurry!" Had he not been so
selfish that he was unwilling to be parted from his loved
ones, Naomi and the boys would be snug and safe at Huntington Castle with Renno and Beth.

He would not allow himself to imagine Naomi dead.
He pictured her alive, defiant but wise enough not to rile
her captors unduly. But his guilt was made more burden-
some by the knowledge of Naomi's ordeal with Bearclaw
Morgan and his moronic sons. He was responsible for her
being in a situation in which, once again, men could force
her to service them, and he prayed that he would catch up
with Calling Owl before he had inflicted still another hu-
miliation on his beloved wife.

As he was pushing his way through dense brush, he
heard Nugee fall. He did not slow, and when he emerged

from the thicket Nugee was not following. He cooed a signal and got no answer. With a muttered curse he retraced his steps and found the young Creek lying in a heap among the brush, his entire side wet with blood. The dark red stain had soaked his clothing and run all the way down his leg to fill his moccasin.

Little Hawk turned the boy so that he could feel his face. Nugee was breathing, but feebly.

"Damn you," Little Hawk whispered as he lifted the boy and carried him to a clear spot on the bank of the creek. He kindled a fire quickly, and when he lifted Nugee's tunic he saw that the wound had ruptured and was oozing blood. The bandage was soaked with it. He rinsed the cloth in the cool water of the creek, cleaned Nugee's side, and packed the wet bandage into the wound.

Time was passing, but the bleeding would not stop. He pressed on the bandage.

Nugee's eyes opened.

"Hawk." The boy's voice was weak.

"Don't move," Little Hawk said. "Why didn't you tell me you were bleeding?"

"Leave me," Nugee said weakly. "Go after your wife."

"Yes, in a minute." He kept the pressure on for what seemed like hours before the bleeding stopped. "Nugee, I am going to have to leave you here for a while."

"Yes, go."

Little Hawk gathered firewood and left it within easy reach, then covered Nugee with his blanket. He left the boy his rifle.

"When I have found my wife I'll come back for you. In the meantime, be still. The more you move the more you're likely to start bleeding again."

"When you find Calling Owl, strike one blow for me," Nugee said.

"I will."

Little Hawk found that he could make better time by

wading in the stream, although he slipped often on slick rocks. The water was cold, the night chill, but he did not feel the discomfort. His consciousness was honed to a fine point, directed toward finding Naomi and dealing violent death to Calling Owl.

Soon he heard the soft, distant sound of the falling waters and increased his pace, for the rush of the waterfall would cover his movements. Just below the falls he saw the glow of a fire in the mouth of a small cave. He moved swiftly out of the water, holding one of his pistols in his left hand, his tomahawk in his right, although he would rather have killed the Creek with his hands than with a bullet. He stormed into the cave, diving past the smoldering embers of the fire, landed on his shoulder, and rolled to a standing position.

The cave was empty. Little Hawk made a torch of dried grass and saw in the dust on the floor evidence of a struggle. He touched his finger to a wet spot and examined it. Blood. His heart hurt, for he could only believe that it was Naomi's.

Holding the torch high overhead, he tried to determine which direction Calling Owl had taken, but the grass burned down, and the flames stung his fingers. It was hopeless. Even if the Creek had left a trail it could not be followed at night. He was faced with a decision. Nugee, weak and helpless, needed care and should be taken to the nearest town, where the women could care for him and the shaman could use his healing magic. That could be done during the remaining hours of darkness.

He hurried down the stream to where Nugee lay sleeping. The fire had burned down, and Little Hawk threw deadwood on the embers for light by which to rig a travois. After quickly cutting several young trees, he lashed one blanket to them, positioning the smaller, springier ends at the rear so they would bend and make Nugee's ride more comfortable.

"I can walk," Nugee protested.

Little Hawk would not hear of it. "Is your head clear?" he asked.

"Yes."

"Tell me, then, in which direction will we find the nearest village?"

"Five or six families live together about ten miles downstream."

"And that is the closest place?"

"Yes. Hawk, leave me. Soon I will be strong enough to walk."

"You need the care of women and a shaman."

He rolled Nugee onto the travois and set out, pulling the wounded boy behind him. After an hour of hard going he struck a well-used trail that followed the stream. In the false dawn he could see groups of houses built in the typical Creek style: rectangular structures of mud mixed with straw plastered on a frame of poles and roofed with cypress bark.

A dog barked tentatively, then more frantically as it caught the scent of the newcomers. Other dogs joined in. A door opened, and a Creek armed with a rifle stepped out into the dim morning light.

"I hail you in friendship," Little Hawk called out in Creek.

The Indian turned toward the sound of his voice, holding the rifle at waist height. "Who comes?"

"I am Captain Hawk Harper, from the agency. I have a seriously wounded boy with me."

The Creek lowered his rifle and walked forward. He picked up the trailing end of the travois and guided Little Hawk to one of the larger buildings. Inside it was warm, for a fire had been kindled. A woman bustled about, clearing a space on a bed for Nugee, who was unconscious, and she shook her head when she pulled off his tunic and looked at the wound.

Little Hawk bent to see. The wound looked swollen and angry.

"Bad spirits," the woman said.

"I will fetch the shaman," the Creek man said. He returned quickly with an older man, who looked at Nugee's wound and spoke quietly to the woman. With water and a cloth the shaman cleaned the wound.

"Who did this?" the man of the house asked.

"People of the red sticks," Little Hawk said.

The shaman spat out a curse.

The man of the house said, "Young cubs who have yet to learn the horrors of war."

"Yes." Little Hawk moved to the shaman's side. "How does it look?"

"The spirits are angry."

"He is my friend," Little Hawk said, "but I must not stay. Will you care for him?"

"I will fight the spirits of evil for his soul," the shaman said.

"I will be grateful, and I will be back."

The shaman opened his medicine pouch and took out dried herbs, ground them between his thumb and forefinger, and sprinkled them on the open wound.

"You go after these red stick warriors yourself?" the man of the house asked Little Hawk.

"Yes."

"Alone?"

"You can help me by pointing me in the direction of the village of a warrior named Eneah."

"He is of the red sticks?"

"Yes."

"His home is not far. It is not really a village but a family compound, such as ours. Go with the sun toward the west on the track toward Coweta. You will find it."

"I am in your debt."

"May the Master of Breath go with you," the woman said.

Calling Owl had demonstrated that when he wanted to cover his tracks he was expert at it, so Little Hawk reasoned that it would be useless to return to the cave to try to find the trail from there. Calling Owl had traveled by night, and he could have gone in any direction. It would be more productive, Little Hawk felt, to find one of the warriors whose names New Man had given him and to ask questions phrased in such a way that an answer was guaranteed, as he had done with New Man.

At the warrior's pace he reached Eneah's village two hours after leaving Nugee with the friendly Creek families. When he was near enough to see smoke coming from holes in the roofs of the houses he slowed to a walk and approached carefully. Three young boys were outside playing warrior, and when they saw the stranger, they gave warning whoops and faded into the trees. Little Hawk walked to the central square and waited until a gray-haired Creek came out of a house. The men greeted each other politely.

"Is the white man lost?"

"The white man seeks the warrior Eneah," Little Hawk said. He held his rifle at his side, ready to lift it and bring it to bear instantly.

"Why is it the white man's business to seek Eneah?" the old man asked.

"Why do you not ask Eneah that question?" Little Hawk answered.

"This family has no quarrel with you," the old man said.

"Old father, is Eneah here?"

A stocky young warrior with both hands on his rifle stepped through the open door of a cabin. "Perhaps you care to ask Eneah a question," he said. "I am he."

"I have but one question," Little Hawk said. "Where is Calling Owl?"

Eneah laughed, but his hands tensed on his rifle.

"Perhaps, Eneah, you and I can ask each other questions in privacy," Little Hawk suggested, "so that if I am forced to kill you, no one else will be hurt."

The old man's eyes went wide. "There will be no talk of killing."

"There has already been killing, old father," Little Hawk said.

"We know nothing of this."

"Ask Eneah where he was yesterday. Ask him if he was the one who split my son's skull. Or was it one of his friends?"

The old man looked at Eneah quickly. The warrior lifted his rifle but did not point it directly at Little Hawk.

"I was here," Eneah said.

"You lie," Little Hawk said bluntly, and as he spoke he leveled his rifle at Eneah's breast. The upward swing of the warrior's rifle halted.

"I have sworn to kill all who were with Calling Owl," Little Hawk said. "I think that the Master of Life will forgive me, however, if I let you and your friends live. That I will do if you tell me where Calling Owl has taken my wife."

"What is the meaning of this, Eneah?" the old man asked.

"The whiteface lies through his teeth," Eneah said.

"Tell me, old man," Little Hawk said, "in your house does this one, this Eneah, keep a red war club?"

The old man's face became expressionless.

"So did those who killed one of my sons, hurt the other, and carried off my wife. Do you carry the red stick, as well?"

"I follow William McIntosh. This family wants no war with the whitefaces."

"And Eneah?"

Movement to his left caught Little Hawk's eye. Holding the rifle with one hand, he freed one of his pistols. A young warrior armed with a rifle leaped from behind a building. Little Hawk's pistol spoke first, but only by a fraction of a second. He fired with his right hand across his body, and his aim was true. The ball knocked the Creek backward, spoiling his shot, so that the rifle ball flew harmlessly in the air.

The old man threw up his hands and wailed. "He is

Little Fox, a friend of Eneah's. There will be no more shooting. There will be no more killing." He turned to Eneah. "Son of my brother, is it true what this whiteface says?"

"He lies," Eneah said.

The old man turned back to Little Hawk. "My women will see to the fallen one."

Little Hawk motioned, and women rushed to the wounded man and carried him into one of the houses. The old man gathered his strength and pushed his face into Eneah's. "Did you make war on women and children?"

"This whiteface, Uncle, was the one who fought beside Big Warrior when Creek brothers were killing one another. Do not believe him."

He put his face closer. "Did you make war on women and children?" he repeated.

"Not I," Eneah said weakly.

"Who?"

"Calling Owl. And others."

"Tell the whiteface captain where he can find his wife."

"I don't know," Eneah said sullenly. "We were all to meet at Calling Owl's hunting lodge four days from now."

"Is that where Calling Owl was taking my wife?" Little Hawk asked.

Eneah leered. "By the time your wife arrives at the bluff over the Chattahoochee she will have become Creek by absorption."

Little Hawk leaped forward, pushed the old man aside, and knocked the rifle out of Eneah's hand. He jammed his rifle muzzle under the Creek's chin. "Already your friend lies dead, and now you have the time it takes to draw three breaths to tell me where Calling Owl was going and by which route."

"Tell him," the old man urged.

"A day's march north of Coweta on the Chattahoochee there is a long bluff on the eastern bank. It is a place

of large trees and rocks. Calling Owl's hunting lodge is at
the northern end of the bluff overlooking the water. Perhaps he is taking her there."

"If you are lying I will come back for you," Little
Hawk said, lowering his rifle. "Old man, I beg your forgiveness for intruding into your home. I hope you can
understand that it was only because I want to find my
wife."

The old man nodded but remained silent. Little
Hawk turned his back and strode away. When he had
taken only ten steps, he heard a scuffle behind him and
whirled in time to see Eneah push the old man to the
ground and dive for his rifle.

"Don't," Little Hawk warned. But the Creek was
aiming the rifle when Little Hawk's ball took him in the
forehead.

The old man sat on the ground and began the song of
death as Little Hawk backed away into the woods. He had
killed before, but this time, after looking upon the dead
and mutilated face of his son, he had killed without feeling regret. Eight men had been in the clearing overlooking the agency. Two of them had died in the attempted
ambush—New Man and Wild Wind. Eneah and Little
Fox were the next to die. Four more were alive, and one of
them was Calling Owl.

As he ran toward the Chattahoochee river, knowing
that at least two days would pass before he reached the
bluff—and before Calling Owl could be expected to arrive
there with Naomi—he called the roll. Aside from Calling
Owl, those who were yet to die were young warriors
named Red Runner, Stone Head, and Gator Toe.

Red Runner and Gator Toe were cousins almost the same
age, twenty-one and twenty-two. Gator Toe, the elder, had
been given his name because the toes of his left foot were
connected by a web. He was a thin, rangy warrior, and
women had told him—and by their actions proved to him
—that to look upon him gave them pleasure. But both

young men were a disappointment to their families, for neither was married.

They came from a Lower Creek family in the clan of Opothie Micco, who had never been willing to live at peace with the land-greedy white man. Both had killed whitefaces before they joined Calling Owl in the raids that followed Tecumseh's visit to Tuckabatchee. Although the willful young warriors did not consider Calling Owl their leader, they were content to let him think he was, so they could go with his war party and kill more white men and women. While they had reluctantly taken part in the capture of the children from the agency, they agreed that it was necessary to kill white boys so that they would not grow up and fight against the Creek.

After the kidnapping of the white woman, Red Runner and Gator Toe traveled quickly to their village near Cusseta and sent a message to Opothie Micco that they were ready to take white scalps whenever he gave the signal. After replenishing their provisions, the two headed upriver toward their rendezvous with Calling Owl, and they waited in the appointed place for two full days before the alarmed call of a crow told them someone was approaching below the ridge.

It was indeed Calling Owl, and he had the white woman with him. A bandanna was tied over his face below his eyes.

"What happened to you?" Red Runner asked.

Calling Owl deliberately loosed the bandage and showed them his abbreviated nose. The two young warriors made faces of disgust.

"This is one more thing I owe the whitefaces," Calling Owl growled.

"Did a rifle ball strike your nose?"

"Yes," Calling Owl lied, not wanting to admit that he had lost his nose to the white woman.

"We thought you would have killed her by now," Gator Toe said, pointing at Naomi.

"No," Calling Owl said, "I have not killed the white witch yet. That will come."

Naomi sat down where she was allowed to stop and hung her head. Her corn-silk hair was loose and matted; it fell forward in pale masses and hid her bruises and blood-shot eyes.

"She is docile," Red Runner said. "Why have you brought her here?"

"Why does one bring a cow to the bull?" Calling Owl said.

"I have never hungered for white meat," Red Runner said with disdain.

"Inside it is all the same," Calling Owl said. "Hot, slick, and red."

Gator Toe laughed. "No doubt New Man will mount the white cow when he arrives." The two friends had decided not to tell Calling Owl that they had run from a bloody encounter with the white woman's husband.

Outside his hunting lodge Calling Owl tied Naomi to a tree by the rawhide noose around her neck. Her hands were bound behind her, and a length of rawhide hobbled her legs.

Gator Toe had skinned a rabbit and was roasting it slowly over the fire. To his delight Calling Owl brought out a bottle of whiskey from a hiding place under the lodge, and by nightfall Gator Toe and Red Runner were singing and dancing around the fire, their faces shiny with grease from their dinner. Now and then one of them would dance toward the woman and kick dust into her face or try to make her flinch by swinging a tomahawk so low that the blade brushed her hair.

The whiskey affected Calling Owl differently, how-ever; he became morose.

Naomi stared into the fire with unblinking eyes. It was as though she did not hear the singing and the happy drunken shouts.

"She has been blessed by the spirits," Gator Toe told Calling Owl, making the sign for madness at his temple.

"Not so," Calling Owl said. "She plays possum."

Red Runner, breathing hard, threw himself down beside Calling Owl. "You have tasted this white meat?"

"Before the Hawk dies I want him to know that his woman has given me much pleasure and that she liked it very much."

"Ha," Gator Toe said. "The woman liked it?"

"Do you call me liar?"

Gator Toe put his hand on his tomahawk. "Do you want me to call you liar?"

Calling Owl saw the defiance in the young warrior's eyes. He didn't want to kill one of his own. He laughed. "Save your fight for the enemy, young cock. If you doubt me, try her yourself. She squirms like an arrow-shot fish."

"Truly?"

"Truly."

"I will taste this white meat," Gator Toe said.

Red Runner shouted in delight, and Gator Toe loosed the thong that secured Naomi to the tree, slashed the hobble at her feet with his knife, lifted her to her feet, and carried her into the lodge.

"If I were you I would not loose her hands," Calling Owl shouted to him. His fingers touched the wound under the bandanna. "And she bites."

While Gator Toe was discovering that Calling Owl had lied, that the white woman did not fling herself about like a fish impaled by an arrow, Red Runner found more of Calling Owl's whiskey hidden in the mud and grass wall. He opened a bottle and later traded it to Gator Toe for the woman whose eyes were dead.

When the two warriors finally staggered out of the house, both were having difficulty standing.

"Where is the woman?" Calling Owl asked, leaping to his feet.

Gator Toe laughed. "You need not concern yourself with her. Not only does she not wriggle like a fish, she does not move at all."

Red Runner fell down beside the fire and immediately began to snore. Deciding that his friend had the
right idea, Gator Toe joined him as Calling Owl left the
warmth of the fire and walked into the house.

Curled into a fetal position, the remnants of her skirts
pulled down to cover her legs and feet, Naomi lay on a
bed of soiled skins.

As a young girl at the mercy of Bearclaw Morgan and
his two sons, she had developed a method of divorcing
herself from reality, and now she was deep in the dark
recesses of her mind. She lived in a white house in Virginia with loving grandparents and her mother and father.
It was a warm, snug house, and she was the spoiled dar-
ling of all the adults. Her grandfather held her on his knee
and told wonderful stories that made her giggle, and her
grandmother baked gingerbread that filled the house with
a wonderful aroma. If a nightmare dared intrude into her
sleep she was taken into her mother and father's bed to lie
warm and protected by her mother's sweet-smelling softness, and in her mind's eye she lay there now.

Lamentably, reason returned, and when she heard
someone come into the cabin, her eyes flew open and her
fist clenched the hilt of the knife she had stolen from one
of the drunks. Even though she had not fought them, she
had new bruises, but the pain helped to clear her mind.
Naomi was lucid when she recognized Calling Owl's
smell, though she could see him only dimly in the moonlight that shone through an open window.

When he jerked at her clothing she submitted pas-
sively, but her hope soared when she smelled the whiskey
and knew that he, too, was drunk. While the drink height-
ened his lust, it diminished his effectiveness, so that it was
a long and painful time before he grunted in completion.
The whiskey had driven caution from him, and he relaxed
and let his weight fall on her. Soon he was breathing
deeply and evenly.

Hate burned white-hot in her as her hand closed over the handle of the knife.

He had told her again and again that a swift death would be too merciful for her. So it would be with him. Moving slowly, she eased his weight off her, and he rolled over on his side and began to snore. She gathered the thongs that had been her bonds and lashed his hands and feet together. Satisfied with her effort, she ran to the cabin door and looked out at the moonlit clearing. The two Creek were snoring loudly beside the embers of the fire. Naomi took a tentative step out the door and made ready to flee into the woods, but suddenly she heard the sound of the ax splitting little Joseph's skull, and once more it drove reason from her.

In a senseless stupor she tiptoed across the cabin and stood over Calling Owl, then leaned down, rolled him on his back, and stuffed a dirty piece of her petticoat into his mouth. He gagged drunkenly, and his eyes flew open. He was instantly alert.

His loincloth was open, his flaccid manhood totally exposed. Frowning with concentration, Naomi seized his male member in one hand and placed the knife at the base of his scrotum.

"Wake up," she said in a flat, dead voice. "Wake up, brave warrior who kills women and children."

Calling Owl jerked against his bonds.

"Be still," she said, pressing the keen blade of the knife upward.

His breath caught, for the blade had sliced the soft skin at the base of his scrotum.

"You are awake," she said simply.

He made a sound that was a combination of hate and sheer terror.

"You told me, back in the cave, that I was not to die quickly. You said that would be too merciful for me."

"Gaaaa," Calling Owl said, for there was nothing he could do but struggle frantically against his bonds.

"Now it is you who will die slowly." She smiled.

Holding his genitals tightly in her left hand, she pulled hard, and as if she were cutting off a slab of bacon, sawed the sharp blade back and forth, keeping the blade close to his pelvis.

Calling Owl strangled on his scream of agony and panic. He thrashed on the bed, lifting and falling, but Naomi's firm grip held him until, as the knife blade overcame the last resistance, she held a bleeding, pulpy mass in her hand.

She removed the piece of cloth from his mouth, and Calling Owl bellowed hoarsely. When he fully realized what had happened, the sound became more shrill.

"Scream," she said sweetly. "You gave my sons no chance to scream."

He bleated like a gutshot sheep.

"I have something for you," she said, leaning over him.

Calling Owl's open mouth was suddenly filled with a softness. He did not want to believe it, for he had done the same thing more than once to the white enemy. He had done it because in his mind it was the most demeaning thing that could happen to a man. Now it was he who lay with his genitals stuffed into his mouth. His mind went red with madness and pain, and he made a sound like a mewling infant.

But the worst of it was the knowledge that what the white witch had done could never be undone. He had known pain before; pain could be endured and overcome. The reality of his loss was the ultimate affliction. Desperation generated a surge of superhuman strength in him, and the rawhide thong on his hands parted. He seized the emasculating white witch by the throat and slowly tightened his grip.

With sadness Naomi realized that she had erred. As his hands closed off her breath she prayed for forgiveness, thrust the knife forward with all her strength, and felt it bury itself in his stomach.

Calling Owl's reaction surprised him. He welcomed the blade. Death was preferable to life as half a man. He knew as the heat and agony penetrated to the depths of his gut that she had struck a fatal blow. His death would be slow and agonizing, but he would take the white witch with him. All the demon spirits in the afterworld would not pry his hands from her throat. He summoned his failing strength and squeezed.

Naomi twisted the blade, and it pleased her when she heard the murderer groan in pain, but she couldn't breathe and was growing weak. She tried to pull the knife from his body, thinking to slash at his hands and arms to free herself from his grasp, but her hand slipped from the bloody haft of the weapon.

She struggled, but his hands were like a vise, and she heard a sound in her throat like stiff paper being crushed. When Calling Owl's hands finally fell away, she could not breathe; his last exertion had crushed her larynx. Naomi's world softened, and she saw the faces of all those who were dear to her. Beth was there, and Renno. Her dead grandparents smiled at her, and her mother held out her arms while her father smiled. Her two sons were there with the golden-haired, sky-eyed boy who had come to free her from the Morgans.

No longer able to see the beams of moonlight coming in the window and the door, she sat down heavily on the bed at the feet of the dying Creek.

"My love," she tried to whisper when Little Hawk's face appeared to her, though no sound passed her blocked throat. Fighting to the last to stay, to await his coming, her lungs began to spasm, but she no longer felt anything. Her pale, corn-silk hair fell across Calling Owl's bloody, mutilated crotch, but neither of them was aware of the contact.

Chapter Fourteen

The garrison at Vincennes and the old post at Fort Knox, just north of town, echoed to the sounds of military preparation. A summer of alarms and rumors was culminating in a gathering of forces, and public meetings were being held throughout the northwestern territories and in Ohio, Kentucky, and Tennessee. Self-appointed orators mounted the stump. Would-be statesmen in Kentucky called for a unilateral invasion of Canada to punish the British for giving arms and supplies to the horde of Indians massed north of beleaguered Vincennes. The governor of Illinois Territory insisted that partial war would go on as long as the Indians were permitted to congregate. Governor William Clark of the Missouri Territory warned of a fast-approaching crisis.

The mood of the west had been clearly demonstrated with the election of the War Hawks, who unseated almost fifty percent of the incumbent congressmen. William Henry Harrison, governor of Indiana Territory, was in consensus with those who wanted to end the crisis by striking preemptive blows at all enemies, English and Indian.

Harrison had had a busy summer. In late August he rode up the Ohio to Jeffersonville to meet the Fourth Regiment of regulars. He traveled with a small party that included Lieutenant Stockton O'Toole and Ta-na.

"Well, Thomas," Harrison said as the little group rode northeastward, "if it comes to war we shall have no shortage of willing volunteers." He smiled wryly. "Perhaps too many. I have received a letter from Major Joseph Hamilton Daveiss, the district attorney of Kentucky. Your father would remember him from Fallen Timbers. Although I have turned down several offers of infantry from the Kentuckians, I have accepted Major Daveiss, and at this time he is on his way to Vincennes with a force of men as eager to seek military glory as he."

"So," Ta-na said.

"Kentucky is also sending a small force of mounted riflemen under Captain Peter Funk of Louisville." Harrison was silent for a while. When he spoke again his brow was furrowed. "You know, Thomas, they don't quite understand the situation in Washington. Secretary of War Eustis tells me that I should need only four companies of militia in addition to the regulars. Now, you tell me if it would be prudent to penetrate the Prophet's backyard with one regiment of regulars and four companies of militia."

Since it was a direct question, Ta-na answered. "Sir, if you march on Prophetstown you must be assured not only of victory but of overwhelming victory. Anything short of that would serve Tecumseh's cause. It would make the bond of confederation stronger among the tribes that support him, and it would bring others into the confederation."

"Exactly," Harrison said.

On the way up the river in keelboats, the governor conferred with militia officers. He had already notified all units that the Indiana Territory militia would be fully mobilized, even though his plan had not been approved by the secretary of war. When the Fourth Regiment of regulars arrived at Jeffersonville, their condition reinforced his intention to utilize the militia. Of the six hundred men who had started the long journey down the Ohio, only four hundred were fit for duty. Desertion had thinned the ranks, and sickness had taken a heavy toll. Moreover, the low water of the Ohio could further delay the arrival of the weakened regiment at Vincennes.

Harrison's party left the ten keelboats to continue down the river and rode overland to Vincennes. There he solidified his plans to use twelve to fourteen companies of militia infantry with sixty to seventy men in each unit. Vincennes and surrounding Knox County raised three hundred fifty militia and eighty mounted dragoons. The Kentuckians under Major Daveiss and Captain Funk arrived. Day by day the force grew, drill sergeants bawled out their orders, and men marched and wheeled on the parade ground.

After a grueling one-hundred-sixty-mile journey along the relatively shallow Wabash, the Fourth Regiment arrived. The men were exhausted, for in order to reach their destination on a river filled with rocks and sandbars, they had hauled the keelboats by cordelle, wading in the chilly water and pulling the vessels against the swift current.

Ta-na watched the keelboats arrive. Eager to make a good impression, the officers of the Fourth marched the neatly uniformed regulars off the boats in parade-ground order, only to be greeted with the wild whoops and derisive yells of a mob of motley frontiersmen dressed in deerskin shirts and trousers and bearskin caps. Drums pounded a tattoo. Flags fluttered in the breeze. The militiamen brandished tomahawks, knives, and hatchets.

On the big prairie north of Vincennes, Harrison

drilled his army. He instructed his subordinate officers in the methods of turning their commands quickly to the right or left to meet a flank attack, and he moved them in two long, thin columns just as General Mad Anthony Wayne had during the war against Little Turtle.

When Harrison staged a sham battle, Ta-na sat watching on his horse, one leg thrown around the saddle horn, and shook his head. When they galloped up and down the prairie, the mounted riflemen made splendid targets for any Indian standing behind a tree, and the infantry companies deployed in the woods sounded like a herd of stampeding buffalo.

Ta-na turned his head sharply when he heard the coo of a dove from the trees behind him. He waited, and the call was repeated. Leaving his horse secured to a bush, he entered the forest, and when Gao stepped from concealment, Ta-na rushed to embraced him.

"Are you so blind, brother, that you do not see an army around you?" Ta-na asked, speaking in Seneca.

"Whiteface soldiers have two eyes, but they see only what they want to see," Gao said with a grin.

"You are well?"

"I am well, brother." His grin widened. "I have a wife."

"Ah."

"Mist-on-the-Water."

"And yet you do not look unhappy," Ta-na teased, matching his cousin's grin.

"Not all girls are like Head-in-the-Cloud," Gao said.

Ta-na became serious. "You should not be here. If someone sees you they will shoot you as a spy for Tecumseh."

"But that is what I am," Gao said.

"Then I think you must go now."

"Brother," Gao pressed, "we have made no threat. Our warriors have not moved toward Vincennes. Why, then, is Governor Harrison preparing for war?"

"Because once too often Indians raided to the south and stole horses."

"Ah," Gao said, feeling a twinge of guilt.

"There was a raid on a wedding party, among which were several members of the garrison and two dispatch bearers," Ta-na said. "When the horses were returned to their owners by the Prophet, a war party took the animals back at gunpoint."

"Is there to be war because I kept my promise to give the bride-price to the uncle of Mist-on-the-Water?"

"It was you?" Ta-na asked.

Gao nodded grimly.

Ta-na threw back his head and laughed at the irony, but the danger of the situation cut short his amusement. "Brother, should we leave all this now, while we can? Should we fetch your bride and take ourselves to the south as quickly as possible?"

"For the first time in my life I am sure that I am right," Gao said. "I could not and will not abandon a cause which heats my blood like life itself. I know where my loyalty lies. It is you, brother, who fight the wrong enemy."

"It has come to that, then?"

"All Indians are of one blood," Gao said earnestly. "It was created so by the Master of Life, who, though called different names by different tribes, made the common ancestors of us all. I will never again shed the blood of my brothers."

"There is still time to avoid war," Ta-na contended. "Messages have been sent by General Harrison that if the horses are returned and certain Indian murderers delivered to us, he will not march. Go, Gao, and repeat this offer to Tecumseh."

"The Panther Passing Across is not with us."

"To Tenskwatawa, then." Questions arose in Ta-na's mind. "How is it that you are now a spy for the Prophet? How is it that he did not kill you on sight?"

"Brother, that is a long story, a tale for a winter's night when the fire burns warmly."

"So."

"I think, brother," Gao said, pointing toward the open field where a troop of dragoons was charging toward them, "that it is time for me to go."

"May the Master of Life go with you," Ta-na said.

"Whatever befalls," Gao pledged, his eyes glistening suspiciously, "my weapons will not be pointed at you."

"Nor mine at you, brother of my heart."

Trailing a herd of cattle and hogs for food, the army moved up the Wabash toward Prophetstown. It was slow going—twelve miles was a good day's march. Ta-na, on foot in order to move in silence, was ahead of the advance guard. Governor Harrison rode at the forefront of the troops. He wore a fringed, calico hunting shirt, and a long ostrich feather protruded from his beaver hat. Indoor living had sallowed his skin, but his dark eyes were alert in his long, slender face.

Several days later, sixty-five miles north of Vincennes, the army paused where a sharp bend in the river allowed a good view in both directions. There were oak and honey locust trees in abundance for use as building materials and firewood. There was also a field of corn that Harrison had ordered planted in the spring, on Ta-na's advice, after the site for the fort had been selected. The corn had been browned by frost, but the stalks were laden with ears.

Ta-na found Harrison sitting on the ground with his back against an oak tree. Men were already at work clearing the site.

"Well, Thomas," Harrison said, "I have noticed that we have not arrived at this place unescorted."

"It is Shabonee, the Potawatomi who follows Tecumseh, who shadows us," Ta-na said.

"The Potawatomi."

"Yes, sir."

"With how many?"

"Only a few. Thirty, no more."

"Just keeping an eye on us?"

"He desires council with you."

"Arrange it," Harrison said.

Ta-na turned to go.

"Thomas?"

Ta-na looked back.

"This is a fine place."

"Yes, sir."

"You were not the first to see its tactical value."

"Sir?"

"You don't know the history of the area?"

"I know what the Wea Indians say. Their village, Weautano, is nearby."

"It is also called Orchard Town," Harrison said, "because of the fruit trees. But before the Wea were here, about a hundred years ago, the French called this the place of the *Bataille des Illinois*. There was a rather fierce little war here. Several tribes who lived along the Mississippi fought tribes of the Wabash. The fight went on for God only knows how long. For days, surely. When it was over only a few warriors were alive. Legends say that hundreds died."

Ta-na shifted uneasily. He knew why, when he was first scouting for a spot to build Harrison's support fort, he had moved his camp in the middle of the night away from the high banks from which the river could be seen both upstream and downstream. The earth upon which he had lain had once been soaked with the blood of warriors. Their spirits haunted the place, calling out to the dead, only to be heard by the living.

"Bring Shabonee to me," Harrison said. "It would please me if we could avoid bloodshed like that of a century ago."

Apparently wanting it known that he and his small band of warriors, not all of them Potawatomi, were keeping a wary eye on Harrison's army, Chief Shabonee made only a token attempt at concealment. He was camped for the night not a half mile away, just beyond the perimeter of Harrison's pickets. He welcomed Ta-na with grave courtesy, and after traditional greetings Ta-na told him that General Harrison had agreed to his request for council.

"If you will follow me, great chief," Ta-na said, "I will take you to the general."

Shabonee walked at Ta-na's side, with four of his warriors bringing up the rear.

Harrison's tent had been set up, and he was seated in a camp chair by a freshly kindled fire. Ta-na squatted by the blaze, for the evening was chilly.

"We have heard your words," Shabonee told Harrison. "Perhaps there is some justice on your side, but you give us not enough time to comply with your demand that the horses be returned. It will take a while for us to find which of our high-spirited young ones played this prank on you."

"Shabonee," Harrison said, "why, when my request for justice was delivered to you, did you not return to your village immediately to pass along to Tenskwatawa my desire for peace?"

"Why do you post such a strong guard at night for your army?" Shabonee countered. "Do you distrust us so much?"

"I ask you, Chief, to go to Prophetstown immediately. Tell Tenskwatawa that neither I nor the Great White Father in Washington wants war. Tell the Prophet of our willingness to treat, and then return to me with a delegation to discuss our differences."

"We, too, are willing to treat," Shabonee said. "I will go."

"Tell Tenskwatawa," Harrison said, "that the distance this army will advance depends on his conduct. If he truly wants peace—if he will come to me and speak the truth about his intentions—then we will go no farther. It is up to him."

Watching the Potawatomi proudly walk away, Harrison sighed. "What will he do, Thomas? Find out if you can."

It was growing dark when Ta-na quietly approached the Potawatomi's camp. The chief was apparently preparing to move, and Ta-na followed as he and his warriors rode slowly northward toward Prophetstown. When they were well away from the army camp, they turned to the east.

"Headed toward Illinois, is he?" Harrison asked, when Ta-na reported shortly before midnight. "Why, do you think?"

"My guess, sir, is that he goes into Illinois to recruit more warriors," Ta-na said.

"So somewhere along the Wabash," Harrison said grimly, "we will select a spot, perhaps a place as beautiful as this, where a great battle was fought. And we will again soak the earth with the blood of men both white and red."

When Ta-na retired for the night, Harrison's gloomy words were still echoing in his mind. As soon as he had wrapped himself in warm blankets and closed his eyes, his lids sprang open, for in his imagination he heard the sounds of battle, the shrill whoops of belligerency, the moans and cries of the wounded, and his nose crinkled to the smells of death. He closed his eyes again and whispered a prayer to the Master of Life, a plea not for himself but for Gao and his new wife and for the men, white and red, who would once more dance to the siren song of the demons of war.

At Huntington Castle Ah-wen-ga, six-year-old daughter of El-i-chi and Ah-wa-o, was filled with maternal fear for her little brother as she stood under one of the pecan trees that lined the long drive leading up to the house.

"Ha-ace," she scolded, "you are not a squirrel, and that is not the way to gather pecans."

Four-year-old Ha-ace swayed on a thin branch a full twenty feet off the ground.

"You knock the nuts from the tree with a long stick," Ah-wen-ga explained. "Now, you come down here this instant."

"You come up here," Ha-ace teased. "But girls can't climb."

"Ha." Ah-wen-ga leaped to a low fork and climbed to a branch near her brother. They sat looking down on the activity.

Up and down the lane, boys and girls from Rusog's Town, the Seneca-Cherokee village, were flailing the trees and picking up the bounty of the season from the dry grass.

One of the older boys had been entrusted with a wagon drawn by a brace of Beth's horses, and he drove up and down the lane gathering gunnysacks full of nuts and loading them into the wagon. The harvest would be shared by all.

Beth, who was supervising, was dressed in a calico work dress. Her flame hair showed isolated strands of silver, and the sun wrinkles around her eyes tattled of her forty-five years. She was walking slowly when she spotted Renno coming down the lane from the house. As she waited, she noted that he was dressed for the woods and that he carried his hunting weapons and a knapsack of provisions. For at least three days he'd been showing signs of restlessness. More than once she had awakened in the night to find him missing from her side, only to see him standing at the window looking out into the night. She knew the signs and was not surprised to see him prepared for a hunting trip.

"With such a work force," he said, "you should have the job done quickly."

She smiled at him. His blue eyes had the look of eagles, the look of a young warrior, not that of a mature, forty-seven-year-old man.

"How long will you be gone?" she asked.

He shrugged. "That decision will be made by my brother the deer."

"So," she said, smiling to show that she was teasing him. "Do you go alone?"

He nodded.

"A kiss, then," she said.

"With this audience?"

"Ah, still the prude," she said, lifting herself to put her lips on his.

A young boy yelled, and there were giggles. Beth hugged her husband, then turned to the young ones. "Hush," she said in Cherokee, "or when we bake the nut pies you will have none."

In Rusog's Town Renno found his brother, the shaman El-i-chi, sitting with Roy Johnson and a group of senior warriors in the common near the longhouse that had been the home of his mother, Toshabe. Formal greetings were exchanged. Although El-i-chi had assumed the duties of chief when Renno gave up the position, Renno was still afforded the honors of sachem of the Seneca. When the ritual small talk was over, Renno motioned to his brother, and El-i-chi walked by his side toward the northern edge of the village.

"You hunt alone?" El-i-chi asked.

"I would welcome your company."

"But you'd prefer that I stay."

Renno laughed. "You read me like a book, brother."

"Well, I've known you for not a few years." He looked at Renno with his head cocked. "There is something?"

They had been conversing in English, in the accent of the British upper class, but now Renno switched to Seneca. "I know not what, brother, but it gnaws at me as the beaver chews at a tree."

"For three nights running, an owl has perched in that tall cottonwood tree near my cabin," El-i-chi said.

A shiver ran up Renno's spine. He laughed to show himself that he was not superstitious. "But we do not believe in the old myths, brother."

"And yet it gnaws at you."

"I have felt the presence of the spirits," Renno said softly. "It is as if I hear the beating of the wings of the bird of death and hear his voice and know not for whom he calls."

"Then you do want to be alone."

"Yes, my brother."

Once clear of the village, Renno increased his stride to the warrior's pace. He circled to the south and by nightfall was a full twenty miles from Rusog's Town. He could not count the times he had made camp in a declivity under a rocky ridge where the overhang would protect him from unexpected weather. Nor could he recall how often he had performed the ritual of fire building and bed making, but he knew that he was at home in the wilderness, more than he was in the luxurious house that Beth had built.

He sat with his back against the rock, a blanket over his legs. Eating and drinking nothing, he soon fell asleep but awoke again and listened to the night sounds. He kept the fire going, and when a cool dawn broke, he walked away from the camp and emptied his bladder. Then he sat cross-legged by the fire, gazing into the embers. Hunger nagged at him briefly as the day passed but was banished by the force of his will.

In the dark of night the manitou came to him. He sensed its presence in the air around him. It was charged with— something—an awareness. Soon he saw a familiar face, the gleam of pale hair and eyes that had once gazed on his face in love.

Emily.

The manitou looked at him for a long, long time, and her beautiful eyes brimmed with tears.

"I know," he said softly. "I know. But who?"

The manitou put her hands to her face, and her body shook with sobs. There was no answer.

"Who, my first love, who?" Renno asked. "Is it

time?" But even as he asked he knew that the manitou did not weep for him.

There was no answer.

The night closed in. The feeling of a presence was no more. Very much alone and far from his Beth, fear for her leaped into his mind. He rose and moved carefully through the darkness, for clouds had come in from the west and blotted out the moon and stars.

Running the last few miles in the dawn, he arrived at Huntington Castle to find Beth asleep in their bed. He stood in the doorway and looked at her long, flame hair spread out over her pillow.

As if she sensed his presence, she moved one hand, opened her eyes, and sat up startled, for she had not expected to see him for at least two days.

"You're back," she said sleepily.

"Yes." He waited.

She smiled, and he knew that the manitou had wept for someone who was absent—for one of his own who was far away. Mentally he called the roll: Little Hawk, Naomi, and the twins; Ta-na and Gao; Ena's Ho-ya and We-yo; Renna and her children in France.

"Come to me," Beth commanded, holding out her arms.

He walked to the side of the bed.

"It would be more comfortable for both of us if you put aside your weapons," she teased.

Who? he was thinking. Who, who, who? But that was what the owl said, the owl that had sat in the cottonwood tree near El-i-chi's cabin, or the owl that had been calling out his omen of death near Huntington Castle for the same three nights.

Beth's arms were warm and her lips tasted of sleep. Her kiss pushed his fear to the back of his mind as she drew him down beside her and began to loosen his clothing.

* * *

At the first light of dawn, death hovered over a riverside ridge in the Creek Nation. A solitary turkey buzzard circled low. Although not even the bird's sharp eyes could see through the bark roof of Calling Owl's hunting lodge, there was a message in the air, a scent that was unmistakable to a creature whose life depended on death.

The buzzard soared higher, alarmed by movement on the southern end of the ridge. A man crept silently through the trees, climbing toward the small clearing in front of the lodge where Gator Toe and Red Runner sprawled in drunken slumber.

The smell of the fire was now nothing more than smoking ashes, and its smell carried to Little Hawk and prompted even more caution. He fought every instinct to rush up the slope, burst into the clearing, and shout Naomi's name.

Waiting motionless behind a tree, he noted the closed door of the lodge and closely watched the chest movements of the warriors sleeping beside the fire. Surprise, he felt, was essential. He did not want to give Naomi's captors the chance to kill her when they discovered that they had been found. He sniffed the morning air. The Creek Indians sleeping beside the fire had been drinking, but the fumes were stale and acid. He took his tomahawk from his sash and moved forward in a gliding, swift run.

Little Hawk felt no mercy, for he had seen the damage done to his son's face by the carrion eaters. He did not aim for the skull. The impact of iron blade on bone made too much noise, so he slashed across the exposed throat of one of the Indians. Blood spurted into the air. Before the dying warrior's eyes opened and his legs began to move in random jerks, Little Hawk smashed the back of the other sleeper's head with his blade.

Seeing no one else around the outside of the cabin, he ran to the door and for long seconds stood there listening. He heard nothing. Nothing. He eased the door open. The interior of the lodge was in shadow, but he saw the pale gleam of Naomi's hair, and his heart leaped in gladness. When his eyes adjusted to the darkness he could see the shape of her. She lay on her side, her head pillowed on something.

The packed earth floor was firm under his feet. He made no sound but lifted his tomahawk and jumped to the side of the bed. There he froze, weapon raised and ready to deliver a death blow that was no longer necessary.

Bile surged into his throat and made it ache. His eyes burned, and he could not catch his breath. No rifle ball, no blade, no intrusion of weapon into the tender tissue of his body could have caused more pain. He heard a thin steady sound, and it was many seconds before he realized that it was he who was emitting the moaning cry.

He lifted her and cursed when he saw her hair matted with blood. Taking a tanned deer hide from the bed, he tried to wipe the dried blood away, all the while moaning softly, making a sound like a hurt puppy. Naomi's eyes were open, and there were livid bruises at her throat. Little Hawk stood and held her with one arm around her waist, one hand at the back of her head.

"No," he said. "No, not you, too."

With tears in his eyes and an unbearable ache in his heart, he looked out a hole in the roof through which he could see the blue morning sky. His throat hurt as he chanted a Seneca song of mourning.

His eyes burned and his tears had formed rivulets down his face when he finally stopped his incantations. Looking out the door, he noticed that the vultures were circling low. One by one they set their wings and arrowed down to feast on the two dead men who lay beside the ashes of the fire. The smell of fresh blood took them first to Gator Toe, and they plucked tentatively at the raw wound that had opened the warrior's throat.

In a moment of unwelcome sanity, Little Hawk looked at the rumpled bed. A storm of fierce satisfaction filled him when he realized the meaning of the bloody mass that had been thrust into Calling Owl's mouth. He also noted the knife buried in the Creek's stomach, and he was filled with pride for his wife, who had acted as a warrior woman and taken her tormentor to death with her. But pride was quickly replaced by revulsion and anger when he realized the source of the blood that made Naomi's hair a clotted, sodden mass. He carried her outside into the sunlight and placed her tenderly on the ground away from the vultures. With shaking fingertips he closed her eyes and, taking a waterskin from a peg by the door, rinsed the blood from her matted hair. He dried it as best he could with a blanket from inside the lodge.

Many times he had watched her wash and dry her hair and brush it until it glistened like white gold. Now, as the sun climbed higher in the sky, he held her head in the crook of his arm and fluffed her hair with his fingers to finish the drying process. He arranged her torn and soiled skirts and unconsciously lifted his face once again to the sky to sing the Seneca songs of loss and anguish.

The squawking and fluttering of the birds penetrated his lonely grief. Black, undulating mounds of them surrounded the two men he had killed. It was right, he thought, for they had left Joseph and the slave girl to the carrion eaters.

"Yes," he said, nodding vigorously. He kissed Naomi's dead forehead. "Wait here, my love. I have something to do."

He lowered her gently to the ground, then went into the lodge. He dragged Calling Owl by his feet off the bed. The dead Creek's head struck the hard-packed earth with a thud.

"Don't be frightened, brothers," he said to the buzzards as he brought Calling Owl to join the others at the scavengers' dining table.

A few of the birds took flight, but others only waddled to a safe distance and waited. Little Hawk left Calling Owl lying five feet from his companions and smiled in grim satisfaction when he observed that the birds had already altered the faces of his enemies. He backed away.

One brave bird hopped to the new source of abundance and with one swift, darting movement of its ugly neck plucked a delicious morsel from the dead man's mouth. Another envious bird contested the coup, but the first bird flapped away, held his treat down with one claw, and tore at it eagerly.

Little Hawk lifted Naomi into his lap again. "You see," he told her. "That is the fate to which they left our son. Now it is theirs."

The hours passed. The sun reached its zenith, and began its slow plunge toward the west, and sank into a dark, rising bank of clouds. The temperature dropped as the clouds moved on, covering half the sky. A chill wind arose, and Little Hawk held Naomi closer so that she would not be cold. He closed his eyes and sang happy songs to her, the songs that Seneca children sang during the time of the new beginning.

As darkness approached, one by one the birds abandoned their banquet. Many of them were so full they had to struggle into the air after a long takeoff run. One engorged bird crashed into a treetop and fell, flapping and squawking through the branches, to the earth and lay still for a long time before struggling to its feet.

"We will need a fire," Little Hawk told Naomi. He considered taking her inside the lodge but could not bring himself to go into the room where he had seen her lying with her head resting on the Creek's bloody crotch. He covered her with the blanket and gathered more wood. Soon there was a blaze. Taking her in his arms once again, he held her and pulled the blanket snugly over her lower body. He had placed a good supply of wood within easy reach, and while the threatening storm had not yet materialized, the sky was dark with the clouds, and there was a smell of wet earth in the air.

The first drops of rain sizzled in the fire, but Little Hawk was oblivious. He stared into the flames and spoke softly, recalling for Naomi the first time he had seen her, how he had felt when she gave him his first kiss. The fire burned low. The heavy rain held off. With his throat aching and his eyes stinging with tears, he told her about Joseph and Magnolia, and about Michael, who was being tended by Lavinia.

He fell silent. When he first heard his name being spoken in Seneca, he didn't open his eyes.

His name was repeated in a deep, resonant voice. "Os-sweh-ga-da-ah Ne-wa-ah."

Little Hawk opened his eyes and was not surprised to see a squat, thick-chested Seneca dressed in the full regalia of a chief.

"Os-sweh-ga-da-ah Ne-wa-ah," the manitou said softly.

"I will no longer be called by that name," Little Hawk said.

"So you have forsaken your heritage."

"My heritage, as you call it, is shared by savages, and I *will* abandon it."

"And yet, in your grief, you sing to the Master of Life in the tongue of your fathers."

"You are Ghonka," Little Hawk said.

"It is so. Os-sweh-ga-da-ah Ne-wa-ah, your woman is dead."

"No."

"You have a son."

"My son is dead."

"One son lives," the manitou affirmed.

"Leave me." Little Hawk held Naomi closer. "I rebuke you. I cast off everything that you stand for. I am Harper."

"You are what you are," the manitou said. "You are Harper because that was the name of the boy I took from the arms of the dead white woman who was his mother. I took him as my own to replace my son who had journeyed over the river before his time. The skin of my new son was pale, more so than yours, Os-sweh-ga-da-ah Ne-wa-ah, but he was Seneca, as are you."

"No, no longer," Little Hawk repeated hoarsely.

"Now you reject the red blood of your fathers," the manitou said, "the blood that marks you as a child of the Master of Life. But hear me, son of my sons: There will come a time when you will hate that which is white in you with an even more intense passion."

"My name is Captain Hawk Harper," Little Hawk whispered.

The wind moaned around the lodge and made the tops of the trees sigh a song of the coming winter. With one hand, Little Hawk added fresh wood to the fire, then put his arm around Naomi and rocked back and forth, holding her tightly to his breast.

"Little Hawk. Son."

At the sound of the voice his eyes flew open. The fire flared up. His eyes filled with tears, for his mother's face was exactly as he remembered it, her pale hair so beautiful, her eyes so filled with love for him.

"You have a son," the manitou said.

"You? But you are not—"

"I married your father. In my heart I am Seneca," said the voice of his mother.

She seemed insubstantial. Her form wavered and faded in the flickering flames of the fire.

"You have a son. You must go to him. She is dead, the woman you loved, she who gave birth to both the son who is dead and the one who lives and needs his father."

"Oh, God," Little Hawk said, the words choking in his throat. "Oh, my God."

"By the river you will find a fallen cypress tree," the manitou said. "You will know what to do."

"Please," Little Hawk said as the manitou faded. His lips formed the word, but there was no sound. "Mother."

By the light of dawn he covered Naomi's body with the blanket and weighed it down with stones to keep the birds away. He went down the slope to the river and used his tomahawk and his knife to peel bark from the fallen cypress, working carefully so that when he finished he had a six-foot length of bark that could be closed into a tubular form.

The birds had arrived for breakfast when he returned to the clearing. "Eat well, brothers," he spat.

He dug Naomi's grave about a hundred yards from the lodge on the highest point of the ridge. Through the trees to the west was a view of the river and to the east the meadow below. He wrapped her in the blanket and encased her in the cypress bark in the manner of his Seneca ancestors. He lowered her gently into the grave, covered her over with small stones to prevent exhumation by digging animals, filled the grave, and covered it with larger stones. There was no marker, but the spot would be forever engraved on his heart.

Little Hawk knelt beside the stone-covered mound and sang one final song of the dead. He began the chant reluctantly, still rebelling against all things Indian, against the senseless barbarity of those who had killed his son, his love, and his heart, but as he sang his voice lifted and soared strongly into the sky.

"Manitous," he whispered. "Forgive me. Spirit of my mother, you who were Seneca in your heart, hear me. I am who I am, and for that I am thankful. I have avenged Naomi's death—seven of her murderers lie dead—and I will kill no more."

He stayed beside the grave until a small rain misted down and beaded on his buckskins, then said one final good-bye.

In the clearing the birds had exposed the bones of his Creek enemy. New, hungry guests were arriving to squabble with the others over the diminishing feast. Little Hawk had one final act to perform. He gathered embers from his fire and dumped them onto the bed inside the lodge, then added dry grass and fanned the embers until a flame flickered and grew. Back outside, he waited until the flames reached the bark roof. As he crossed the meadow to the east he could see a column of smoke marking the site of the burning lodge.

The rain fell steadily, lightly. He called out one more farewell, an undulating paean of grief in the language of Ghonka, then turned his face away and ran until his lungs burned fire. The spirit of his fathers surged up in him and gave him new strength.

The words of the manitous rang in his ears. "You have a son."

Chapter Fifteen

Gao and Mist-on-the-Water lay entwined. The wegiwa was warming slowly, for he had risen to kindle the fire from coals kept hot by insulating ashes. Mist clung to him sleepily, but he knew that his teasing touches and his lips on hers were awakening the woman in her. A brittle, brilliant sun sent rays arrowing through the roof hole to be outlined by rising smoke. The smell of burning wood was pleasantly familiar.

"Greedy, you are," Mist whispered as Gao's hand sought the heated softness between her legs.

"Of this greed I am not ashamed," he said, his lips brushing hers.

There was a magic about her, a thrilling newness of which he never tired. That she was his own and that she was as eager as he to bond together in love was life's greatest miracle. He liked best to make love in the morning while her mouth tasted of sleep and her body retained the warmth of their cozy bed. When he heard Main Poche's voice at the door he groaned in frustration.

"Nephew."

"I hear."

"The Prophet has called a grand council."

"I hear, Uncle."

Mist clung to him, giggling when he tried to leave her. "I will not let you go."

"I will be there, Uncle," Gao called.

She positioned him skillfully, and in the never-ending wonder of becoming one with her he forgot everything but the tender young love in his arms.

His knees still wobbly from a night and morning of passion, Gao ran through the village to the Prophet's medicine house and stood at the back of a growing group of warriors. Tenskwatawa was wearing his most impressive regalia, and a red pebble glared from his eye socket. Gao gathered that he had said nothing of importance as yet, for he was reaching for the sky with his hands while chanting a prayer to the Shawnee god.

"The whitefaces have built a redoubt, which they are calling Fort Harrison," the Prophet said when he had finished his prayer. "I fear that they plan to use this fort as a support base for a march on our town."

The gathered warriors muttered in anger and threat.

"If the whiteface army marches up the Wabash we will have no choice but to stop it. We will throw ourselves on these invaders and destroy them."

A great shout went up.

"Tenskwatawa," said a warrior from the front of the gathering, "we are few."

A buzz of protest came from the crowd. Gao managed to get a look at the warrior who had voiced the mild dissent. It was Wasegoboah, Stand Firm, an old compatriot of Tecumseh's.

"The bulk of our strength is missing!" Wasegoboah shouted. "In the absence of the Panther Passing Across, most of our warriors have gone home to their families. We could muster no more than three hundred and fifty men for this fight."

"Hear me," Tenskwatawa said, his anger apparent in his shrill voice. "Remember what happens to traitors, Wasegoboah. Remember the price paid by Leatherlips for his cowardice."

"No man accuses me of being a coward," Wasegoboah said. "If Tecumseh were here he would say that Wasegoboah has been at his side since he was a boy."

"Traitor!" someone shouted, and others took up the cry.

Wasegoboah would have faced any of them man to man, even Tenskwatawa, but he was wise enough to know that those who had remained at Prophetstown were fanatic followers of the man who stood before them. He lowered his head and was silent.

Gao's heart went out to him, for he knew the warrior to be stout of heart and unwavering in his loyalty to Tecumseh. Main Poche looked back and caught Gao's eye, shaking his head with a small, quick movement to warn Gao to remain silent.

"Hear me," the Prophet cried in his shrill, grating voice. "Moneto has spoken to me. He has said—mark this well—that we have no reason to fear the whitefaces. If we are forced to attack in order to protect our town, bullets will pass through us without harm. Fear not, for my spirit will be with you. I will direct you. And we will never stay our blows until the last whiteface is dead."

Gao lingered until Main Poche had finished conferring with the other war chiefs. He walked beside his uncle-by-marriage.

"He will fight," Gao said.

Main Poche nodded sadly.

"Uncle," Gao said in a quiet, serious voice, "I have told you that my cousin, the son of my uncle, is with Governor Harrison."

"Yes."

"I will have no part in this fight, lest by some design of the evil spirits my blow should fall on my brother."

"That is your right," Main Poche said. "I will not fault you for that."

"You are wise and generous, Uncle," Gao said.

Sergeant Jeb Martin sat playing cards with three of his men in front of his tent. He had just returned from leading a patrol northward along the riverbank, where he had seen Indian sign, and then reporting as much to his immediate superior, Lieutenant Stockton O'Toole. Martin looked up as two Delaware scouts sauntered arrogantly toward the makeshift card table.

"Injuns," Martin growled.

"These Delawares ain't too bad," said one of the players.

"They're Injuns." Martin spat in contempt as the two scouts paused to watch the play.

"How goes it?" one of the card players asked.

"It does not go well," one of the scouts said. "This army is too small to march against the Prophet."

"Bull hocky," Martin said.

"The men are talking, Sergeant," said another of the card players. "They're saying that an American can whip almost anyone, but if we don't outnumber the Indians two or three to one we're in trouble."

"Bull hocky," Martin repeated. "I don't want to hear any more of that—"

Martin's invective was cut short by the bark of a rifle. He and his men sprang to their feet. From the edge of camp a man screamed in agony, and Martin grabbed his rifle and ran toward the commotion. Other men had already congregated there. A sentinel was down; a rifle ball had passed through the meaty portion of both thighs, and he was bleeding profusely. Martin ordered a small patrol into the darkening woods, but they found nothing. Major Joseph Daveiss led a mounted squad of dragoons into the night, but he, too, returned empty-handed.

The spirit had gone out of the card game when Martin returned to his tent. Throughout the night the militia guards saw hostile Indians in every shadow and in every wind-driven movement of a bush. The troops' sleep was regularly interrupted by shots and cries of alarm, but the gunfire was all outgoing; there were no further attacks.

An hour after sunrise, while Harrison was at breakfast, Ta-na returned from a quick scout. He reported to the governor that he had seen a few signs, but that the incident of the night before had evidently been the work of a lone Indian.

Harrison sighed. "One brave fires from behind a tree and the whole army is spooked. I need an estimate of the Prophet's strength, Thomas."

"The two Delawares were on the outskirts of Prophetstown yesterday," Ta-na said. "They estimate that no more than four hundred warriors are there."

"I wish I could believe them." Harrison was uncomfortably aware that his army, which consisted mostly of undisciplined militiamen, numbered slightly more than a thousand men, many of whom were sick. "Thomas," he went on, "I'm going to send Lieutenant O'Toole back to Vincennes with orders to embody four more companies of militia and get them on the move toward us as quickly as possible."

Daveiss, known in Kentucky for his skilled oratory, broke a bottle of bourbon at the gate of the completed fort and said in a soaring voice, "In the name of the United States, and by the authority of the same, I christen this Fort Harrison."

Cheers were mixed with groans protesting the waste of good Kentucky whiskey.

Harrison spoke briefly, concluding with the promise that the waiting would soon be over and the army would see some fighting. The cheers, whether or not they were sincere, were loud.

The army moved. On the advice of Harrison's chief

scout, the soldiers forded the river to avoid marching
through dense woodlands. On the western side lay the
prairie. The supply train, with the cattle and hogs, would
have easier going through the frost-withered bluegrass.
Harrison issued an order giving the men permission to
shoot any Indian on sight. At the mouth of the Vermilion
River, three days' march from the Prophet's stronghold,
the general ordered construction of a small blockhouse to
shelter men who had fallen sick and to protect flatboats
that were now making their way up the Wabash. Indians
had already killed one man on a flatboat heading toward
Vincennes, so Harrison considered the blockhouse a necessity.

"I wonder, Thomas," he mused, "if the Indians have
scattered." He was concerned about the attack on the flatboat between his position and Vincennes. "Bring Lieutenant O'Toole to me, if you will."

When O'Toole arrived, Harrison gave orders to send
a militia officer with twelve men back to Vincennes
straightaway with instructions to the citizens to barricade
all public buildings.

"We wouldn't want the Prophet to steal a march on
us and attack Vincennes while the army is not there to
protect it," Harrison explained. He did not mention to
anyone, not even Ta-na, that he was thinking about St.
Clair's defeat. It was November 4, the anniversary of that
disaster, and although he was not superstitious, he posted
extra sentinels that night.

On the next day's march, Indians were sighted, and
Harrison circled the wagons and sent dragoons ahead
with instructions to engage them in talk, to bring them to
a parley. A chief named White Horse came into the camp
under a white flag and expressed his concern at the presence of the army so near Prophetstown.

"Your men are trampling our cornfields," White
Horse complained. But he agreed to a council to be held
the next day.

*   *   *

Lying on his stomach five hundred yards from the outlying buildings of Prophetstown, Ta-na looked across cornfields and fallow cultivated areas. He ran back and reported to Harrison that nothing would do but for the general to follow him to the vantage point overlooking the town. When they got there Harrison raised his telescope.

"They've fortified the place," he said.

"There are many canoes on the riverbank," Ta-na said.

"Yes," Harrison agreed, shifting his glass. "And there are Indians everywhere."

Harrison mounted his gray mare and rejoined his forward troops. That night Chief White Horse came to see him once more, protesting that the move toward Prophetstown was contrary to their agreement.

"Then, perhaps, Chief," Harrison said, "you could suggest a suitable camping area where there will be ample wood and water for my troops."

White Horse pointed toward the northwest, where a small creek wound past the village.

"Take a look, Thomas," Harrison ordered.

Ta-na found an elevated area of about ten acres. Shaped like a blunt flatiron, it rose several feet above the swampy land that surrounded it, with woodlands on two sides and marshy prairie on both ends.

Including officers, Harrison's force had dwindled to nine hundred and fifty men, three hundred of whom were regulars. Ta-na rode beside him as the governor moved into the area and positioned a third of his force facing Prophetstown. He ordered three hundred men to line up along the creek, and when he was satisfied that his perimeter was secure, he passed the word that the riflemen were to tether their horses inside the lines. He decided to hold the Kentucky dragoons under Major Daveiss in reserve.

As fires were built and tents pitched, a cold, light rain began to fall. The order for the night was, "Sleep

with your rifle under you and with your bayonet fixed.
Keep your cartridge box at the ready."

In the early darkness Ta-na moved with great care
through the cornfields on the outskirts of Prophetstown.
The fires had not been allowed to burn down, and there
was much activity in the village. Circling toward the
north, he moved closer. Dogs barked from the nearby
wegiwas, but so many warriors were moving about that no
one paid any attention. Ta-na was ready to withdraw and
return to camp to report to Harrison when he saw his
cousin Gao walking with a Potawatomi chief. They halted
in front of a small dwelling and talked for a few minutes,
and then the Potawatomi left. Gao entered the wegiwa,
and Ta-na cautiously moved closer and cooed like a dove.

Gao's head popped out the door, and he looked
around with forced casualness before he darted into the
darkness behind the wegiwa. With another soft coo Ta-na
guided his cousin to his location.

"Are you blind, that you don't see hundreds of warriors around you?" Gao teased, for that was how Ta-na had
greeted him the last time they met.

"Tonight the Prophet will fight?" Ta-na asked.

Gao said nothing.

"Brother, you march with the wrong army," Ta-na
said. "It is not too late to bring your wife and come with
me."

"No."

"If Tecumseh were here, there would be no battle,"
Ta-na said. "He would know that he is outnumbered."

"But he is not here." Gao's voice was bitter as he
continued. "Two British soldiers have come to the village
and are at Tenskwatawa's side day and night. It is they
who incite him to attack."

"Is this true?"

"It is true." Gao laughed and sneered. "They have
discarded their red coats, and dress as Shawnee. They tell

us how to fight like redcoats and have no conception of Indian tactics."

"Our forefathers fought against the redcoats," Ta-na said. "Do you side with them now?"

"I am with my brothers in blood," Gao said. "But as I have promised, I will not raise my weapon in this fight."

"Nor I," Ta-na said. "You will stay here?"

"Yes."

"It is this night, then?"

"See for yourself," Gao said.

Ta-na turned. In the distance, visible between the wegiwas, he saw Tenskwatawa emerge from his medicine house. Warriors gathered around him, and he made odd motions over the head of each, after which they disappeared into the night.

"I must go quickly," Ta-na said.

"Go with care."

"And you."

He circled far outside the village and could just detect shadowy forms crossing the cultivated areas toward the woodlands surrounding Harrison's camp. He had waited too long. In order to get back into the camp he would have to pass through hundreds of Indians in carefully concealed positions in the woods.

Tenskwatawa the Prophet slept little that night. In his medicine house he brewed more of his sacred concoction, and, one by one, grim-faced warriors stood before him to be anointed.

"Hear me," the Prophet repeated to each group of men. "When I have touched you with my magic, the gunpowder of the Shemanese will be sand. Their bullets will be no more deadly than soft rain. Already Moneto, the Supreme Being of All Things, has killed half the whitefaces. The rest will run at the slightest noise in the night."

The Prophet raised his voice. "Hear me, women of the tribes. Here you will wait for victory and its spoils. Each of you will have a white soldier to use as you see fit.

He will be your slave, or he will be an evening's entertainment before he dies."

Several women shouted shrill cries of approval.

"Hear me," Tenskwatawa told each group of warriors in turn. "The white chief rides a pale horse, a mare. Make him your target, all of you. Cut off the snake's head and the body dies. I want a hundred warriors to rush immediately toward the white chief and kill him."

In small groups the Indians crept through the darkness just before dawn to take up positions behind trees and in thickets of brush. Their fever for war kept them warm as the light rain continued.

A few early risers in the camp were kindling fires when Harrison, relieved that the night was almost over, pulled on his boots. It was pitch dark when he stuck his head out the tent flap, and he could barely see the drummer who was standing by to sound reveille when the hour arrived.

At the edge of the woods on the left flank of the army, a sentinel heard movement and, in a whispered conversation, consulted with a comrade nearby, wondering whether or not to fire toward the brush. The whiz of an arrow past his ear and its thud as it struck a tree made up his mind. With his fellow sentinel he raced toward camp.

Nearby, a man from Kentucky saw movement in the dark and fired instinctively. He missed, but his shot gave the alarm. The movement he had seen in front of him materialized into the forms of Indians, and he turned to run, but a single shot felled him.

Now the darkness burst into wild, ear-splitting war cries, and a volley of musketry tore through the tents. Live coals were tossed into the air when bullets struck the newly kindled fires.

Half-dressed men poured out of the tents and were greeted by chaos. The Indians were already among them, and with hoarse cries the defenders met the charge with hand-to-hand fighting. In the dim light the American lines were infiltrated, particularly on the angle held by the Kentuckians. Iron blades rose and fell, slashing through flesh and hacking at bone.

Ta-na took the risk of joining the charge; in the dark he was indistinguishable from the other Indians. Units were organizing, and a respectable hail of rifle fire tore through the trees. When he was clear of the woods he went to earth and crawled forward, keeping below the line of fire from the militiamen who held the area in front of him. Suddenly he appeared before a young soldier and knocked the man's rifle aside.

"I'm on your side," Ta-na yelled.

The soldier yanked the rifle out of Ta-na's hand and lunged toward him. Ta-na easily sidestepped and kicked the soldier in the crotch. He fell, clutching himself and moaning.

"I told you that I am on your side," Ta-na repeated. He ran through the misted, dawn-gray woods, dodging spirited fire from the enemy.

"Ah, there you are, Thomas," Harrison said calmly when he reached the general's tent. "Have you seen my boy?" he asked, referring to his servant. "I want him to find my gray horse."

Unable to find either, Harrison commandeered a large black horse, mounted, drew his pistol, and rode off to try to make some sense of the confusion. As he approached the scene of the fighting he was joined by Colonel Abraham Owen of Kentucky, who was riding a white horse. Although the Americans were unaware of it, the Indians acted in accordance with the Prophet's orders; thinking that the rider of the pale horse was Harrison, warriors aimed dozens of rifles, and Owen toppled over, dead.

"Get away from the goddamned rifle fire!" Harrison yelled when he saw the man fall.

Most of the soldiers had sought the protection of shadows and were blinded by muzzle bursts in the predawn darkness. Many of the Indians had painted their

faces black and were invisible. Kentucky marksmen
loaded their squirrel rifles with number-twelve buckshot,
fired at any hint of movement, and were often rewarded
with yells of agony.

Harrison turned as a rider drew up alongside. Ta-na
had mounted the horse of a fallen rifleman.

"Thomas," Harrison said in puzzlement, "they're not
fighting like Indians."

A second charge of Indians hit the line facing
Prophetstown, but the regulars there stood firm. The
fiercest attack smashed into the camp from the right. Harrison spurred his horse toward the roar of musketry, and
Ta-na followed. Rifle balls peeled bark from the trees
through which they rode. Most of the officers in that area
had been killed when large groups of Indians rushed forward, fired, and then retreated to reload.

"Sir," Ta-na said, pointing. To their rear a militia
company was being pounded hard and showed all signs of
getting ready to run.

Bellowing encouragement, Harrison rode into the
thick of the fight, his hat knocked askew when a bullet
went through the brim and grazed his head. A rifle ball
struck his horse in the neck, and the animal screamed in
pain but stayed on its feet.

Major Daveiss found Harrison. "I want permission to
dislodge the enemy from behind those logs, there!" he
shouted.

"You are in reserve, Major," Harrison said.

"Twenty men, sir. Just twenty men."

"Act on your own discretion, Major."

With a whoop Daveiss led a troop of his dragoons
toward the fallen logs. Despite a hail of fire, their horses
lifted gracefully over the obstacles. Daveiss went down
with three bullets in him, dead before he hit the ground.
The dragoons continued to fire their pistols as they soared
over the logs, but the Indians had faded into the woods.

When daylight came, Harrison called to Ta-na. "Go

tell Major Wells to shift the regulars to the left. Tell Boyd to move his men to the right."

Harrison had decided that the Indians were hesitating to mount a new attack for two reasons: the coming of daylight and the determined resistance of his army.

From the village, Gao heard the opening shots of the battle. He was standing in the morning darkness with Mist-on-the-Water.

"This I must see," he said.

"You promised your brother that you would not lift your weapons in this battle," she said, her voice filled with fear.

"That is so," Gao said, "but it does not mean that I can't watch."

"Please," Mist begged.

"The bed will be warm," he said. "Go to it and wait for me."

He ran across the fields. The battle was heating up; the first shots had swelled into a continuous roar. By the time he reached the marshy area leading up to the high ground where the battle was raging, he could make out forms in the dim light. A warrior with a gaping hole in his breast was walking slowly toward him, head down, blood filling his cupped hand.

"Today I will be with my fathers," the warrior said in Seneca. He was, then, a Mingo, long since displaced from the Seneca homeland to the east.

"May the Master of Life make your journey swift and easy," Gao said.

On the upslope, a young man, not much more than a boy, leaned against a tree and clasped his stomach. Gao recognized him as one of the boys he and Ta-na had guided to Tecumseh only a short time ago. Something tubular and purplish hung over the boy's fingers. Other Indians sprawled in the abandoned positions of death, and the continuing curtain of fire from the whiteface army scythed through the woods, dropping small branches to the earth and thudding into the tree trunks. Quavering war cries blended with the roar of rifle fire.

Gao took a position of relative safety behind a fallen tree and waited as the light grew. The noise of battle quieted, then roared up again. All around Gao were men in the throes of death. Their moans and cries of mortal agony took on the bitter edge of despair, for the new charge against the white enemy had failed. The surviving Indians left their dead behind them as they ran for cover.

Hoarse yelps of triumph from the whiteface soldiers followed the warriors into the trees.

Ta-na delivered Harrison's orders to majors Wells and Boyd. Militiamen armed with squirrel rifles gave covering fire as the dragoons mounted their horses and formed a line. The regulars, too, were in position. Ta-na rode fast to inform Harrison that all stood in readiness, and the general gave the order. A bugler sounded the charge. The regulars rushed forward from both right and left, and the dragoons thundered after the fleeing enemy.

In panic, Indians rushed past where Gao was concealed. A few stopped to give aid to the wounded, but others ran as though pursued by evil spirits. Only the marshy ground saved them from total disaster when the dragoons' horses became mired and the pursuit was called off.

Gao lay as if dead as the dragoons struggled back to the high ground. Gradually the sound of gunfire faded into silence. Somewhere near him a wounded man was breathing with great difficulty, his breath bubbling in his throat. It was over. As Wasegoboah had warned, their numbers had been too small, their tactics ill conceived. The whiteface army held the field, and now nothing stood between them and Prophetstown.

He thought of Mist-on-the-Water and was tensing himself to rise and run, to go to her, to take her to safety before Harrison marched on the village itself, but movement in front of him froze him. A uniformed soldier was moving slowly in his direction. The man paused, bent over a fallen Indian, and muttered a curse. The soldier's tomahawk flashed, and the sound of bubbly breathing ceased abruptly. When the white man straightened, Gao's vision blurred with red fury, for it was Sergeant Jeb Martin who had just killed the wounded Indian.

Martin's rifle was slung over his shoulder, and he carried a pistol in one hand and his tomahawk in the other. He looked around, then put the tomahawk and pistol in his belt, drew a knife, and bent to slash away the dead Indian's scalp.

At that moment Gao forgot his pledge not to participate in the battle. Jeb Martin was the man who had killed Mist's mother, who had tried to rape Mist herself, and who had twice seen to it that Gao was thrown into the guardhouse on false charges. While he had bungled one opportunity to kill Martin, this time Gao would not fail.

Martin must have heard a twig snap because he turned in a rush and reached for his rifle, but Gao swung his own rifle sooner and knocked Martin's weapon from his hand. He wanted the satisfaction of killing Martin in close combat, and he wanted to feel the impact as his blade split Martin's skull. He crouched as the sergeant reached for his own tomahawk and then bore in, flashing his blade low, aiming at the whiteface's crotch. Martin danced back expertly and sent a counterblow swishing toward Gao's head. Iron met iron with a reverberating clash.

The sound quickly restored Gao's sanity. The noise of hand-to-hand combat could easily be heard by the whitefaces who were no more than a hundred feet away. He had two choices. He could turn and run, or he could end the battle quickly before others could come to Martin's aid.

"I've been dreaming of a chance to break your skull, Injun," Martin snarled. He lunged forward, and his wild swing swished through Gao's hair. Gao ducked under the blow and buried his blade in Martin's stomach. He tried to jerk his blade free to protect himself from the downward swing of Martin's tomahawk, but it was entangled in something. He fell away just as Martin's tomahawk slashed down. The blade glanced off Gao's shoulder, and for a time he was not sure whether or not his flesh had been opened.

Martin took two stumbling steps toward him, spewing out his hatred. Gao waited, knife in hand, but Martin's legs gave way under him, and he fell. With one foot Gao rolled his enemy over onto his back. Martin's eyes were open.

"Injun bastard," he spat.

Without hesitating Gao slashed the sergeant's exposed throat. He waited for a few seconds, watching the light die in Martin's eyes, before wresting his tomahawk free.

Suddenly a rifle ball whizzed past Gao's shoulder, and he could see two soldiers running toward him. The second rifle spoke even as Gao turned and ran.

The wounded Indians were moving slowly, painfully, toward the village. Other warriors ran past them but did not stop to help. Gao's eyes filled with tears because he knew that he was looking at the bloody remnants of Tecumseh's grand dream. He began to jog, lengthening his stride into the warrior's pace.

Because there was no safe place where he could watch the battle, Tenskwatawa waited in his medicine lodge until the first survivors reached the village. He went outside, frantic for news, and his heart grew heavy when he saw the faces of the warriors. He did not have to ask, for he could see defeat in their eyes.

He sat at the door of his lodge with his head between his knees, remembering the last words spoken to him by Tecumseh before his brother left Prophetstown.

"No open hostilities of any kind are to break out between us and the whites," Tecumseh had said. *"It is in my mind that Governor Harrison will attempt something in*

*my absence to make you act foolishly. This must not hap-
pen. If he attempts to destroy Prophetstown, let him have
his will. The town can be rebuilt. Our union, if it becomes
ruptured, cannot.*"

A warrior approached the Prophet. "You lied," he
accused bitterly. "You said that the white soldiers were
dead or crazy and that they would run away. They did
not. Yours is a false magic."

Others muttered against him. Tenskwatawa rose and
in a desperate voice said, "My magic failed because without my knowledge a woman touched the sacred kettle,
thus robbing the magic of its potency. I will cast another
spell, and this time I will lead you. I will be in the forefront when we drive the whitefaces screaming in fear
down the river."

The warriors turned away without a word, leaving
the Prophet to stand alone.

The survivors of the early morning battle were yelling to their families to make haste. There was no time to
gather possessions. Those who were alive were aban-
doning Prophetstown, leaving behind the homes they had
built to protect them from the cold and snows of the coming winter, leaving the unharvested fields of corn and the
storehouses of provisions. They had only one thought, to
get away, to be out of range of the deadly rifles when the
white chief's army came, as it surely would.

Main Poche was more methodical. His followers
were taking time to pack blankets and skins, cooking pots
and provisions.

"Uncle, where will you go?" Gao asked.

"To the north."

"We will follow you."

"You saw?"

"I was there," Gao said. "And the Prophet?"

"I've just heard that he fled. It is said that he will
seek sanctuary in Canada among the redcoats."

"He did not fight as Indians have always fought,"
Gao said.

"He forgot the lessons of the past and listened to the redcoats," Main Poche said bitterly. "He ordered us into the very muzzles of the whitefaces' rifles. We wasted many lives in wild charges in the dark. Moreover, he lied. There was no spell on the white chief's army. The gunpowder did not turn to sand. The bullets were not like soft rain, but like the hardness of death itself."

Mist-on-the-Water emerged from the wegiwa where she and Gao had spent so many wondrous nights. She carried a heavy pack on her back.

"I have brought our bedding, husband," she said.

"I will get food," Gao said.

"Hurry, husband."

"There is no need for haste," Gao said. "The whitefaces will be content to rest and lick their wounds and take the scalps of those who fell. Only then will they come here."

"Still, I am frightened," Mist-on-the-Water said.

"Better to be frightened without reason now than to be hungry when the snows come," Gao said.

He made a pack of food, gunpowder, and shot and collected their cooking vessels and Mist's spare clothing that she had left behind. By the time he was finished, Main Poche and his family were gone.

Gao had made his choice. Tecumseh, and Tecumseh alone, had the power to revive the lost cause, to put the hunger for freedom back into the hearts of those who had believed the lies of Tenskwatawa. The whitefaces had won again, but the war was not over. When the Panther Passing Across returned, he, Gao, would be there, for the cause was still just.

Gao took Mist's hand in his and looked at the sun riding at its winter low in the southern sky. That way lay home and family. Sadly he turned away.

A group of Illinois militiamen had butchered a dead horse. Generous roasts of the rich red meat were searing over open fires and giving off a mouth-watering smell. It was not the first time that Ta-na had eaten and enjoyed horse meat.

Frightened into stampede by the battle, the hogs and cows were scattered everywhere. The surviving officers were at work counting casualties, and by day's end, when Ta-na reported to Harrison that the Indians had abandoned Prophetstown and left behind stores of food and provisions, Harrison had the grim total. Three hundred fifty-one soldiers were dead, one hundred fifty-one were wounded, and two were missing.

"Well, Thomas," Harrison said, "the dead are the lucky ones compared to the two missing men, if they've been captured and burned alive according to the Indians' threats. Thomas, I wish you'd find Lieutenant O'Toole and tell him I want the men to stop taking scalps. The things stink awfully as they age."

"Sir, I fear you're too late."

"Oh, well." Harrison shrugged his shoulders.

The morning of November 8 was cold, although the rain had finally stopped. A detachment of soldiers rode into Prophetstown and found it abandoned; only a few dead warriors were in the wegiwas, and one old squaw had been left behind because she was too ill to travel. The scouts summoned the troops, who emptied the storehouses of dried corn, peas, and beans. Men loaded kettles and other things of value onto the wagons along with a large supply of the highest-quality British gunpowder and some fine English rifles still in their original wrappings.

The soldiers put the torch to the town and destroyed the unharvested corn. To make room for the wounded on the wagons, the officers' baggage was tossed onto the fires. Saddles taken from dead horses were also destroyed, and Harrison set the example by throwing his camp chair and his bed into the fire. He also sacrificed a campaign chest and a fine saddle.

As the weather worsened that day and became bitterly cold, the bloodied army traveled only eight miles.

Ta-na came up alongside a wagon in which Dr. Henri was treating the wounded, and the old surgeon greeted him with a smile.

"I see, *mon ami*, that you came through unscathed."

"Thanks to the manitous," Ta-na said.

"And your brother, that Gao? Did you see him?"

Ta-na saw no reason to lie. Dr. Henri had healed Gao's leg wound.

"I saw him. He is well. He did not fight against us."

Henri held up a small, dark object. "The enemy chewed their rifle balls."

"How do you know?"

"A chewed bullet, with the lead made rough and jagged, makes an enlarged wound and tears the surrounding flesh. They probably poisoned them, as well, for many of my men will die of septic wounds."

Fourteen soldiers who had lived through the battle died in the first two days. Fifteen more would expire before reaching Vincennes as the wagons bumped and rolled over the rutted roads. Harrison left fresh detachments of men at the blockhouse and at Fort Harrison. At last the tired, hungry army reached Vincennes on November 18, fifty-four days after their departure.

"Well, Thomas," Harrison said, "we did it. The fears of those who said that our force was not strong enough were groundless, after all."

Harrison went to Grouseland to write his official report to Washington. He sent it with a trusted officer, Major Waller Taylor, to be delivered in person to Secretary of War Eustis. In Louisville, where Taylor paused briefly to rest before riding on toward Washington, he took time to give a brief description of the battle to a Kentucky member of the House of Representatives, who immediately released the information to the press, and the storm that developed stunned William Henry Harrison. Regardless of his victory, in spite of his official account of the battle, the press described an army and its commander surprised and thrown into confusion. In Kentucky, Major Daveiss's brother-in-law said that Daveiss had been sacrificed to jealousy and unmilitary orders in what was nothing less than a horrible and inept butchery. To compound the situation, an argument broke out among regular and militia officers, with both sides claiming that it was their units that had won the battle.

Although the legislatures of both Kentucky and the Indiana Territory passed resolutions of thanks to Harrison, the praise did not last as long as the criticism. A Virginia congressman said that Harrison was guilty of graft and dishonesty, that he had personally dipped into annuities intended for friendly Indians.

The storm continued into December, with winter lying heavy on the country. A new accusation surfaced, one that had a measure of truth behind it. So many men had died, Harrison's critics charged, because he had allowed the Indians to choose the ground on which he had encamped the army.

Ta-na was the first to learn that Harrison intended to resign as commander in chief of the western armies.

"Thomas," Harrison said, "I believe that even the greatest generals would admit that they could fight a second battle on the same ground better than the first, but since I will not be given that chance, I think it is time for me to strike my colors."

He made his resignation official on December 20, 1811.

Chapter Sixteen

For thirty nights Opothie Micco had ceremoniously burned a section of the last of the red sticks given to him by Seekabo, the Shawnee prophet who had accompanied Tecumseh on his visit to the Creek Nation. Seekabo had stayed in the village as Tecumseh's ambassador so that he might continue to instruct willing young warriors in the mystic rites and dances of the northern tribes. Now he watched impassively as Opothie Micco performed his nightly ritual.

Opothie Micco had heard Tecumseh's words and seen the promised green fire in the sky, and he believed in the prophecy yet to come.

Angered by the reluctance of some of the Creek chiefs to join his cause, the Panther Passing Across had said, "I will stamp the ground with my foot and shake down every house in Tuckabatchee." He had named the day and the hour, and now it was time to signal all tribes to rise up and reclaim what had been given to them by the Master of Breath as their right of birth.

On a night when the warmth of the great gulf of salt water flowed upward from the south to moderate the winter cold in the Lower Creek towns, Opothie Micco had a silent and respectful audience as he lifted his arms to the lights in the sky and intoned a prayer to the Master of Breath. Finished, he looked around, gazing at each face in turn. He was dressed in his finest ceremonial costume. His muscular torso was adorned by silver gorgets; his neck was heavy with gold and silver chains, and when he moved his hands his bracelets jingled. The lobes of his ears stretched under the weight of ornate earbobs, and his central comb of hair was accented with feathers. His shaved scalp glowed in the firelight.

Slowly he lowered the thirtieth and last piece of the red stick into the fire. He crossed his arms on his chest and waited.

The same ceremony was taking place in dozens of Indian villages from the Creek Nation to the shores of the wide lakes.

At the Flint River Agency, Christmas had come and gone. For Little Hawk the holy day that had been important to his mother, a day that was always observed in Huntington Castle with the singing of carols, good things to eat, and presents for all, would have passed without notice had it not been for the cheerful efforts of Lavinia. She saw to it that no one was forgotten. There were gifts for the smallest child in the slave cabins, and in the Hawkins home the smell of gingerbread and plum puddings filled the rooms.

That good woman had become a second mother to Michael, tending him as though he were one of her own. With youthful resiliency the boy had rebounded from his injuries, and his broken ribs had healed with gratifying swiftness. That there were still wounds to his spirit could not be denied, but he was, after all, only five years old and not fully capable of understanding the meaning of death.

He knew only that he was very lonely for his twin brother and missed his mother so much that he often cried himself to sleep.

As the old year dragged itself to a cold and miserable close—two days of freezing rain had been capped by a heavy sleet storm followed by four inches of snow—Michael's splint was removed from his leg. The limb was weak and pale and somewhat withered from its long encapsulation, but with the aid of a cane whittled for him by the Creek boy Nugee, whose wound had also healed, he began to move about.

"Look, Father," he said, "I can walk. We can go home now. I want to see Grandfather Renno and Grandfather Roy Johnson and Grandmother Beth."

In the dead of winter Little Hawk's duties at the Flint River Agency were negligible, and he had isolated himself and become a silent, withdrawn man. In the depths of his depression he could not force himself to visit the Creek towns and talk to the chiefs to assess their collective mood. He, too, thought often of home, of Huntington Castle and his family, but he was an officer in the service of the United States, and he had his orders from the President himself.

"Soon, my small Hawk," he said to Michael. "We will go home soon."

"If we don't have horses we don't have to ride. I can walk now."

"Yes, yes. Hush now."

Lavinia served a feast on New Year's Day. The Hawkins brood and Michael stuffed themselves on a variety of meats and sweet treats that left their young stomachs bulging. Benjamin Hawkins did trencherman's duty with the repast, as well, which may or may not have contributed to his becoming quite ill that night. In spite of Lavinia's nursing, the agent's condition worsened as the new year came in with clear, cold skies that left the accumulation of ice, sleet, and snow on the ground for a longer time than any remembered by the older Creek Indians at the agency.

Hawkins diagnosed his condition as pleurisy and told Lavinia that it was fatal. On the ninth day of the year he called in everyone who lived in the enclosure. As they filed past his bed he shook hands solemnly, telling each one of them, "I am going."

His affairs were in order; his will had been written. There was only one thing left to do.

"Lavinia, my dear," he said, "I want you to call Brother Petersen."

Lavinia wiped away her tears. She thought that Benjamin wanted the Moravian preacher to say a dying prayer for him, but when Petersen arrived Hawkins said, "I am going, Reverend, but before I do, you will make this good woman my wife."

Lavinia's tears were a mixture of sorrow and happiness. For fifteen years she had lived with Hawkins without the blessings of matrimony. She had given him children, and although they were called by his name, they were bastards in the eyes of the law and of God.

Lavinia was not the only one who shed copious tears. The sickroom was packed as the minister performed the service. Little Hawk's name was recorded as one of the official witnesses. After the ceremony Brother Petersen stood a deathwatch over the new bridegroom, staying throughout the night. Hawkins was fifty-seven years old. It was common for a man of those years to die, but Hawkins did not go. He felt better the very next morning, and as the month progressed, he recuperated nicely.

News of the spirited little fight at Tippecanoe arrived at the Flint River Agency along with a packet from Washington for Captain Hawk Harper. The heavy bundle contained back pay in gold and a set of official orders drawn up by the War Department and initialed by President Madison.

"Well, Colonel," Little Hawk said to Hawkins, who

was propped up in a comfortable chair in his sitting room, "I'll be leaving you."

"We'll miss you, my boy. Orders, eh?"

"I'm Washington bound," Little Hawk said.

"May I inquire?"

"It doesn't seem to be urgent," Little Hawk said. "I'm to report to the White House, where I will be President Madison's military liaison officer."

"You're going to go far, Hawk," Hawkins said.

Little Hawk smiled, but he was thinking, *I have been far, but never so far from happiness as now.*

While the all-consuming ache in him had diminished, it was never totally absent. Sometimes it concentrated in a hard knot in his stomach and lay there, heavy and acid, so that the thought of food was hateful. He slept fitfully, for he dreamed. Of late he'd been dreaming of a Heceta Indian girl named Twana who had given herself to him warmly and willingly before she fell to her death on sharp rocks beside the Columbia River. He had mourned her, but he had not felt the debilitating loss that had come with the death of Naomi.

Was he dreaming of Twana because he had failed to protect her in time of peril? Were the manitous sending him thoughts of the little Heceta girl to heighten his guilt for having brought his family to a place where they could be defiled and slain by enemy Indians?

Much had been taken from him, but he still had one son. His duty to that son overrode all obligations to the President and to the United States.

"My small Hawk," he said, as he sat on the side of Michael's bed that night, "you have asked that we go home."

"Yes, sir."

"We will leave tomorrow."

Michael sat up and gave his father a hug.

It was the evening of January 23, 1812.

*   *   *

Shabonee and two other defeated war chiefs headed west
to tell Tecumseh of Tenskwatawa's folly. It was not a
pleasant journey. They rode through freezing rain and
iron-cold days when the ground was as hard as stone under the unshod hooves of the horses. One of the animals
died from shock when it was forced to swim behind canoes across the frigid waters of the great river. It was
known that Tecumseh had planned to search for his sister,
Tecumapese, who had become the woman of a French
trader in the area around a white settlement in Missouri
called New Madrid.

Shabonee and his companions had some difficulty
finding Tecumseh, and the search consumed weeks. They
finally found him camped near New Madrid, and it fell to
Shabonee to give him the disastrous news.

"Nearly four hundred warriors died," Shabonee
said, his throat tightening at the memory, "because
Tenskwatawa listened to the redcoats who were among
us."

"Where is Tenskwatawa?" Tecumseh asked. His face
was set in hard lines, and his eyes burned with a terrible
anger.

"The enemy dead lay with their hair in place,"
Shabonee went on, the memory of his personal humilia-
tion making him rigid. "Three white scalps were taken,
and two of those were recovered by the long knives, taken
from the hands of our dead."

"Tenskwatawa," Tecumseh said in a soft voice.

"All day long the white-eyes harvested the scalps of
our people," Shabonee continued. "Some of them were
sliced into pieces so that they could be shared. The
soldiers carried them by punching a hole through them
and threading them on their ramrods."

"Where is Tenskwatawa?" Tecumseh thundered.

Insulted, Shabonee fell silent. One of the others
spoke up. "We have him. He tried to flee to Canada, but
he was caught. Some wanted to kill him then and there,

but Wasegoboah said that it was up to you to determine your brother's fate."

"We will go tomorrow morning to Prophetstown," Tecumseh said.

"Of Prophetstown," Shabonee said, "there is nothing left. The whiteface soldiers carried away our food and goods on their wagons."

"We must see what can be done to salvage our union," Tecumseh said, "and we must determine what is to be done with Tenskwatawa."

Slowly he got to his feet and pulled his bearskin mantle close around him. He walked away from the campfire, stood on a small hill, and looked out toward the distant village. The news Shabonee had brought put the weight of the world on his shoulders. His heart shriveled like a dried apple. He lifted his face to the sharp-edged stars and whispered, "Ah, Tenskwatawa." It was a sad and melancholy sound. Then he raised his voice and wailed, "Tenskwatawaaaaaaaaaaaa!" In anger and pain, as if his stomach hurt, he raised one leg high.

"Damn you, Tenskwatawa," he whispered, the leg still held up next to his belly. He stood there unnaturally, like a crane in cold weather warming one foot in its feathers.

Consumed with frustration, the Panther Passing Across stamped his foot.

Benjamin Hawkins was awakened by someone moving his chair. He looked around, expecting to see Lavinia, but he was alone in the sitting room. His chair danced across the wide pine planks of the floor. A tobacco tin clattered its way to the edge of his desk and fell, spilling the fragrant leaf. A picture fell from the wall with a crash. From the kitchen came the sounds of breaking china.

As Little Hawk stood beside Michael's bed, the floor of the cabin moved under his feet. He kept himself from falling by grabbing the headboard. Michael tried to sit up and was bounced off the bed; his father leaned to pick him up and then sat down heavily. As the cabin groaned and shuddered, Little Hawk gathered his son in his arms. All around them things were rattling, falling, and crashing to the floor.

Ta-na had left Vincennes following the resignation of William Henry Harrison as commander in chief of the western armies and had crossed Kentucky into Tennessee. Wrapped in his blankets, he was comfortably snuggled in loose, clean hay in the loft of a friendly settler's barn. He had just closed his eyes when the structure began to sway, and he rolled off the edge of the hayloft. He awoke in midair, landed on his feet, and stood unsteadily for a moment until the ground lifted and fell under him and sent him tumbling to the floor. Staggering as if he were drunk, he untangled himself from his blankets and ran outside. One wall of the settler's cabin was starting to buckle. With a crack like thunder the solid earth rocked under his feet, a chasm opened, and the cabin disintegrated and fell into a huge cavity even as the settler dragged his wife and two children to the dubious safety of the undulating front yard.

Ta-na ran from a spreading abyss that threatened to eat him. The barn collapsed inward. Squealing with terror, his horse burst out of the tangle of falling planks. Ta-na fell to the ground and lay there, feeling waves of motion roll through the solid earth. The settler and his family struggled to stand but kept falling, and when they finally managed to stay upright they ran and kept on running.

"No, damn it, no," William Henry Harrison said. He sat up in bed as sturdy Grouseland groaned and cracked with the sharp movements of the earth. "Not again, damn it." He was remembering how Tecumseh had predicted the eclipse, then the meteor, and now this. But he forgot Tecumseh when his wife screamed and his children crawled into the bedroom to join their parents.

* * *

In the White House, James Madison awoke from sleep, aroused by a rumble of sound that he could not, at first, identify.

At Huntington Castle, Beth was dreaming she was at sea. The ship rolled in the force of a storm, but the crash of books falling from the shelves in the library woke her. She sat up and clung to Renno, who was bolt upright, his head cocked as he listened to the eerie rumbling that emanated from the earth beneath the house.

At Tuckabatchee, Opothie Micco and those who stood vigil with him sat in awed silence as the sturdy thatched-mud houses of the village began to crumble. The earth danced under them. Opothie Micco lifted his head and sang out praise for the Master of Breath. The Panther Passing Across had said that every house in Tuckabatchee would fall. Now it had come to pass.

Tecumseh's party was near the epicenter of the great earthquake, and he was violently thrown to the ground. He heard the sound of cannon, but as he dug his fingers into the infirm earth and fought to hang on, he saw that the wild bucking and falling was snapping scores of trees as if they were no stronger than straws. The sudden break of huge boles made sharp sounds like gunfire. A roar louder than thunder, louder than a twisting storm as it scythed its way through a forest, filled his ears and made them ache.

The campfire sent showers of sparks into the air as it was scattered, and one of the men cried out in terror. The world had become a terribly potent and utterly alien enemy. Then a new roar was added to the already unbearable din. Tecumseh could not know the cause. He knew only that when he stamped his foot the world had responded with unbelievable violence.

* * *

The roar heard by Tecumseh and others in the vicinity of New Madrid was, first, the sound of the earth's indigestion, a grating of rock on rock from deep within the belly of the land. To that sound was added the rush of water. Directly across the Mississippi from New Madrid, near the Kentucky-Tennessee border, an area of land one hundred fifty miles long and forty miles wide within seconds sank three to nine feet. The waters of the Mississippi joined with those released from subterranean stores and rushed into the huge depression in a tumultuous flood of biblical proportions.

Near the juncture of the two great rivers, the Ohio and the Mississippi, in Kentucky, Illinois, Missouri, Arkansas, and Tennessee, the earth opened in raw abysses, swallowing whole forests. The Mississippi River roiled as if in storm, and riverside bluffs sheared away and crashed into the heaving, muddy waters. The Father of Waters reversed its flow and churned northward, sending oceanic waves exploding over the land.

Throughout Tennessee, Kentucky, Arkansas, and Missouri, and in the Illinois and Indiana Territories, stone and brick chimneys made clouds of dust as they collapsed. Windows shattered at Grouseland, and barns were flattened.

It was not only man who suffered. Domestic cattle and the wild buffalo of the plains west of the Mississippi lost their footing, rolled helplessly on the unstable ground, and struggled to their feet, only to be thrown down again.

As new fissures opened, lakes were drained and streams ceased to flow. Fish flopped helplessly on dry riverbeds. Lakes Michigan and Erie danced as if their waters were being agitated by a powerful storm. Waves pounded the shore. For a thousand miles in all directions from New Madrid, the eerie, grinding sounds made by the tortured earth were like bone scraping on bone. In the major cities of the west, in Detroit, Cincinnati, Pittsburgh, Chicago, Cleveland, and St. Louis, and in every

town and hamlet, the movement of the continental plates
far below the surface of the earth caused massive destruction.

In the southland, where Opothie Micco lay on his stomach trying to cling to the frantically shifting earth, Creek,
Choctaw, Chickasaw, Cherokee all heard the bellowing of
a world in torment. As houses collapsed about them, people rushed into the open, and one word was spoken again
and again.

"Tecumseh!"
"Tecumseh!"
"Tecumseh!"

In the eerie silence that followed an interminable period
of movement and cacophony, Tecumseh lay on his face
with the scent of freshly disturbed earth in his nostrils.
He sat up. A small aftershock caused his eyes to widen.
After a time he stood and looked toward the town of New
Madrid, where something was burning. He looked at the
unchanged sky, and his eyes filled with tears.

He had stamped his foot.

Moneto and all the good spirits were with him. He
had said there would be signs, and Moneto had given
them to him; but this sign—this great wonder that could
not fail to convince the tribes that he was blessed by the
Great Spirit—had been wasted. Once, the event would
have rallied thousands to his side, but now it meant nothing. The fragile union of Indian tribes was shattered, destroyed by the ego of the man who, because of the words
that Tecumseh had put in his mouth, had come to believe
that he was truly the Prophet.

"Tenskwatawa," Tecumseh whispered.

A large group of refugees from Prophetstown was encamped by a small creek north of the junction of the Tippecanoe and the Wabash. Gao had constructed a wegiwa,
and although the house wasn't as snug as the one in

Prophetstown, it kept out the worst of the cold winds and kept Mist and him dry. It was, at least, more substantial than the tepees that sheltered some of the families.

It was cold. Winter held the north country in an icy grip, and there was not always enough food.

Gao and Mist-on-the-Water were warming themselves by a fire on the rock hearth in the middle of the wegiwa when they heard a voice from outside.

"Tecumseh. Tecumseh is coming."

Gao wrapped Mist in a warm fur robe, pulled his own furs about his face, and went outside. Eight riders approached from the south. The horses lifted their hooves high because the snow was fresh and deep, but there were no smiles and no glad greetings. Every one of the two hundred people in the camp knew that the Panther Passing Across had seen the blackened ruins of Prophetstown.

Wasegoboah stepped forth as Tecumseh dismounted.

"Tenskwatawa," Tecumseh said.

The Prophet was tethered to a stake in a wegiwa, his hands tied behind his back. As soon as Tecumseh entered the house and looked down at him, Tenskwatawa began to whimper in fear. With one hand Tecumseh took his knife from its sheath, and with the other he seized Tenskwatawa by the hair. In his fear the Prophet's bladder overflowed, making a dark stain on his buckskins. Tecumseh pressed the blade into his brother's neck, and blood welled up and slid in droplets down the Prophet's chest. He made moaning sounds.

"No," Tecumseh said. "That would be too merciful."

He cut away Tenskwatawa's bonds, lifted his brother to his feet, and shook him so hard that his nose began to drip blood. When Tecumseh thrust him violently away, Tenskwatawa crawled to a corner and cowered. Three warriors drew weapons but were stopped by an order from Wasegoboah.

"In one day, Tenskwatawa, you have undone the work of a decade," Tecumseh said in a voice laden with sadness. "In one day you destroyed the hope of all Indians." His voice became softer. "I will not kill you, but each day you will die a little, for you are no longer the Prophet. You are a liar and a cheat, and you are without a people. When death does find you, no one will mourn your passing." He raised a hand. "Leave me. I have done with you."

Tenskwatawa crawled like a beaten dog.

"My heart hurts because I have failed you," Wasegoboah said to Tecumseh.

"We await your word," said another chief.

Tecumseh turned his face to Gao and Mist-on-the-Water. "So, Seneca, you are still here."

"I and these few are with you," Gao said.

Tecumseh spoke softly. "Once more I have stood in the ashes of my home. And as I stood there I called upon the spirits of those who fell. I had the scent of their blood in my face, and once more I swore eternal hatred for the Shemanese. The great sign that Moneto allowed me to predict has been wasted, just as the lives of those who listened to him whose name I will never again speak were wasted. Many will turn their backs on us because of what happened, but there will be others who will continue to be strong, who will take up their weapons when the time is right."

He was silent for a long moment, and when he looked up his eyes were as hard as iron. "We will rebuild our homes, but no longer will the town be called Prophetstown. From now on it will be known only as Tippecanoe."

In times long past when the great Ghonkaba led the hawk and bear clans of the Seneca Nation to the land of the Cherokee, the customs of the homeland came with the band in the memories of the shaman, Casno, and of the women, among them the principal matron, Toshabe. Even though most of those who had made the long trek were with their ancestors in the west, the traditions they had brought with them lived on. The tales and legends of the League of the Iroquois, the Ho-de-no-sau-nee, were still recounted around the winter fires. The matrons saw to it that Seneca morality was observed. In its winter sleep, when the world gave the appearance of death, the festive celebration of the new beginning was observed as it had always been. It was so from the time when the prophet Degandawida envisioned the Great Peace, embodied in health of body and mind, peace between individuals and tribes, good conduct and clean thought, justice, preparedness for defense, and spiritual rightness —orenda.

The Master of Life had promised that there would be a new beginning, that there would be green grass and warm days, and that promise had never been broken. In the time of celebration the grotesquely carved wooden false faces hid the faces of pranksters, and there were singing and dancing and cries of joy and surprise as the young ones acclaimed life with unabashed enthusiasm.

Little Hawk and Michael arrived at Huntington Castle just before the festival began. As it happened, Renno saw two horses turn into the tree-lined lane that led to the tall house. His heart leaped in gladness, for he recognized his son immediately by the way he sat his saddle. That joy was dampened as he waited for other horses to appear, horses carrying Naomi and another small boy, for Little Hawk held only one of the twins in the saddle in front of him, and the second horse carried nothing more than a pack. As he stood on the front porch and waited for his son, he knew for whom the manitou wept. Little Hawk lowered Michael to the ground, and the boy ran into his grandfather's arms.

Renno's eyes misted. "And who is this?" he asked.

"I am Soaring Hawk," Michael said in Seneca.

"It is good to see you, grandson."

"Standing Bear and my mother got dead," Michael said quietly.

Pain knifed through Renno's heart. He held Michael

in one arm and walked to Little Hawk, who had dismounted.

"Oh, my son," Renno said. "Oh, manitous, my son."

Little Hawk clasped his father's arm.

"It is true, then?" Renno asked.

"I want to tell it only once," Little Hawk said, "for it is still tender in me."

"Yes," Renno said.

"I broked my leg," Michael said in English.

"Well, it looks as good as new," Renno said, holding the child close.

Beth rushed out onto the porch and welcomed the newcomers. Servants were summoned to care for the horses and to unload Little Hawk's necessaries. Michael, showing that he had an excellent memory, rushed off to the kitchen, where it took him only seconds to cajole old Aunt Sarah into opening the cookie jar. In the small sitting room Little Hawk told his tale, and Beth wept quietly.

"That poor, gentle girl," she said.

"In the end she took the enemy with her," Little Hawk said, his eyes turning to ice, his voice grating. "And he will spend eternity as a man who is not whole."

Beth went to her stepson and gathered him in her arms. For the first time Little Hawk's control left him, and he wept unashamedly on Beth's shoulder.

Ta-na rode up the lane on the first day of the festival of the new beginning and found Huntington Castle deserted. He told Aunt Sarah that he would enjoy some of her superior cooking, which, as he had learned in his travels, was the finest in the entire country east of the Mississippi. She smiled proudly, and her skirts rustled as she put heated leftovers on the kitchen table and heaped them on Ta-na's plate until he begged for mercy.

Ta-na had two fathers. He had spent his childhood in the longhouse of his uncle and aunt, El-i-chi and Ah-wa-o. He had suckled at Ah-wa-o's breast side by side with Gao.

There had been times when he was unsure of his feeling for his biological father, the sachem Renno. It seemed to him that Renno loved his children by Emily more than he loved the dark Seneca boy who was the son of An-da. Although he considered himself too mature to harbor such juvenile sentiments, he had been marked by his childhood, and now he made his way first to the log cabin with which El-i-chi had replaced his large and drafty Seneca longhouse.

El-i-chi, both sachem and shaman, was preparing to officiate at certain activities and was painting his face in time-honored pattern. He put down his paint pots and shouted with joy when Ta-na stepped into the room. He leaped to his feet, threw his arms around the boy, and squeezed hard.

Ah-wa-o made it a three-way embrace as she kissed Ta-na on the cheek. She looked past him, her eyes searching for her other son.

"He is not coming, Mother Ah-wa-o," Ta-na said.

"So," El-i-chi said.

"He is not—"Ah-wa-o could not finish the terrible thought. Already death had visited the family; the news of it had been brought home by Little Hawk.

"No, he is well," Ta-na said. "And you have a new daughter-in-law."

"By the spirits," El-i-chi said. "Tell us."

Ta-na spoke of Mist-on-the-Water, of her beauty and her gentleness and her obvious love for Gao. He avoided as long as possible the revelation that Gao was with Tecumseh. When, at last, he had no choice but to tell the whole truth, he was surprised by the bitterness of Ah-wa-o's outburst.

"Damn the Shawnee," she said. "He stole two children from Ena, and now he has taken my son from me. May all the evil spirits of the darkness gnaw on his bones."

"He fights with the Shawnee, then?" El-i-chi asked. "He was with him at Prophetstown?"

More explanations were required, but none of them helped Ah-wa-o. She did not brighten until Ah-wen-ga and Ha-ace ran into the cabin to tell their father in shrill, excited voices that everyone was waiting for him.

"You have not said hello to your brother Ta-na," Ah-wa-o said.

"Hello, Ta-na," Ah-wen-ga said. She seized her little brother's hand. "Come, Ha-ace. It's time for the dance of the False Faces."

Ta-na laughed. "I can see that they have missed me sorely."

"Well, I certainly missed you," Ah-wa-o said, touching his cheek with her hand.

At the celebration Ta-na eased up behind Renno and Beth, who were watching a spirited false battle between two horribly masked demons. He put his hand on Beth's shoulder and kissed her on the neck. She gasped in surprise and turned into his arms.

"Ta-na, you rascal," she cried. "You made me think that I had a suitor."

Renno was beaming. It seemed to him that his second son had grown taller. He clasped a strong young arm and pulled Ta-na to his breast. Once again it was necessary for Ta-na to answer questions about Gao.

"He'll come to his senses," Renno said. "I wouldn't be surprised to see him and his new bride before spring."

Little Hawk came into the common with Michael on his shoulders, and there was a warm reunion between the two brothers, one blond and bronzed, the other dark and coppery.

Word of the antics performed during the festival of the new beginning had spread into the white settlements in neighboring Tennessee. Although white participation was discouraged, no one really minded spectators as long as they did not interfere, criticize, or blanch in horror when, at the height of the festival, a white dog was ceremonially killed. Among those spectators was a frequent visitor to Rusog's Town, and he sauntered over, having spotted several members of Renno's family together. He had heard of the death of Little Hawk's wife and son and had already offered his condolences.

"Well, look who's here," said Andrew Jackson, extending his hand to Ta-na. "Did you ever make it to Vincennes to join up with Harrison?"

"That I did, Colonel," Ta-na said.

"And your cousin?"

"He, too." Ta-na added nothing more.

"If you boys are still eager for adventure and a little action," Jackson offered, "I'm smack dab in the middle of raising a militia to march south and teach the Creek Indians some manners."

"Ask me tomorrow, Colonel," Ta-na said. "Right now I'm trying to get my toes thawed out from the frozen northland."

"When do you march, Colonel Jackson?" Little Hawk asked.

"Hard to say, right now," Jackson answered. "You considering joining me?"

"My orders are to report to Washington," Little Hawk responded.

"Too bad. Reckon you got as much reason as any man to want to see the Creek Nation broken up so that they will never again be a threat to a white woman."

Little Hawk did not answer. He turned away. On his shoulder his son shouted in glee as the two false faces struck simultaneous blows and knocked each other to the ground.

"You have a pair of fine sons," Jackson said to Renno.

"So," Renno responded.

But his heart was full as he let his eyes linger first on the finely molded copper face of his younger son and then on the bushy blond curls of the elder.

"Two fine sons," Beth said, giving his arm a squeeze.

Author's Note

The ponderous flow of history does not often lend itself to the self-defined requirements of a work of fiction. So it is with knowledge aforethought—but without malice —that we sometimes compress the years and shift events in the interest of the yarn while doing our best to retain the sense and the spirit of the period.

At times there are contradictions in the historical records. For example, some respected sources state that three large shocks followed by over a thousand aftershocks were associated with the great continental earthquake centered near New Madrid, Missouri, in the early nineteenth century. Dates given for the three main temblors are December 16, 1811, January 23, 1812, and February 7, 1812. Opinions differ as to which quake was the most severe. Since our story deals with events in the Creek Nation in the area that is now Georgia and Alabama, we have selected the shock felt by Benjamin Hawkins at the Flint River Agency on January 23, 1812, as the event predicted by Tecumseh.

For readers who would like to know more about the events leading up to Mr. Madison's war against the British and the two tragic wars born of the preachings of Tecumseh and the fiery defiance of Creek warriors who brandished the Shawnee's red sticks, we recommend the collected works of Angie Debo and specifically, for the history of the Creek Nation, *The Road to Disappearance* (Norman, OK: University of Oklahoma Press, 1941).

Grant Foreman's *The Five Civilized Tribes* (University of Oklahoma Press, 1977) and *Indian Removal*, another in the University of Oklahoma's Civilization of the American Indian Series (1976), complement the Debo books.

To know Renno's friends, the Cherokee, we suggest Grace Steele Woodward's *The Cherokees* (Civilization of the American Indian Series, No. 65, University of Oklahoma Press, 1988) and John Ehle's *Trail of Tears: The Rise and Fall of the Cherokee Nation* (New York: Doubleday, 1988).

The Southern Indians and Benjamin Hawkins, 1796-1816 (University of Oklahoma Press, 1986) is a valuable reference for life in the Creek Nation prior to and through the Red Stick Wars and Andrew Jackson's campaign of extermination.

Among the many works consulted by the author were such biographies as *Old Tippecanoe, William Henry Harrison and His Times* (Freeman Cleaves, American Political Biography Press, originally published in 1939), *The Life of Andrew Jackson* (Robert V. Remini, New York: Harper and Row, 1977), *James Madison, A Biography* (Ralph Ketcham, Charlottesville: University Press of Virginia, 1971), and *Thomas Jefferson, A Biography* (Nathan Schachner, Appleton-Century-Crofts, Inc., 1951).

The monumental and definitive work by Allan W. Eckert, *A Sorrow in Our Heart: The Life of Tecumseh*, presented to the reading public in 1992 by Bantam Books, the publisher that also gives life to the White Indian, has been invaluable for its insight into the times and character of the warrior who was not a chief.

DONALD CLAYTON PORTER

THE WHITE INDIAN—BOOK XXVII
CREEK THUNDER
by Donald Clayton Porter

Following the battle of Tippecanoe in November 1811, Tecumseh's Pan-Indian movement appears crushed, the tribes scattered to the wind. But when the New Madrid earthquake is felt all the way from Canada to the Gulf Coast, Tecumseh's Red Stick warriors see it as the fulfillment of his promise to "stamp the ground with my foot and shake down every house in Tuckabatchee." New converts join their ranks, and again war looms on the horizon.

Andrew Jackson, eager to see action, at last receives the assignment he has been seeking. With 2,500 volunteers under his command, he intends to cut a swath through the Creek Nation and destroy the Red Stick rebels.

Standing on opposite sides of this conflict are Renno's sons, Ta-na and Ta-na's cousin and closest friend, Gao. But they do not stand alone, for as the beat of war drums is replaced by the clash of muskets and cannon, their family is drawn into the fray. Hawk Harper finds himself torn between conscience and duty, while his sister, Renna, returns from Europe to discover her family in disarray.

Renno, great-grandson and namesake of the original White Indian, fears that when Creek blood stains the ground, it will be mixed with the blood of those he holds closest to his heart. He vows not to let that happen—even if he must take up lance and shield and walk the path of the warrior one final time.

Look for *Creek Thunder*, on sale in November 1995, wherever Bantam paperbacks are sold.